INHERITING ARMAGEDDON

Also by R. D. G. Lover

Angels' Compass
Tempest of Angels
Inheriting Armageddon

The Tides of Amelia Island
The Storm & the Sea
Rose Tide & Rust

the wisteria collection
wisteria, vol. I

Coloring Books
The Amelia Island Coloring Book

INHERITING ARMAGEDDON

BOOK I OF ANGELS' COMPASS

R. D. G. LOVER

4pocalypse Arts

4pocalypse Arts

First Paperback Edition November 2025

For information about special discounts for bulk purchases or to book an event with the author, please contact R. D. G. Lover at www.4pocalypsearts.com or via email at racheldglover@gmail.com.

ISBN 979-8-9904778-7-2

For the child that survived.

*I thank my God every time I remember you. In all my prayers
for all of you, I always pray with joy because of your partnership
in the gospel from the first day until now, being confident of this,
that he who began a good work in you will carry it on to completion
until the day of Christ Jesus.*

Philippians 1:3-6 (NIV)

AUTHOR'S NOTE

When I first sat down to write *Inheriting Armageddon*, I was at rock bottom. I'd just come out of a three month psych-drug withdrawal, during which I'd lost my best friend and watched the woman who taught me how to write lose her best friend and sister and her will to write. The culmination of these loses—as well as the fact that the psych medications I was on had caused me to not be able to draw or write for over a year during treatment—left me feeling broken and empty.

I remember the exact moment that the withdrawals lifted, though the sorrow from this rock bottom had lingered. I sat down and decided I would go back to what I loved—drawing and writing.

I was inspired, and in the matter of a week, I plotted an entire four-book fantasy series that followed the lives of four unlikely friends who found themselves joking about being the Four Horsemen. It was like lightning striking; this story was *given* to me in order to keep me alive.

I've always known, since that moment in 2018, that God called me to write this story. The events in the time that has passed since then have lead me to believe that this story may be purely for *me*. This story healed me in many ways—more than anything else in my life. These characters were there for me when no one else was. This world was my home when I felt like I didn't belong. This story is my heart on a page, blood, pulse, and heartbreak, all in one.

That said, this story includes many elements that I have faced in my own life. This is *not* a young adult novel, despite the age of some of the characters. This is an adult novel with adult themes. The choice of the characters ages comes from my own experiences in life before I turned eighteen—I was abused, I self-harmed, I considered that death would be much easier than life. These are very real, very serious issues that young people go through, though I have been convicted that this is *not* something I want to advertise to the young adult audience. This novel is an exploration of what it means to make sense of the senseless violence and heartache that some of us have experienced in our youth.

Please understand that this novel is an epic urban fantasy at its core; it is a bildungsroman with a literary bent. This series will span the lives of these characters—well into their adulthood and beyond. Please note that any use of angels and demons and the like in this book is purely fictitious and my own creative twist; it is not meant to be a serious or accurate portrayal of these matters. This book contains adult themes such as violence, swearing, sexual content, graphic content, abuse, self-harm, suicide, child abuse, assassin activities, use of drugs, alcohol, and weapons, and more. If these are sensitive or triggering topics for you, *please* do not read this novel and perhaps recommend it to a friend who might enjoy it more instead.

If you're in for the ride, hold on tight.

Seven years, seven drafts, seven Iterations…

Welcome to Angels' Compass.

GLOSSARY

— HIERARCHY —

ANGELIC RANKS (IN ORDER OF POWER)

Archangels – the highest ranking angel to walk the Earth, they oversee human affairs; they are placed on Earth every few hundred years to chart humanity's progress; they can compel humans to choose to be virtuous rather than sinful; they represent the Eight Virtues: Joy, Humility, Liberality, Patience, Diligence, Chastity, Abstinence, and Kindness

Archangel Heirs – the children of two Archangels

Nephilim – the children of one Archangel and one human; human women often die giving birth to the children of male Archangels

Angelborne Halfbreed – children conceived by an angel and a demon, delivered by an angel

Sentinels – guardian angels who take the angelic form that is the lower half of a land-dwelling creature (Landborne) or a sea-dwelling creature (Seaborne); (slang: *nymph* {for Landborne Sentinels} and *siren* {for Seaborne Sentinels})

Authorities – another name for avenging angels, especially the Four Horsemen of the Apocalypse; known for having some sort of power or authority over a certain topic, such as famine or war

The Four Horsemen of the Apocalypse – Conquest, War, Famine, and Death (reference: Revelation 6)

Saints – humans who have been ordained by Archangels or the Church for a holy purpose

DEMONIC RANKS (IN ORDER OF POWER)

Deceivers – the highest ranking demons to walk the Earth, they are shapeshifters; they tempt humans in the form of a human or as an invisible force; they represent the eight Cardinal Sins: Sorrow, Pride, Greed, Sloth, Wrath, Lust, Gluttony, and Envy

Demonborne Halfbreed – children conceived by an angel and a demon, delivered by a demon

The Fallen (slang: *swampers, cerebus*) – fallen angels

— IMPORTANT TERMS —

GENERAL

A History of Hierarchy – a book written by Saint Michael that details the angelic and demonic hierarchy on earth, along with information about the Iterations, Four Horsemen, and RUST; the information on RUST is only included in the Revised Edition (republished in 2085)

Fallen – a term used to describe an angel who has "fallen from grace"; for Sentinels this means breaking the Sentinels' Law (drinking blood) and for other angels it means to turn their back on God

Iterations – this refers to the different incarnations of the Archangels, Archangel Heirs, and Four Horsemen on Earth

Armageddon or *The Battle of Armageddon* – (also: the Final Battle) the final battle waged between angels and demons at the end of the world

Unseen Wars – invisible battles between angels and demons that happen on Earth, during day-to-day life, especially during storms or other natural disasters

God-Given Names – angelic names given by God to high-ranking angels and avenging angels, such as the Archangels and Four Horsemen

Sanctuary – a land, building, or area protected by memory altering affects of some angels; places where angels can go without keeping up an act; humans may encounter angels and be aware of it but will forget the happening as soon as they leave the Sanctuary; demon Sanctuaries also exist

Marks – protections cast by angels, much like spells or enchantments; some examples are Binding Marks, which suppress the affected's power, and Cloaking Marks, which hide one's true nature from being detected

Archangel Tattoo – a tattoo which Marks the ranks of Archangel, Archangel Heir, Nephilim, or Halfbreed

Holy Water – water which has been prayed over by high-ranking angels or saints

Black Magic – magic granted by the Devil or other high-ranking demons

Deathbenders – assassins employed by Cephan in RUST, they are able to die and come back to life repeatedly

The Soul Stitch – a compass brand, burned onto Deathbenders' skin with Hellfire, which is able to prevent one's soul from moving on to a different plane; it keeps

the Deathbenders' souls in the Abyss so they can be
brought back to life

THE SWORDS

Ferro, "The Sword of the Sentinels" – this is the sword that
was forged by the Archangels for Mars; in a past Iteration,
it was sheathed in a stone as Mars died in battle, then
renamed *Excalibur* in human legends

Scriptor de Mortem, "The Author of Death" – this is the
sword that was forged by the Archangels for Mori; it was
reforged in Hell to be a double-sided scythe

Scriptor de Exitium, "The Author of Destruction" – this
is the sword that was forged by the Archangels for Hades;
it was reforged in Hell to be a bident

— LOCATIONS & ORGANIZATIONS —

THE FIVE PLANES

Heaven – the first and highest plane; this is where God and
the angels reside

The Mediating Grounds – the plane between Heaven and
Earth; this is where angels and demons alike come to
report to God's Spokesperson

Earth – the midplane, where humans exist; angels and
demons also have the ability to move about in this plane,
interact with humans without revealing their true nature,
and sway Earthly battles

The Abyss – the plane between Earth and Hell, this is where
RUST exists; there is no light in this plane

Hell – the last and lowest plane, where Satan and the demons reside

OTHER LOCATIONS

North Academy – an advanced high school academy for those with angelic blood, founded by Valentine North

North Institute – a medical institute well-known for curing cancer, founded by Valentine North

North Tower – the headquarters of North Institute; located in the heart of Jacksonville, Florida

RUST – blacklisted assassin organization, banned from killing besides after dark; the assassins employed here exclusively wear black; founded by Cephan, located within the Abyss

Hell's Alley – a portal to Hell, located within the Bermuda Triangle

The Angels' Diner – a Sanctuary owned by Joshuah Braidensen

The Angels' Archive – an archive that includes the angels' history and knowledge which any angel descendant can access via pressing angelic blood to a library door handle

The RUST Archive – an archive that includes files of RUST targets, located in The Abyss

— CHARACTERS —

438 A.D. ROME (BY APPEARANCE)

Venatici – the daughter of the Canes patrician family, whose family has been accused of treason (earlier incarnation of Venatrix Canes)

Orion – one of the Gemini assassin twins (earlier incarnation of Orion Jude)

Ophiuchus – the other Gemini assassin twin (earlier incarnation of Ophiah Jude)

Serpens – a Scandinavian thief who's befriended Corvus and Ophiuchus (earlier incarnation of Jayren Omans)

Corvus – the slave driver for the Canes family (earlier incarnation of Corvun Khlyde)

Carina – a notorious pirate, friend and lover of Corvus (earlier incarnation of Carina Blackrock)

2106 – 2107 A.D. NORTHEAST FLORIDA
(BY FAMILY)

CANES

Samuel Canes (God-given name: Suriel) – Archangel, the Virtue of Chastity, husband to Rachael Canes, father of Caeleb, Erin, and Venatrix

Rachael Canes (God-given name: Raquel) – Archangel, the Virtue of Abstinence, wife to Samuel Canes, mother of Caeleb, Erin, and Venatrix

Caeleb Canes – Archangel Heir

Erin Canes – Archangel Heir

Venatrix Canes (God-given name: Victoria) – Archangel Heir, the Authority of Conquest

KHLYDE

Michael Khlyde (God-given name: Michael) – Archangel, the Virtue of Liberality, father of Corvun and Cynthia

Valkyrie Khlyde – deceased – Saint, mother of Corvun and Cynthia

Renee Khlyde – human, second wife to Michael and stepmother to Corvun and Cynthia

Corvun Khlyde (God-given name: Fames) – Nephilim, the Authority of Famine, firstborn son of Michael and Valkyrie

Cynthia Khlyde – Nephilim, daughter of Michael and Valkyrie

OMANS

James Omans – deceased – Seaborne Sentinel, father of Lacey and Jayren

Mia Omans – human, plagued by demons, mother of Lacey and Jayren

Lacey Omans – Seaborne Sentinel

Jayren Omans (God-given name: Mars) – Seaborne Sentinel, the Authority of War

JUDE

Tristan Jude – the Deceiver of Sorrow, father of Orion and Ophiah

Ariel "Missy" Jude (God-given name: Uriel) – Archangel, the Virtue of Kindness, mother of Orion and Ophiah

Orion Jude (God-given name: Mori) – Angelborne Halfbreed, the Authority of Death

Ophiah Jude (God-given name: Hades) – Angelborne Halfbreed, the Authority of Destruction

NORTH

Valentine North (God-given name: Valor) – Archangel, the Virtue of Joy, father of Cassie and Casper, headmaster of North Academy, founder of the North Institute

Gabrielle North (God-given name: Gabriel) – Archangel, the Virtue of Humility, mother of Cassie and Casper

Cassie North – Archangel Heir

Casper North – Archangel Heir

OTHER CHARACTERS (BY APPEARANCE)

Carina Blackrock (God-given name: Azrael) – Seaborne Sentinel, the Angel of Death

Leroy Blackrock – Fallen Seaborne Sentinel, mentor and adoptive father to Carina

Lynx Direlight – Nephilim, daughter of Remington Direlight, Corvun's cousin, Venatrix's best friend

Avon – the Deceiver of Greed, the "Kraken"

Cephan – leader of RUST

Empress Amy – the Deceiver of Sloth, ruler of Hell's Alley

Joshuah Braidensen – Landborne Sentinel, owner of The Angels' Diner

General Remington Direlight (God-given name: Remiel) – Archangel, the Virtue of Patience

Krista Martin – Saint decadency, girlfriend of Caeleb Canes

Dr. Ralph Bennett (God-given name: Raphael) – Archangel, the Virtue of Diligence

God's Spokesperson (also: the Spokesperson for the Lord) – an angel that resides in the Mediating Grounds, to which angels and demons report

I

THERE'S A STORM COMING

Ever since the crucifixion of Christ, the Eight Archangels have been sent to Earth in order to chart humanity and persuade humans into being virtuous and good. In every lifetime that the Archangels are sent to Earth, their children are also reborn. These lifetimes are known as Iterations.
— A History of Hierarchy

NOVEMBER 3RD, 2106 A.D.
ATLANTIC OCEAN
CARINA BLACKROCK

The sky is red.

The dress in your hands is red, too.

As the sun bleeds across the morning sky, you throw the ruined garment in the sea. The dress is heavy with salt water and blood. Saturated, like your body. Exhaustion weighs heavy on your chest as you watch the dress drift up and down on choppy waves and finally disappear behind a white cap. Down, below deck, Leroy is filling you a bath. To wash the blood from under your nails. To comb the blood out of your hair. To soak the war from your bones.

You do not think the mark of killing can ever truly be washed away, though. Not really.

You descend below deck, and Leroy offers you a towel and a bar of perfumed soap. He gives you a sad smile of wrinkly, red skin and a wiry gray beard. The eye patch over his left eye is pinched in that familiar smile. "Take ya'r time now, ya hear?"

You nod.

You step into the washroom and close the door. The ship lulls. The bath splashes gently. Your clothes—a borrowed shirt and a pair of shorts—fall to the ground in a soft thud. You listen to your heels thump across the wood beneath, grateful for the quiet sound of home. It is your heartbeat, the song in your soul.

Your feet slip into the metal tub, and your eyes close.

Screams begin ringing in your ears. Shrieking. The clash of swords. Teeth gnashing. All of it, hauntings of the war you have just won, singlehandedly. Leroy predicted it—predicted that God would come with the storm. In a way, he was right. You acted, as God's hand of vengeance, to wipe out every demon that lived on the island you had been held captive on. It was called Hell's Alley, it was hidden in the Bermuda Triangle, and it was a portal to Hell.

Your arrival had been an unfortunate mistake—you had been lost at sea months before. Once you arrived, neither of you were permitted to leave. The residents there—the demons—had worshiped you as a prophesied princess, and Leroy had called their bullshit. You were hostages, but treated like royalty, until Leroy uncovered a plot to sacrifice you to the Devil.

That was the night before.

And by God's grace and mercy, you survived.

NOVEMBER 3RD, 2106 A.D.
NORTHEAST FLORIDA
VENATRIX CANES

The party bumped downstairs. Uninterested in whatever trouble her brothers were conspiring with all the other students from her classes, Venatrix held her Glass phone in her hand. On the screen, hovering above her own palm, was a picture of two bikers in a social media post.

One rider wore a casual get-up: faded jeans with a slit across each pale knee, a gray band tee, red Converse, and a wine-red scarf around his neck. The visor of his firetruck-red helmet blocked his eyes from sight.

The other rider wore all black—something too bold and controversial to do in their time. Wearing all black was a sign, in their day and age, a promise of violence. Only assassins wore black, and the biker in the picture was sworn to become one. His visor was up, leaving only a strip of his eyes visible to Venatrix; they peered at her darkly, menacingly, and in a way that Venatrix had known all her life.

Still, her blood boiled.

Venatrix locked her phone. The images faded from view, leaving her see-through cell dormant in her hand. She placed it on the desk beside her and turned back to her computer. She spread her hands over the pulsing, blue keyboard, electricity thrumming in her fingertips. On the screen of her gaming PC, a browser displayed a checkout screen and a bright white sportbike in the cart.

She reached for her parents' credit card, anger simmering just under her skin.

He promised we'd buy bikes together. He promised.

A loud knock sounded on Venatrix's door frame.

"Go away!" Venatrix yelled. Her eyes scanned the shipping address listed on the screen.

Another knock.

Venatrix groaned. *I wish I could move out,* she thought bitterly. She fantasized about running away for a moment, considered where she could go and hide out. But running away meant she'd have to drop out, and she *wanted* her education; it was important to her. Not to mention, she couldn't get this education anywhere else.

Another knock.

"Leave me the fuck alone!"

If she heard one more knock, she thought she might bust a blood vessel in her forehead.

Bangbangbang.

Venatrix shot up from her gaming chair and launched herself at the door. She swung it open, fixing the most vitriolic death glare she could manage on her older brother.

Caeleb stood there with a lazy grin on his pale face. Long, dark strands of hair coiled over his shoulders like drips of an oil spill. "Why don't you come downstairs?"

"You know why," Venatrix gnawed at the words. A feeling of emptiness and despair gnawed at her heart, too.

Caeleb gave a lazy, careless smile. "Still mad Corvun's not talking to you?"

Venatrix slammed the door in her brother's face. She turned and pressed her back to the door, exhaling through thinly parted lips. Wrong move. Of course she was still upset over her falling out with her best friend, but making a scene over it would only worsen things. Her brothers picked at any weakness she showed.

Venatrix listened to the sound of Caeleb's footsteps disappearing down the hallway. She was in the clear. She sank to the floor, hugging her knees. She thought of the picture on her phone—of Corvun and his new motorcycle and his new friend. Jealousy burned inside her.

Footsteps returned, slowly, one by one. Two by two.

More knocking.

Venatrix hauled herself up, resolution settling inside her. She'd tell her brothers to not so kindly *fuck off*. Her friendships—or lack thereof—were her business. She was tired of hanging around in her brothers' friend circles; Corvun had gotten tired of that a while ago. Venatrix wished she would've come to her senses at the same time.

She opened the door.

Caeleb stood in the doorway with Erin this time. Her brothers looked strikingly similar. The only difference between them was their years, the style of their hair, and their eyebrows. Erin had a shorter haircut which left his black locks cut choppy and sharp around his angular jaw. His eyebrows were a little thicker than Caeleb's, but they both shared the same, ice-cold, knife-like eyes that cut way too deep into her insecurities.

"Come downstairs and party with us," Caeleb said again.

Venatrix's stomach bottomed out. She pleaded with Erin silently—staring at him with as much horror and self-pity as she could manage. He used to be on her side, too.

"C'mon, it'll be fun," Erin's pale lips moved slowly, his voice detached from his body.

Venatrix's world spun. Her free will slipped from her grip on it, and just like that, she felt the need to do whatever it was that Caeleb and Erin asked.

Somewhere deep inside her mind, she watched herself. She could brush the edge of her consciousness with mental fingertips, but she no longer had control of what she did. Venatrix observed herself from faraway as her body followed her brothers down the hall and down the stairs into the neon-lit, liquor-drenched party below.

Her bedroom door gaped open behind her.

She would have shut it.

She should have never opened it.

The party was a blur of half-clad bodies and glossy bottles of aged wine and bourbon and whiskey. Her parents' liquor cabinet sat open in the corner, like her bedroom door. The inside was dark and hazy. She couldn't tell what was left.

Venatrix tried to think of something else as her body moved of its own accord. A red cup at her lips, the burn of whiskey in her nose. She closed her eyes and saw Corvun. She was sitting in the corner with him, in her mind. They were at the outskirts of the party, talking about everyone there. Who's who and what's what. Corvun always knew more about the hierarchy of angels and had tabs on what kind of angels or descendants attended their private academy. In her mind, Corvun was telling her about their classmates. Flashes of their faces between blinks. Venatrix knew everyone's name. She knew everyone's secrets. Her brothers and Corvun had made sure of that. Venatrix had navigated the popularity scene with ease with the three of them.

Liquor ran down her throat.

Stomach acid and bile backtracked up.

She was dancing with someone who had his hands under her shirt and on her waist.

Venatrix drank again.

She opened her eyes and placed Corvun's face over his.

They used to dance together at these parties, too.

Warm breath on her neck. Cool air on her back.

Corvun used to make a spectacle. He used to get them both on the table and dance traditional ballroom dances. They used to be the life of the party.

Venatrix found herself back in that moment. She was on a table again.

Only this time, she was on the table in her memories, in an out-of-body vision. Her body moved with the music. Her skin buzzed with the alcohol that pounded through her veins.

Rage was there, too.

It settled in, like a poison.

Every twist, every turn.

She would make them pay.

NOVEMBER 4TH, 2106 A.D.
NORTHEAST FLORIDA
CORVUN KHLYDE

"God, I hate the South," Jayren mumbled through his helmet at the stoplight.

Corvun hummed in response to his friend's gripe. The Florida sun reflected off Jayren's deep red sportbike. Corvun was more than aware that his friend had no interest in being here. Corvun didn't know too much about Jayren's past, only that he'd reluctantly moved from Indiana some time ago.

The light turned green, and the two of them took off down the road. This was their morning ritual: ride their motorcycles to North Academy together. It was the best way to get close parking and avoid walking with the other students and being subject to unwanted bullying. They pulled their motorcycles up to a small spot in the shade of the academy building and kicked their stands out. They left their helmets hanging on the backs of the bikes, and Corvun pocketed his small key. Jayren did the same, but kept his hands stuffed in his pants.

As they walked towards the school building, Corvun checked his phone. A sickening feeling roiled in his stomach.

There were new messages on his phone; he knew what that meant. Instead of reading the texts, he said, "The Canes' siblings threw another party last night."

"You go?" Jayren asked.

"Hell no." Corvun had stopped going when Caeleb and Erin Canes had started busting out their parents' liquor at the parties. Jayren had said that seemed like the right time to *start* going, but Jayren had never been invited to any of the parties. Jayren always said it was probably because he was still wearing glasses and braces at seventeen, but Corvun didn't have the heart to tell him that it was because he wasn't in Caeleb's inner circle.

"Was Vena there?"

"Yeah," Corvun said. "Always." He wasn't happy about it. Then again, he hadn't felt happy about anything in a long time.

Jayren changed the topic. "Did you hear *cleopatra's* new song?"

"No," Corvun said.

"It's pretty dope. She's got an all-acoustic setup in the song," Jayren said.

Corvun didn't respond.

"It's pretty damn cool if you ask me. Humanity hasn't seen a real musician since before World War III. There's too much dumb artificial bullshit out there if you ask me. I think people are finally getting sick of it. *cleopatra*, though, I think she's gonna make it big among the 'bots." Jayren picked at his braces.

He made a point, and Corvun agreed. About eighty years ago, there had been a wave of new art, the "New Era Art" that had run most creatives out of jobs—artists, writers, musicians. There were plenty of old-school connoisseurs that listened to pre- and early 2000s music that was written by real humans, but it was mostly a lost art. Corvun and Jayren shared that in common; they both made a point to support any human artists they found.

Corvun had a bunch of music he pirated from OneStream back at home, too. He'd put it all on CDs with an old converter he found at a vintage shop. He had one called *THE SICKEST MIXES* that Jayren swore by.

Jayren asked if they could plan a game night and give their homemade record a spin.

Corvun agreed absently.

Ever since the start of the month, it'd been hard to focus on anything but the impending sense of doom that hung over him.

Corvun's nineteenth birthday was in seven days. It wouldn't have been so bad if it were just any other birthday. Corvun wasn't one to draw attention to himself much either, at least not recently; his birthday was just another day. But this birthday would be the day he was sworn into RUST.

Corvun had known about it since he was twelve. His father, the Archangel Michael, had been a member of RUST—an underground assassin organization. Michael never told Corvun the exact circumstances in which he got caught up with the criminals, but he told Corvun the way he got out. What Corvun did know: the RUST pact is meant to be for life. Only a sacrifice of pure, selfless intent can break the RUST pact. His father had no way out, but the leader of the RUST assassins, named Cephan, offered him a deal: If Michael signed a blood contract, promising that his firstborn would return in his place at the age of nineteen, Michael could escape RUST.

Corvun was Michael's firstborn.

It was just a shitty hand he'd been dealt, paying for his father's mistakes. *It is what it is,* Corvun thought. He'd been training for this day for years, learning how to street fight among all other forms of fighting, learning how to use weapons and guns. Learning how to defend himself. Learning—or at the very least, being told—how to keep his faith. As if killers could have faith.

But this is who he would be. It was who he was already becoming. It's who he was, somewhere deep down, because in the end, he had a rank just as high as his father's.

All of this swam in his head as he stood there numbly. Jayren was talking, but Corvun barely heard him.

His phone gleamed with a text from Caeleb, a picture of Venatrix dancing shirtless on her family's dinner table. Her long, raven-black hair was a silky swirl around her nimble shoulders. Her shorts could barely be considered shorts. 'You missed a good one,' was the text Caeleb sent with the picture. Corvun couldn't imagine how many more people got the same photo, the same text. His stomach tightened uneasily. Things felt like they were all spiraling, all at once. He wasn't sure what the catalyst was, but he could feel the shift.

Things had been set in motion.

Something changed.

NOVEMBER 4TH, 2106 A.D.
NORTHEAST FLORIDA
VENATRIX CANES

Raven-black hair fell to the ground in eight-inch-long clumps. Dull kitchen scissors sawed and sawed and sawed. Cool air brushed her neck. Finally, the braided elastic in Venatrix's hair slipped loose and fell to the ground, too.

Venatrix's hair hung short and choppy around her sharp jawline. She used the bathroom mirror to trim fistfuls of hair and even out the severe cut. It didn't do much, but that was okay. Venatrix was going for severe. She checked the back of her hair with a handheld mirror, and she looked at the tattoo on the back of her neck.

The tattoo was composed of thin black lines, and it depicted a coat of arms—a shield with four feathered wings fanning from it, upward in victory. It was a Mark of her heritage as an Archangel Heir. Her father and mother were two of the Seven Archangels—Samuel and Rachael—but they took human forms to walk among people. The Archangels were sent to Earth like this to chart humanity, to sway humans into being virtuous and good. The Archangels were powerful too—with the ability to change common knowledge, to influence people with a power of persuasion, and they were dangerous.

Venatrix was powerful and dangerous, too.

That's what she intended to show. Her Mark. Her rank. Her power.

All because of what happened the night before.

Venatrix was almost always the center of attention in North Academy. North Academy—under the guise of a prestigious, private school—was dedicated to all who were angels, saints, or descendants of anyone with angelic blood. Venatrix maintained a level of stardom there for her rank as an Archangel Heir. Her brothers, Caeleb and Erin, were popular too, but Venatrix was convinced they controlled the school with their power of persuasion. The three were known for the parties they put on when their parents were out on Archangel business, and Venatrix thrived on the attention. Originally, she liked the new attention she got for her developing body—her slight curves and dainty, tall stature. She was growing into the body of a runway model. Now she felt different. At fifteen, she wanted to show off her body. At fifteen and a half, she stopped.

Cutting her hair was an act of defiance, a way to warn anyone against testing her the way her brothers had done.

She wouldn't let it happen again.

Venatrix turned and glared into the mirror. Her pale blue eyes were electric with anger, with ambition, with power.

She refused her brothers' carpool, making an excuse that she was on her period, and then she walked to school on her own. She was late. Fashionably late.

Venatrix stood in the double-door entrance to the grand hall of North Academy. She looked nothing like the other students because she had done everything *not* to. Venatrix wore her blouse untucked and unbuttoned, a pair of jeans instead of her uniform skirt, and hadn't bothered with the obnoxious tie required for everyone. Forget the suit jacket.

The Archangel tattoo on the back of her neck flashed at her audience as she stalked down the hall. She liked their horrified attention. She wore her tattoo like jewelry today. Showing her Mark was strictly prohibited; it was an act of rebellion against the Archangels. She knew the repercussions—from her brothers, her parents, the school. She didn't care. All she knew was that her nerves were alive and buzzing, that adrenaline was shooting through her veins like Novocain, numbing everything but her sky-high ego.

She swept her eyes down the school hallway, locked sights with seniors from the night before, and she plotted her revenge. One after the other. Onto the next. But she wasn't ready to meet *his* hard, defiant gaze. He stood to the left side of the hall and watched her. Corvun Khlyde. He'd watched her like a vulture ever since he stopped going to her brothers' parties. In the regal school—its high, cathedral-esque ceilings, gold inlay lockers, and white pillared doorways—Corvun was a shadow, a bad omen. Hollows caved his pale cheeks, and cynical, pessimistic lines wore at the sides of his lips. He looked as if he already knew everything he needed to know about life, even just at eighteen. But Venatrix was always drawn back to his eyes. If eyes were the gateway to the soul, then his gate stood open and gaping in a sinister challenge, a dare for her to step inside.

Beside him, his blond sidekick, Jayren Omans, slouched against the gold-and-silver lockers. His green eyes flashed behind thick, black-rimmed glasses; he hissed a comment between his braces. Venatrix gave his red tie a second glance when she realized it wasn't a tie at all—it was a knotted scarf, the scarf he wore in their social media post. It seemed she wasn't the only one breaking the rules this morning.

"So this is the real reason you missed our carpool," Caeleb said behind her. Venatrix turned to glare at her brother, and he raised his eyebrows in return. He eyed her hair. Caeleb was tall and cruel and underhanded. Nothing about Caeleb was likable, not even his long black hair that he wore in a glossy ponytail behind his back. Venatrix was glad to be rid of hers. "You could've at least worn some makeup to knock the edge off that death glare. You look terrible," Caeleb said.

"You can shove that makeup right up your ass, Caeleb." She pushed her brother in the chest and tried to side-step him.

Caeleb grabbed her arm. "I hope you realize how much trouble you're about to be in. I'd rather you behave than be neck-deep in detention slips."

Behave, Venatrix scoffed. She looked away from her brother's cold blue eyes. She gritted her teeth, weighed her options, and glanced pathetically in Corvun's direction. She doubted he would help her. They grew up as best friends, but their latest feud was too new, wounds were still open and bleeding. He had no reason to help her.

Corvun raised his hand to his mouth and brushed his knuckles against his lips. He watched her with an eyebrow cocked in amusement. Jayren prodded at Corvun's arm; Jayren's stream of chatter was inaudible but quick and on edge.

"You're going to ruin my reputation, Vena," Caeleb warned under his breath.

"You mean no one's going to come to your parties because your sister won't strip and dance on tables anymore." She struggled against Caeleb's vise-like grip.

Cold, sweaty hands plucked the grip from her arm.

Venatrix gaped as Jayren stepped between them. She looked to Corvun in surprise, but Corvun just shrugged.

"Dude, back off. You shouldn't be treating her like that," Jayren said in a voice that was soft and timid and nasally.

Venatrix opened her mouth to interrupt.

Caeleb slammed Jayren against the lockers in a clatter.

Jayren's hands shot up in surrender. His glasses slid crooked on his nose. Caeleb's massive height shadowed Jayren's small, disheveled stature. "Alright, alright. Fine! I'm sorry! Forget I said anything, man," Jayren uttered frantically. "Sorry."

"Didn't your father teach you not to pick fights you can't win?"

Jayren twitched.

"Oh, of course not. I forgot—he's dead."

Venatrix held her breath.

Corvun yanked Caeleb away from Jayren. He nailed Caeleb in the nose in a silence-shattering crack of cartilage. Caeleb collapsed.

"*Khlyde!*"

Venatrix spun on her heels. Her heart raced.

The headmaster of North Academy stalked in their direction, hair windblown and wild.

She glanced back to see Caeleb hunched over on the blue mosaic floor, holding his nose. Blood leaked through his fingers. When she turned back, Professor Valentine North towered over the four of them.

Professor North's strong shoulders made Venatrix wonder if he wore armor beneath his three-piece suit. His tan skin and golden-brown mane of hair created a glowing aura around him. The righteous resentment in his eyes silenced the murmuring in the hallway. Time halted in his presence, and not even Caeleb dared to speak. "I want the three of you in my office. Caeleb, find your way to the nurse," Professor North said. He looked at each of them one at a time, then turned and marched back in the direction he came from.

Corvun followed first, shouldering Venatrix as he passed. Venatrix tensed.

The lockers behind her rattled. Jayren sulked up beside her. He tugged at the knot of his makeshift tie until the scarf unraveled. He pulled it out from where it coiled beneath his collar, offering it to her. "Here. I'm sure you don't want any more attention at this point, or at least I would hope not. You can use it to hide your tattoo." He pushed the red scarf into her reluctant hands. He walked away.

Venatrix stared down at the worn fabric. Her mind spun. The frayed threads were comforting in her hands. It held no sentimental value to her, but all at once, it meant the whole world. She wrapped it around her neck, and it eased the lump in her throat. It was the first time a boy offered her clothing, not taken it away. "Wait!" She called after Jayren. He paused, and she caught up to him. "Thank you."

"Yeah." He fixed his glasses, kept his head down, and didn't acknowledge her for the rest of the walk to the office.

· · · ·

It was the first time Venatrix had been in Professor North's office. The room was wide, the walls paneled with dark wood and decorated by framed portraits of people Venatrix vaguely recognized from her history lessons. She was pretty sure the one with curly, cherry-blond hair was Christopher Columbus. His crew stood with him, bordered in gold. Upon closer inspection, Venatrix swore she spotted Valentine in the picture with a somber expression. She wished she could ask the story, but she knew now wasn't the time.

Despite the warm colors and homey decorations, Professor North's office was cold. It smelled like firewood, and the massive windows behind the professor's desk blazed with smog-filtered, midday light. Their professor stood in the center of the windows, looking out at an oncoming storm front, and the daylight created a hazy, glowing halo around his figure. "Venatrix Canes," he started, his voice cutting through their silence.

She winced.

Corvun scoffed, and Venatrix shot him a glare. He slouched in his chair, arms crossed.

Without looking, North said, "Sit up, Khlyde."

Corvun straightened in obedience, glared back at Venatrix, and she crinkled her nose in disgust.

"Miss Canes, you know better than to act this way," Professor North scolded. The words should have burned, but the professor's voice buffered the sting. It was as smooth as a lake at dawn. It was a trait of the Archangels, to have calming effects on those around them. Professor North was the leader of the Archangels, and his powers far surpassed hers. Venatrix didn't know the extent of his abilities, but she knew they didn't stop at simply a calming voice. North turned, and his gold eyes settled on Venatrix. "I should throw you out for cutting your hair. Revealing your tattoo is strictly prohibited. It is a prideful act, Miss Canes. Do you wish to end up like Lucifer, too? Had Mr. Omans not been so kind as to loan you his scarf, I'd have you sent home. I would've let your parents worry about it if it weren't for what you are."

"Who," Venatrix corrected.

Professor North sat in his chair and steepled his hands on the desk. His gaze held her captive, and even if she'd wanted to, she knew she wouldn't be able to stand, much less walk out of the office. The professor looked to Corvun, and the weight left her shoulders. "Mr. Khlyde, your father taught you better than to be a bad influence."

Corvun gripped the armrests of the chair he sat in. "I did nothin' wrong," his voice dripped like venom—steady, callous, and cold. A small, lisp-like falter caught the end of his words.

"You cannot attack other students. Whether or not you were defending Venatrix, this isn't good behavior. There are better ways to stand up for your friends."

"I wasn't defendin' her. She's not my friend," Corvun bit back sourly.

"Dude, seriously? You were just talking about her right before she walked in! You were literally saying you wanted to go to her brothers' parties to—"

Venatrix's ears rang, drowning out Jayren's rambling. Her skin burned.

Professor North studied something behind them.

Corvun interrupted Jayren and said, "She's not our friend."

The silence that followed shattered Venatrix. Her ears and neck flushed red. She wanted to knock Corvun's front teeth out for brushing her off so naturally. She'd make him sorry.

The headmaster scratched a note on a small piece of paper with a black and gold fountain pen, then handed the Corvun the slip. "Alright. Corvun, I'll be giving your father a call, nonetheless. You will report to detention Monday after school. Don't let it happen again. Dismissed."

Venatrix jumped at the offer, hands on her armrests and ready to stand, but Professor North glared at her. She froze.

He clicked his tongue and leaned back, saying, "Not you. Not yet. I want to have a word with you alone."

Venatrix looked away. She listened to Corvun and Jayren exchange a few words regarding Jayren's lucking out of detention as they exited the office. She heard Jayren yap, "Hell on Earth!" when the office door swung open. She glanced over her shoulder to see another student standing in the doorway.

"Well, you're not totally wrong," the student noted.

Venatrix agreed in a way. He was clean-kept and tall and handsome as hell in her opinion. She had never seen red hair as rich and dark as his. A stray strand slipped loose by his freckled cheek; he stared back at her with gray-green eyes. She knew him through mutual friends. His name was Orion Jude, and the whole school spread rumors about him as if he were some sort of infamous killer walking among them. Still, she hadn't talked to him much and knew little about him besides those rumors.

Orion's expressionless face looked forced. Venatrix stared into his eyes, and she recognized something of herself in his reflection. She was pretty sure it was chaos in his eyes which he controlled so well. But something about him was much more attractive than her, she thought. Maybe it was the warm tone of his skin, or his reserved demeanor, or maybe it was because he looked like he'd just walked off the set of a fashion magazine photo shoot. *He could make the front cover of any style or beauty magazine he wanted to,* she swore to herself.

"It seems our time has been cut short," Professor North said to Venatrix. He sighed, soft but exhausted at the same time. "Go on. You will report to detention on Monday with Corvun. I'd like to speak with Mr. Jude for a moment."

Venatrix stood and turned to leave, but a life-sized mural hanging on the wall opposite the headmaster's desk stopped her briefly in her tracks. The painting composed a fury of colors—reds and deep blues and golds, darkness and light—into a clashing, brilliant cacophony that she could hear through the stillness of the frame holding it. She recognized the illustration as the Four Horsemen of the Apocalypse. On her brisk walk out, she realized that the riders lacked eyes. In their place, immaculate white.

ORION JUDE

Orion's spine ached from his posture and composure. He tried to hold Professor North's unwavering gaze, but he faltered and glanced away. The office door clicked shut, and Orion's façade crumbled to the floor. His neck beaded with sweat. His hands curled into fists behind his back, fingernails digging into his palms. He hadn't wanted to interrupt the professor, but he was on the edge of losing control. Again.

The headmaster's silence crushed Orion.

"I'm sorry, sir," Orion said, looking down. He studied the hardwood floor, the worn hem of the royal blue and purple oriental rug, the flecks of bronze on the ends of the tassels. He listened to Professor North tap his black and gold fountain pen on the desk.

"How is your mother, Orion? And your sister?"

"Fine, sir," he lied. His throat was scraped and sore as if it was lodged with broken glass.

"Has your father burned the Bibles again?"

Orion hesitated. Finding words was as hard as trying to pry that shattered glass from an inch-deep wound. "He's not my father, sir."

"Father or not, you have his blood. Do you know what that makes you?"

Halfbreed, a faraway voice whispered. Orion became accustomed to the voices over the years; the demons always spoke to him when they tried to take control.

"I'd rather not answer that," Orion said.

The professor set his pen down.

Orion closed his eyes. "Evil. Isn't that what I am to you? The dirt you walk on, a disgrace to your legacy and all the other—"

"Powerful, Orion," Professor North interrupted. "It makes you powerful."

Orion looked up at the headmaster's silhouette. In the light of the bright, gray-tinted window, Orion watched black smears paint his vision into monotone. Blood trickled down his top lip. A headache crashed into his skull like a sledgehammer.

"Why don't you come have a seat?" the headmaster offered. He opened a drawer and took out a pill bottle. He slid the medication and a water bottle towards Orion.

Another clash of stone splintered against his skull, and the sound of shrill, shrieking metal flooded his brain. He knew that before long he would lose consciousness, so he took slow, unsteady steps across the office. The ground quivered like crumbling concrete under his feet, as if the world shook with a tremulous warning of an oncoming rupture, a crack that would split beneath him and swallow him whole. He figured falling to the pit of the Earth and burning alive would be better than the entire hierarchy of angels telling him he was no good. As he gripped the armrests and lowered himself into the office chair, he wondered if Hell would abandon him the same. He wondered, in fleeting, if he could live among humans in secret, fading into a world that was oblivious to the spiritual wars happening all around them. He wanted somewhere to belong.

Professor North watched him and took a deep breath.

Orion hesitated again before reaching for the pills. He noticed the shaking in his own hand as he reached further; his muscles melted as he fought to keep a hold of the bottle. It was his only means of survival. The demons didn't like it because it would temporarily ward them off. Orion knew. The demons knew. Professor North knew, too.

"Why did you come to see me today?" Professor North asked.

"I want to know about the deal my mother made with the demons," Orion said quietly.

Orion managed to open the bottle but dropped the lid by accident. He shook two pills out into his palm. The sweat on his neck plastered his hair against his own mandatory Archangel tattoo. He caught a glimpse of Venatrix's tattoo during her dramatic entrance. It was the first time Orion realized his design was different. Hers was beautiful. His was simple, lesser.

He raised his palm to his lips. The pills stung his mouth like stale poison, sour and bitter and chalky. The water didn't do much, and he felt as if he was swallowing forest burs that had been rolled in bile. He tried to suppress the gag reflex that washed over him.

"I'm sorry we haven't educated you better."

Orion's sight had almost gone black, and he kept his head down to try to hide the fact.

"Your father is the most powerful demon that walks the Earth. He leads the other seven Deceivers. He threatened…" Professor North paused, "he threatened to kill one of the

Archangels in this lifetime—something he is very much capable of doing—and we rushed into a solution. The death of an Archangel would be detrimental to the plans our God has for us. I don't know that there was a right answer. Orion…your mother agreed to be a peace offering, a sort of truce between both the Archangels and the Deceivers. In exchange for her hand in marriage, the Deceivers agreed to an armistice for sixteen years. Your father…"

Orion had always known in his gut that his father was a demon, but he didn't know enough about the hierarchy of angels and demons to even begin to guess which kind of demon he might be. He wasn't surprised to learn his father was a Deceiver. It made sense to him. "He burned the Bibles again," Orion's voice cracked, and his words dragged dry out of his throat like smoke from a dwindling fire. The tears that formed at the sides of his eyes didn't ease the burn. "All of them, even the one Ophiah keeps hidden inside her baby blanket at the top of our closet. He took our phones and snapped them in half."

Professor North was silent for a moment. "Like it or not, you are his son, and that makes you just as dangerous. You must—"

"I thought you said powerful!" Orion accused. He looked up to the professor, squinting against the black in his eyes.

"You must first choose your side, Orion."

"How does this help the situation? Even if I side with the angels, none of you will ever really accept me."

"I need you to understand what you are. Orion, *you* are the Authority of Death. You are one of the Four Horsemen."

There it is, Orion thought. *That's the piece I've been missing.*

"The Archangel your father threatened to kill was your mother, Ariel. You would have never been born," a rare emotion threatened Professor North's voice. "Though, it seems, your father has dealt a hand against you—against us. Does this make you stronger or weaker?"

"It makes me *abused*," Orion said with half a sigh, aghast.

"You cannot change the past, Orion. And you must understand the stakes here. This trauma—you could pass this on, inflict on others what has been inflicted on you. You must forgive him; it is the only way to move forward."

A shadow cast across Orion's heart inwardly. "I don't think I could ever forgive him for what he's done. No matter how hard I try."

Valentine's lips pressed thin. "Regardless, you have to accept who you are and what you've been through before you get better."

"Better?" Orion bit at the word. "Really? That's an option?"

"We've talked to Ophiah about this, and she agreed to get help. She's already started on a medication and—"

Orion stood and threw the pill bottle back onto the headmaster's desk. The pills cast small, dancing shadows across the glossy surface before falling to the floor.

"—they're working wonders on her. Orion, sit down."

"That's because she chooses to believe these crap lies you angels feed her. Kind of like the placebo effect, yeah?"

"You will lose yourself fighting this battle alone. We are not the enemy." Professor North was clear in Orion's vision now. The professor's tense muscles and stiff grip on his fountain pen made his frustration evident. "We need you to get better."

"Why? So you can spit on me and tell me I'm still not good enough?" Orion glared down at his headmaster, gritting his teeth. He could see normally again, and he saw the prescription Professor North had written on a small, blue paper.

The stray pills dotted the teacher's desk, but amid the chaos, Professor North kept his composure. He offered Orion the prescription. "If nothing else, do this for your sister, Orion. She hates to see you like this."

VALENTINE NORTH

Orion took the prescription before he turned and stalked from the room.

Valentine sat silently, watching him go. As Orion slipped out the door, Valentine's eyes drifted to the mural opposite his desk. The Four Horsemen of the Apocalypse were painted in great detail there—so much so that the similarities between the four students that had just been in his office and the four warriors painted were uncanny. It was always their growth that astounded Valentine; to see them go from awkward, lanky children to dangerous, avenging angels was a miracle, the hand of God at work.

So much was different in this latest lifetime—things that Valentine hadn't anticipated. The sixteen-year armistice had put an end to the Unseen Wars waged between angels and demons so that Valentine and the other Archangels could focus on raising their children. But that time was over now. They had hoped it was long enough to instill peace and build a righteous foundation under the feet of the Four, especially. What Valentine hadn't factored in was the abuse Orion and Ophiah now faced from their father.

What awaited the Four worried Valentine, too. Their purpose was unique among angels, especially the ones on Earth. Each lifetime—each Iteration in which the Archangels had come to Earth and the Four Horsemen reborn—served as a trial. They were born into eras with major wars or world conflict. The Four Horsemen were to train, to ready themselves to fight in that human war. In each of their past lifetimes, the Four had died in combat. Valentine knew that the war in which they fought and *won* would be the catalyst for the Final Battle of Armageddon. Their victory would serve as their readiness to fight for the end of the world. Valentine had no doubt that this would come to be.

But Michael, Valentine's right-hand Archangel, had brought something else to Valentine's attention, something worrying. The Four Horsemen had influence in the Final Battle. If they fought for Heaven's Army, the Earth would be reclaimed for Heaven, but if they fought for Hell's Army, the Earth would be forever under Hell's reign. It was all dependent on their alignment. If the Four continued to walk in righteousness, to acknowledge God as their commander, they would fight for Heaven; if they fell—turned their backs on God and His Law—they would fight for Hell. Valentine was hopeful the Four would honor their origins, but Michael had pressed that between the twins' abuse and Corvun's upcoming initiation to RUST, there was room for concern. Valentine tried to calm Michael, reminding him they were doing everything in their power to save Corvun from his fate, but even he wasn't sure if the things already set in motion could be stopped.

VENATRIX CANES

"Hey! Hey, wait!" Venatrix chased after Corvun as she fled the office. She sidestepped Jayren, caught Corvun's sleeve, and yanked him around. "Wait," she said firmly, catching her breath.

Corvun raised his eyebrows, and she saw the sly, demeaning amusement in his eyes. It was the first emotion he'd shown towards her in months.

She didn't like how his emotions felt.

"What?" he snapped.

"What do you mean, you don't even know me?" She shoved him in the chest. Her blood pounded in her ears.

"Well, I sure as hell don't feel like I know you anymore. We were supposed to be on each other's sides."

Venatrix glanced at Jayren's staring eyes, and he looked away quickly. His face was red with embarrassment as he chewed on the dry skin of his bottom lip.

"You were supposed to be on my side, Vena," Corvun pressed. "Best friends forever, 'til Armageddon and after. Remember?"

The line shocked her, cut deeper than she wanted it to. It was a vow they made to each other when they were only kids. Venatrix thought back to the night before. She was ashamed to admit it, but she'd looked for Corvun in the crowd of students at the party more than once. He used to come to the parties until he and Caeleb got into a fight a couple years back. Venatrix had tried to break it up. He'd asked whose side she was on then, just like he was asking now. Venatrix's confidence stripped away as Corvun's hard gaze picked apart her face. She knew he could see the remnants of makeup, the beginning of a hickey which she had put an immediate stop to.

"You changed," he said coolly.

She looked away, focusing instead on the rip in the left hem of Jayren's slacks and a bloodstain that looked as if it'd had several failed attempts to be scrubbed out. "Then why did you stand up for me? Why did either of you bother?" Venatrix asked.

"I was standin' up for Jayren," Corvun said.

"Dude, don't be an ass," Jayren said.

Corvun rolled his eyes. "Your brothers are idiots. We like you more than we like your brothers. It's like pickin' the lesser of three evils."

"C'mon, stop!" Jayren stepped between them, nudging Corvun back.

"I did it because it's what you deserved," Corvun said finally. "It's what I deserved. It's what I wish you would've done for me."

"I thought…" Her words grew heavy, and it became hard to breathe. "I…"

"That's your problem, Vena. It's all about you. Try thinkin' about someone else for a change."

Venatrix searched Corvun's black eyes, but his emotion vanished as quickly as it had made its cruel visit.

Corvun turned his back and walked away. Venatrix looked to Jayren, but he looked down—pausing on his scarf—before turning and following Corvun. She stood in the circular, terrace-like lobby and watched their figures get swept away into the wave of students beyond. She blinked away frustration. She would prove him wrong. She hadn't changed, not like he said she had.

Venatrix wore her tennis shoes to ballet class that night.

CORVUN KHLYDE

"No way. There's no way you're actually going to ballet class. What the actual flying duck." Jayren created a few more clever, off-brand swears, stood, and dropped his gaming remote into the low-sitting sofa behind him. He followed Corvun across the room. "Dude, that's mortifying. Yes, I'd love to go pirouette around in a tutu 'til our brains fly out of our ears. Are you crazy?"

Corvun grabbed both their backpacks, tossed Jayren's into his chest, then slung his own over his shoulder. He shot Jayren an exasperated side glance. "Let's go, Jay."

Jayren threw his backpack onto the couch and grabbed the cord of his lamp off the floor.

Corvun turned, unsuspecting, and tripped over the makeshift booby trap. Corvun catapulted into the closed bedroom door and collapsed, defeated.

"Listen, you ass!" Jayren said. "I don't want to go. And you don't want to go just to humiliate yourself, so what's the deal?"

Corvun slumped against the door. His arms and legs were numb with exhaustion. He thought about the weightlifting and workout regimen his father insisted on daily. He considered he should've opted for a five-mile run instead of his training that morning before school.

"Dude," Jayren's voice was monotone for once. Jayren knew about Corvun's training, about how much it wore him out. "How are you gonna dance?"

"You know, I still go sometimes. On those days you make excuses to ditch class because you're quote-unquote *sick*."

"Thanks man, but panic attacks are an actual thing. Can you just answer the question? Why are you going?"

"Vena," Corvun said. "I'm goin' 'cause of Vena."

"Yeah? You got the hots for her?"

"No."

"What, then? She's the Class A bitch of the century. Let her be. Emptying a whole clip of bullets into virtual zombie brains is a lot more fun than debating a popular girl with an ego bigger than her brothers' balls."

"She's not like the other Archangels," Corvun said.

"*Oh my god.*"

"Yeah, okay, you got me. She's hot. I like her," he lied. He made a face, scrunched his nose at the thought. He'd grown up too close to Venatrix to ever see her as more than a sister. Corvun grabbed the strap of his backpack again, stood, and turned to leave. As soon as he put his hand on the doorknob, the TV remote smacked into the back of his head. "Ow! Jayren, cut it out!"

"'Fess up, man. Tell me the truth."

Corvun stared down at Jayren's off-white carpet. Old, dried mud smeared the baseboard by the doorframe. It had been there ever since the summer Jayren convinced Corvun to try out for the soccer team with him. Loose change was scattered by the dirt from the night the two of them had made an unsuccessful trip to a local 1980s-style arcade. They'd lost every game they played, and Jayren swore by the hair in his armpits that the games were rigged. And just above the door handle, a yellow smiley-face sticker stared back at Corvun with beady black eyes. It was from Jayren's most recent trip to see his mom in the hospital, two years ago. It had been taped back to the door each time it came unstuck ever since. This room was their safe place, and it had collected more secrets than any of his past friends had been able to twist out of him. He let his guard down. "Have you ever met an Archangel Heir that would risk their standin' like that? Showin' off her tattoo has consequences," he said.

"No," Jayren said. "They usually just accept the angelic limelight with dry-cleaned church clothes and holier-than-thou smiles. I'm actually starting to think this 'angel' thing is bullshit. It's just a conspiracy."

Corvun sighed. "And the Illuminati and the Bermuda Triangle and the flat Earth theory?"

"Yeah, but there's *proof* of the Bermuda Triangle and—"

"Listen, Vena doesn't like what she is. I don't like what I am. You don't like who you are. Do you see a common thread?"

"Sure, self-haters. Let's make a squad. Our slogan can be 'Why let the haters make us famous when we can make ourselves famous?' Trademarked!"

"Shut up, Jay. I'm not doin' this for attention or popularity. She's human like we are."

"I thought you were half-Archangel."

Nephilim. Corvun wanted to correct him. *An angel stuck in a human body.* It wouldn't be any use. Corvun had tried to explain to Jayren the hierarchy and where they stood within it, but Jayren dismissed it each time. Corvun stood up and glanced over his shoulder at his friend. "Let's go. You'd argue a point 'til the grave. I'm not askin' anymore. We're goin'."

Corvun didn't wait for Jayren. He heaved his bag onto his shoulder and walked out of Jayren's room. He listened carefully for the sigh and shuffle of Jayren giving in behind him. Outside, both of their motorcycles sat side by side in the driveway, just behind Jayren's sister's car.

Corvun left the helmet hanging on the back of his bike as he mounted it.

Jayren swung his leg over his seat, no helmet in sight.

They walked their bikes off the driveway then steered onto the road. As they rode, the wind picked up. Luckily, the route to North Academy was all back roads for them. Corvun watched a few leaves fall—some browning from the changing season and others ripped from their branches as the wind flared up. The sky in the west was dark and churning. The oncoming storm would be vicious, relentless.

The two pulled up to the recreation center and parked.

"You didn't actually have to break his nose, you know," Jayren told Corvun.

"Yes, I did."

Jayren scoffed. "My sister's pissed. She thinks it's my fault."

"Blame it on me," Corvun said.

"I will," Jayren said.

Corvun rolled his eyes. He stared at the recreation center. A cool breeze whipped his shoulder-length hair up around his face and pricked his neck with goosebumps. He flattened it back down against the nape of his neck by habit, against his own Archangel tattoo. Half status. He made more than sure to abide by the rules to hide his tattoo. Even though many of the students at the North Academy had angel descendancy— and even though his own rank as Nephilim was one of the highest—he still felt as good as dirt to the Archangels, to Venatrix, and to his own father.

"This is your worst idea yet, Corvun."

"Shut up, Jay," he said through clenched teeth. He tightened a fist around the strap of his backpack and stalked towards the building.

"You didn't even wear your ballet shoes. They won't let you in there." Jayren struggled to keep up with Corvun's long strides.

"I'm not askin' them to let me in. I'm *goin' in*. I'll dance barefoot if I have to."

Inside was hardly warmer but more humid from sweat. They navigated the halls of the building, smelling chlorine as they passed the pools and the stale smell of chalk as they rounded the corner of the boxing ring. Corvun led Jayren down the last hall to the rehearsal stage. He heard a faint piano melody twinkling from within the chamber in the distance. Each step he took towards that little door on the right weighed more and more, until finally he stopped. He stood at the open door, his feet as heavy as anchors.

Venatrix swiveled past the door, a few yards in.

Of course, she was killing time before practice with a solo ballroom dance routine—something they used to do together.

"Last chance to back out," Jayren said to Corvun.

Corvun shook his head and sighed. "If you've got nothin' better to do than complain, at least hold onto my bag and work on your homework or somethin'."

"Fine."

Corvun glanced down at his worn sneakers. A brash slap of a shoe made him look up; he saw Venatrix wearing her own, stark-white tennis shoes. He wasn't surprised. She hadn't obeyed the rules either. They'd first become inseparable in school when Corvun came to class breaking dress code and sat with the only other student who had done the same: Venatrix. They'd both worn vintage band shirts that day, and suddenly their parents, their ranks, and the rumors vanished. He wanted that simplicity back.

Corvun paused, checking the perimeter for teachers, then slipped onto the rehearsal stage and walked to Venatrix. She was early, as was he, and the only thing he noticed was the line of broken-in, spare pointe shoes by the edge of the stage for kids like them—who'd either destroyed, forgotten, or refused to bring theirs. They would both have to eventually change into the shoes if they wanted to dance anything more than the ballroom warm-up Venatrix was doing now. Corvun continued to Venatrix slowly, warily, until her eyes darted to him. She looked away as if she had only seen a shadow.

Venatrix leaned into a stretched pose. Paused, disciplined. She continued through her dance, but she refused to keep time with the faint piano playing in the corner of the room. She danced to something only she could hear. She spun into each perfected form in her routine. She faltered, lost her balance, and he stepped up and caught her and held her up. No one watching would have been able to tell that Venatrix's fall and Corvun's save was anything but what the two had meant for the dance. Venatrix swiveled away, but Corvun stepped in time with her defensive counter and followed her side-by-side. She yanked her hand back; he snatched her wrist before she could spin away again, caught her waist, and dipped her dangerously low.

Venatrix's short hair brushed the floor. "I don't want to talk to you," she said.

"What if I want to talk to you?" he asked.

"Too bad. Let go of me."

Corvun quirked an eyebrow at her, and she glared back like a feral animal, biting at the bit to attack him. He lifted her back up and loosened his grip on her. She hesitated, didn't move. She stayed there in his hands. "Are you sure you don't want to talk?" he asked slowly.

"Yes."

"Dance, then."

"With you?" She scoffed.

He felt the sticky, nervous sweat on her palm and between her thumb and pointer finger. "You're a horrible dancer, anyway. I wouldn't be missin' out," he lied.

Venatrix lifted her chin and held his gaze evenly. She saw right through it. They both knew better; they used to love dancing together. "Teach me then, if you're so much better than me, Nephilim."

"Low blow."

"Speak for yourself, Ben."

The childhood nickname softened the sting of her use of his rank. He remembered their youth—growing up on and off with her. He remembered how she'd struggled to pronounce his name when she was only a toddler. She'd called him

"Corben," and the name "Ben" stuck. He stared at her wide, blue eyes. He still saw her as that young girl.

Corvun flattened his hand on her back, formed her in his arms how he wanted. He pushed her posture as hard as he could and lifted his chin, knowing she'd mirror it. She did, and he tilted his head patronizingly. Even though he was four years older than her, she had never had an issue challenging him.

Venatrix lifted her chin higher and looked to the side. She followed Corvun as he stepped into a lunge that twisted back upright. Her breath shook as she danced with him. She wasn't tired, and Corvun noted it by her ready ability to keep up with every step he led her through unannounced. Something was bothering her. Corvun sped up the dance, dipping her and swinging her back up. Her glassy eyes locked on his, and she tightened her jaw.

"You dance like a robot," he whispered, trying to lure out her trusting side. "You just follow me blindly. Do you know why I'm better?"

"Humor me," she said.

"Art is emotion. Dance is no different. It's expression. Put your heart into it. If you're angry, dance like it."

Venatrix spun out of his arm, and he pulled her back like a whip. Her hand gripped his shoulder; her body heated with newfound aggression.

"Better," he said.

They danced around the stage for a while longer. Corvun felt the energy that buzzed through Venatrix like lightning. Her anger was a storm, black fury and thunder, as she exhaled the frustration next to his face.

"They did it again," she said. Her voice cracked like electricity. She was near enough to him that she didn't have to speak very loud for him to hear. "I was volunteered against my will," she seethed, "for a drinking-stripping game."

Corvun's hands pricked with pins and needles where they rested on her back. He let go of her and stepped away. He only stayed close enough for her to continue without risking anyone else overhearing. He swallowed. Her light eyes grew distant, and he fought the urge to look at the ground. "I'm sorry," he said.

Venatrix rubbed at her dark lashes, cleverly wiping away dampness in her eyes, and made it look as if she'd just fixed her hair. "That's why I cut my hair. I'm tired of them making me out to be a slut. I'm never going to wear makeup. I'm going to prove to everyone that I'm *better* than them."

"You don't have to do all that, you know," Corvun said. He looked at the hardwood floor between their sneakers. He glanced up at her meekly. "You were always better than them. Still are."

Venatrix fell quiet.

"I'm sorry," he said again. "I should have been there."

They stood facing each other.

"Can I sit with you at lunch?" she asked.

"Yeah," he said. He offered his hand again, and she took it.

This time, they dueled for control of the dance.

JAYREN OMANS

Jayren stood in the same spot Corvun had left him, just to the side of the door. He watched Corvun and Venatrix stalk through their silent routine. He picked at a piece of loose skin on his finger absently, leaned back against the wall. He stared, and his heart sank. He wondered—now that Corvun and Venatrix were on speaking terms—if Corvun would forget he existed. Jayren worried he was a burden as a friend anyway. Between hearing voices in his head every now and then and the gossip passed around about his mom and dad, even Jayren wished he could just disappear sometimes.

He sighed, thought about fishing his headphones from his backpack and cramming them in his ears to distract himself. That's when he heard the shy piano melody in the corner and realized he knew it from somewhere. His mind revved up and raced at two hundred miles per hour to place the song. He'd heard it plenty, and he put a finger on it. The song was by one of his favorite, obscure dubstep artists. The genre had gone so far out of style that Jayren never expected to hear it anywhere but in his wireless headphones. Jayren glanced to his right, where the piano was tucked behind thick, red velvet curtains.

The student from earlier that day in the office—the six-foot-something guy carved straight from dinosaur-DNA-preserving amber—sat at the piano. *Hell on Earth,* Jayren thought. *More like "Hell, what on Earth* wouldn't *I give to look like you?"* He was gorgeous. He continued to pluck twinkling notes from the familiar song, making his own clever rendition. It reminded Jayren of running through sprinklers in summer and the feeling of droplets of water racing out of his wet hair and down his sunburned back. Jayren rubbed his neck and walked over. The boy's fingers danced over the keys in a light trance, and Jayren wondered how loud he would've played if no one were listening.

Beside him on the steps just above the top of the piano, a girl sat with a notebook in her lap. She looked exactly like him—with skin the color of creamy, spice tea and really pretty, long, red hair.

Jayren cleared his throat.

The girl looked up first.

Jayren's face flushed. "Hi," he managed in a crack of a voice. He suddenly regretted tagging along. This was his *own* worst idea yet.

The girl's cheeks quirked into a small but genuine smile. Her green eyes were beautiful and tired. She had wiped smears of concealer beneath them—Jayren could smell it—and it didn't fully hide the dark rings on her skin. A sudden quiver of her lips and chin gave her away; she was nervous, but Jayren didn't understand why. She closed the notebook in her lap.

Jayren picked his brain for their names. He knew them. He'd seen them a lot. They were the only students who probably got a worse rap than he did. Jayren wondered if that was why the girl was nervous—because she thought Jayren had come to bully them like the other students did. Jayren refused to believe the rumors about them were true, and instead, he liked to believe they were just generally too beautiful to talk to. "You guys are the Jude twins, right?" his voice broke again. He swallowed hard.

The boy's playing changed. He elicited jagged notes, nailing each one down with terrifyingly swift precision. Then his fingers began hammering wrong notes. He gave up with a swiping slam across the keys, a jumbled mix of muted and disoriented harmonies. He sighed.

"Orion, right?"

Orion looked up and stared straight ahead, ignoring Jayren.

"Dude, keep going! That was really good. Was it that song *Forget Me Not* by that dubstep—"

Orion glanced at Jayren. His eyes were a bright, sea glass green.

"—artist who did all of the…"

"The flower-themed songs? Yeah, actually," Orion said. "Wait, you know him, too?"

"Hell yeah, he has the coolest stuff." Jayren took a step forward.

Orion scooted over on the piano bench.

Jayren hesitated then plopped down beside Orion.

Orion traced his fingers down the keys, lightly tapping at the notes to encourage the same, gentle song. His fingers were thin and his knuckles were bruised, but he touched the instrument with care. The piano purred like a happy cat as Orion played. It was as if Orion spoke to the instrument and it to him; they carried on a conversation which had been spoken a hundred times in their own special way.

"So," Jayren said, "it is Orion then."

"You can call me Rian. That's my sister, Ophiah."

Jayren looked at her again, and she smiled back, a bit wider. If Venatrix's extraordinarily good looks came from "being an angel," then Ophiah one-upped her in every way. Jayren wondered. "Are you guys Archangel Heirs? If you believe in that sort of stuff, I guess."

Orion shook his head. "Not Heirs."

Jayren's brow furrowed. "Okay."

"Do you want to come sit beside me?" Ophiah asked. Her voice was warm milk and sticky-sweet honey.

Jayren swallowed up her offer, set his bag on the bench next to Orion, and jumped up to the steps where Ophiah sat. He perched beside her, and she opened her notebook back up. His eyes devoured the scribbles inside her journal, but dismay punched through his heart when he noticed it wasn't feelings about boys. Ophiah's journal was full of handwritten sheet music without lyrics. *This could be a good thing,* he thought to himself. *Maybe she doesn't have a boyfriend.* He settled into his spot beside her. "This is cool. Did you write it—I mean, come up with it?"

Ophiah tucked a strand of hair behind her ear. She laughed. "It's our studies. Mother has us handwrite old scores to memorize them."

Jayren watched her hands as she flipped over her journal pages like they were ancient scrolls in a museum. Her brown nail polish chipped away from her fingertips, and soft watercolor blues and purples bruised the skin just beneath her sleeve. He almost asked, but she spoke again.

"When you study really far into music theory, you learn some of the lore. Most of it isn't written anywhere. Mother taught us those parts. The basics are, 'Music is a gift from God that can be used to counteract demons and other evils.' There are a lot of different ways, but one of them is the intent in which the music is played."

Jayren looked at Ophiah again, and he noticed a small patch of freckles she had missed with concealer. They were cute, and Jayren didn't understand why she covered them up at all. He studied her face for clues. He found a spot—on her other cheek—that was slightly darker than the rest.

Ophiah caught him looking, brushed her hair back into her face, then turned away to grab the violin case behind her. She opened the clattering latches and pulled the instrument from its bed. She touched the body of the violin lovingly, raised it to the crook of her neck, and laid her chin on the small, black plate. She didn't use her bow but instead plucked at the strings. She mirrored Orion's playing style, and she matched his melodies with shy harmonies. "When you play an instrument with love, it becomes your weapon."

Jayren put his chin in his hands and watched her fingers flit over the strings like she was picking wildflowers for a crown. Her music sounded like spring, like rebirth, like the joy Jayren suspected dogs felt when they saw their owners. Each note she plucked tugged on his heart. He tried to hold back his unsolicited smile. He covered his mouth with his palm so she wouldn't see.

Ophiah glanced over her violin at him and smiled even brighter.

Jayren blushed nervously.

"Do you believe in angels and demons?" she asked.

"No," he said.

Orion scoffed.

"Do you believe in God?" Ophiah asked.

"Do you guys sing?" Jayren changed the topic.

"No. For what we are, our voices are tools of evil," Orion said.

Jayren recalled earlier that day in Professor North's office, when Venatrix had corrected "who" instead of "what." Jayren noticed Ophiah's lack of correcting her brother. Orion didn't change his words.

"We are the hands and feet of God—the instruments God uses—but the tongue is set on fire by Hell," Ophiah said. "We are not allowed to sing."

"Are you kidding?"

Ophiah stayed quiet, lowering her violin. She turned to put her violin away and accidentally knocked her notebook from her lap. The pages flipped open to a score with *Star Wars Main Theme* written across the top in small, neat handwriting.

Jayren reached down and grabbed the notebook then stared at Ophiah, eyes wide. "You know this?"

"Yeah. Orion and I are leading the theater's orchestra for the play. Are you trying out?"

"I—uh, no. I mean yes. I love Star Wars."

Dimples poked in Ophiah's smile.

Jayren's heart lodged in his throat.

"Who are you auditioning for?"

"Pffft. Luke, of course," he half-choked.

Orion stopped playing the piano. His eyes were fixed on Corvun and Venatrix, who still marched around the room in a combative dance. Jayren watched, too, and beside him Ophiah turned a few pages and began drawing small notes on the music staff.

"She's smart, right?" Orion asked.

"I mean, yeah. She's ahead a few years. She's in some of Corvun's classes. I mean, Corvun and her used to be really good friends, and he said she always did better than him in everything—in grades, too, and he's smart. They grew up together, I guess. He doesn't really talk about that, though. He never really talks about her at all. I don't actually know why they're not friends anymore. I tried to ask him—"

"She's in my Religious Studies class," Orion interrupted.

Jayren stopped talking.

"Do you have her number?" he asked Jayren.

"Nah, I just know she lives down the street from Corvun," Jayren said.

"Ri," Ophiah chastised softly. "If you want her number, go ask her for it yourself."

Orion picked at the piano keys again. He didn't look down, but rather kept his sights up, watching Venatrix. "I like her hair," he said.

Jayren rolled his eyes. He realized anything she would do would be considered a statement or a new trend. Jayren wished he were so popular he could get away with anything he wanted—and at the same time, do it in style. He thought the first thing he'd do (if he was ever so lucky that the opportunity presented itself) would be to start a food fight and launch mashed potatoes into her face.

CORVUN KHLYDE

By the time practice ended, plans were made, and Venatrix was tagging along. Even though Jayren gave them both the silent treatment, Corvun didn't change his mind. Venatrix rode on the back of his motorcycle, and he and Jayren parted ways. Corvun dropped Venatrix off at her house.

Corvun stood on the sidewalk, and Venatrix started up her family's driveway.

She turned around. "Do you forgive me?"

"What for?"

"For not being there for you," she said. "For not taking your side."

Corvun held her gaze, but he couldn't speak.

Her eyes were the saddest shade of blue. "Because I'm sorry."

"Yeah…" He paused. "I forgive you."

VENATRIX CANES

Venatrix stared at the mashed potatoes on her plate. Her hair clung to her face in small, annoying licks, still damp from her shower. Outside, rain continued thrumming against the rooftop, shifting through the trees.

Forks clinked against plates.

Her mom spoke, the first to break the dinner's silence. "Vena, honey, do you want to talk about what happened today?"

Venatrix blushed angrily. She stabbed the prongs of her fork through her steak. She was sure Valentine had called and filled in her parents with full, unbiased detail.

Erin sat—wisely—in silence.

Caeleb, on the other hand, scratched his fork across his plate, and Venatrix shot him a glare. His face blurred together with dark blues and purples, and his eyes were puffy on the inside corners. A piece of white medical tape stuck crookedly to his nose.

She gritted her teeth and made a mental note to thank Corvun. "Do you know that Caeleb treats other angels like shit?" she seethed. Venatrix met her mother's soft, blue-eyed gaze, saw the change in her expression. Venatrix continued. "Do you know he walks all over the Nephilim like they're lesser than us? It's kind of funny he didn't foresee Corvun busting his nose. I thought Archangels were supposed to be the most powerful entities on Earth these days."

Caeleb dropped his fork. "Can she be excused? She's making me lose my appetite."

"Your face is making me lose my appetite," Venatrix said. "Thanks, sis."

Venatrix stood and carried her plate to the sink and scraped the rest of her still-warm food into the drain. She rinsed the food down and flipped the disposal on. It churned loudly, and at the table, her mother flinched. Venatrix burned in anger and embarrassment and in an inkling of regret as she stalked away from the kitchen and fled upstairs to her room. The air chilled the sweat beading on her neck. Venatrix slammed her door behind her and heard her father raise his voice and yell at Caeleb and Erin; her mother chimed in too.

Venatrix flung herself across her bed. She stared across her room to her backpack, deciding she'd skip her homework and take a low-end A for the semester.

Her phone buzzed on the bed beside her.

She ignored it.

Venatrix glared at her desk lamp for a moment, leaving blind spots in the back of her eyes, then rolled onto her back and looked at her phone. It was Lynx—her closest friend and Corvun's cousin. A text popped up on the screen saying, 'Call me.'

Venatrix sighed. She listened to the rain clattering on the rooftop and on the window for another minute before calling

Lynx. Venatrix didn't speak, but Lynx began spewing on the other end of the line.

"Girl, where were you at lunch? I looked everywhere. I saw Caeleb leavin' school this mornin' and—and Corvun won't even talk to me! I texted him, and he read it and ignored it. He never does that. He always says somethin', even if it's 'okay' to a yes or no question. I tried to call him and he picked up then hung up on me! What happened?"

"He punched Caeleb in the face."

"He *what?*" Lynx shrieked.

Venatrix closed her eyes. "Yeah, we both have detention on Monday."

"Hey girl," Lynx's tone changed suddenly. Usually she'd dig more into the drama, but she continued as if it were an afterthought. "Come to your window."

"Why?" she asked. Sometimes Lynx would sneak over and come in through her window, but Venatrix wasn't up for a surprise girls-night-in visit tonight. "I don't want you here right now. My parents are yelling at Caeleb and Erin downstairs. It's not a good time. I just want to go to sleep," she moaned. She was surprised her parents even had the time or energy to scold her brothers; they usually didn't. All the Archangels were usually so busy with either fighting or planning defense or other strategies for the Unseen Wars against the demons that they couldn't see their own children turning into demons, themselves.

"No, it's not me, I mean… Just, c'mon! Go to your window!"

Venatrix stood and walked to her window, brow furrowed. She peeked through her curtains to see a boy crouching there, his freckled knuckles ready to tap on the glass. His rosy-auburn hair and distant green eyes gave him away. It was Orion. And it was the last place she ever expected him to be. He looked up at her, and she stared back. "I gotta go," she whispered to Lynx.

Lynx giggled. "Who is it?"

Venatrix hung up. She cracked the window and knelt to talk to Orion. "What are you doing on my roof?" she snapped. "And how did—where did you get my address?"

"Uh, Jayren got it from…Corvun's sister? I think…" He smiled, a bit unsure.

Venatrix clenched her jaw.

"Are you going to let me in?" Orion's face shone brightly, despite the storm and the rain plastering his long hair to his face. There were dimples in his smile, but they felt forced, fake.

"No, my parents would kill me. They'll kill *you* if they find you here! Go home. It's raining," she felt as if she needed to state the obvious. Something told her he didn't care.

"I know, so let me in…" He touched her fingertips on the window like a cat reaching his paws under a door, begging for attention, wet and soft and small.

Venatrix pulled her hand back. "Tell me why you're here."

"I know what you are. I want to ask you about something." His smile vanished. "Please. I have to get home soon, anyway. I won't stay long."

"You have to be quiet," she whispered.

"I will."

Venatrix hesitated, mulling over the odds of getting caught. His touch on her fingers replayed in her head. She couldn't resist him. She opened the window all the way, and Orion slipped in. He stood by her curtains, dripping with water. He smelled like the earth and the ocean all at once; the dirt and the salty-fresh air, calloused and raw, worn and tireless. He was a juxtaposition; he didn't make sense. "Don't move," she said as she scrambled to find a blanket and give it to him.

He looked a lot smaller than he had at school, wearing his drenched tee and baggy jeans, but he was still tall and lean and toned. His arms were covered by old-style gothic text and deep, blood-soaked bruises.

She shut her jaw tightly to keep from gawking. "Dry off," she said, but her voice was choked. She wanted to ask to see if that was the reason he was there with her. Her heart plummeted in her chest, dragging her words with it. *So the rumors are true,* she thought. *His father does abuse him.* But it was so much worse than she expected it to be now that she laid eyes on the evidence of it. She pushed the quilt against his chest, and his hand touched hers again. She pulled away.

Orion tousled his hair in the blanket. "I'm sorry for—" his voice was thick and rich.

"Shhh!" she hushed him. She stared in his eyes and saw the flinch, the hurt. He looked scared, terrified, and vulnerable, but Venatrix didn't understand why. He was safe with her, and she would make sure of it. "You have to be quiet," she reminded.

Orion looked away from her and studied her room instead. He walked around her room with bare feet, looking at the five-by-seven cards she'd pinned all over her purple-gray walls. The Christmas lights that hung around her ceiling turned his skin honey-gold. "Do you do art?" he asked in a whisper; she almost missed it.

"No, I… I just print them. They're…" The conversation seemed fickle, and her chest weighed heavy with emotion. "I just like the pictures."

He touched her record player. "You listen to records?"

"Yeah."

Orion thumbed through the box of vinyl next to the player.

Venatrix noticed a small, white-lined tattoo on the back of his neck peeking through dark tendrils of his hair. She recognized the shape instantly—a shield with four, fanned wings. All Archangel descendants were required to get the tattoo, but she had never seen it in white ink before. "You're part Archangel," she said out loud.

"And…part Deceiver," he finished evenly. He stopped browsing her music and looked up to stare at her wall. Polaroids she and Lynx had taken spotted the space above her record player, strung in with the lights. She felt vulnerable suddenly, to be alone with him in her room, for him to see inside her personal space, the pictures, her bed. "You can see the tattoo," Orion said, "so you're full-fledged. Your mom and dad are both Archangels. Only Archangels and their Heirs can see it."

Venatrix occupied herself with pushing divots into her rug with her heels. Her mind spun. She wondered if maybe Orion could be a new start, if maybe she could redefine what friendship should be with him. Not because of popularity. Not for benefit or gain. Just companionship. *No more rumors*, she thought. She would get to know him herself. "Who hurt you?" she asked finally. She wanted to hear it from him.

The question made Orion twitch. "Don't you know?"

She took a step toward him, and he turned.

Venatrix froze.

Orion searched her face. "My—uh…blood father. I don't know what to call him anymore. The demon that conceived me, I guess."

Venatrix listened to the ins and outs of his voice, the falters and flickers of doubt and hatred. She'd bet money that the angels instilled that into him. She wanted to believe she heard hope somewhere, but she couldn't be sure. She walked to her door and locked it. Venatrix grabbed another quilt, motioned for him to give her the wet one, then handed him the dry blanket. "Take your shirt off and wrap up. You'll warm up faster."

Orion shook his head.

"Do you have more?" She eyed his bruises again.

He nodded. His hands clutched the quilt, and tears filled the lower half of his eyes. He turned before she could watch one escape.

Venatrix faced away when he lifted his shirt. She hoped it would make him more comfortable, or maybe it was for her own sake.

"Thanks," he said.

"Is that why you're here?" She listened to him sit on the edge of her bed.

"No, I—" he struggled. "I mean kind of, but not really. Here."

Venatrix turned and watched him fish a small plastic bag from his pocket. Inside, there was a folded piece of blue paper. She took the bag when he offered it to her.

"I wanted to see if you could tell me what this is," he said.

"Why not just look it up online?"

Orion's eyes were wide and empty.

"No phone?"

He shook his head.

Venatrix sat in her swivel chair and spun to face her desk. She pulled up a browser on her computer and unfolded the paper to read the handwritten prescription. It was a medication she hadn't heard of. "Who gave you this?"

"Professor North."

She typed the name of the prescription and scrolled through the results. It didn't take long to find the use. The drug was an extreme sedative, a tranquilizer for wild animals. It wasn't meant for humans. She slumped in her seat. "Does your mom know about this?"

"Not yet."

"Do you want it?"

He paused. "No."

Venatrix glared at the prescription, snatched it from her desk, and tore it to shreds. The weight on her chest started to lift. She closed her computer and threw the remnants of the paper in the trash. "I hate it. I hate that they treat you like shit," she said, "like somehow you're lesser. You, Corvun, Lynx. It's not fair."

"You do the same."

Venatrix spun in her chair to face him. Embarrassment reddened her cheeks.

"Your little scene this morning?" He tilted his head patronizingly, yet somehow still shy. "You showed off your tattoo to people like me. The lesser ones."

"Yeah, but I didn't prescribe you an anesthetic strong enough to put out a five-hundred-pound lion."

"That's what that was?"

Venatrix shrugged.

Orion slouched, too. He laid back on her bed, and the quilt around his shoulders flipped open to reveal more intricate tattoos on his side. Still, Venatrix didn't think he looked dangerous enough to take drugs—prescription or recreational—at all.

Venatrix stood slowly and walked over to sit beside him. "Why do you have all those tattoos?"

"Mother made me get them. Ophiah has them too. They're supposed to be reminders." Orion didn't protest when Venatrix tugged the blanket open. "The sleeves are passages from the Psalms."

Venatrix traced his tan skin with her eyes. Across his upper chest, bold script spelled "Memento Mori." On each of his sides, a tree stretched its intertwining arms out. One was full of leaves, and the other had bare branches. As beautiful as they were, Venatrix couldn't ignore the swells of bruises or the way his ribcage protruded past his stomach. Her insides welled with emotion again. "They're cool. I wish I had tattoos like yours," she managed. Her heart ached when she saw the tears on his cheeks.

"I wish I had cool hair like yours. It's awesome."

Venatrix forced a thin smile. Before she could respond, Orion began drifting in and out of sleep. His eyes rolled back until they were only whites, and it reminded Venatrix of the mural in Professor North's office. She looked to her bedroom door, back to her still-cracked window. The wind howled outside, threatening to slip inside her home like a thief and shatter her normal life. It fluttered the papers on her desk, the journal entry she'd written that very morning before searching the kitchen for scissors. She held her breath, collapsed back onto her bed, and exhaled.

Sleep came for her with swift arms; it carried her deep into the quiet dark.

II

WHAT THE STORM BROUGHT IN

The Eight Deceivers are the direct enemies to the Eight Archangels. Each Deceiver represents a cardinal sin and can persuade humans—much like how Archangels can—into sin. The Deceivers have walked the Earth since the beginning of time, and this has resulted in much lore and legend. Each Deceiver has its true form as a beast most commonly known to humans as a dragon. Though, over time, these legends have twisted, turning into many different stories. For example, what once might have been considered a giant squid might have originally been a beast that no man had truly laid eyes on.
— A History of Hierarchy

NOVEMBER 5TH, 2106 A.D.
ATLANTIC OCEAN
CARINA BLACKROCK

"Hello, Phoenix," a voice scoffed, "or should I say Calypso? The pirate in the red dress. A genocidal *angel!* The irony." A laugh. "And the list goes on…"

Carina's skin prickled with anger, with fury. Rope sawed through her wrists which were bound to the wooden post behind her. She thrashed against the rope, twisting and turning but never catching sight of the man who spoke. She listened for his footsteps. "You are a fool to think those names mean anything to me." The ship rocked under her knees; the water beneath groaned. The storm raged with untamed wrath of a hurricane.

"Carina Blackrock," the man clicked his tongue. "Protégée of Leroy Blackrock. Oh, but *his* name does! Where is he?"

Carina clenched her jaw. The demon was right. That name did mean something to Carina. Leroy had been her caretaker for years now. He taught her many things, including the names and forms of the Deceivers. The demon behind her was one of those Deceivers. His name was Avon, and he was the Deceiver Greed, the dragon that lurked in the seas. Carina closed her eyes to the dark cabin around her. "I would never tell you, even if you skinned me and picked the bones from my body."

"So be it."

A sharp blade drove through the sole of her foot. Her breath choked from her lungs, and pain ripped through her leg, deep into her bones. Shock gripped her neck, silencing her scream. Her blood pumped loudly and pulsed with the heat of rage that formed around her eyes and ears.

"What good is a siren with no tail? I will cut off your feet and let you bleed in the sea, serpent, if you do not tell me where he is. The Fallen have no place among the angels, so why does he continue to stand by you? His fate has been sealed!"

The Fallen? Carina didn't know any fallen angels. Surely Avon didn't refer to Leroy. But doubt gnawed at her heart, and thunder shook the hull of the ship. Was there something she didn't know?

"So has hers," Leroy growled from the deck above. Rain sheeted in from the open door. "She has a big responsibility ahead of her, Avon, and I'll be makin' sure she gets to it."

The sword withdrew from her foot.

Leroy jumped down with a heavy thud.

Lightning illuminated his silhouette.

Carina struggled again, but the ropes tightened on her skin. She panted as a sharp slicing and clashing of swords began behind her.

"Carina!" Leroy shouted.

Carina ducked below a strike of Avon's sword. A second blade lodged into the post, cutting her free of her bindings. Carina gasped, stumbled away. She unwound the rope's remnants, turned to run.

Avon stood in her way. His eyes flashed with gold and silver reflections of the lightning above. His face reminded her of statues in Hell's Alley—carved from marble—but lines cracked around the edges of his mouth, his eyes. Avon lunged at Carina.

She stumbled back. Pain shot up her leg, and she collapsed. Crates exploded beneath her; splinters cut into her palms as she scrambled back further.

Leroy grabbed Avon from behind, and the two tumbled to the other side of the cabin.

"Get out of here!" Leroy shouted over the storm.

Carina wanted to argue, to say she couldn't. She would die if she jumped into the ocean now. The storm would pull her under, and her blood would lure the sharks. She couldn't swim near as fast as she needed to. Not wounded.

"Now, Carina!"

Carina held her breath and heaved herself up. She watched, judged, anticipated the fight. Avon tumbled violently to the right, and Carina ran for it. She flung her legs up the stairs, limping, her foot stabbing with pain. Avon's sword nicked her calf, but she didn't look back. On the top deck, the storm's fury blew her over, and her wounds were forgotten.

She collided with the railing of the ship. Wet tendrils of hair plastered her face. Carina stared at the churning, black waves below.

Thunder.

Two more bright white flashes. White foam below.

Tears of blood and rain on her bare arms and legs.

A bellowing crack of wood split through the storm. The ship creaked again, moaning and crying as the hull ripped apart.

Carina spun. She searched for Leroy.

Above her, the main mast teetered.

Snap.

Carina lurched, her heart skipped.

The railing behind her gave, and she plummeted down into the water. The waves dragged her under, and she tumbled deeper in. Her hearing changed first, hollowing the sound of the thunder above. Her eyes adjusted next. She watched the small glimmers from deep down, flashes of scales. She inhaled the water, smelled for predators, and prayed for her safety. She fought herself free of her blouse and her shorts, twisting in the tumultuous current.

Carina swallowed back her fear and the ache in her chest. The ocean had always felt like home to her—like the embrace of a mother she'd never known. Sometimes she felt like the sea was the only place she could belong, but now, nothing felt quite as it had. Not Leroy, not herself. Not even the sea. The water became the feeling of that embrace being torn from her, a torrent dragging her into blackness.

Carina's skin changed, sealed by a fine layer of hook-like scales. Membrane connected her fingers, and her legs wrapped together in a long, finned tail. But the bleeding didn't stop, and her wound had left a hole in her bottom fin. She was no better than an exhibit in a museum—something pretty to look at, something useless.

She turned, analyzing her surroundings, anticipating her end.

Death wasn't the friend she thought he'd be.

The surface broke again, a faraway *boom* as someone fell into the water just as she had.

Her breath hitched. She twisted again.

Was it Avon? She wanted to use her echolocation to find out, but fear drained the thought from her mind. If it were Avon, she would soon be dead. She'd heard rumors of what he really was—the "Kraken," the sea dragon that haunted the ocean and all its sailors.

Something swam around her, shifting the water, pushing it against her skin and through her hair.

Carina closed her eyes. She couldn't breathe. Instead, she prayed. She wished she'd felt happiness on the day she died, fulfillment. She wished her lifetime had been more than being a hostage in the Abyss and in Hell's Alley. She didn't want to die. Not like this. Not today, in this cursed storm, in the sea that had forsaken her.

The water pulsed violently with anger and aggression. Yet, instead of being directed at her, there was defense in the movement. Carina fought the urge to swim away as a face neared hers. A glowing gray eye stared back at her, somehow warm in the dark ocean, a lighthouse shining to guide her, the silver lining when all else had forgotten her. *Leroy.*

Leroy pulled her near, and Carina held tight to his chest. He sliced through the sea in the same way he wielded all his weaponry—faster than she dreamed to be. Water rushed through her hair as he fled with her. All around them, piece by piece, the ship drifted deeper down towards the ocean floor.

Carina couldn't differentiate truth from lies anymore as she watched the crumbling hull of the ship dissolve with distance. Her heart snapped in her chest, leaving her to question everything again, cradled inside the ocean and the only arms she thought she knew.

· · · · ·

Dawn hesitated to break through the sky as Leroy dragged Carina up through the shallows and onto the shore. Carina's body ached with exhaustion. She collapsed on the sand. Her scales withdrew into her skin, and her tail turned back into legs, but she was too tired to acknowledge her nakedness, much less do something to cover herself.

Leroy removed his coat and hauled it over her.

She opened her eyes to see the beach smeared ahead of her with gray-blue morning light. She couldn't lift her head. The air she breathed into her lungs felt like fire yet again. She longed for the ocean.

"You alright, kid?"

"Is it true?" she rasped. "Are you a demon, like Avon?"

"Not—"

A chilling voice interrupted him. "Oh please, Leroy. Don't continue this lie when you've long lost the war. Tell her the truth."

Fear struck Carina like the lash of a whip. Recognition surged through her at the sound of the voice; adrenaline kicked in her heart. She forced herself up to look at the black dress shoes crunching through the sand.

The man stopped just before them, his feet shoulder-width apart. He wore a black three-piece suit. His face was clean-shaven and his blond hair was combed back neatly. In his hand, he held a cane—one she knew was not for balance or walking. She met his cold, pale eyes and recoiled back to Leroy's side. Even a demon was better than the devil that stood in her way of freedom. Cephan. His name was a curse in her mind, a brand on her memory. She would never forget what he'd done to her and to others. Cephan addressed Carina, "Azrael, how good it is to see you again, dear. Leroy? No? I'll tell her."

"No," Leroy growled. "Let her be."

"Are you scared she'll look at you differently? C'mon," Cephan crooned. He took a step towards the pair. His cane fell away in black shadows to reveal a gleaming, silver sword. He pointed the sword at Leroy. "Azrael, dear, rather than a demon, your friend was a guardian angel, a Sentinel, much like yourself. He broke the Sentinels' Law. He drank blood—your kind's most forbidden fruit—and for that reason, he fell. He cursed himself to become what the humans call a 'vampire' and to be locked out of Heaven."

Carina heard the disappointment through Leroy's silence, in the falter of his breath and his hesitance to speak. He always had a counter for every insult thrown his way. But not this time. Carina fought for words to spit back at Cephan. She had none.

"It was an accident, Carina," Leroy whispered. "He isn't tellin' you the whole story."

"Didn't you ever think it strange of him to never show his face in the sun? A sailor?" Cephan tipped Carina's chin up with the end of his sword, and she glared into his hollow eyes. "His skin would've appeared as bone in the sunlight. *You* would have recognized it, the mark of being Fallen, even though you may not have known what it truly meant at the time."

Carina did not move from Leroy's side.

"Come back to me, Azrael. I can't have you walking around freely, causing trouble like the renegade you are."

"Never," she forced between her teeth.

"Pity." Cephan clicked his tongue. He swiped his sword away, right across Leroy's throat.

"No!" Carina cried.

Leroy gripped his throat. His face twisted with pain.

Blood poured from the wound.

Carina reached for him.

Cephan stepped on her arm. He rolled it with the sole of his shoe, exposing her wrist. There, a white scar raised her skin, the shape of a compass rose. It was a brand that Cephan gave her years ago, marking her as his property.

She panted and hissed at the pain, unable to do anything but watch as Leroy—her only friend, her rescuer—fell still in a lake of his own blood. Words wouldn't form in her rage. Tears seared her eyes.

"Stupid girl. I'll ask you again," Cephan said. He pointed the tip of his sword at the center of her wrist and pressed. His blade pierced the skin of her scar. "Would you come back and be employed by me, Azrael?"

"Never," she choked again.

"It would be your best option."

Her blood beaded in the center of the scar.

"Must I remind you that you are just as bad as he is—as a Fallen—because you belong to me? To RUST? You will have nowhere to go. But humor me, what do you want the most?"

"Nothing. There is nothing this life could give that I could possibly want."

"Not if I offered to bring him back, contingent on your reemployment?" Cephan removed his sword and took a few steps away from Carina.

Carina glanced at her wrist. The blood in the center of the compass trickled in Leroy's direction, leaving a red, needle-like line. She wiped the blood away angrily and crawled to Leroy's body. The tears in her eyes blurred him into a heap of white and gray and brown. She clung to his body and felt the absence of heat on his skin. Cold set in.

"When the sunlight shines on him, he will turn to dust, and my offer will be gone."

"Never," she repeated. "I would never."

NOVEMBER 5TH, 2106 A.D.
NORTHEAST FLORIDA
ORION JUDE

Soft thumping woke Orion. Footsteps. His stomach sank like a twenty-ton weight in still water. Fear clutched him, a grip tight enough to paralyze. His eyes snapped open, staring at a white canopy stretching over him. It took him a moment to realize he'd never made it back out of Venatrix's window and that it wasn't his own father walking down the hall to his bedroom.

It was hers.

"Vena, are you awake? Your brothers are leaving in a few minutes," her father spoke through her door.

Venatrix flinched beside Orion, startling him. She jumped out of bed and ran to the door. Her heels stuttered across her floor in her frenzy. "Yes! Yes, but no! No, Dad, I'm not driving with them today! I'll walk," she said, palms pressed flat against her door. She shot Orion a glance over her shoulder, nodded at her closet, and mouthed, "Hide!"

"Venatrix, I wanted to talk to you," her father said.

"Dad, I really don't want to talk. It's fine. I just want to be alone."

The door handle rattled quietly as her father turned it, and chills pricked Orion's skin with instinctual horror. Panic yanked a leash around Orion's neck and dragged his stumbling feet across her soft rug and into her closet. He collapsed on the floor, taking a few shirts and hangers with him. He rolled the closet door shut.

"What was that?"

"Dad!" Venatrix cried. "You're messing me up! I'm trying to style my hair. I dropped my blow dryer."

Venatrix's clothes smelled like sugar, icing, and freshly baked cupcakes. Orion scooted deeper into the far side of her closet. A long dress fell over his face, blacking out his vision. His breath hitched. He hated the dark. He could never see the demons coming in the dark. It was why he still kept a night light, well into his seventeenth year.

Orion heard the door open. He held his breath and listened.

"Where's your hairdryer?" Venatrix's father asked. His voice was low and calm.

Venatrix didn't respond.

"We've talked about this, Venatrix."

"I'm sorry," she said.

"What fell?"

"My backpack. I left it on my bed by mistake last night, and it fell when I got up," she explained.

Her father sighed. "We talked to Caeleb about what he said to the other students. He was unfair and cruel, but that gives you no excuse to be out of line, too, Vena."

"I cut my hair."

"Rules are rules. You abide by God's Law, so it is no different. Think of concealing your Mark as an act of respect to Him. Now," he paused, "do you need me to wait for you to get ready and drive you to school in a little while?"

"Can I stay home? Please?"

Orion blinked a few times. It grew darker in her closet.

"Dad, I just want to be alone. Please. I don't want to be seen with them."

Orion closed his eyes and prayed. Venatrix's bickering faded as he focused on reciting the prayers his mother had taught him religiously since the age of six. He formed each word on his lips, devoted his heart and mind, but it wasn't enough. The shadows cast over his mind and blanketed the world into eerie silence.

Venatrix swung her closet open, and morning light flooded down on Orion. "Wake up."

Orion shook his head and blinked away the fogginess on his brain. Unconsciousness slipped off him. He decided to let Venatrix believe he'd been asleep. It was easier than trying to explain that he'd been possessed by demons in the dark corner of her closet. Orion brushed her shirts from his shoulders only to apologize, pick them up, and fold each one quickly. "Are you going to school?" he asked.

"It's noon," she said. Her newly washed, black hair left wet spots on her old, vintage tee. All the remnants of yesterday's makeup were gone now, and her skin glowed like clean, expensive ivory.

Orion's heart burned in his chest.

"I let you sleep. I didn't want to wake you," she hesitated, "and you were too heavy to drag."

Orion stood, flustered.

Venatrix stared straight ahead, her expression blank. Her eyes were level with his lips. She didn't look up.

"I'm sorry I fell asleep on your bed. It was soft and clean, and you—"

Venatrix turned and grabbed her backpack off the floor.

Orion noticed her jeans. They were loose and stone-washed, out of style. "You're nice," he finished.

"You're the first to think so," she said. She sat on her bed, cross-legged, as she pulled her homework from her bag. She still didn't look at him. "Look, you can hang around, but does your mom know where you are?"

"Yes, I mean… No. I told her—" Orion ran a hand through his hair. "I told her I spent the night at Jayren's and that I'd carpool to school in the morning with him."

"You're friends with Jayren, too?" Venatrix asked in disbelief. She glanced up from under her dark eyebrows. Her blue eyes stole the breath in his chest again; they woke something daring in him, too.

"Yeah," he said decidedly.

"He's one of those hipster kids."

"And? I'm a hipster, too," Orion said. His voice sounded almost strong, he thought.

Venatrix laughed. "Please! You're a church boy. Gaming is a sin, a waste of time, and a distraction from reality, and *most importantly*," she stressed dramatically, "the Unseen Wars between angels and demons. Caeleb and Erin don't have gaming systems."

"And you? You'd only say it with such spite in your voice if you didn't feel the same way. I bet you have one. You're a liar to the bones. I heard you lying to your dad. It's second nature for you. You don't even have to think about it."

"I don't have a gaming system." She looked down.

"Liar," he called her. "You're a hipster, too. Admit it. The vinyl? The polaroids? You can only find those at vintage shops. And all the good systems are at those vintage shops, too. What system?"

"I'm not lying. It's not a system," she said suddenly. Orion's face lit with a smile. He sat on the edge of her bed beside her homework. He pulled her book away, but she tugged it back. "Stop," she said. "Leave me alone. Give it back."

"Tell me," he heard the smile in his voice.

"It's my computer, alright? I don't use systems. Hell, that's the worst way to game. PC gaming only."

Orion laughed brightly. The chiming of his own voice startled him, and Venatrix looked up with wide eyes, too. Her eyes shone beautifully in the tender light coming through her window. She was a deer in his headlights, whom he'd never expected to run into. Their collision tangled his heart up in tight strings in his chest. "You're a liar and a hipster, and I love it."

"I swear, Orion, if you tell—"

"I have no reason to tell anyone. Besides, who would I tell? I don't talk to your friends or your brothers, even if I do hang out with them. They think I'm a lowlife. One of those hipster kids," he drawled, "as you like to call us. They only keep me around because Ophiah makes them."

Venatrix closed her textbook.

"Do you want to go to the beach with me?" he asked.

"With a hipster?"

"Yeah, like a hipster date."

"No," Venatrix said. She scooped her books up, stood, walked to her desk, and dumped them there. "I have homework."

"It's Friday, and I'm betting you don't want to do it anyway."

"Don't you want to talk about it?" she asked. She turned to him, brows knitted in a frown on her stark face. "Doesn't anyone know? Someone who could help you? You look like you haven't eaten in a week. What does your father do to leave bruises like that? How hard does he hit you?"

Orion recoiled at the anger in her voice. Her defiance crippled him.

"Well?"

"It's not that easy," he whispered.

"Why not?"

Orion couldn't speak. His father would beat him for just being there at her house, twice if he found out she knew now. A quiet hope deep inside him wondered if she could help.

Venatrix clenched her jaw.

He thought she was pretty, even with the icy rage in her eyes. The daggers she bore into him couldn't change his mind. Her frustration wasn't directed at him, but he figured he wouldn't mind even if it was. He wanted to change the subject and go to the beach.

"Does Professor North know?" she demanded.

Orion studied the permanent marker graphic on her worn band tee. "You wouldn't like the answer either way."

"You have to tell someone. Or I'll do it, damn it."

"Please don't swear," he muttered, "and please don't tell anyone. Can it stay between us? I just don't want him to find out that you know." He glanced up at her bitter face. He wondered what she thought about. She would probably avoid him at all costs from here on out, and he hated the idea of being completely rejected by another angel. It wouldn't be the first time or the last.

She sighed. "What beach?" she asked finally.

"What?"

"What beach do you want to go to?"

NOVEMBER 5TH, 2106 A.D.

NORTHEAST FLORIDA

CARINA BLACKROCK

Sometimes, when Carina had resided in Hell's Alley, she wasn't sure if it was a dream or reality. Sometimes when she dreamed, she still couldn't tell. Light shone in a warm, bright, creamy pink haze. White silk curtains hung from the banisters twenty feet overhead. The draperies smelled like the skin of the rich, an aroma of hibiscus and lavender, and they adorned every light-bearing window. The marble walls and supporting pillars swirled with flecks of gold. Shiny coins and precious gems could be found at random, littering steps and tables. Wealth came as readily as oxygen, but Carina could never find anything she wanted there.

Carina turned, looking back down the halls she wandered. She moved slow, twisting as if she were drowning in water. Light pierced her skull, a hammer to the head, and the memories hit her one after the other. Children bounded past, and their figures trailed like taillights on a highway. They disappeared. Their voices hollowed into echoes. Their laughter sounded like glass breaking.

She turned again. She found the hall's exit—a wide, high marble arch—and she took heavy steps toward the daylight beyond it. Under her bare feet, she felt the woven carpet—slaved over by human captives and made with only the finest material. Carina could hear their souls calling from beyond the grave, begging to be avenged. She could smell every drop of blood lost for this empire, every life destroyed for its fleeting conquest.

Carina stepped into the sunlight. It was cold.

She looked down on the city, but it was empty. Her vision flickered. Black, then a smear of the golden city. Black again. Feather-soft hands bound her, the action rough in contrast. The split second passed. She was back in the palace on the island in Hell's Alley. Bodies littered the streets now. She could see them for miles where she stood above them all.

"We gave you everything!" Amy screamed. Amy was the empress of Hell's Alley, the Deceiver Sloth, and Carina's personal mentor. Amy had taken Carina under her wing at first, before Carina realized she could not be trusted.

Satin blindfolded Carina. Gagged her. Strangled her. Cold gasoline poured over her.

Her breath stuttered in her chest. Another second, another flash. The feelings—gone. She was in the palace again. A cold wind rushed over her skin; a shadow fell over the kingdom hidden in the Bermuda Triangle. The portal to Hell. *Demons,* she reminded herself as she looked over the bodies once more. They had doubled. They looked to be men and women and children. *Demons. All of them, demons.*

The streets wailed with inhuman cries, a sound like the shrieking of metal, of a gas too close to combustion, of a sizzling fire itching to destroy everything in its path. Thunder boomed overhead like the voice of God, and the noise deafened everything. Carina turned to run, but instead she fell through the absence of the dream.

She woke.

Thunder rumbled in the distance, tired, lazy. Bored.

Carina breathed deep. She gathered her surroundings and found herself in a bed. The covers were warm and coarse. Nothing like the silk she'd slept on in Hell's Alley. They were welcoming, she thought, and she imagined it felt like the embrace of a friend. She had never had a friend so hospitable as to give hugs; Leroy never cared much for physical contact. Handshakes were a lot for him. She wondered now if that had been due to his Fallen nature. Her throat tightened as reality came back to her next, along with a dull throb in her sole.

"Good morning," someone said. His voice was smooth, rich.

Carina propped herself up to look over the footboard of the bed.

A young black man sat there. He smiled at her. His hair was dyed red like a burning bush in the fall. The sun illuminated the spark of heavenly fire that flickered above his crown. He was like her, she realized. A Sentinel, a guardian angel. "I know what you're probably thinking—since you can see my halo. Sentinel, obviously. You're right. I live on an island, so probably Seaborne, like you. But no, I'm Landborne."

"H-How did you find me?" she rasped, her voice dry. "Wh-Where am I? Was I alone?" She didn't want the answer. Not really.

He hesitated.

"What is your name?" she asked.

"Joshuah. Josh is fine. And you? I already know who you are." His smile appeared again, small but sad. "I found you on the beach just down the road."

"Where am I?" she asked again, firmer.

"Amelia Island. It's the northernmost barrier island on the east coast of Florida."

"Florida," she repeated in a whisper. She swallowed, blinked back the tears that threatened her eyes.

Joshuah started slowly, "When I, uh, found you…you were alone. Your friend was gone, and you were unconscious. I gathered his things, and I brought you back here. Here are his things," he said. He motioned to a dresser on his left where Leroy's bag sat next to a small stack of clothes. "I had a friend of mine drop off some clothes for you, too. I own this place, so you're safe here. My bar, the Angels' Diner, is—uh—a Sanctuary. This loft has a bathroom and a shower. You're welcome to stay as long as you need."

Carina nodded, thankful.

"I'm not sure if you're familiar with Sanctuaries," Joshuah said. "They're owned by Sentinels, usually. Humans can come and go and have interactions with you—might even realize you're an angel—but by the time they step back out the door, they'll forget all about it. Might come back and remember you, but never outside of this place. Like I said, you're safe here."

Carina stared at Leroy's taupe bag. His belongings spilled out limply. "What about his coat?"

Joshuah nodded towards the door.

Carina spotted the long leather jacket hanging in a lifeless manner. "Thank you," she hesitated, "Josh."

"I wanted to stay with you until you woke, so I closed my bar for a few days. If you want to be alone—"

Carina nodded.

"I'll be downstairs then," Joshuah said as he stood. "You can come down if you get hungry. I'll make you something. The bar is closed 'til Wednesday."

"What is today?"

"Friday."

She nodded again. "Thank you."

Joshuah smiled and left the room.

Carina's heart sank. She counted her breaths, and she studied the mirror that hung opposite the bed, framed by two windows. It reflected her broken composure, her tangled hair, and her tired, bloodshot eyes. She slipped back down onto the bed and drifted back into sleep. Safe. She was safe.

NOVEMBER 5TH, 2106 A.D.
NORTHEAST FLORIDA
ORION JUDE

Wind whipped Orion's hair as he walked, hands in his pockets, side by side with Venatrix. The roar of the ocean rushing in his ears made it hard to hear anything—even Venatrix's crunching footsteps beside him. They'd walked for fifteen minutes, and the sun refused to peek out from behind the thin haze of storm clouds. They didn't speak, but words clogged his throat like condensation.

The sky and the ocean melted together in the distance, one and the same, with the mist uniting them. On the white-gray sand, the still tide pools reflected perfect mirrors, portals back into the heavens. The atmosphere trapped the two of them together, somewhere between reality and absence, between pain and healing.

Orion wished he could stay there forever, or maybe even simply dissolve into the mist that settled over the beach and the horizon. He felt the question coming even before it reached her lips. It was inevitable, like death itself.

"Why does he abuse you?" Venatrix asked, her voice barely loud enough to hear over the howling in his ears. She looked to Orion. Her face was washed out, drained of emotion, and her hair snapped in vicious spikes around her face. Her perfect façade and pretty makeup had gone out with the tide, crumbled like the sand beneath their feet. Orion wondered if it had really been there at all. She didn't look less pretty, though, only more human as they walked together. He figured she might still blame him for the wreck her hair would be once they got back to her house. Despite his hesitance, Venatrix did not push him to answer.

Orion breathed steadily. "I guess over time, I accepted that not everything has an answer to 'why.' Some things just happen because they have to," he said. "Some things have to break you to shape you into the person you're supposed to be, you know?"

Venatrix stopped walking. "Everything happens for a reason," she said.

Orion almost missed her reply.

Her face pinched as she squinted through the pale light. She sighed heavily and stared off into the distance. Silence hung between them like a sickness they were too scared to breathe in. Finally, she said, "Do you know which one he is?"

"What?"

"As in Deceiver. Which Deceiver is he?"

Orion's heart weighed a billion pounds in his chest, sinking him into quicksand he would never escape. He'd become all too familiar with that feeling lately. "I don't know," he whispered, "but Professor North said he's their leader. He would know. We could ask him."

"No, we can't."

"Why not?"

Venatrix paused. "Well," she said pointedly, "because we're going to find out who he is, then we're going to do some research, and we're going to banish him back to Hell."

"What? No! Are you crazy?" Orion's heart skipped a beat. "I won't let you."

"I wasn't asking you to let me," she argued.

"This is something I just have to deal with! On—On my own."

"You don't have to do this on your own. I can help you, and I will," she bit the words.

Orion thought her eyes were almost prettier gray, calm, and glaring. That drive to achieve the unachievable turned them steely in the fall fog. Jayren's red scarf—which was tied around her neck to hide her tattoo—made her lips rosier in the blanched afternoon. He wished she would smile. Then he'd have something better to think about, something beautiful.

She didn't smile.

III

THE BATTLE OF THE NORTH ACADEMY CAFETERIA

In the hierarchy of angels and demons, the Archangels and Deceivers make the top of the list. At the bottom of the hierarchy are lesser spirits and lesser demons. Lesser spirits are responsible for good; they inhabit animals and move with the wind and storms. Lesser demons are responsible for evil; they are to blame for rabid, possessed creatures, for causing small anomalies that injure the physical or wound the psyche. Multiple lesser demons in a single body can cause mental disorders, such as depression, anxiety, symptoms of PTSD, OCD, and more.
— A History of Hierarchy

NOVEMBER 8TH, 2106 A.D.
NORTHEAST FLORIDA
VENATRIX CANES

Venatrix's morning couldn't have been slower. It had started with a review of World War III in her History class, something everyone in her generation suffered the repercussions from. And though it touched on the human problems of their world, it was made very clear to Venatrix and her classmates that the Third World War had been an Unseen War at its heart.

The catalyst of World War III was a computer virus that spread across the internet too quickly to be stopped. With tensions already high in the world, each world superpower blamed the next, resulting in all-out war. In a desperate attempt to win the war, each superpower sent a nuclear device to wipe out the power in their neighboring countries. No one noticed what was direly wrong until it was too late: the virus had disabled all the systems in place to cool the world's supply of nuclear reactors. Meltdowns happened all across the world. A total reset. The world quickly abandoned the war, each country turning inward to deal with their own catastrophes at hand.

Everyone who survived in the States moved into major cities for safety's sake, but the government required anyone seeking shelter in those cities to surrender their weapons to prevent further tension.

Some backup emergency power stores kicked on, but they were out by the end of the week. Slowly, any new construction was purely solar-powered, and it took over fifty years for new skylines to light the horizon. Night had been so pitch black for those fifty years that, rumor had it, RUST was born out of World War III. Most believe it, too. RUST had risen from the ashes with all the weapons that were previously surrendered— stolen from the government—leaving RUST to be the only armed force in the States and most of the world.

To make matters worse, RUST assassins only hunted at night, so it made them incredibly hard to ignore. The existence of RUST had altered everyone's day-to-day lifestyles.

It was all a downer to Venatrix, and today's Religious Studies class wasn't much better. The lecture dragged on: "Just as angelic intervention has changed the history of the world to what we learn today, demonic influences have done the same."

Venatrix's chin dimpled with the fabric of her sweater. The lesson wasn't boring, but it picked at her mind like burs and thorns, tearing at her façade. Orion shared this class with her.

"Demons manipulate animals the same way that angels persuade dogs to rescue humans. Demons, however, will possess the same creatures to attack. For this reason, demonic influences have been deemed one of the most powerful forces in day-to-day life."

A book slammed shut in the back of the classroom.

Venatrix sat up and turned.

Orion struggled to gather his books. He flushed, and—illuminated by the blue projector light—the red on his face looked like a brand new bruise.

"Demonic influences, huh?" someone said from across the class. A snicker broke out like wildfire.

Orion shuffled, a deer stirring up leaves in his frantic haste to get away. He clutched his books, pinched his bag beneath bone-white knuckles. He lost a few papers as he whisked out.

Venatrix stood and glared. "You asshole," she accused into the darkness. She looked around, but the blackness swallowed up the culprit.

The room hushed.

"Venatrix, sit down," the professor said.

"No," she bit. "You're an asshole, too…sir." She glared at the teacher's black outline, and he stiffened. "He didn't do anything. Demonic. Like hell! He's not evil! Pick a different day to give this lecture."

Murmurs.

"Miss Canes."

What does it matter? she thought. *I've already got detention.* She snapped her book together, shoved her stuff into her bag, and stalked from the room. She twisted on her heel—ready to run after Orion—only to find him pressed to the wall just outside the classroom. She hesitated and took a deep breath.

He didn't look at her, and she studied his shoes absently. His gray tennis shoes looked as if he'd run through a forest and tripped and fallen face-first into a puddle of mud. Dirt crusted the nose of his shoes like scabs—new enough to still be painful, old enough to almost be healed.

Orion was too quiet.

Her own anger quivered through her. Part of her wanted to go back, to find the kid and break his nose. It was a lost cause, so she focused on the cause right in front of her. *He's a chance at a real friendship*, she thought, *one I choose*. She looked at his hands. He held his belongings in a clustered mess. Slowly, she reached out and coaxed the limp, brown mass of a backpack from his arms. She opened it and held it out for him. "Here," she muttered. She pushed the bag closer when he hesitated; she closed her eyes when he flinched.

"You can't be seen with me," he said.

"May as well. I'm on your side now."

He closed his eyes, exhaled shakily. He whispered, "Thank you…for what you said in there. I heard."

Venatrix blushed. She hated the feel of the heat on her skin, and she tried to quickly deter the emotion. "C'mon. Put your books away. We'll go hang out in the cafeteria."

He dropped a book as he tried to put his belongings in the outstretched bag.

Venatrix knelt and picked up the book. She slid it in with the others. She prayed he didn't think of her like the rest of them, like her brothers. She stepped closer, handed his bag over. She smelled the nervous sweat on his shirt and saw the dirt stain near the shoulder.

"Are you hungry?"

Orion nodded. He shifted his weight.

"Let's go. This is the last place we should be when that class lets out. I'll buy you a soda," she said.

"Just water, if that's okay."

He walked past her, and she followed him. She liked the challenge of keeping up with his long-legged stride. "You don't like soda? I'll get you whatever you want, honest."

"It tastes like chemicals steeping in metal," he mumbled.

A smile tickled Venatrix's face. She laughed.

"Water's good for the soul anyway."

"Okay. Well, speaking of water," she said. She watched him, but he didn't look back at her. "I did some research last night. Have you thought about Holy Water? Like to use on your dad?"

He scoffed, hesitated. "Can we not call him my dad? His name is Tristan."

The words pierced Venatrix's thoughts like ice. Cold, hard, jagged spikes of fear. "Tristan, then," she started again. "Have you thought about giving him Holy Water like in a drink or something?"

"If I could get close enough, maybe. But I've never seen him drink. Ever."

"No water?"

"No."

"He probably dried up his soul." Venatrix joked. She nudged Orion gently. He glanced at her, and she saw the hint of a smile at the corners of his mouth.

"I have thought about it. But Holy Water wouldn't banish him. If anything, it'd make him mad and…" Orion fell silent.

Venatrix's heart tied in tight knots. "Fine, okay. Do you have any better ideas?"

"How 'bout a library date?"

Venatrix paused. "I don't think the term 'date' should have anything to do with it. We're trying to banish your d—

Tristan. The demon, Deceiver, you know," she faltered. She cursed herself.

Orion laughed, but his tone was half-hearted, a lesser pitch than the music she'd heard him play. She wanted to make him laugh loud and bright and brash. It was as if he were an instrument—but one covered in tarnish. His polish had been gone for years, she could tell. "Okay," he said, "but make me a deal. If we banish him, we do a real date. I'll take you out for sushi."

"Sushi and water?" she asked.

"Yeah."

She peeked sideways at him. "Alright, deal."

CORVUN KHLYDE

"I think I'm gonna try out for Luke's part," Jayren said through munches of chips.

Corvun stirred his soup absently.

Jayren continued to ramble as they sat together in the empty cafeteria. His voice echoed like a choir in a cathedral. The familiar acoustics put Corvun at ease; he'd become fond of Jayren's nasally narration, as if he were the morning radio or his favorite audiobook.

"What made you decide that?" Corvun asked.

"I—uh—yeah," Jayren paused, his cheek full of food. "Well, when you were flirting with Vena, I did some flirting of my own."

"Oh, really?" Corvun looked at his soup. Muddy-orange carrots, green beans, and shavings of beef floated in the broth. "Did you land a date?"

"Hah! I wish. She's too pretty for me."

"But you're tryin' out for the play to impress her," Corvun guessed.

"Sure, I mean, why not? I've always wanted to be a Jedi. I know all the lines from the movies." Jayren twirled a small braid that was longer than the rest of his hair around his fingertip. "Plus, I already have a Padawan braid, too."

As Jayren continued to talk, Venatrix and Orion appeared in the hall carrying lunch trays. Corvun knew Orion well enough to know he wouldn't be a fling Venatrix's brothers put her up to, but it surprised Corvun that the two had talked. Orion and his twin sister, Ophiah, had the reputation of being outcasts due to their heritage—which Corvun knew well, thanks to his father's brutal honesty. Only in the past couple of years had they settled into one friend group—with Caeleb and his gang—because of Ophiah's boyfriend. Corvun had watched them from afar, and they had remained outcasts, even within their friend group.

"Hey! Hey, that's Rian!" Jayren piped.

Venatrix muttered to Orion as they approached, her eyes darting back and forth from Jayren to Corvun. She gave them a tight-lipped smile when they stood before the table. Venatrix maintained her ever-confident posture, but Orion was lanky and awkward. The difference was startling. "I double-booked," Venatrix said. "I hope you guys don't mind."

"Dude, Rian! What's up, man?" Jayren beamed.

Venatrix put a hand on Orion's back as he tried to turn away.

Jayren's smile faded.

"I'm okay, how are you?"

"Just tryna figure out how to land a date," Jayren said. His face quirked into a friendly smile. "I like your shirt."

"I meant to wash my other sweater last night. I forgot." Orion rubbed his arm to cover the indie band logo stamped on the front of his chest. His shirt was a dusty gray, washed-out color with loose, worn hems. Orion had attempted to cover the tee with another old garment—a button-down sweater with stripes on the ends of the sleeves. It was unlike Orion to break dress code, and neither garment abided by the rules.

Corvun noticed a bruise on Orion's collarbone.

"Can we join you?" Venatrix asked.

Corvun waved his spoon at the other side of the table in invitation.

"In case you haven't already been introduced: Corvun, Jayren, this is Orion. Orion—" She waved her hand in order, "Corvun, Jayren. Though, I heard he's already met you." Venatrix's voice hitched when she said Jayren's name, as if it were a profane or offensive statement she could lose her status for.

"Nice to meet you too, Trixie," Jayren said with a toothy grin.

Venatrix gripped her fork like a dagger.

"Don't cut his throat out, Vena. He's the only friend I've got," Corvun said.

Venatrix turned her gaze to him with a faint look of dismay—one only he was familiar enough with to know.

"Can I call you Trixie?" Jayren asked.

Corvun held Venatrix's gaze; she took a deep breath, exhaled evenly. She knew it was a test as well as he did. Jayren was his new friend, and if Venatrix wanted to restore her friendship with him, she'd have to befriend Jayren. "I guess," she muttered.

Corvun's heart skipped a beat when Jayren grabbed a handful of peas off his plate and piled them into his white, plastic spoon. He didn't have enough time to detain Jayren before he launched the food into Venatrix's face. Jayren let out a cackle, Venatrix gasped, and Corvun couldn't feel his arms or legs.

Orion's breath fell from his lips in a shy, half-hearted snicker.

Venatrix's expression changed from shock and disgust to surprise at Orion's gentle laugh.

"I got one down your boobs," Jayren said.

Corvun backhanded Jayren's arm.

Venatrix looked back to Jayren. Her eyes were cold as ever, but Corvun could see warmth melting them like spring snow. She grabbed two handfuls of chips, crushed the greasy, flaky junk food in her palms, and stood to rain the crumbs into Jayren's blond hair. "Looks like you have dandruff now, you little shit."

Jayren turned pink with laughter.

"Vena," Corvun chastised, only to find her face flushed the same.

Orion's cheeks were red as he tried to contain the humorous tickle in his mouth.

"Food fight!" Jayren hollered.

"No!"

"There are only four of us!" Orion interrupted.

"Two-versus-two. Let's go!" Venatrix chimed. "I call Rian!"

"Nope. No, Orion's on my team," Corvun said. He jumped the table to protect the quiet kid. "I want to see you and Jayren work together. You two will lose in two minutes flat."

"No we won't," they griped together.

"No way," Venatrix said firmly. "C'mon Jay."

Corvun laughed as Jayren stared up at Venatrix, dumbfounded. He took the opportunity to flip his now lukewarm soup into his best friend's lap.

Jayren tumbled backwards off his seat, swearing the whole way down. He crashed onto the floor, and spears of plasticware clattered and clanged on the ground next to him. Venatrix stepped up onto the table, then back down to offer Jayren a hand. Jayren grabbed Venatrix's arm, and she heaved him back up into the cafeteria campaign. He swiveled around and struck an offensive pose, wielding a plastic knife as a sword. "For Narnia!" he cried.

"For Narnia!" Vena bellowed, louder. She began flinging string cheese across the table, and Jayren mirrored her attack.

Corvun snatched a lunch tray and shielded himself. "Grab a tray!" he shouted to Orion. Cheese pattered relentlessly against the plastic.

Orion picked a tray off the floor and hid his face behind it. Corvun kept his focus on Orion amidst the friendly fire of cheese and green beans and soup remnants; Orion held his small smile like a torch. He peeked over his pale tray and threw a stray orange at Jayren.

The orange smacked Jayren square in the forehead and sent him stumbling backwards. He collapsed again.

Venatrix stormed atop the table, a scepter of a fork in her hand. She aimed it down at Corvun and Orion. "You've slain my best knight. For that, I will get my revenge!" Her words resounded like a cruel queen's decree in the vacant lunchroom. Her authority carved itself in stone, unwavering and unchallenged.

Until Corvun stabbed her showing ankle with a spork.

She yelped and hissed down at him. "You cowardly rat! You cannot stop me from my quest to avenge my slain squire!"

"Hell yes! Yes! She's one of us!" Jayren deteriorated into fits of giggles on the floor.

"But I, dear queen, have somethin' you do not!" Corvun called back dramatically. He felt young again, weightless. Free, if only for a moment. "I have the wheels of this damn table.

Somethin' your stupid kingdom hasn't invented yet. Pathetic!" He kicked the lunch table, and Venatrix fell with a shriek.

Orion caught her; his movement reminded Corvun of a shadow, come and gone too soon. Venatrix's face flushed, and Corvun grinned. "And now, the final blow. Death's lethal strike. You're finished, you white bitch—I mean witch," Corvun said breathlessly. He heard the smile in his own voice.

"How could I kill her? She's pretty. It would be a shame," Orion said.

Venatrix sank in his arms.

"Kiss her!" Jayren popped up on the other side of the table. His bright eyes flashed above his barricade, eager with curiosity. He ducked when Corvun chucked a brownie at him. "Death's kiss could take even the most beautiful life. She must die for her sins! She's conquered too many hearts with her deceitful beauty! Let not Death be defeated by her, too. Rian, her eyelashes are probably *fake*."

Venatrix sank further into Orion's arms, and he stared at her with a longing Corvun had never seen in anyone's eyes. Envy or adoration, he couldn't tell. It burned bright as a wildfire in the depths of night. Too bright, even, to let the stars shine.

"What on God's good Earth?" a lunch lady squealed from behind the four.

Corvun spun and stared. The excitement in the room dropped like a wrecking ball from a crane. Their castle crumbled; their imaginary masterpiece turned to dust. It was over, just as quickly as it had begun.

· · · · ·

"I smell like beef," Jayren said with a gag. Orion fished a string of cheese out of his shirt. The four of them stood in Professor North's office, together, for a second time. "Can't we just go shower in the locker room?"

"A food fight," Professor North started, disregarding Jayren.

"Sir, it was fun," Orion said.

"It is not the way to handle drama."

Corvun saw Orion's jaw gape out of the corner of his eye. Corvun's back stiffened, and he closed his eyes.

"We weren't fighting! Not *actually*," Orion said.

Professor North sat back in his leather throne, flipping a pen in his hand.

Corvun felt captive in Professor North's gaze. He knew their headmaster held them to a higher standard, all four of them. His pulse beat with steady disappointment in himself. "Professor, I started it," Corvun said. Jayren's eyes snapped to Corvun, and Corvun glared back. "I take full responsibility for all of this."

Jayren looked away. "Professor, I'd like a shower."

"You'll all report to detention tomorrow. Venatrix, you have detention again on Wednesday."

Corvun gritted his teeth. "If she has more, then so do we."

"Her discipline is greater because she's acted out of line more than you boys."

"Are you sure it's not because you consider her greater?" Corvun bit back suddenly. He felt Jayren and Venatrix and Orion all tense beside him; they remained silent.

Their professor sighed. "And what would you be referring to by saying that, Mr. Khlyde?"

Corvun raised an eyebrow in challenge.

"Mr. Omans, do you know what he's referring to?" Professor North asked.

"She has better grades than all of us combined, doesn't she?" Jayren said.

The professor glanced back to Corvun, and Corvun gritted his teeth. Professor North's eyes returned to Jayren.

"Doubt wages a powerful war inside the mind, Jayren," he said softly. "Your sister accepts this, and she removed the doubt in her mind. You're protected here, and you're safe. You don't have to pretend you don't believe."

"I want a shower," Jayren snapped.

Professor North stood, and the four of them shrank back. "Corvun, if you take responsibility for them, detention won't be your worst consequence."

Corvun didn't change his mind at the headmaster's warning.

"Dismissed," North said.

Corvun waited for the other three to leave first, and he turned to follow. He walked out behind Venatrix and closed the office door.

"What's he talking about?" she spun and asked.

He avoided her cool eyes only to find Jayren and Orion staring at him, too. He rubbed his neck and found a disk of carrot stuck to his collar. "Let's go to the locker room. We can shower, and I'll tell you. Alright? But we block the door. She's comin' with us."

"No. I'm not going in a guy's locker room. You guys can come in the girls' locker room. We barricade the door," she agreed.

"Sick," Jayren said.

"We can't keep breaking the rules," Orion said. "We'll have detention all year."

"You heard North," Venatrix said, tilting her head at Corvun, "detention won't be the worst consequence. But we better go now. Girls' swim meet is one period after lunch."

Corvun let Venatrix lead the four of them through the wide, empty halls of the school. They weaved in and out of the doors and side halls as teachers came strolling down the corridors on patrol. They reached the girls' locker room, and

Venatrix whispered for the other three to stay put. She snuck across the last hall and slipped into the girls' locker room. A few moments later, Venatrix popped her head out and motioned for the others to come over. Corvun held the door for Orion and Jayren and went in behind them. He helped Venatrix push a bench against the door and secure the trash can beneath the handle.

"There are towels folded by the showers. Leave them on the floor when you're done. And be decent. I'm not asking," Venatrix said.

"What about our clothes?" Jayren asked. His pants were already on the way off.

Venatrix turned and stared at the ceiling, biting her lips together. Anger fumed on her cheeks.

Corvun couldn't help but chuckle. "I'll wash them by hand real quick. Where's the dryer?"

"Around the left corner."

"Why do the girls have a washer and dryer and we don't?"

"We do, Jayren, you've just never used them."

"Can I shower?" Orion asked quietly from the far end of the locker room. "I haven't been able to at home. I'd really like one."

"Of course. Take your time," Corvun said. He walked to Orion as the redhead stripped down to his underwear and handed his clothes over. Corvun looked at the bruises covering Orion. He could feel the sour pain on his own skin, but he knew Orion's hurt cut bone deep. "I'll wash yours, too."

Orion tried to smile.

Jayren stayed quiet behind them for a second then loudly said, "I have to take my boxers off now, so everyone look away!"

"Gross." Venatrix swore and shoved past him. She stalked deeper into the locker room and disappeared. "Decency, guys! Not asking."

ORION JUDE

Hot water kissed Orion's skin with kindness he wasn't used to. He didn't hesitate to use generous amounts of shampoo and conditioner. It didn't matter that they smelled like lilacs and vanilla. It felt good to be clean and to take his time; to not need to worry about Ophiah in the meantime or if his next beating was just around the corner. Still, he'd asked Venatrix to sit outside his shower just in case. Fear was still a constant noose on his shoulders, ready to scoop him up at any given second. Venatrix lifted that noose when she was close by.

"So I, uh, meant to apologize," Venatrix said. "I didn't consider they might see your bruises."

Orion stared at the water that beaded against the white tile like sweat. Bruises kept him company, kind of like friends, he thought. He guessed he'd rather have real friends who knew about his demons instead. He couldn't form those words to say aloud, though, and instead, his mind thought through all the ways Venatrix and Corvun and Jayren could use him for their own gain. Shame scorched his skin, but he told himself it was just the water.

"I'm so sorry," she said.

"I forgive you," he said, barely a whisper.

"Thanks for not kissing me," she said next. Her hesitation to bring it up was small but obvious, but her words were genuine.

"You're welcome," Orion turned to rinse his hair in the water. His shoulders and neck and ears pulsed with embarrassment as he recalled holding her that close, her lips parted and rosy, and her eyes wide in shock. "I mean, I just figured—I don't know. You and Corvun?"

Venatrix laughed. She sounded like wind chimes and songbirds in the springtime.

"You grew up together, right? You guys seem close. There's a lot of tension when he looks at you, and when you glare at him. I mean, you glare at everyone, but you glare at him more."

"No. No, it's not like that at all," she said with a smile in her voice. "He's like my brother, but it's different because I hate my brothers. Corvun makes it hard to hate him with all this. You know, standing up for people. Being nice to you. He's got a good heart, but I know he doesn't like people knowing that. My brothers have black hearts, but Corvun," she paused, "his heart is gold. He's just painted it black."

"So you don't like him, like…"

"Romantically? No way."

Orion hesitated. "Well, that's all that matters to me."

Venatrix fell silent.

"Can we all be friends?" Orion asked, changing the subject. "We make a good team." Orion turned the water off and wrung his hair out. Words came easier when he was out of sight, he realized. He thanked God for the two curtains separating him and Venatrix. "I hate being alone," he confessed. "I hate thinking I have friends only to find out it was all fake. Sometimes they see my bruises, or Ophiah's bruises, and then want nothing to do with us. I mean, I get it, but Corvun didn't even look away."

"You know why he didn't look away?"

"His heart of gold?"

"No, he…" she breathed, "he's used to that kind of stuff. He's not abused like you, but his father started training him really hard when we were little. It's why we grew apart. He's intense. He knows what pain is, like you. We didn't really see eye-to-eye after that. He thinks I'm a pampered bitch."

"You are. I-I mean only the pampered part!" He squeezed his eyes shut and braced himself.

Venatrix tossed a towel over the shower curtain. "Dry off." Her voice was happy and relaxed, and he relaxed too.

Orion pulled the towel into the steam with him. The fabric felt like a baby blanket on his skin, kind and caring and safe. He dried off quickly. The curtain ruffled, and his eyes darted up; there he found Venatrix's hand holding freshly dried clothes between the curtain and the wall. "Thank you," he said. He grabbed his clothes and dressed, wrestling the fabric over his humid skin. He was clean, and he smelled like flowers, and he loved it. He opened the curtain.

Venatrix stood waiting. "Can I ask you a question?" she asked. He nodded as he studied her exciting features, the pink on her nose that reminded him of the winter wind on his own. Her eyes were bright without makeup, snow reflecting the sparkling sun. But guilt and uncertainty shadowed her face; he'd seen the same look on himself. "Why do you like me?"

"You looked deeper than my bruises. Like Corvun did, just earlier."

Venatrix reached out to take his towel, and her fingers touched his hand. It reminded Orion of how her fingers had felt on the windowsill, cold but not bitter. Sad, almost. Unpredictable like the weather. Her fingers didn't move away immediately. Her magnetic touch drew him in and pushed him out at the same time, like the moon to the ocean waves. Her fingertips traced the tips of his as she took the towel out of his hands.

JAYREN OMANS

Jayren felt better with clean clothes. The lack of meat stench eased his headache, and the perfume of clean clothes reminded him of his mom in the early mornings she'd wait by the bus stop with him and his sister. He missed her encouraging hand on his shoulder and the lullaby of her voice. He was left with the empty memory, sitting on the girls' locker room counter, facing his loyal friend and two new acquaintances. He could feel every time any of the three looked at him. Their eyes were scalpels and knives, dissecting his silence. He wasn't really sure what shattered him. It had come suddenly and violently, and it left him broken again. He wanted his parents.

"Professor North was hinting at a prophecy," Corvun said. He tossed Orion a new towel to finish drying his hair. "I'm not sure how much you guys have been told."

"About us?" Venatrix asked.

Corvun nodded.

Venatrix looked around—at Orion then at Jayren. Orion kept his eyes down, and Jayren thought it best to keep his lips zipped. "*Us?*"

"Have you looked closely at his mural?" Corvun asked. "It does look like us. I put it together that day in his office. The three of us. I couldn't place the fourth until I walked out and saw Orion heading in. I've known that I'm the Authority of Famine for some time. I was never told who the others might be, but I always had a feeling, like a sixth sense. *This* makes sense." He waved his finger at the four of them.

Orion meandered over to Jayren and leaned against the counter he sat on. Orion's silence felt the same as the dawn, the serene quiet before the honey-gold light of day washed over the world.

Jayren leaned closer to Orion and quietly asked, "What are they talking about?"

"Professor North has a painting of Revelation's Apocalypse in his office," Orion said. He tipped his head in Jayren's direction but didn't lift his face. He looked at Jayren's wine-red Converse. He breathed deep. "I think he means to say that we're the Four Horsemen."

Jayren plunged into a bucket of ice. He stared up numbly, watching Corvun. Much to his horror, he saw stars circling in his vision, around Corvun and around Venatrix.

"Why wouldn't they tell the rest of us?" Venatrix crossed her arms tightly across her chest. She became distant, unsure, and all her confidence vanished.

"I don't know," Corvun said quietly. He scoffed. "Michael—" he said, then shot a wary glance at Jayren and Orion, "my father, he takes it on himself to tell me everythin'. I'm not sure why your parents haven't told you, Vena. But Orion's and Jayren's... I mean, it doesn't surprise me they don't know."

"Tell us, then," Venatrix said.

Corvun turned his dark eyes on Jayren. "The Four Horsemen—Conquest, War, Famine, and Death—have been reincarnated throughout time, every few hundred years after the crucifixion of Jesus. We're born into the same eras as the Archangels, and while the Archangels are meant to be a charter of humanity, we're... We're a test."

"A test of what?" Venatrix pressed.

"A test to gauge the timing of the end of the world," Corvun said. "We're born into eras with major wars, turnin' points for civilization. Like, say, the Revolutionary War or World War III. When we fight in that war and win it, we trigger Armageddon. In previous lives, we've failed."

Humiliation burned in Jayren's chest. He couldn't believe Corvun would pull a joke like this. It was bad enough he was even hanging out with them, but to make a joke out of it? He jumped off the counter, and the other three looked at him. He was suddenly painfully aware of his wimpy stature and the zit on his nose. "You've actually lost your mind, Corvun. Even if it is true—which it's not—I'm a nobody. Are you doing this 'cause you pity me, or want to make me feel like part of something? I don't *belong* with you guys. You're all beautiful and good at things."

Corvun tensed, and Venatrix looked at the floor.

"And you," Jayren turned to Orion, "God, I wish I looked like you, but even if I did, I'd just mess it up somehow. I'd probably blow my eyebrows off trying to light up homemade fireworks." He sucked in a breath. His chest was tight. "Angels *aren't* real. This is some stupid setup I got thrown into because my sister had to listen to some idiot with an ego bigger than this country. Now she's in debt to this douche, and I'm stuck here. I don't even really want to be seen with any of you."

"War," Corvun whispered to Venatrix.

"Fuck off, Corvun," Jayren said.

"Hey, c'mon," Orion said. He threw his towel under the sink. "He didn't do anything to you."

Jayren stalked to the bench that blocked the door and collapsed on it. The door was cool against his burning back.

"What about Orion?" Venatrix asked.

"Death," Orion said.

"You're just picking that because it's cool and edgy," Jayren snapped at Orion. "You could be whatever you wanted."

"Anything I wanted, sure, but never good enough for them," Orion said, motioning at Venatrix and Corvun. They seemed not to notice, and suddenly Jayren felt a little less alone. "And that's beside the point. North told me."

"And that leaves Conquest," Venatrix named herself.

"Can I leave now?" Jayren asked. Exhaustion and defeat made his arms feel numb, like after weightlifting in gym class, and the threat of tears squeezed the back of his throat. "This is stupid. Besides, it's Pestilence. Everyone knows that." The other three looked at him, and his composure crumbled like a fortress. He was pretty sure he'd built it with super glue and Legos. They could pierce the most calloused foot; no one should've been able to get to him. Yet, here he was, surrounded. "Are we done?"

"Yeah," Corvun said.

Jayren stood, tossed the trash can back on the floor, and pushed the bench out of the way. He swung the door open only to come face-to-face with a young brunette. She stared at him in horror. The world stood still, and her shriek split the atmosphere in time with the school bell. His hand dropped to his side. "Guess we're gonna have detention with Trixie whether we like it or not," he said.

INTERLUDE

I

THE ARENA

*The stars in the heavens were named to be a sign for the angels. Canes
Venatici, known as the hunting dogs, was chosen for the Archangels
Suriel and Raquel and their three children. The constellation was
named for their daughter, Victoria, the Authority of Conquest.*
— A History of Hierarchy

438 A.D.
ROME
VENATICI

"Your prize is your freedom," the announcer's voice boomed.
Venatici stood in the corridors, preparing to enter the
gladiator arena. The bumpy, stone walls echoed the voices of
guards and prisoners alike. She listened to the announcements
resounding outside in the arena. The challenge. Their names.
She heard the stories of the gladiators, too, and it included
herself: the daughter of an esteemed patrician family. No
fighting skills. No fighting chance. The crowd's roar
crescendoed, a rising clash of fanfares and shouts. "Survive,
and you will wear your victory like a crown."

Venatici slid her whetstone down her spear, trying desperately to remember her training. Friction heated her hand. She gritted her teeth and watched two leather-and-metal-clad guards drag away two bodies. She didn't need to see their long, black ponytails to recognize them; her brothers were in the arena before her, and they were slaughtered. Her brothers were always more skilled at combat than she was. The reality of it all hadn't quite hit her yet; maybe it never would. Her fate loomed over her like an oncoming storm.

A sharp pain seared in her thumb, and her eyes burned with tears. Venatici dropped her whetstone and looked down to where she'd caught her thumb with her spear. The wound severed her skin and muscle, a thick ribbon of red.

"I believe wounds are meant to happen in the arena," a smooth voice said behind her.

Venatici spun and swiped her spear at the one who spoke.

A tall, bronze-colored man caught her weapon and aimed it away. He snatched her other wrist and held it tight enough to examine the cut steadily. In his vise-like grip, Venatici glowered. He was beautiful—handsome like a Roman god from her studies with auburn hair and emerald-green eyes—and it made her even angrier. He was just another prisoner she was pitted against in this cursed competition. He would kill her, she was sure of it. She wondered if he would enjoy it. "Let me wrap it," he said.

"No," Venatici bit. She spat on his shoe.

The tall man disarmed her with a twist of her spear. He shifted the weapon in his free hand, testing its weight. He pointed it at her chin, lifted her face with the flat side. All the while, he kept a firm hold on her wounded hand. Venatici felt useless. Chills clutched her as his twinkling eyes studied her face. "I know you," he said.

She willed herself not to talk.

"You're the youngest of the Canes siblings. Your family just committed treason against the throne. Quite jarring, coming from patricians." Venatici grabbed for a jeweled dagger hanging on the man's belt, but he twisted away. He clicked his tongue. "Please. You're too small to fight me. What does that life get you besides pale skin and a pretty face? Ignorance, maybe. They say ignorance is bliss. Is it true?"

"Let me go," she said.

Playfully, he raised a slim eyebrow at her. "May I wrap your hand, traitor?"

Venatici felt a second set of shadowy eyes watching her. The sickening feeling of being hunted like prey fell over her, and like a lethal strike, realization hit her, too. She knew him as well. His amber-red hair and cat-like eyes and ruby-and-amethyst-studded weapons fit the rumors passed around by her friends and family. He was a skilled assassin, and he wasn't alone. "Gemini," she whispered his renowned name. His name, *and* his twin sister's name.

"Good, so you've heard of us," a woman spoke.

Venatici broke Orion's grip and spun to face his twin.

Ophiuchus was just as elegant as him, composed of warm tones of earth and flame, of rust and gold. She leaned into Venatici's face, and Venatici could smell the rose of her red lip paint. "So, you'll know who's going to win this fight. Sit this one out, darling. I'll let the vipers kill you. It'll sting less."

Venatici snapped her elbow up, knocking Ophiuchus in the chin. Behind her, Orion wrapped his arm around Venatici's neck and dragged her away. Her heels scuffed the ground, kicking uselessly. Her body weighed her down, crushing her windpipe in his arm. She clawed at his skin; he only chuckled at her futile attempts. Just as Venatici's head began throbbing with pain, Orion dropped her, and she collapsed on the ground. She scrambled backwards, away from the approaching twins, coughing and gasping and stirring up dust in her wake.

"Orion! Ophiuchus! Please, give her a break!" another voice said. He had a Scandinavian-sounding accent, one she'd only heard in passing on the streets. "We need her. She's our straight shot out of here. Take her with us and we have money! We'll sell her for passage at sea. Help her up and wrap that wound on her hand. Where did she get it?"

Venatici stared up at the new stranger who split the Gemini twins apart. He was just as stunning as the twins but in a different way. He was fair skinned with hair the color of bone ivory. His sharp face pinched into a mischievous grin as he leaned down. "You are quite pathetic in person," he told her. "You're much prettier in the paintings." He turned and sauntered away.

"Wait!" Venatici shouted. She struggled to get upright on her weak knees. She pursued the blond man, but she didn't get far; the twins held her back. "Wait, you're breaking out?"

"Breaking out? No. Making a game to remember and a daring esscape?" He hissed the words. The blond turned, and he bared four fangs at her. His green eyes narrowed into snake-like slits. "Well of coursse."

SERPENS

"Serpens, you were meant to collect weapons," Corvus said under his breath when his friend returned to his side. Corvus dreaded being alone, and Serpens knew it. Corvus stood with his hands chained in heavy, black metal because he was a threat, a slave driver. Someone who knew his way around weapons and retaliation. Serpens was the only one who didn't look at Corvus exclusively that way; Serpens viewed Corvus as a friend. "Why have you brought me the Gemini twins and that piece of noble trash?" Corvus asked.

Serpens looked at Corvus's bound hands and picked at his fangs absently. "You said, 'Get us tools to escape,' and I couldn't possibly think of a better way to do that than with the Gemini twins and that piece of noble trash," he responded. Serpens glanced over his shoulder to see the two redhead twins examining the slender girl. They poked and prodded and questioned her. "Listen, Corvus, the others don't dare look in your direction. The twins joined this fight for fun. They're the ones to beat."

"They will kill us," Corvus snapped back. "We will be betrayed. They don't pity us. They don't pity *her*. What do we have as leverage on them? The emperor treats those killers like jewelry, like gold on his neck. They are his treasure. They will win this game and return to their bed with the king."

Serpens held his friend's dark, black-eyed glare. He had a secret; he *did* have leverage, although he planned to keep it locked behind his teeth, prisoner to his own intentions. The Gemini twins thought they were sterile. Ophiuchus never dreamed she could have a family, but in the recent weeks, Serpens smelled changes in her hormones. He wanted to keep it a secret, keep it sacred and personal between Ophiuchus and himself, but he would use it as a last resort if he needed to. He just hoped she would choose him—a family of their own— over endless riches and a posh life with the emperor. So he said, "That's exactly why they'll choose our side. They don't like belonging to the emperor. I don't like it. You don't like it. We are slaves to a king, and we crave to rule our own lives. We never want to bow to anyone. We can give them that life. We can give them *freedom*. If they win, with our aid, we can get them out of the city. You and I know this city better than anyone. No one will be able to stop us."

Corvus didn't seem convinced. (Truthfully, Serpens wasn't convinced himself.) "You let your adrenaline control you. She will slow us down." Corvus shot a glare at the black-haired girl. She'd become tangled between Orion and Ophiuchus's arms as they flattered and patronized her. "She does not know anything but eating from a silver spoon."

"We're pawning her off. At best, she makes it to the port where we can trade her for safe passage." The cheers in the stadium grew louder, and Serpens's heart clenched in his chest.

"Cut her hair and make her look like a boy," Corvus said quickly. "Others will be watching for her, but we'll take her with us. Her family studies the stars. She can help navigate the seas. I have seen enough slaves sold that I pity her enough not to condemn her to the same fate."

"A slave driver, sparing a potential slave," Serpens scoffed. "You have a heart of gold, Corv. I'll give you that."

"Remember the mercy I showed you," Corvus lowered his voice. "Do not treat anyone with cruelty, especially after you've been shown mercy yourself."

Serpens bit his tongue and walked back to Venatici. Quickly and without warning, he pulled her hair behind her head and cut it with a few swipes of his dagger. He grabbed the silver and glass pendant around her neck, snapped it, and threw it into the sand. "Looks like you've got yourself a team, girly," he said to her. "Don't act too poised. You're our slave boy now."

Venatici stared at her jewelry and hair on the ground around her.

"Head up. Eyes open. Stay alive."

Venatici looked to Serpens. Her bottom lip quivered.

The gates opened with labored clamoring, and the sun pierced through the doorway.

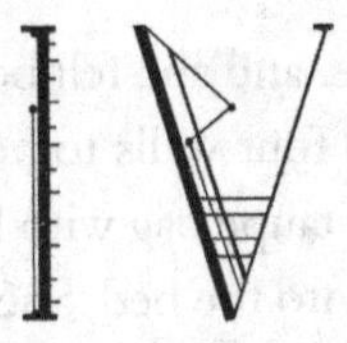

THE COMING
OF (AN) AGE

Guardian angels, which are called Sentinels, have two different categories—Landborne and Seaborne. In their angelic form, Sentinels take the upper body of a human and the lower body of their respective classes. Landborne Sentinels often take the lower-half of a deer, horse, panther, or other kinds of land-dwelling mammals. Seaborne Sentinels take the lower half of sea-dwelling or reptilian creatures, such as snakes or fish.
— A History of Hierarchy

NOVEMBER 9TH, 2106 A.D.
NORTHEAST FLORIDA
CARINA BLACKROCK

Carina's head was underwater, full of tears, drowning in fear and anger and rage. Plotting revenge was like white noise in her head. Constant. Calming. She would tear Cephan apart for taking Leroy's life.

She stood in the loft bedroom of Joshuah's Sanctuary, showered and dressed in a sky-blue blouse and brown leggings. Her reflection in the glass before her was shallow and hazy in the morning sun. She looked and felt out of place. She didn't belong. Not in Hell's Alley, and not here. She'd never had a place to call home, and she felt best when she was at sea with no boundaries, no four walls to hold her in.

Carina grabbed the taupe bag with Leroy's belongings and dumped the contents onto the bed. She rummaged through it; Leroy had been a pack rat even in his own trench coat. Gold and silver coins and precious gems winked back up at her, but she didn't have eyes for any of that. It was simply their currency. The other souvenirs held more value to her. Little black sharks' teeth from their stops at various beaches spotted the light purple quilt. Leroy had also had a knack for collecting and preserving stamps from all over the world, and he'd kept the cut-out postage in a wrinkled plastic bag. She picked the bag up and smiled. Their job wasn't one looked fondly on. Mail couriers were often considered outlaws, and they were called pirates. Civilian communication across different countries had been banned after the Third World War, and people like Leroy and herself had taken up the highly sought-after service. They had secret mailboxes all over the world. She longed to be back on the water, to stop at each rickety house and collect the small treasures left there—payment, and those scraps of paper that bore the writers' souls and secrets.

All of this had been stolen from her.

She picked a dagger out of a fine, silk scarf that Leroy had wrapped it in. The hilt and guard of the dagger were gold, and the blade itself was bone-white with ridges like sharks' teeth. A decorative red line flowed from the handle to the tip of the dagger, just between the two serrated rows. She wondered if she would ever have a chance to use the dagger on Cephan. She twisted the blade in the sunlight, but something else caught her eye.

It was a coin that didn't shine. She picked it up and rubbed her thumb across the brass-colored surface. On one side, there was a woman with a child in a sash across her back; the other side showed an eagle with its wings spread in flight. The coin was etched "2000" but looked to be new despite the year being over a century away now. It surprised Carina that Leroy hadn't tossed the coin in the sea. He'd never failed to remind her that birds were a sign of bad luck, that they were dark omens that symbolized imminent death. Now she wondered if Leroy hated birds because of their wings. Did they remind him of the angel he'd been prior to his fall? All she saw was freedom on those wings, and she craved it deeply. She slipped the coin into her pocket.

Carina glanced at the loft door. She convinced herself to limp carefully, to make it to the door and steady her breathing. She opened the door. Artificial light from one lantern hanging overhead painted the tavern walls and spiral staircase a deep gold-brown. She smelled tomato soup cooking downstairs, mingled with faint mildew from the building's walls. There was no trace of meat to turn her stomach. She'd always remember the verses of the Bible—or rather, the secondhand stories Leroy told her—that God loved the smell of burning animal sacrifices. It made her stomach twist more.

Slowly, she made her way downstairs.

Joshuah bustled around the counter, which entered her sight first. He paused and looked at her.

Carina looked around the rest of the tavern. With the counter to the right, the rest of the bar stood open and at the mercy of her bird's-eye view. Round tables speckled the floor with friendly, worn chairs scooted about from the come and go of regulars and locals. It was quiet and empty, but she could feel the memories that had been made there. It was safe, and her heart rested. She took a few more steps down and looked back to Joshuah.

"I made you some soup. I'll grab you a bowl if you'd like," he said. "How's your foot feeling?"

"Better, by some," Carina said. She approached Joshuah, and he folded his cleaning rag in half in his hands. "How does a Sentinel fall?" she asked.

Joshuah sighed. He tossed the rag over his shoulder and leaned forward as she sat down at the bar counter. He looked down at his hands, laced his fingers. "As guardian angels, our purpose is to protect. Our kind has vowed to protect *all* life, so we swore to never consume blood. Surely you know this."

"Cephan said—" Carina noticed the change in Joshuah's face. He touched her clenched fists, soothed them open, and turned her wrist soft-side up. He looked at the compass scar she could never rid herself of. She'd burned over it with fire, tried to carve the brand off with a knife. Nothing worked; it always returned the same, like magic. He sighed again, and she swallowed hard. "Cephan said," she started again, stronger, "that it turns a Sentinel to a vampire."

"He told you the truth."

"What does that word mean? Vampire?" Carina clenched her jaw. Knowledge dangled in front of her, only close enough to brush her fingertips on. Her frustration grew like a wave in her chest.

Joshuah furrowed his brow. "When a Sentinel drinks blood, they fall. They become cursed as the Devil was in the Garden of Eden. Some," Joshuah nodded at Carina, "the Seaborne, are cursed with their tails, to slither like the Serpent was. Others, the Landborne like me, are cursed to their respective guardian forms. Hooves, four legs… The Fallen must continue to drink blood to return to their human forms. Many of them do—drink blood, I mean—to continue to *look* human. They crave it, too, but that's the nature of the Fallen, to crave the forbidden."

"Leroy was not like that." Carina shook her head. She wanted the doubt to shake off with it.

Joshuah paused for a moment. "But if he *was* Fallen, he must've continued to drink blood of some kind to appear as a man."

"He was not like that," Carina said again. But she couldn't stop the memories—Leroy had hunted every night, yet forbade Carina from hunting with him. Could there have been some truth there? She was never allowed to eat the fish he ate himself; Leroy always offered her their dried rations they'd purchased at land. *He was not like that,* she thought firmly.

"I believe you," Joshuah said softly. He paused. "Do you know who you are?"

"Does it matter? *You* must know if you ask that question."

"Every Sentinel knows you by the flame above your head," Joshuah said. "You guard the Apocalypse."

"What the hell does that mean?"

Joshuah shook his head. "That's all we know. Leroy knew your destiny by your God-given Mark. He knew he had to protect you. I know I must do the same. All Sentinels will. It's sort of like instinct, you know?" He wrung his hands, distant. "It's possible God granted your friend mercy in order to look after you."

Carina stood suddenly, her heart throbbing in her chest. Her friend had turned to ash on the beach, washed away with the morning tide, and now Joshuah was trying to tell her that she was special. No one should have had to die for her, even if she was Marked by God like Joshuah claimed. Especially not Leroy. He'd given everything up to raise her. Rage quivered in her bones as she stood, and she walked to the door. "I am going to the beach," she said. She needed air, the salt water, and the sound of the waves.

"Will you be back?" Joshuah wondered aloud.

Carina paused. "Yes."

It was a two mile walk to the beach, but after the disaster of the nights before and with her energy restored, it was refreshing to walk. To smell the salt on the air, to feel the wind in her hair, to have steady, safe ground beneath her feet—it was a reminder that she was out of reach of danger, if only for now. The low-lying marsh and the heavy green of the landscape took her mind away from the disaster, if only for a moment. She was lucky that her body healed at an excelled rate, but pain still tingled through her leg with each of her steps. When she reached the shore, the prior feelings returned twofold. She watched the ocean and its restless waves. Anger tore at her skin, and questions ripped at the seams of her mind. She fished the small coin from her pocket and held it between her fingers.

"Carina, we leave tonight. We sail in the storm front," Leroy said to her from the shadows.

Carina looked to his sturdy shoulders, the silhouette that stood behind the white marble pillar of her balcony. The balcony of her bedroom was big and airy and ethereal, planted with exotic flowers and foliage, and it was watched. She pretended she was studying the city below. Leroy spoke to her in low whispers, and she hissed back through her teeth. "I cannot leave. There are five guards outside my door now."

"Some princess," Leroy scoffed, a little too loud.

Carina stiffened. Hell's Alley had dubbed her their long-lost princess when she and Leroy first arrived. They said it was a prophecy, something they had been awaiting for centuries. Leroy didn't trust any of it, and he had quickly been separated from Carina because of this.

"That storm will destroy this Godforsaken city." Leroy said, "God himself is coming with that storm."

"God has forsaken me."

"Carina," Leroy chastised.

"Why are we here, Leroy? We are abandoned! Trapped!" she snapped.

Leroy looked over his shoulder. *"I leave tonight, Carina. I've heard rumors. They plan to sacrifice ya. I can't let them kill ya. God has other things in store for ya. Come with me."*

"You are not my father." Carina almost stepped in his direction. Fear kept her still.

"Ya don't belong here."

"I do not belong anywhere, Leroy, and neither do you. That is why we are called pirates, no matter how many letters we delivered, how many stranded sailors we saved, no matter our intention—"

"Please, Carina…"

Carina's fingertips grew cold. The wind twisted her hair in spirals around her face. The storm front passed the shore here; it had moved inland, and here she was with it. Here, where she still didn't belong. She should have left with the storm front, not behind it, because she could still feel blood on her skin. Leroy had been right. God came with that storm, and by God's hand, Carina had slaughtered every last demon in Hell's Alley.

Her genocide left a mark on her, too.

Carina sat on the sand. She thought of Leroy again. She realized his skin *had* looked bone-like in the sun. She remembered too how she'd rarely see him choke down their rations and insist she eat instead. Still, she wished to have her friend back. Maybe it would have been different if she had listened.

She should have listened.

NOVEMBER 9TH, 2106 A.D.
NORTHEAST FLORIDA
CORVUN KHLYDE

By detention, the day felt like summer again, not fall. The sun peered from the top of the sky as Corvun walked into the classroom with Jayren by his side. He chose a seat next to Orion, and they sat in silence. Corvun glanced at the little doodles Orion drew on his page. Pencil-sketched skulls of small rodents and all types of plants growing out of the decay dotted his page.

"Do you do art a lot?" Jayren asked, breaking the silence.

Orion dropped his pencil on his desk and held his head in his hands. He opened his mouth to reply, but sharp arguing cut him off.

Behind the three of them, Venatrix and Caeleb spun into the room like a thunderstorm. Their words cracked like lightning, aimed at one another. Venatrix's short hair whipped over her electric blue eyes. Corvun stood, and Caeleb's eyes struck Corvun like a hurricane-force wind. Corvun tightened his jaw and held Caeleb's wild glare.

Caeleb scoffed. "Ben! Seems you've replaced Erin and me as Vena's brother. I thought we were done with you, all of us," he spat sideways at Venatrix.

Venatrix shoved past her brother and threw her stuff into the chair in front of Orion.

"How unfortunate you won't be able to look after her for very long." Caeleb smiled wickedly. "I heard your soul's already been sold."

Corvun's hands went cold.

"Hey loser, go pick on someone your own size," Jayren bit.

Caeleb looked pointedly to Orion.

Venatrix sat down in front of the quiet redhead, giving her brother a deadly glare.

Corvun's chest tightened with worry. Caeleb had habits of picking on the weaker, just like any bully, but Corvun wasn't about to let him say two words to Orion. Venatrix turned and engaged Orion in a soft conversation. Even Jayren showed Caeleb the same flippant dismissal as he immersed himself in the math homework splayed on his desk. Corvun looked to Caeleb once more, and he saw the clench of his jaw and a muscle twitch in his neck. Corvun shrugged, and Caeleb sat a few desks ahead of them.

Professor North walked into the classroom, and Corvun sat down slowly. The only thing to be heard was Venatrix's kind whispering to Orion and Orion's small replies. Corvun relaxed back into his seat, and he watched Venatrix. She glanced at Corvun then looked back to Orion. Her fingertips were on the edge of Orion's paper, awaiting an invitation. Her other hand cradled her face. Corvun knew her better than he knew her brothers; Venatrix never flirted intentionally, but rather her body language gave away her interest in someone. When Orion offered her his pencil, her fingertips touched his hand. She drew little sticks and stones around his shy drawings of nature and life. Corvun noticed the blush on Orion's face, too.

Corvun crossed his arms and sat back in his seat, thinking. He observed the room around him, the bulletins and corkboards and tidy announcements that lined the wall, the murals that hung higher than all of it that rivaled a Catholic church. The blackboard in the front of the room bore white scars of chalk: facts from the Bible, the laws of man's science, and the world as the angels taught it. Corvun focused on Professor North.

Valentine North, his name, was sort of an alias. Corvun disliked the name because it was a cover-up for Valor. Corvun didn't hate the angels or what they did (or the questionable reasons they had), but he did blame his father and the Archangels for solidifying their holier-than-thou reputation. Corvun felt small next to them, insignificant, and that was something he truly hated. But that wasn't something he'd let on.

When Professor North looked up at Corvun, Corvun couldn't see past the exterior of his eyes. Corvun had seen bone-deep cuts through Orion's eyes, his wary hesitation to trust which was often mistaken for weakness. Corvun always saw too far into Venatrix's eyes because she let him. She was always taunting him, wanting him to see her disaster. And Jayren's eyes held a multitude of lies and stories and voices that Corvun learned to decipher over the years. Professor North reflected an entire sky full of stars, an endless knowledge that held Corvun at arm's length from the truth. But Valentine knew what Corvun was. Corvun was an Authority, an avenging angel that would bring destruction to every corner of the Earth. They both knew it was only a matter of time before Corvun grew into that calling.

Corvun watched Professor North stand. He glanced at the clock. Only fifteen minutes passed. The headmaster exited the room.

Jayren smacked his math book closed and chucked it at the back of Caeleb's head. The book collided with Caeleb's shoulder and neck with a loud *thwack*.

Caeleb turned around, and Jayren pointed at Venatrix. "Vena!" Caeleb said.

Venatrix smiled bitterly.

"Do you know why no guy likes you?"

"Humor me," she said.

"Because you behave really well until you have to get naked."

Corvun stood before anyone could move. He held his blunt pencil up in defense, raising one eyebrow. He stepped past Orion and Venatrix and Jayren and walked to the pencil sharpener. Only the grinding of the manual sharpener made a sound in the room. Corvun walked back, stopping at Caeleb's desk. "I'll give you one chance to apologize to her."

"No way in hell," Caeleb said with a smirk.

Corvun grabbed Caeleb's wrist firmly and stabbed his pencil through the top of Caeleb's hand.

Caeleb yelled out in pain; his eyes welled with tears and anger. He glared at Corvun pathetically, flexing his arm in an attempt to pull away.

"Corvun, stop!" Venatrix yelled. She stood, and Jayren stood beside her.

Corvun let up.

Caeleb writhed away, yanking the wooden shard out of his hand and swearing through sharp breaths.

Professor North reentered the room, and Jayren let out a heavy sigh. "God, we've got the worst timing."

. . . .

"One more act of violence, and you will be expelled, Corvun."

"Good," Corvun snapped. He ducked away from his father's swing. The two of them sparred in the garage with nothing but wrapped fists. The room was heavy with humidity and the smell of sweat. He caught his father's wrist, spun and slung it over his shoulder. He attempted to flip his father, but a sharp blow to the ribs stopped him. Knuckles jabbed his back. Once. Twice. Corvun staggered away and spun back around. He held his fists above his mouth, glared at his father.

"You cannot be expelled."

"I'll be expelled if I punch Caeleb again, and he makes it really temptin'." Corvun deflected a punch. Heat plumed in his face. Sour sweat was slick on his skin, plastering his hair to his neck. He panted. He didn't want to train tonight, but his father advanced with more jabs and slams of his fists.

"Focus," Michael said.

"You know I'm not like you. I don't *like* this." Corvun waved his hands at the fight and grimaced. He took a swing at his father. Michael knocked it away. The second nailed his father under his ribcage. "You know the prophecy," Corvun said between breaths, "about us. Tell me the rest."

"Fight for it." Michael took two steps toward Corvun, and Corvun drew a knife. "Make me beg for mercy, and I'll tell you."

Corvun flattened one hand, held the dagger in a tight grip with his other. He swallowed hard and darted back into the fight. Corvun swiped the knife towards his father five times. Each, a miss. He ducked under a high kick, backed away from a punch. He lunged forward, locked an arm around Michael's neck. His father wrestled to get free. A swift punch to Michael's nose hindered the protests. Corvun yanked Michael's long sleeve up to reveal his compass brand. He dug the blade into the star-shaped scar, breaking the skin.

Michael winced. Blood welled at the compass on his father's wrist. It dripped onto the blue wrestling mat on the floor.

"Does it still work? Can you still find direction with it?" Corvun asked. He heard rumors about the RUST compass brand—that when opened, the wound would point in the direction of what one wanted most.

"Corvun," Michael warned. He winced again, finally saying, "Mercy."

Corvun released Michael.

"You and the others were reborn throughout the past. We call them Iterations, the past incarnations we've lived," Michael said. He braced his hands on his knees and caught his breath. "You've been given different names in your past lives, always named after the stars, but your God-given names have always been the same. They're Latin names, after your authorities. Yours is Fames, for famine. The others are Victoria for conquest, Mars for war, and Mori for death. Hades, for the one who follows the Horsemen, the final destruction. You'll recognize the names when you are addressed by them." Michael stood, continued, "You've died in battle in your past lives. You have to win this time, Corvun. The Deceivers will go to no end, and each Iteration they try harder to stop you and the others from winnin' your war. If you and the others win the war in this life, you will bring the Final Battle of Armageddon. You would end the Deceivers' reign on Earth. They will do anythin'. This Iteration… Son, they're goin' to try to make you and the others fall."

Corvun pinched the bridge of his nose. He felt like passing out. *Focus,* he told himself. *Focus, focus. Breathe. Just breathe.*

"Corvun," Michael said, rubbing his wrist. The wound on his wrist healed shut like a superficial scrape. "They're usin' this, this *situation*. What you endure there, it will test your faith… Violently."

Corvun closed his eyes. He found comfort in the absence of light, the silence of his mind for a few precious moments. When he opened his eyes, he looked around the old, unfinished garage where he'd trained for the past ten years. Dusty light shone through the windows, and the two-by-four framework reminded Corvun of a skeleton. Rusted metal boxes and tools cluttered the ribcage of the garage. His sister's lime green bike hung on the bike rack next to the exercise jump ropes made of thick black and gray plastic. Their childhood dog—Strike—had been memorialized with a water bowl hung and used as a frame for a picture of him and Cynthia and the black German Shepherd. Strike had died from a leg tumor five years back. He didn't want to leave all this behind, his life and the memories of his childhood. But he would take one thing from this garage with him—his years of training, whether they'd really prepared him or not.

"I need you to promise me somethin', son."

Corvun looked at his father.

Michael stood straight now, his shoulders square and his lips pressed thin. "Promise me you will never take a life in vain."

"That's what assassins do," Corvun said.

Michael shook his head. "Find a way to make it matter. Never forget the value of every human life. Find a way."

· · · · ·

"Is it really true?" Venatrix whispered on the other end of Corvun's cellphone.

"Yeah, it's true. We had past lives. Michael told me." He listened to her sigh; she fought for words and failed. Corvun stared at the black sky overhead. Trees waved in the breeze, shuffling and shuddering with the oncoming cold. His skin pricked with chills, but he didn't move from his place on the roof. "He told me we've always been named after the stars, after the same constellations."

Venatrix was quiet on the other end.

Corvun filled his lungs with the cool oxygen. A sprinkle of rain misted his face.

"What does it mean? If we *are* the Four Horsemen?"

"It means we live the same tragedy we've always lived."

"What's that?"

"We die at war, or…" he paused, "we win this war and bring the Apocalypse."

"You mean the end of the world, lake of fire, Battle of Armageddon Apocalypse?"

Corvun smiled wryly. "Yeah, somethin' like that."

JAYREN OMANS

Jayren walked through the front door of his house later that night. He tossed his school bag on the sofa next to his sister, and she jumped. "Why are you always so finicky?" he asked. He noted that his voice sounded too tired, too defeated, so he whistled an uptight tune.

"Did Professor North talk to you during detention?"

"Nah, he was more interested in the other teenage screwups."

Lacey sighed.

Jayren glanced at the TV as he opened the fridge. The weatherman spoke in a boring, monotone hum of words. Jayren was more interested in the forecast itself. The temperatures on the screen showed record lows, and despite the cheery, preschool-sticker-style storm clouds and snowflakes, the thought chilled Jayren. The snow always reminded him of his home state, and his skin pricked anxiously. He grabbed the orange juice from the refrigerator, and his fingers froze to the bottle. "We're expecting snow?" he asked. His voice broke, and he swallowed hard.

"Yeah," Lacey said.

"Aren't we in Florida?" he asked dryly.

"Jayren."

He rolled his eyes. "Why did we move here anyway? You know if we'd gone farther south there wouldn't be any stupid snow."

"Jayren, stop complaining."

"We had to move away from all our family—for this."

"Mom's side of the family didn't want our dead weight, that's why," Lacey bit back.

That, or the family hates the sight of Lacey because she's the spitting image of mom, he thought. A lump formed in Jayren's throat. He glared at his glass as he poured the juice.

"I don't want to have this conversation with you. It doesn't help either of us."

"Yeah, if Dad were here, he'd be able to help both of us. Mom's more of a dead weight than we are."

Lacey's shoulders pinched, and she stood and spun to face him. "Go to your room. I don't need this." Her eyes were sliced thin, knifing into him like daggers; her lips flattened. She stopped wearing makeup years back, and it allowed a corpse-like emptiness to sink into her features. Lacey looked more like mom than he liked to admit.

Jayren clenched his jaw. His heart thumped in his chest. He wanted to yell back, but his nervousness kept him stone-still. He forced himself to turn and leave, fighting all the pins and needles that picked at his skin. He hadn't noticed the snake-like slits of his sister's eyes. At least, that's what he told himself. His eyes welled with hot tears, and he slammed his bedroom door. Jayren left his orange juice on the desk and collapsed on the bed. He didn't move again.

. . . .

His nightmares stirred his brain.

Jayren came around to the sound of a mourning crowd, the hazy rain knocking on the church windows, and a droning eulogy for his and Lacey's father. Every word was a tick on a clock, the countdown of a bomb, a speck of sand in an emptying hourglass. His heart was suspended on a thin thread, a feeble harness holding back a landslide. When that rope snapped, he felt everything at once: fear, hurt, anger, sorrow.

Jayren's legs pounced off his dull, green pew. He ran to his father's open casket.

A few adults grabbed for him before he made it to the black box that held his dad.

Jayren bit a woman's hand, stepped on another man's toes, and struggled away from yet another. His fingertips gripped the cold coffin. Jayren heard his own screaming, his pleas and cries. He wanted his dad back. He touched the body in the casket, but the man wasn't his father. A part of him thought his skin would still be warm, or that his eyes would open and recognize him, but his dad's skin was cold, empty, and suddenly the coffin was, too.

Jayren realized his father wasn't there anymore. The body in the coffin now was void of a soul, hollow with nothing inside. Screaming filled Jayren's chest, tore his throat raw. Jayren's fingers tangled in the red scarf tied around the neck of the body. The following moments were always a blur. The yanking as Jayren was pulled in five different directions like a doll between angry children; the profanities tossed like candy into Halloween bags; the yelling was laughter, and his name was a curse. Jayren gripped the scarf, held his ears to block the noise, and the red blotted his vision.

The dream suffocated him, again. It was always the same. Again and again.

And Jayren woke the same, again, jerking out of bed and reaching for the resting place of his father's scarf. His heart sank when he flattened his palm on the hardwood nightstand. He'd given the scarf to Venatrix.

It was different, this time.

This time, light shone through a crack in his bedroom door. Lacey stood staring at him. Jayren couldn't ignore her snake eyes now, and he felt the cold tears on his face and the icy sweat on his skin. Something was different.

OPHIAH JUDE

Ophiah stared into the pale eyes of the snake facing her.

No matter the day, the night, the week or month or year she lived, she always felt trapped by this moment. She wasn't sure it was a dream, but rather a suspension in time where her mind left her body and tangled itself in another reality. She shook the fear urging her to look away. Even if she wanted to glance away, the snake always followed her, face to face and tongue slicing the space between them.

Ophiah felt the ground beneath her, the dirt in her hands. She molded the raw ground in her palms and inhaled the Earth's rich scent.

The snake leaned closer.

"Be still," she whispered the verse. "Be still and know."

The snake's tongue flickered against her greasy hair that hung like limp, mud-covered grass around her face.

"Be *still*," she hissed at the snake. Her lips quaked.

Scales coiled against her thumb and paralyzed her with horror and fascination alike. She stayed on her knees, hypnotized, until the snake bared its fangs, and she woke.

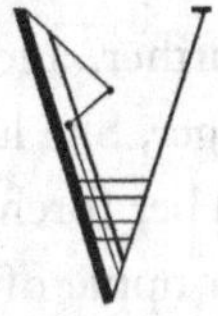

TWIN FLAMES

Sentinels have heightened physical abilities that correlate with their angelic forms.
— A History of Hierarchy

NOVEMBER 10TH, 2106 A.D.
NORTHEAST FLORIDA
JAYREN OMANS

Venatrix moved around the busy lunch room like a flame following a trail of gunpowder. Jayren chewed on the white plastic spoon he carried in his mouth, holding his lunch tray numbly. He gazed after his red scarf, which Venatrix wore now. Jayren watched her sidestep a gathering of girls waving their hands and a herd of football players belting heaves of laughter. Venatrix stopped in her tracks when she saw that Jayren watched her, blinked as if in a daze, then looked away.

Jayren's heart sank.

Venatrix stumbled back when Erin stepped up to her.

Somehow, Jayren could hear the words Erin spoke, nearly twenty feet away and underneath all the cafeteria chatter. He zeroed in on the conversation.

"The popular girl had lunch with the nerds as an act of charity, I heard," he said. "How nice. Are you volunteering all your time to help them survive high school?"

Jayren's heart sank further, and his hands went cold as Venatrix's eyes lit with anger. She lunged forward, red lunch tray in hand, and slammed her forehead into Erin's nose. The cafeteria shuddered with a ripple of whispers and gasps, and Jayren flinched too. Students quickly moved on, clearly not interested in getting involved, and Venatrix walked away as if nothing had happened at all.

"Wow," Orion muttered from beside Jayren.

Jayren jumped again. "Fuck!"

"Don't cuss!" Orion said. "Shit, she's coming over here."

Jayren narrowed his eyes at Orion. "Dude…"

Orion stared at Venatrix, absent and awestruck at the same time, like she was the only thing that existed, the sun in the middle of a night sky.

"You have a massive bruise starting," Jayren told Venatrix as she walked up. His voice cracked, and he was pretty sure he was about to pass out. "You're eating with us? Even after…" He realized he probably shouldn't have been able to hear what her brother said, so he stopped talking.

"Duh. Four Horsemen for life," Venatrix said. "Where's Corvun?"

Jayren cleared his throat. "He didn't come to school."

"I talked to him last night…" She looked away. "Never mind. Let's just find a seat, alright?"

Jayren hesitated to follow Venatrix and Orion. His heartstrings plucked like a sad song on the radio with every step they took away. "Trixie—I mean, Venatrix. Wait. Can I—"

She didn't stop walking, but she slowed and waited for him to catch up.

Jayren stared at his mashed potatoes. He'd promised he'd still shove them in her face one day, but today wouldn't be that day. He set his tray down at the table that she chose.

Orion pointed his thumb at the bathrooms and walked away, leaving the two alone. Jayren looked back to Venatrix with his heart lodged in his throat. The last thing he wanted was to cry in front of her. *But when do I ever get what I want?* he thought bitterly. "Can I have my scarf back?"

She smiled, a small but bright smile. "Yeah, sure."

"And why don't you like me?" he blurted.

Venatrix took the scarf off and handed it to him.

He grabbed the red scarf, and the familiar fabric soothed his sweaty hands.

"I was actually pretty sure Corvun had told you enough that *you* hated *me*," Venatrix said, head hung.

"What?" Jayren blinked away tears. "No. He doesn't talk badly about you. I don't hate you."

"What's with the scarf?" Venatrix asked. "I wouldn't have taken it if I'd known it was so important to you."

Jayren's eyes filled with water as he looked at the red-and-purple-hued fabric. "You know when something hurts too much to talk about?"

Venatrix didn't respond. Slowly, she sat backwards on the bench next to him. "Keeping the salt in the wound hurts more than washing it out," she said.

Jayren sniffled loudly. "It's my dad's." A tear raced down his face. Three more followed. "My dad hung himself," he said through the balloon of sadness that inflated the top of his chest. Helium pitched his voice too high; the pressure made his head feel like popping.

Venatrix put her hand on top of his, and she sat beside him while he cried.

CORVUN KHLYDE

Corvun stepped into the Angels' Diner that afternoon. His head was bursting with excruciating pain, and the bright gold-tinted sunlight reflecting off glossy tables and amber-filled bottles didn't help. He couldn't believe the temperature had dropped with such a powerful light in the sky. His breath turned from steam to the smell of his own morning coffee as he adjusted to the indoors.

"Corvun!" Joshuah belted from the counter.

"Hey Josh," Corvun replied. A smile forced its way onto his face.

"What's going on? It's Wednesday! I won't sell you your family's liquor if you have some shit excuse for not coming by Friday instead." Joshuah's smile shone through his words. His arms stretched wide as he rounded the bar and walked to Corvun. Corvun would never tire of Joshuah's hearty hug, the slap on his back, and the way Joshuah beamed into his face like the sun itself. After Corvun had turned fourteen, he'd been sent to the Angels' Diner every second Friday of the month to pick up his parents' liquor, but as the years had gone on, it was obvious to Corvun that Michael had pushed him right into Joshuah's path. And for good reason; Joshuah was Corvun's guardian angel.

A redheaded woman darting around behind the bar counter caught Corvun's attention.

Joshuah laughed at his fleeting attention and cupped Corvun's face in his hands. "You look like hell! What's the matter?"

Corvun removed Joshuah's hands from his face. "Michael's inductin' me to RUST tomorrow, so there's a good chance I won't be awake much on Friday."

"Khlyde," Joshuah scolded, and Corvun wasn't sure if it was meant for him or his father.

The woman behind them stiffened.

"Who is she?" Corvun asked. He eyed the flame above her head. He'd been taught to see an angel's halo. Joshuah had a flame, too, but his was a white-yellow glow that danced with the wind. The woman's flame was red like war. "What's her name?"

Joshuah hesitated, his lips breaking and sealing again.

Corvun walked past Joshuah and approached the counter.

The woman turned. Her face was reserved and young, and she looked a little older than he was, but her eyes were set on fire like none he'd ever seen before. The sight of her struck Corvun; he lowered his guard a moment too long. She leapt the counter, drew a knife from her boot, swept her leg around his neck, and dragged him to the ground. She knocked the oxygen from his lungs, and his head slammed against the wooden floor. He blinked away the double-fold pain crushing his mind, squinting up at the girl and taking a deep breath. Corvun studied her round features to make sure he'd never seen her before. Not the sun-kissed freckles powdering every inch of her exposed skin, the matte-petal texture of her lips, the wild flare of her nostrils. Her orange-yellow slitted eyes pierced through him like a sword. She dug her serrated blade into his throat. Her legs held his chest and neck still.

"Carina!" Joshuah shouted.

"What is your name?" Carina demanded.

Corvun gasped, hands held away in surrender. He stretched away from her blade. He hesitated, but when she pressed harder, he yelled, "Corvun! My name is Corvun! Okay? Corvun Khlyde!"

Carina leaned closer to him, her wind-whipped hair poking his face. Her eyes seethed with rage he'd never seen in anyone. Her weight on his chest made it incredibly hard to breathe. "You," she said, breathing ragged, "You are one of those damned Archangels."

"No! I swear."

Carina's knife broke his skin, and he winced at the hot pain.

"Carina, stop! He isn't an Archangel. Trust me," Joshuah coaxed.

"Khlyde is one of them," Carina said.

Corvun raised his eyebrows and said slowly, "My father."

Carina grabbed Corvun's right arm and yanked his sleeve away from his wrist. She stared at his unblemished skin, and he stared back at her. He began to realize; she was mistaking him for his father. But why? Corvun nodded warily, and she shot him one last swift glare before standing and stalking away. Corvun sat quickly, stood, and pursued her. He caught her wrist, pulling her sleeve back. She swiveled, but not soon enough to pull away and hide what he was looking for. There was a white compass brand on her freckled skin.

"Who are you?" he asked her.

"Which name do you want first?" she spat.

Corvun hesitated, and he searched her eyes. They had returned to a calm, gold color. Human eyes. "The name you call yourself."

She remained silent.

"So it's true," Corvun said. He looked back to Joshuah, who looked to the ground. "'The Guardian of the Apocalypse has many names but none for herself.' She's not just a myth."

"I thought she might be for a while," Joshuah said. "I kind of thought you were, too. You know, you being one of the Horsemen… But none of it is. I'm sure *you've* realized that by now. It's like a part of me wished the stories were just stories, and then she showed up, Corvun. Do you remember when we used to laugh at the thought? Gladiators! With Christopher Columbus, too? Hah! And then to think it did happen…"

Corvun watched Carina.

"You are the Apocalypse," she said, soft like a mother's lullaby. Then she turned to Joshuah. "I guard the Apocalypse," she said, realization dawning on her, "the *Four Horsemen* of the Apocalypse?"

Corvun's throat tightened. Suddenly, he wanted to shut them both out, because he knew how it would end. He'd been told—just as he'd relayed to Joshuah in their midnight walks on the beach in heart-to-heart conversations as brothers— that his title, if it were true, and the titles of the other three were a curse 'til the end. They would lose and lose and lose. They would lose 'til they won, but they'd still lose everything and everyone along the way. "You're our guardian angel," he whispered, feeling the weight of her sentence pull at his heart.

"I am no angel," she said. Her lips pressed thin.

"Then am I any better?" he challenged.

"You are just as evil as I am," her words had an ancient, religious dialect that hissed out like an antique lamp being extinguished in a church. Corvun concluded she hadn't been raised near modern civilization, never mind growing up with an education.

Before she turned, he caught her wrist again. "Evil, or just hurtin'?" he asked. "What did my father do to you?"

The look in Carina's eyes held every swear and curse and condemning thought she lacked words for. Her hurt cut as deep as Orion's, built up with more lies than Jayren could tell, and just like Venatrix, Carina let him see every broken shard of her. She reminded him of a technique he'd done in art class—kintsugi—and thought that sometimes broken things could be mended more beautifully than they were before. He wondered if she'd ever let anyone try to put her back together. He released her arm, but this time she didn't walk away.

JAYREN OMANS

Jayren hesitated before he opened the heavy theater door. The room was half-empty, and the students already sitting in the dim-lit auditorium turned in their seats to see their next contender. He couldn't see the entirety of anyone's face, and it bothered him. Jayren tried to ignore the onlookers, grabbed one of the spare scripts, then walked to an empty seat on the far side of the stage.

"Omans! Who are you trying out for?"

Jayren thought about not replying. He hated it when people used his last name to address him. "Luke," he said.

"The orphan's trying out for an orphan's role," a student said, and several more laughed.

"I'm not an orphan," he said. *And neither is Luke. Not like any of them would know. Fake fans.* He rolled his eyes. Jayren dropped his backpack into the seat next to him. He collapsed into the pew and opened his script.

He regretted his decision already. The room smelled like stale mildew, like some room-temperature, buttered popcorn, and like nervous sweat. He could smell the gag-worthy perfume that the nearest cheerleader had bathed herself in before blessing the room with her presence, too. Jayren hoped she'd do terribly so they'd send her out soon. All the sounds— the crinkling of scrap paper and scripts and the clicking of pens and the dings and pings from cellphones—combined with the smells gave him a headache. He had a horrible gut feeling that no one here had seen the Skywalker Saga beginning to end (in order) as he had. He hated the fact he'd cried today and drained his mental battery down to five percent. He hadn't had time to plug in some earbuds and recharge to movie soundtracks or dubstep or random twenty-first-century pop songs. *Shake It Off* was prime for a day like today. Silently, Jayren cursed the New Era Art that had taken over after the war. He didn't think any machine could make good art—like Star Wars or Taylor Swift's discography—but it was all that saturated the market because it was cheap and easy and fast. Jayren stuck to the old world art like a lifeline.

He leaned his head back on the pew and closed his eyes. No sooner had he done so, he overheard more whispers behind him. He peeked over his shoulder, only allowing his eyes to graze over the top of his seat. No one was behind him. The other kids weren't looking his way, never mind caring enough to make fun of him. Cold chills gripped him, and he slipped back down into his seat.

Did you see him speaking to Ophiah? the whispers continued. Snickers.

Jayren told himself not to listen.

He thinks he has a chance with her, hah!

Boys like him always do.

Jayren dug his nails into his arms and sank further into his seat. He considered copping out and hurrying home to make a microwave pizza instead. A black hole consumed his insides, folding in on itself, and the fear turned him inside out with a sudden cold sweat and a sickening dizzy spell.

Be still, he begged inwardly. He couldn't place where he'd first learned the prayer, derivative of a verse he couldn't—and didn't care—to quote. Jayren squeezed his eyes shut, covering his face with the red scarf at his neck. The fabric caressed his face and filled his lungs with Venatrix's perfume like some sort of distant hug. He wondered if she'd unfriend him in real life once she found out he heard voices. *If Corvun hasn't already told her, that is,* he seethed inwardly. The fire and ice of his emotions never mixed; they just left him burned and confused.

Quiet. Be quiet. Be still.

His eyes stung from Venatrix's perfume.

"Jayren Omans, you're up first."

He winced.

"*No,*" he rasped through the scarf. A stray strand of fabric caught in his mouth, and he fished the string off his tongue as he stood. He brushed his hair back with his palms and stared at the theater teacher. Her silver-gray hair hung around her jawline like the helmet of a warrior, and her old, worn eyes sized him up. Jayren felt like a soldier marching into a war he'd die in. He passed her with a knot in his stomach and jogged up the stage steps. He stood at the back of the stage so that the glare of the spotlights blotted out his vision of the kids watching him. He tried to fix his posture, straighten his spine, but he felt like a noodle. He closed his eyes and waited.

"What piece of music have you prepared to sing for us?"

"What?" Jayren asked, suddenly choked.

"This is a musical."

"Star Wars isn't a musical," he said brashly. He opened his eyes and heard a soft wave of amusement pass over the audience of tryouts.

"Singing pleases God. It was requested by Professor North."

Mr. North can go fuck himself, is what Jayren wanted to say. A different, gripping thought slipped out of his mouth instead: "What do you mean? What about Rian? And Ophi? They're not *allowed* to sing. Did you turn them down for roles in the play? Is that why they had to play for the orchestra instead?" A hush fell over the room, and Jayren held them all by that accusation, a sword on a sweet spot.

Aw, he likes the demon spawns!

Jayren stepped forward out of the light and narrowed his eyes. He glared across the room, but the seats were covered in shadows and he couldn't tell who'd spoken. He fought the urge to scream. The last thing he needed was proof to back up the rumors that he heard voices—on a stage nonetheless.

"If you don't have a song prepared, I'm going to have to ask you to step off the stage and let the other students try out."

Tears clouded Jayren's vision again. He stalked from the stage and snatched his things from the pew and whisked out of the room. The door slammed in a theatrical *boom* behind him. One wish from a magic genie would've taken him five states away. Instead, he fled to the closest hideout: the bathroom. That was where he stayed, camped out on the top of a toilet tank, hands over his ears and begging the voices to stay quiet.

CARINA BLACKROCK

Carina stood on the beach in the middle of the night, barefoot, with no more than Leroy's gold-hilted dagger, which she'd pulled against Corvun. She couldn't shake Corvun's features, those which made him the spitting image of his warrior father. He shared the low, dark eyebrows and the deep ravines below his eyes and the same strong cheekbones. Corvun was beautiful, and she hated him for it. She hated him for looking like his father and for reminding her of things she didn't want to remember. She hated that he was the one—she knew too well—that she'd be bound to for her whole life. And if she admitted it to herself, Michael and Corvun were a good outlet for her anger, somewhere to point her pain for her loss of Leroy, right or wrong.

Carina sat on the ground. She balled her hands in the cool, damp sand. The wind threw specks of shells, worn from years of restlessness, into her teary eyes. Joshuah walked up beside her and sat down, too. He inhaled, held his breath. His hesitation to speak was obvious, so Carina chose to speak before he could ask her anything. "Have you heard of the Kraken?"

"Well, yeah," Joshuah said. His façade crumbled, his shoulders fell, and he leaned back on his arms.

"He is real, and he is not only a sea monster," Carina spat. "He is worse than anything you could dream of. Luckily, he is bound to the sea." The ocean roared, distant, crashing and turning the sand at the shore. The air smelled of salt and rain. "He is a demon. Do you know of the Deceivers?"

"Yeah."

Carina threw a ball of wet sand at her feet. "Avon, Ava. He takes two names and endless faces—of men, women, children, and royalty. Avon is the sin of Greed. He often follows pirates because many will do their job in *search* of treasure and gold. That is why the pirates tell stories of the Kraken."

"Like you and Leroy?"

Carina laughed. "Please. We did our job out of passion. Leroy wanted to travel the world; delivering illegal mail brought in the pay he needed to do so. That is why Avon could never find *us*. We sailed for freedom, never money. It was word of mouth that led Avon after us when we fled Hell's Alley," she said. "But he is out there, Avon. I can feel him searching like cold water on my skin. He will not rest until he finds me. I must refrain from every selfish want to stay hidden. He tracks by the scent of sin," she explained. "He can smell greed on a sinner's skin. It is like the smell of coins when you rub them between your fingers."

"You can smell it, too?"

Carina nodded.

Joshuah looked back out to the black water lapping at the break of the tide.

"You never desire things that way, in greed," Carina said. "But Corvun is different. I could smell it on him."

"Corvun's never been materialistic," Joshuah defended. "He's not like that."

"He may not be chasing the material. Those Archangels want something different. He wants power, not treasure, whether he knows it or not. He could be a tyrant if he tried, and he will lead Avon back to me." She fell silent, wondering what would happen when he did.

"Never hunt for treasure, Carina." Leroy's voice was the sound of wisdom. He choked down a swig of water and fought a cough. The dim lights of the cabin warmed her skin and made Leroy glow softly. Flames danced in the creaking metal lanterns as their ship swayed, adrift at sea. "If ya do, the Kraken will be huntin' for ya in the blink of an eye."

She had been only a child back then, and she had called him father, friend, family. She stared at his eye-patch and wondered what other stories he held behind it.

Leroy shook his head and offered Carina the mug. The cup was too big for her to fit both her hands around, so she stood on the bench, tipped the glass, and lapped water out of the mug. Leroy chuckled and helped her take a better drink of their rations. "Y'are clever. Ya'd have to be," he concluded, sitting back. He crossed his bulky arms over his chest, gleamed at Carina with one gray eye. "How did RUST catch ya?"

Carina felt lost suddenly, and the water backtracked up her throat.

"Where were ya'r parents?" Leroy asked. He eyed the crown of her head, her halo.

"Cephan found me," Carina said. "He raised me."

"Why did ya run from him?" Leroy asked, quiet and soft. "Why were ya runnin' when I found ya at the docks?"

Carina couldn't speak. She could see everything again, flashing back with strikes of a nine-tailed whip—on men and women alike, on children, on any assassin employed by Cephan—as punishment. For failure. For anything. Cephan had called himself a hand of justice when he thought Carina wasn't listening or didn't know better. And she'd run. Demons had chased her down wide, gaping halls that threatened to swallow her up and trap her in darkness forever. She'd run, not looking back once. She chewed out the words, a lie, "I cannot remember."

"He sent Valentine and Michael after ya," Leroy said.

Carina looked at him.

"Those bastards." Leroy shook his head again. He smiled. In the years to come, Carina would become familiar with the fondness Leroy held in his voice when he spoke about Valentine and Michael. "They let ya escape. They would. God knows they would."

Carina watched Leroy run his wrinkly hand over his wiry beard. He twirled the single braid that hung from his lower lip, which fell over a tuft of gray growing from his chin. He pinched the three gold beads at the end of the fine braid. They shone, catching Carina's attention. Leroy clicked his tongue to distract her. Carina realized now. Leroy had defended her from every form of greed as she grew under his watch.

"Carina," Leroy always said her name like a distant charm or a spell. It was a name he'd given her, a name from the stars, the only one she was fond of. "Promise me ya'll never consume blood, not cooked and not raw. No matter what they tell ya, and no matter how temptin'."

"Yessir," she said.

"Captain," he corrected.

"Yes, Cap'n," she repeated.

He smiled, flashing sharp teeth at her.

"What did Michael do to you?" Joshuah asked, pulling her gently out of her reverie.

Carina still felt water in her throat. "Michael never did anything to me. Neither did Valentine," she said. "Michael and

Valentine and Leroy were a team in RUST. Leroy never told me the whole story. I do not think he could, for how much it hurt him. He said only a truly selfless sacrifice can free an assassin from RUST. Their sacrifice to free Leroy—they planned it—and it went wrong. Leroy fell in the process, on accident. That must have been what happened." Carina tried to reason with logic, and she was infuriated that she'd never really know. All she could do was guess. "He went free of RUST, with their help. That much I know. But they hurt him in the process. He never saw either of them again, not until he found me at the docks when I escaped from Cephan."

Joshuah listened, and Carina continued.

"He turned to ash in the sunlight because he was Fallen."

"Carina," Joshuah said, but Carina heard Leroy's voice instead. She picked at the raw skin around her fingers, tearing at a broken nail. "Do you know the story of Samson?"

Carina shook her head.

"He lost his strength because he disobeyed God's Law— the one given directly to him. He'd fallen, in a sense, as a human. But he prayed to God to restore his power in order to destroy a city full of wickedness. He died in the process," Joshuah said. "Sentinels were granted something similar. It's the same concept, really. Even after Sentinels fall, they still have their halo, and their halo can be used to save the life of the one they guard. Most of the Fallen turn their backs on God and their calling to the one they guard. But if they don't—if they use their halo after their fall—they are redeemed. He protected you, Carina. He's redeemed."

Carina's throat squeezed tight. She leaned into Joshuah, resting her head on his shoulder. She felt small, worthless, and cold. But somewhere in the mix, there was peace.

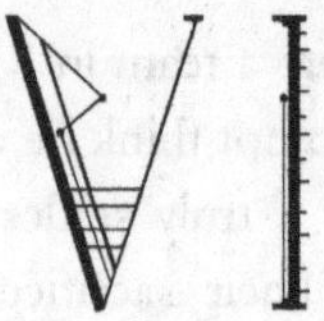

HELLFIRE AND SNAKE EYES

The abilities of Sentinels develop alongside brain development. By the time the brain is fully matured, so is the Sentinels' full-fledged power. This often happens quicker than average human brain development, as Sentinels' brains and physicality mature faster.
— *A History of Hierarchy*

NOVEMBER 11TH, 2106 A.D.
NORTHEAST FLORIDA
OPHIAH JUDE

Ophiah hated waking up. Every time she did, her reality clung to her like a million demons, scratching at her skin, trying to drag her back to Hell. She rubbed the tears out of her eyes and tried to shake off her dream. It was the same, again. As if she needed another reminder that she "worshiped the Devil" with her mere existence. She'd already heard it three times at school that week.

Ophiah rolled over and squinted through the dark. Orion slept facing away in his bed across the room, his figure as thin and wiry and bony as a corpse. Ophiah thought about telling him about the snake in her dreams, to ask if he thought it was a bad omen too, or maybe a good one. Orion was always trying to see the bright side of things, the side she was never able to see.

She saw the hallway light flip on, and her heart raced. Nothing could compare to that sickening dread, the fight or flight mode that jumped into her skin. She wanted to call out for her mother, but her mother could not help; she was unable to for the deal she made with the demons. Ophiah desired so deeply to hide and never be found again.

There was nowhere to hide in this bedroom.

Orion woke at the sound of the door handle twisting. His eyes flashed at hers. She felt his fear, his hurt, his panic down to her bones, rushing through her veins. She felt the same. He moved to her side to stand in front of her, but she stood beside him. What he endured, she would endure too.

Their father entered the room. He never seemed to take the same form or appearance. Sometimes he looked inhuman, with skin like a glowing ember, red around the edges. Sometimes he was more human, bearing self-harm scars and cuts and stabs from street fights. Tonight, his skin was like jasper, flecked with black freckles across his cheeks. His hair was the darkest shade of black that reminded her of fossilized sharks' teeth in the sun. His eyes were even blacker, and they didn't reflect any light.

Ophiah never looked in his eyes when he looked at her. She knew when to expect the collision by the movement of his feet; she'd learned when he braced himself and how many seconds it would be before he hit her. But she couldn't defend herself. She and Orion had begged for self-defense lessons that could save them from a beating; they were always turned down, told it was too risky for them to know how to fight and how to wield a weapon.

Their father spoke to them, but his words were in a different language.

Orion spat something back at him, a curse in the demonic tongue, warning of God's wrath. Ophiah refused to learn the language, but she recognized the meaning as if the translation was carved into her bones.

Tristan grabbed Orion by the arm and threw him across the room. Orion crashed into the bookshelf. The impact elicited a cry from him, and Ophiah felt the snap and pop in her back, the sharp pain as the shelf collapsed on him. Books fluttered helplessly from the shelves. Ophiah lunged for Orion, an instant reflex to ease the pain as if it were her own. She was stopped by a tight grip on her shoulder; it swung her around. Tristan struck the side of her face. Her skin burned. His iron fist released her, and she fell, reeling back to find shelter between her nightstand and bed.

Ophiah thought she'd kill Tristan if he touched Orion again, but she didn't own any weapons, not even anything sharp. *Hopelessness like this,* she thought, *only happens in Hell.* There was nothing else to do besides wait it out. Sobs riddled her chest, shook her ribs, and her back ached from Orion's pain. Her father shadowed Orion's unconscious figure, and Ophiah screamed. "Don't touch him!" Fire burned her lungs. The smoke in her throat threw her into a coughing fit. "Leave him alone!"

Tristan turned, and Ophiah closed her eyes and shrank back.

Fingers tangled in her hair, yanking. A hand jerked her neck, and pain ripped through her muscles. Her head was forced around, close to her father's face. "You belong in Hell, too, child."

Ophiah's will to fight slipped away like the last light of day, and shadows trapped her behind her own eyes. She squeezed them shut, and she prayed. She remembered the story of the fiery serpents that bit the Israelites, and the snake made of brass that saved them from certain death. In her blindness, she could only think of the snake from her dreams, and in that safe haven, the suspension of time in her mind, she could see his eyes. Green snake eyes.

Falling to the ground was a mercy.

From the floor, she watched her father's footsteps recede. Slowly, the black smears left her eyes.

After a moment, Ophiah crawled to where Orion laid in the debris of books. She mustered every ounce of her strength to push the bookshelf off her brother. She held his head in her lap, and she cradled him. His nosebleed stained her white pajama pants. His eyes stared at nothing, wide and empty and black. She whispered a prayer over him, recited the verses their mother had taught them, over and over, a chant that marched the demons away from the circle they danced around her and her brother. She whispered the words until they became a melody on her lips, a lullaby she sang over him, forbidden. She prayed her mother wouldn't find them in the ruin.

Orion woke with a violent fit of vomiting beside Ophiah's thigh. The black, tar-like vomit burned to breathe in. Orion gathered his surroundings, then he held her tightly. His tears on her legs were as hot as the sting on her face. She sniffled, and she smelled the tangy metal of blood dripping from her own nose.

"What time is it?" he rasped.

"Almost seven," she managed. She looked to the window and wondered if light was always this hard to see.

JAYREN OMANS

'Are you okay?'

Jayren winced against the light of his phone screen. He narrowed his eyes to make sure he read Venatrix's text message right. He considered texting a '*No,*' back; he felt like all his bones were breaking, like his skin was on fire. He dropped his phone on his nightstand and rolled over instead.

. . . .

Jayren stood a couple of paces away from the cast list posted on the bulletin board. His stomach twisted in knots. He peered between the other students, too mortified to be seen as *caring too much* for the results of the roles. He knew he had a fat chance at even being considered after the scene he made on stage, but he was curious to know what goody-two-shoes choir boy might have secured the role instead. Jayren narrowed his eyes to read the name listed beside Luke Skywalker—Casper North, Mr. North's son. Jayren begged himself to walk away and forget about it.

"Jayren!" someone called from behind him.

He closed his eyes. Too late. *Too late.* He turned.

Caeleb approached, crossing his arms and smirking at Jayren. Casper was in tow, a less amused look on his face.

Jayren glanced nonchalantly at the bruising on Caeleb's nose that looked like an oversized paintball had left a permanent stain on his face.

"You know," Caeleb walked up to Jayren, "Luke didn't have four eyes." Caeleb snatched Jayren's glasses off the bridge of his nose.

"God, you're so lame!" Jayren said. His stomach somersaulted. He and Lacey didn't have the money to replace the glasses, and she'd be furious if he even asked.

As if Caeleb had read his mind, he dropped Jayren's black plastic frames and stepped on them.

Jayren felt the crunch. His heart sank.

Caeleb kicked the glasses down the hall. They continued to be kicked accidentally, bounced in different directions, lost in a foosball game of real feet.

Two figures parted the sea of students—one fuming, and the other on one knee to retrieve his glasses. They were a smear of royal blue uniforms and gold makeup. It was the Jude twins, the last people Jayren expected to come to his rescue.

"You're a piece of shit, Caeleb!" Orion spat as he stalked up.

"Oh, c'mon! You two would have so much fun if you'd just lighten up." Caeleb laughed bright and loud, like hospital lights.

"You think this is fun? Piss *off.*" Orion bared his teeth.

"I can't even believe you're here, condoning this," Ophiah said in a dark voice that made Jayren's hair stand on end. Her sights were fixed on Casper. "Just because Caeleb's a damned Archangel Heir means nothing of his loyalty to God. Pick your friends wisely."

Caeleb gave Ophiah a seething look. "Come on, Casper."

Jayren could hardly believe that Casper actually listened— actually turned and followed Caeleb away from the scene of the crime and his girlfriend. Jayren gained a newfound respect and sense of friendship for Orion and Ophiah. He'd often thought beauty and cruelty went hand in hand, but the twins were proving him wrong.

"I have somewhere to be," Orion struggled to say. "I have to go. I'm sorry."

Ophiah thanked her brother quietly.

"Thanks, Rian," Jayren said, too.

"Welcome, dude," Orion said. He shuffled off.

Jayren was left standing face-to-face with Ophiah. He didn't realize, until that moment, that she was just as tall as he was. It wasn't much of an accomplishment; most of the girls at North Academy were taller than he was. "You look nice today," he attempted. He smelled salt welling faintly in her eyes, felt the shudder in her breath when she half-laughed. Startled, he asked, "Are you okay?"

"What are you going to do about your glasses?" she asked. Her voice broke here and there, but she never let it fall apart. In her hands were his crippled glasses.

"Uh…" He reached out when she offered the glasses to him. His fingers brushed her soft hands, and his heart fluttered in his chest, sending a rush of blood straight to his head. He smelled blood on her—with the sudden peak of his senses— not a blush, but bruises. His eyes tried to focus on her, and her image came in and out of clarity.

"Your eyes," she whispered.

"Yeah, my sister is gonna skin me." Jayren's hands dropped to his sides. "I can't see for shit. She's gonna be so pissed when she sees these."

Ophiah sniffled. She reached up to wipe away a tear, and Jayren touched her arm lightly. Her sleeve pulled away from her wrist, and a purple bruise peeked out. There was no way to mistake it—not after the first glance and not after knowing what Orion endured.

Jayren didn't know what to do, so he asked again. "Are you okay?"

The hall emptied, and the second period bell rang.

"I'm ditching," Jayren said suddenly. "Come with me."

Ophiah hesitated.

"I have to go buy fake glasses. I can't show my face to my sister without them. We'll take my bike and go into town. Just for an hour. We'll be back in no time. I-I'll buy you lunch— please—"

"Yes," she said.

As Ophiah blotted at the shine on her cheeks, her makeup wore away. Beneath it, there was another darker bruise. He clenched his jaw, and the sight of her came into full focus as if he had new glasses already. Her makeup was too sloppy to be convincing. The rich brown around her eyes looked like burnt sugar, sticky and wet. The tears in her eyes shimmered, and it boiled his blood. He grabbed her hand, careful not to cause her any more harm but strong enough to make sure she knew he wouldn't let go.

The intensity of *her* flushed his body. Like facing a burning building, he felt her sorrow and fear lick against his skin and fuel the wildfire burning inside him. He wanted to hold her and burn together. And in that moment, he swore his life to destroying anything or anyone who threatened Ophiah or her brother. He got angrier as he remembered he was just a seventeen-year-old nerd with now-broken glasses, braces, and zits like the plague. But he felt like he'd loved her for years; her hand felt like it belonged twisted in his.

VENATRIX CANES

Venatrix's research on the Deceivers took her deep into the religious section of the school's library where books weighed as much as burial kits and pages smelled like old garments from a tomb. Carrying the books to her desk was like heaving a coffin into the ground, where it would lie forever and become one with the Earth. *Dust to dust,* Venatrix thought dryly. It was all rather morbid to her, what she researched. Even brushing her fingers across the words *demon* and *Deceiver* was like dancing with death.

The most useful book she'd found so far—*A History of Hierarchy*—was open on her desk. The other books she'd pulled from the shelf had proved fruitless; it was as if the Deceivers didn't exist outside of the book she studied now. She slumped down into the bench and flipped through the pages again. Back to the table of contents. She ran her fingers down the ladder of words, down, down, down until she reached the Deceivers again.

The fine-printed, gothic text contained lore and legend of the well-known "Cardinal Sins" as Deceivers. The Deceivers were the first Fallen angels to follow Lucifer, and they were in direct opposition to the Seven Archangels and the virtues the Archangels represented. But there were eight, not seven. That was new to Venatrix; she'd been familiar with the "Seven Deadly Sins" but never heard of an eighth. As the book explained it, the lesser-known Eighth Sin, the Eighth Deceiver, was the highest ranking and the most deadly. He was their leader. There were Latin names listed below each respective Sin and the Deceiver who embodied it. She read them over and over, flipping through the pages to revisit the words. *Gula, Luxuria, Avaritia, Superbia, Ira, Invidia, Acedia, Tristitia.* The last word had her staring at the page in her hand. Tristitia. *Like Tristan,* she thought in horror. It was listed under the Eighth Sin, the Sin of Sorrow.

ORION JUDE

Orion broke into a run when he reached the courtyard. He hadn't run in weeks, and pressure stabbed through the muscles in his ankles and thighs. His chest heaved with pants. The cool breeze nipped at his lips and brushed thin, wispy fingers through his hair. He jumped the curbs and dodged stones in his path on his sprint across campus. He couldn't run to Venatrix fast enough. He knew she'd be there; it was where they agreed to meet today, and he needed her presence, her reassurance. Orion burst through the heavy double doors, and they slammed against the walls. His own strength surprised him.

Everyone turned to stare at the thunder-like disruption he'd caused.

Venatrix's eyes widened, too, and she jolted out of her seat.

Orion started towards her. He heard the voices around him whispering. Some stood, some went for the librarian. But he didn't care. All he cared about in that moment was *her*. He collided with Venatrix and buried his face deep in her shoulder, smothering out the chaos of judgment around him. She smelled like faint sweat, like honey and lemon and rosemary. He realized he'd never hugged her before, but he held her tighter when the voices started and hot blood tickled the inside of his nose.

"Rian—"

"Say a prayer," he begged.

Her head turned in question, a soft caress between his head and shoulder. She whispered a prayer in his ear.

His tears would stain her shirt with black, he already knew. He couldn't stop the chemical sting of hellfire wrapped up in his tears. "We have to find a way to banish him," Orion whispered, "I won't let him beat Ophi again."

Venatrix went rigid, and she said, "Let's go before we get in trouble."

Orion noticed that she didn't blame him for the trouble they could get in for hugging in the middle of the library. He wanted to correct her, to tell her it was his fault and she should blame him. But that's what he'd been conditioned to think. The feel of her cold fingertips on his hot neck told him she'd burn beside him before she let him burn alone.

She was hugging him back.

. . . .

They walked from the library together, Venatrix clutching a book to her chest. They crossed the campus grounds to find

a bench on the side of one of the buildings. Venatrix sat first, looking numbly at the book in her hands. Orion sat beside her.

The courtyard was still, and the bushes around them created a cozy, quiet nook for their conversation. Rain lingered in the air, old drops slipping from the dewy leaves around them. It was cold, but not uncomfortably so, just enough that it made Orion lean into Venatrix for warmth.

"Do you know what the Cardinal Sins are?" Venatrix asked.

Orion nodded. He tried to list them by memory. "Pride, lust, greed, gluttony, envy…"

"Sloth and wrath," Venatrix finished for him, nodding too. She opened the book and thumbed through the pages. "There's an eighth sin in here. Sorrow. Each of them have Latin names beneath their English names. Tristitia is beneath Sorrow, Orion," she said slowly. Then, a whisper, "Like *Tristan.*"

Orion looked away from the book. His throat tightened, as if someone had cut off the water supply to a garden hose. Oxygen pinched in his throat, and his face and knuckles felt hot. He popped a few of his fingers, unsure why he was embarrassed by the revelation. *It makes sense,* he told himself. Orion's head swam like an overwatered potted plant, and the debris of his thoughts twirled in the flood.

Much to his surprise, Venatrix's face was blotchy with emotion, too. "It just feels like the whole world is falling apart," she blurted.

Orion watched her.

"I want to save you, and I want to save him, too—but I just *can't.* There's nothing I can do."

"Save who?" Orion interrupted.

Venatrix nearly punched the tears off her face before they fell. "Ben," she whispered. "He's getting inducted into RUST today. And what about you? Hell, I want to kill your dad! I've studied in all my free time for a way to kill a Deceiver—and this book—it's the only book that even *mentions* Deceivers! It's not possible. They're immortal." She sniffled. "The only thing—literally the *only* thing—in here is that the Four Horsemen kill the Deceivers near the end of Armageddon. The author called us dragon slayers or something stupid like that," she said with her palm against her nose, wiping away snot.

"Hey, that's good." Orion leaned closer to Venatrix and watched her; she watched his lips. He knew he shouldn't even touch her, that the Archangels would see his fingerprints as if on a crime scene, but he touched her arm lightly anyway. "*We're* the Four Horsemen. That should count for something, right? If we kill them in Armageddon, maybe there's still a way to banish him now."

She nodded, her breath dancing across his lips in a shy tremor.

"We'll figure it out," Orion reassured her. He pursed his lips, and she stared back at him. Her hand moved from the book to brush his fingertips. Sparks flew in the periphery of his vision, but he wrote it off to be nothing more than his lightheadedness and excitement, not thinking twice that it could be something more.

NOVEMBER 11TH, 2106 A.D.
THE ABYSS
CORVUN KHLYDE

Corvun had never been more afraid in his life. He'd been dreading this day since he was first told about the Abyss. It was a plane between Earth and Hell, a place with no sun and no stars. It was the home to RUST, and it was where he would become a killer. Cephan—the leader of the assassin organization—acted as a king in the Abyss, an authority presiding over all its power and inhabitants. The inhabitants were assassins.

Corvun couldn't remember the journey here, as if a fog had settled over his mind. His last recollection was of his stepmother's goodbye and the firm kiss she'd pressed to his forehead.

Michael guided Corvun through the dark world, down alleys and narrow passages through identical rows of warehouses. All of them looked to be abandoned, standing three stories tall with darkened windows and boarded-up doorways. They saw by way of artificial, blue light shed by tall metal lampposts, which flickered in and out as they pleased.

Michael stopped, and Corvun's legs locked up, too.

A man stood a few yards ahead of them. Corvun hadn't even noticed him for the darkness of the world around him. "Lucifer sends his warmest welcome, Michael."

"Cephan," Michael acknowledged dryly. He drew a dagger from the side of his belt and swung the weapon to the side. In a blaze of white light, it extended into a sword. "Swear to me that the Devil is not here."

"Even if he was, your Heaven-forged weapons are useless in the Abyss," Cephan said.

Corvun looked to his dad for some sort of reassurance that they wouldn't see the Devil today, but his father did not look at him. Corvun stared back at Cephan, and the smile on the blond man's face chilled Corvun's bones. Cephan's eyes were ice blue and losing color. They reminded him of the living dead, something between a vampire and a zombie, gleaming with insatiable hunger. Corvun's veins buzzed with the instinct to run, with adrenaline that threatened to break him in half.

"Do you know the friends your son keeps, Michael?" Cephan looked back to Corvun's father. "Azrael is back in town."

"Azrael eludes us all. I can promise you she's done the same with my son."

A shadow lurked in the street over, darkening the narrow alleyway. Corvun turned to look. The mass moved low to the ground, silent. It crept closer, and Corvun swallowed hard. The silhouette lurched forward, stretching from the shadows. Green-brown eyes of a dragon flashed at him, the color of a wilting forest, of death and rot and decay. Corvun collapsed, scrambling back, heart thumping in his chest.

The dragon's lips pulled back in an inhuman, vicious smile. Orange-yellow fangs framed the grin, the color of bloodstained bone. The hot breath the monster breathed stunk of rotting flesh and of blood and ash.

Michael struck the ground with his blade, a barricade between his son and the dragon.

"It seems Corvun has also met the Son of Sorrow," Cephan said. He clicked his tongue, motioning at the dragon. "The Deceivers have an incredible sense of smell, and those twins reek of their shortcomings. You know I won't let them even have a chance at coming into their power, Michael, don't you?"

The Deceiver lunged forward, and Michael struck the dragon across the muzzle, leaving an open gash across the bridge of its nose. The dragon reeled back and swung its head towards Cephan; Cephan did not move. Michael seethed at Cephan. "They have faith stronger than you anticipate," he spat. "They will come into their power. Of that much, I am sure."

Corvun panted, numb. His chest burned, exhausting the muscles that held him together. He felt like he was going to fall apart.

His consciousness slipped away.

It came back in a different place, a later time.

Corvun sat in a hard, metal chair in a slate-gray, boxy room. Fire sizzled ahead of him, and footsteps fell muted on the ground.

Cephan came into Corvun's periphery with his eyes downcast and focused. Cephan locked a metal contraption around Corvun's palm, thumb, and forearm with a harsh *clack*.

The steel was cold against Corvun's skin, and fear danced in Corvun's mind, telling him the metal was sticking to his skin like ice to a tongue. Corvun wanted his father. He looked around, frantic, only to find that Michael was nowhere to be found here. Corvun closed his eyes and tried to steady his breathing; it didn't work.

Cephan grabbed Corvun's face, sudden and without mercy.

Corvun stared back, wide-eyed, into Cephan's heartless smile.

"I have waited decades to have you," Cephan said.

Corvun leaned away.

"Have you ever felt Hellfire?"

Corvun's stomach twisted violently. He yanked against the metal restraints.

"It leaves a burn that can never be healed," Cephan said. He turned and strode towards a grand furnace that stood against the far wall. It looked like it should've been the centerpiece of a wicked ballroom, for a party that demons held to celebrate Jesus's short-lived death. Dust and ash collected on the twisting, horn-like curves, the mock, thorn crown that decorated the mantle. Cephan opened the black gate, and the pit hissed and flared with fire hot enough to burn the room around them, had it not been made entirely of stone. "And for angels," Cephan crooned, "it is most torturous."

Corvun pressed back against the metal chair, desperately trying to pull his hand loose of the metal cuffs. He would claw his way back to Earth if he had to, dig through the dirt with his fingernails just to get back home.

Cephan took a metal rod from the stand beside the fireplace.

Corvun thought of Carina, the wild look in her eyes, and the angry flame over her head. *This is the fear she felt,* Corvun assured himself. He closed his eyes, but he could still see the metal turn white in the flames. Flames coming up from Hell itself, no doubt. Corvun's mind blazed with panic, a static buzz. He imagined that if he had been someone else, someone greater like his father Michael, he could escape this fate. He bruised his wrists the harder he pulled.

"Fames," Cephan hissed the name, and a deep part of Corvun's waking mind recognized it, almost responded to it. "Welcome to RUST." He clamped a hand on Corvun's arm. The white-hot metal stamped down on Corvun's right wrist.

Corvun's head clouded. He couldn't hear himself scream over the ringing in his ears. Hot air tore his throat raw. Panting only shook his chest, never giving him enough oxygen. The burn in his wrist blistered up his muscles. The pain coursed through his veins. Tainted. Unworthy. That's how it made him feel. The pain was more than physical; it was like being ripped from Heaven.

He prayed for salvation.

He didn't know how long he begged for it to end. Everything was a blur, a haze of pain and desperation. Sweat beaded on Corvun's neck and chest and dampened his shirt, matted his hair to his forehead. Sandpaper lined his throat, and chalk powdered his mouth. Numbness tingled in his hands and feet, and the muscles of his legs had turned to liquid. His head rolled to his right. He stared at his wrist.

The sight of the red, swollen wound stabbed through his mind. The compass brand. A blacklist to society. As for the rest of the world, it was incorrectly considered the "Mark of the Beast." This was never Corvun's will, nor would he deny his faith for anything. This was slavery, a brand to show he wasn't his own.

Corvun glared back in the last direction he'd seen Cephan, finding his blurry figure by the hearth again. He turned, holding another rod, a white-hot fire stoker. "Don't worry. The worst of it's over," Cephan said. He came closer, and horror rushed through Corvun again. Cephan lifted the stoker and pierced Corvun through the heart.

Time slowed. Breath trickled from his lungs, and he slipped through dark, black fingers, through the cracks in his mind into unconsciousness.

· · · ·

Corvun woke lying flat on his back in the middle of a desert. He jolted up onto his hands. He stared at his surroundings. Distant canyons stretched across the horizon. Skeletons of massive creatures laid beside him and around him with ribcages like empty prisons. Skulls gaped with carnivorous teeth, some bloodstained and some broken. Dry cracks cut across the ground.

Corvun forced himself onto his feet.

Only the sun was suspended in the sky, a harsh red orb that glared down on him.

He smacked a hand to his chest, feeling for the stab wound Cephan inflicted. There was no wound, but the pain remained. He looked to his wrist next; the compass was still there.

A black root stretched up out of one of the cracks in the ground. It crept towards him then wrapped around his ankle. Startled, Corvun tried to shake it off. It tightened, and his heart punched through his lungs. Adrenaline kicked through his system again. He stumbled back, and the root yanked his foot out from under him. It dragged him a few feet towards a wide gap in the sandy ground.

Corvun clawed at the cracks around him, hoping to find one he could pry his fingers into and hold on to. He gripped the edge of a break, held on with all the strength he had left. Five more roots reached up and tied him together. The coarse roots sliced against his skin as he struggled. Another root wrapped tightly around Corvun's neck. He scratched at the wiry, black noose, but the dying plant pulled tighter. It suffocated Corvun.

Pathetic. Corvun heard his own voice in his mind, just before blackness consumed him. *Again,* he said.

. . . .

Corvun woke again. His breath was the sound of the ocean rushing—high tide to low tide, over and over, crashing violently. He sat up to find himself in the same place as before, a godforsaken desert with no drop of water but the sweat on his brow. Corvun scrambled backwards as lashing black vines shot up from the dry cracks in the desert ground.

Corvun jumped up and ran.

Two roots whipped around his ankles, tripping him. He slammed down, and his skull cracked against a stone. He exhaled, staring sideways at the expanse of sky. The black returned.

Weak, he said. *Do not run from yourself.*

. . . .

The third time, Corvun was ready when he woke. He found the nearest abandoned skeleton and broke a rib from the bones. He held the rib up as a decoy when the roots flew in his direction. The black tendrils wrapped around the bone.

Corvun breathed hard.

The roots spiraled down towards his hand, and Corvun dropped the bone to break another. He climbed into the skeleton to wield off the hissing vines with the help of the ribcage around him. No matter how he fought, the vines kept slinging towards him. They knit a dark hide around the lifeless dragon, trapping Corvun inside the starved, dead beast. The whip-like weapons blotted out the sun, twisting and winding, snapping like leather as they tied together.

Better, he said.

NOVEMBER 11TH, 2106 A.D.
NORTHEAST FLORIDA
JAYREN OMANS

"There's a dollar store at a shopping center just a few blocks around the corner," Jayren said. "There's a sub shop right by it, too." Jayren stood over his motorcycle, one foot on the foot peg and the other on the ground, as Ophiah straddled the back of the bike. The fall air around them was sticky and cool yet somehow refreshing. Jayren was grateful the humidity masked his sweat, but it also made cute, haywire curls in Ophiah's hair. They were adorably distracting.

"Okay," she said.

"Hold on," he said. He took one of her hands gently and laced her arms around his waist. He melted at the feeling of her palms resting flat on his stomach. Jayren's stomach filled with lethal butterflies—the type that had razor blade wings and pins and needles for feet and laser beam eyes. "Okay," he managed. "Let's go."

Ophiah laughed a soft, fluttering melody.

Jayren drove slowly out of the school lot, testing the balance of their combined weight on his motorcycle. At first, the world around him was all smears without his glasses. Green overwhelmed his vision, blotted with obscure colors (of strangers' tee shirts, he guessed, of orange and green and white and navy blue). The sidewalk ran like a stream of gray water, liquid concrete. Dizziness struck him. Then, colors started flashing. He saw pedestrians in bright neon oranges and reds and purples. Their footsteps left behind fading yellow lights. Ophiah shuffled behind him, and hard, jagged material appeared in grayscale. The world around him continued to come to him in these bits and pieces. Jayren swerved around a lump on the road—a tortoise crossing their path. He sucked in a breath, heart pounding. He swore to himself he hadn't had any drugs and wondered if maybe his water bottle had been spiked with magic mushrooms in class.

"Can you see alright?" Ophiah asked.

"Not really," he admitted.

"Do you trust me?"

Jayren swallowed and blinked a few times. The world was chaos around him. He nodded.

Ophiah unraveled his scarf from his neck and folded it neatly around his eyes.

Colors seared through the blackness of the makeshift blindfold, like computer screen burn-in. He panted, heart hammering harder than before, and every noise he made brought back black and white and gray box-like visions of mail drops, power lines, parked cars, and buildings. Much to his horror, he realized between the neon colors and the hard, gray shapes, he could see his own version of the world around him, and he had no trouble steering at all. "I think I'm tripping."

Ophiah giggled. "Breathe through your nose," she said.

Jayren closed his mouth and did as she told him, and the scent of the whole world came back to him nearly strong enough to knock him off the bike. He smelled a pizza joint— but the nearest one had to be at least a mile away. The ever-present Florida humidity clung to the streets, and the scent of damp grass filled his lungs. And then there was Ophiah—a sweet mix of lilac shampoo and sugary lip gloss, her pasty concealer, and the smell of her half-washed laundry. Her skin smelled strangely of ash, like she'd suffered a burn wound; she smelled of bruises, too. Everything hit him too fast, too soon, and the motorcycle wobbled beneath them. Ophiah steadied him. "I think I'm gonna puke," Jayren said.

"Okay, let's slow down."

"I'm gonna puke, like right now."

Ophiah helped him stop the bike.

Jayren yanked the sash off his eyes and darted to the nearest bush. He fell to his knees and shoved his head through the leaves. He lost the soymilk and banana and granola he'd had for breakfast, and acid stung the back of his nose and throat. Jayren wiped the vomit off his nose and lips only to dry heave again. His head hurt. Badly.

Ophiah touched his back. "Hey, are you alright?"

Jayren didn't want Ophiah to see him. "Maybe you should just take my motorcycle back to school and leave me here. This was a terrible idea! I'm so sorry."

"Don't be silly," Ophiah said. "Besides, I don't know how to ride one anyway. Here." When he didn't move, she laughed his name.

Jayren thought he might puke again. *Damn those evil butterflies.*

Ophiah took his arm and encouraged him to stand up. He faced her, and she smiled. He couldn't understand why because he could feel that there was still vomit on his chin. "Here," she said again, handing him a tissue.

Jayren took it and wiped his face vigorously. "Stop laughing at me," he begged quietly. He furrowed his brow at her, and she came into full focus.

Her makeup was ruined from the humidity, but she smiled so brightly it surprised him. She tucked her crimson hair behind her ear and pursed her lips as if she were about to say something or maybe laugh again. She eyed the distance above his head.

Jayren looked up, too. "I don't have stars floating around my head, do I?"

She smiled and shook her head. "Come on. Let's go find you some glasses, Snake Eyes." She took his fingertips in hers and tugged him towards the shopping center.

Jayren desperately tried to convince himself she'd called him "four eyes" instead.

OPHIAH JUDE

Thunder grumbled in the distance as Ophiah and Jayren dashed, side by side, for the dollar store. The sliding doors *whirred* open, greeting them with a dry blast of warm air. Ophiah spun to face Jayren, gazing at his eyes. The pretty, pale green reminded her of a lily before bloom; the snake-slits of his eyes soothed her like spring after a long winter. She knew enough about Sentinels, about their abilities and role in the human world, but she had never known one personally. Seeing Jayren's abilities of infrared vision and echolocation manifest right before her was incredible. She was enchanted.

The store around them was white and half empty, so Ophiah knew they'd draw attention. She needed to get Jayren to the glasses without anyone seeing his eyes. The Archangels may have been able to make humans brush over a sight like that with their power of persuasion, but Ophiah didn't know that skill, and Jayren clearly couldn't control any of his skills yet either.

The cashier looked their way, and Ophiah stepped into her line of sight. She pulled Jayren by the hand, deeper into the store. The clothing aisle smelled of stale, dirty fabric, sweat stains from potential takers, and post-party filth on the floor. Ophiah tugged Jayren close to her as they reached the back corner, where turning displays held fashion glasses like a hundred precious stones.

"Do you two need any help?" an employee asked.

Startled, Ophiah plucked a set of plain black sunglasses off the rack and slipped them onto Jayren's face. She turned and smiled sweetly and shook her head. "No thanks."

Jayren stood so still that Ophiah couldn't hear him breathe. The store attendant walked away, and Jayren slid the sunglasses up his forehead to hold his hair back. He gazed at her. His pupils became human again, stretching like a cat's eager eyes.

A sudden sweet and playful feeling rushed over Ophiah, a type of careless feeling that made her want to run away with Jayren and never look back. *This is what childhood should have felt like,* she told herself. But she wondered if it was all just a side effect from Orion. She knew he was falling in love with Venatrix. All their life, Orion and Ophiah had been tied together with a divine red thread that kept their feelings so in tune with each other that they could speak without using their voices, feel without knowing what the other felt directly. She tried to tell herself it was only Orion who was falling in love, not herself. She couldn't be falling in love because she was already committed—betrothed by her mother and the parents of another. She'd gone with it because it was what seemed safe at the time. She liked Casper's family. It secured her future without pain and with a promise of a bright path. But all she cared about in that moment was the blond boy standing in front of her. He stared back at her with a million stars in his eyes, and the knots in his hair painted him like a distant, messy galaxy. She could see her whole fate, her whole future, studying him like this.

"I need something to trick my sister," Jayren said, clearing his throat. He struggled to get the sunglasses' tag out of his tangled hair. "She's probably still gonna kick me out."

"Here," Ophiah said. She handed him a pair of clear-lens glasses. "These look like your old ones."

He tried them on.

"They look great," she said, smiling.

"Let me buy you lunch," he said.

"Let me buy the glasses for you." Ophiah did quick mental math. She had seventeen dollars—three fives, two ones, and one ripped dollar bill from an encounter with the lunch lady—tucked on the inside of her bra. It was enough for both pairs.

"Deal," he said, clutching the sunglasses in his hands like a good luck charm.

"Deal," she said with a laugh.

INTERLUDE

II

THE VOW AND
THE SACRIFICE

The constellations Serpens and Ophiuchus were chosen for the Horseman and Authority of War, Mars, and for the Authority of Destruction, Hades. Their paths will cross in every lifetime, for there is no war without destruction, nor destruction without some form of war.
— A History of Hierarchy

438 A.D.
ROME
OPHIUCHUS

Ophiuchus couldn't stop thinking about the nights leading up to the games. Those nights Serpens held her, his hands touching her in reckless worship, his words as sacred as vows, etching promises into her skin and bones, eternal. She felt golden in his embrace, and he rewarded her endlessly with his breath on her chest and his body between her legs.

Serpens's hand touched the small of her back, reminding her how out of reach those nights were. They walked into the arena—paraded by guards into the middle—burned by the spiteful sun and victim to the shouting and jeers of the bloodthirsty crowd. "I swear I'll get you out of here," Serpens whispered into her ear. His hot breath tickled her neck. "I will spare you, but you and your brother *must* spare Corvus and the patrician. Do not lay one finger on them."

Ophiuchus turned to look at him, and his lips brushed her face.

"Fight like you're with child, assassin," he said, his tongue slashing across her lip, "because you are."

The gates of the arena clanked and clamored shut.

Ophiuchus stumbled away from Serpens and drew her two swords. He gave her one steady look before turning away to evaluate the sandy playing field and the handful of other strangers—criminals, no doubt—she was pitted against. Shock dizzied her head. *How can I be pregnant?* She and Orion were both sterile—an unfortunate curse of being born half-angel and half-demon. *Is Serpens lying? Why would he lie?* She stared after him. She'd never known Serpens to lie.

Orion flanked her side, wielding blade-like weapons similar to her own. Where her swords were curved, Orion's curved blades were attached to the ends of staffs, kin to a pair of scythes. "What did Serpens say to you?"

Ophiuchus studied her surroundings. She spotted Venatici struggling to steady her spear.

"Sister?"

"Do you remember what we were taught growing up? Find any means to survive?" Ophiuchus backed up to Orion so they could see a three-sixty span; his firm back pressed to hers. Her chest tightened uneasily, and she said, "Save the girl and the slave driver."

"That damned Scandinavian," Orion spat Serpens's name at the ground. "I will slit his throat. What did he say to you?"

Ophiuchus shook her head. "I'm carrying his child," she said, still unbelieving.

Orion fell silent. After a pause: "It's not possible."

"I know," she whispered, "but what if it's true?" She hated to voice it because Orion knew just as well as she did how much she longed for a child—that one thing out of her reach. *What if? What would we lose if it were a lie?* She would lose her respect for Serpens if it were a lie. But what if it were true? She would have what she always wanted. "If we spare the others, he'll get us out," she told Orion. "Do you trust me?"

"I don't trust *him*," Orion said. "Do you?"

"I don't have a choice," Ophiuchus said. And to herself, *I have to trust him.* Ophiuchus looked to where Serpens fought. He ducked under an attack, a heavy shield strapped to his forearm. His arm flexed under the weight and the clash of the mace on his shield. He heaved the weapon off, kicked his offender in the stomach, then slung his sword across the gladiator's chest. His opponent fell, and fear reared in Ophiuchus's chest. "I trust that his loyalty is as much with us as it is with his slave driver, *if* we do not cross him or the patrician. Save her."

"I will not leave your side, sister. Now that you tell me you're pregnant?" Two gladiators approached Ophiuchus, and Orion whipped around in a fluid movement to put him between Ophiuchus and her offenders. He deflected an attack from the first, stabbing the man in the shoulder. Orion ripped the weapon away, sliced it through the second man's thighs. The men staggered, and Orion finished them both with two quick strikes to their throats. Orion's expression flared with wild eyes and raised brows. He turned to Ophiuchus. "I will kill him."

Ophiuchus raised her sword to Orion's chest. She took a step back. She knew he was furious at the concept: If it were the truth, their close friend had impregnated her. If it were a lie, Serpens was using her in the worst way possible. Neither sin would be easy to return from in Orion's eyes. Slowly, Ophiuchus said, "I made a deal to escape. We follow through with that deal."

"How long has it been going on? Between the two of you?"

Ophiuchus's jaw tensed. She turned to meet a gladiator head-on. His sword was raised above his head, and his throat was exposed. Ophiuchus stabbed her sword through his neck. Blood coated her hand like a glove. "Return to my side when they are safe," she said through her teeth. She didn't look back.

ORION

Orion's heart pounded in his chest, harder than the beat of the drums high up in the stadium. The arena roared louder, a rhythm chanting for survival of the fittest, for the game of life and death, gambled by fate. Orion spun his scythe-like blades, balancing the weight of the weapons. He searched for Venatici.

He noticed Corvus first.

The slave driver's hands were still bound in heavy metal cuffs, and a man twice his size was approaching him.

Orion sprinted to Corvus's side. The giant gladiator—whose chest guard alone could have knocked Orion down—barreled towards Corvus. Orion pushed himself harder, defying the ache in his calves. He tackled Corvus and collapsed, shielding the slave driver from the gladiator's blow. The sword penetrated Orion's shoulder instead. Orion cried out. He strained to hold himself up over Corvus, arms shaking.

Corvus's eyes widened. He stared at Orion, eyes flickering to a spot on his chest where silver flashed and dripped with red. Panting, he said, "Break my cuffs. Hurry!"

Orion reached for a stone in arm's distance. His fingers brushed the sandy stone. Above him, the gladiator yanked the sword out of his back only to puncture him again a few inches from the first wound. Orion yelled out, smoke stinging his lungs. Hot tears streaked his face.

"Hurry!" Corvus yelled.

Orion clutched the stone, forced himself up on searing muscles. Corvus held his hands to his side, and Orion bashed the stone into the metal. Five strikes broke the chain binding his cuffs.

Corvus caught Orion's midriff with his legs and rolled them over. He grabbed Orion's discarded weapons, crossed the blades over his head and behind his back. He caught the gladiator's sword and disarmed him. Corvus got to his knees, stood. He spun and locked the hooks of the blades on the gladiator's metal breast plate, threw the weapons downward, and the gladiator stumbled forward towards Corvus; Corvus dropped both staff weapons and slipped a dagger from his pocket. He thrust the dagger through the exposed shoulder of the man's breast plate, ripped the weapon back out. He slung an arm over his offender's neck, forced him down, then swiped the dagger across the underside of his throat. Corvus's face snapped up at the sudden cheering of the crowd. He looked feral, like an animal on a hunt, and his black eyes sank into Orion's.

Orion's heart skipped a beat. *This is it*, he thought. *This is where I die*. He looked to his discarded weapons, wondering if he could get to them in time. He couldn't feel his arm anymore, he realized, so he readied himself to be bled out at the neck just as callously as the gladiator before him. Corvus straightened and stalked towards him, picking the weapons off the ground; Orion fell flat on his back. He coughed as the dry dirt billowed into his lungs.

Corvus flipped Orion's weapons in his hands, offering the handles to him. "Get up."

No time for second-guessing, Orion told himself. He struggled to stand on his weak knees then took the hilts of the swords. "What will you fight with?"

"Anything," Corvus lifted his dagger again, then he tore a whip from the side of the slain gladiator, "and everything. Where is Vena?"

The friendly name startled Orion. "Do you know her?"

"Where is she?" Corvus demanded.

Orion looked around with Corvus. He pointed towards the black-haired girl who sprinted away from another warrior.

"I need a chariot."

"What?"

Corvus fixated on the horses pulling a gold chariot around the perimeter of the arena. A Roman fighter was atop the moving throne.

"Are you insane?" Orion spat.

Corvus turned and ran.

CORVUS

Corvus unraveled the whip at his side. It felt natural, like an extension of his body, and rage pumped through his bloodstream. These games had gone too far; where it used to be a sport for assassins and warriors like the Gemini twins, they'd made *this* game a free-for-all execution for traitors to the crown. Venatici's family had rebelled, and naturally, as their slave driver, Corvus had been ushered into the same fate. He wouldn't accept this fate; though at the back of his mind, he wondered, had the Gemini won the game, would they have risen to even higher glory? Despite being elusive, they were still well known. And—did Serpens really think they would abandon that glory?

The Roman guard turned as Corvus neared the chariot. The fighter drew his bow and arrow. Corvus flung the whip towards the chariot, catching the thin, wooden weapon and yanking it out of the Roman's hands. Corvus ran faster, winding the whip around his fist, and lunged onto the chariot. He tackled the Roman fighter, hammering three swift punches to the man's face. The leather wrapped around his hand took the blunt force; Corvus threw the unconscious Roman from the back of the cart.

The crowd roared again.

Corvus lapped the pit of the arena once as he searched for Venatici. He found her again. Reigns in hand, he lashed the horses, and they ran faster. Corvus came up behind Venatici and her pursuer. Corvus flung his whip out, striking the man's ankle; he stumbled and fell beside the chariot and was left behind. "Canes!" Corvus shouted at Venatici.

She ran beside the chariot. Corvus stretched his arm out for her, and she didn't hesitate. She grabbed his forearm, and he heaved her up into the racing cart with him. He could hear her panting through the sound of thundering hooves and frantic whinnies.

Corvus grabbed a spare bow and quiver that was tucked under the steer of the chariot. "Do you know how to aim?" Corvus asked Venatici.

"My father taught me, long ago…" Her voice faded.

"Shoot at the other prisoners." Corvus helped Venatici up on the shaking chariot. He handed her the weapon.

Venatici almost lost her balance, but Corvus quickly grabbed her arm to steady her. She stared at the broken chains on his wrists.

He leaned in and said, "And don't fall off."

SERPENS

Serpens was surrounded but not outmatched. Three gladiators circled him, and he waited for their attack with his sword in hand. *They have no idea what they're getting into,* he thought. Serpens grinned at each of them in turn, twirling his sword and deflecting each gladiator with ease.

"They call you the Snake! Why don't you show us what they mean by that?" one of the warriors called, teasing. She belted a strong laugh. She was lean with dark, braided hair and warpaint across her face. "Let us battle with the *real* beast in the arena."

Serpens turned to her. "Don't *s*speak to me," he hissed.

"Skin him," the woman said to the two men gladiators. The three neared Serpens.

Serpens cut off the hand of the man who attacked first. His sword clattered on the ground, and the man grabbed at his wrist. Serpens spun, slicing his sword across the bicep of the second man. He ducked under the man's arm then drove his sword through his back. Serpens looked up and spotted Orion and Ophiuchus fighting back-to-back across the arena.

In his moment of distraction, the woman neared him. She plunged a knife into his thigh.

Agony lit Serpens's bones. He felt her twist the knife, smelled raw meat, cracked pepper, and rich spices on her breath. He let go of his sword and grabbed a fistful of her braid. He yanked her head back and bit down on her neck. His jaw clenched; hot, syrup-like blood spilled into his mouth. She went limp in his arms.

Focus, Serpens begged himself. He reminded himself of the consequences of indulgence. Swallowing her blood meant eternal damnation. Still, the temptation was there. His body changed without his permission, and he hated it. It pinned him between pain and pleasure, weakness and power. His skin molted, with churning in his muscles. Seconds passed. The sour ache in his muscles turned to acid then to strength he could feel. Scales bound his legs and his blood ran cold.

Serpens dropped the dead woman and spat her blood on the ground. He looked up again, and Ophiuchus caught his eyes.

VENATICI

A flash of white blinded Venatici. She spotted Serpens in the center of the arena, and her stomach turned. Words refused her in her shock. She managed only Corvus's name, a fragile chime of warning.

Corvus turned to look then swore violently. He handed Venatici the reins. "Steer," he commanded.

Venatici watched, horrified.

Iridescent white shimmered in the beating sunlight. Serpens slid across the ground with scales sawing against each other, scratching and scraping in a dry, barbaric challenge. Serpens tripped two opponents, caught a third with the end of his serpent's tail and dragged him across the ground. He coiled his tail around the prisoner, tightening until the man's spine snapped under the pressure.

Two arrows whisked through the air, striking two fighters who fled Serpens.

Venatici looked for the archer, only to find Orion approaching Serpens.

"Orion!" Corvus yelled. "Stop!"

Venatici circled closer to Orion and Serpens. Her heart beat high in her throat; fear choked her.

One stray arrow lodged into the end of Serpens's tail. Serpens snapped around, anger cutting his pupils to wild slits. His eyes landed on Orion.

"Serpens!" Corvus called. He turned to Venatici, frantic. "Jump."

Venatici dropped the reins and followed Corvus's lead. They both jumped, tumbling onto the ground. She couldn't feel anything save for the adrenaline numbing her body. She looked up to see Serpens wrestle the bow out of Orion's hand; Serpens's tail wound around Orion. Corvus scrambled to his feet and ran towards the two. Venatici stumbled after him. Corvus stopped when they were close enough to speak but far enough to be out of Serpens's range. Ophiuchus met them there.

"Serpens," Corvus chastised, keeping his voice low.

Serpens glared in Corvus's direction. His gaze wandered to Venatici.

Chills bit Venatici's skin as she looked in his eyes.

Serpens tightened his coils around Orion; Orion winced in the vise-like grip. Serpens's scales appeared as metal, a silver shimmer, as a cloud dimmed the sun. The makeshift chain mail ticked, clacking like the sound of breaking bones. "Thiss iss a traitor, Corvuss."

"Serpens, listen. It was a mistake. He is not a traitor. He will not betray us. That's what you told me. Remember?"

Serpens arched Orion back, threatening to break his spine, too.

Orion yelled out in agony.

"Stop!" Ophiuchus cried suddenly.

The crowd had gone quiet. A murmur of whispers spun like the wind around the five.

"Please," Ophiuchus begged.

Serpens looked at her.

"Take me instead," she said. "Spare him."

A savage smile pulled the sides of Serpens's cheeks. He bared razor fangs at Ophiuchus. "You'd *ssacrificce* your*s*self for him?" he challenged.

Ophiuchus laid her weapons on the ground and stepped towards him. "Yes."

OPHIUCHUS

Ophiuchus couldn't keep up with the speed of Serpens's movement through the blur in her eyes and the hazy heat around them. Serpens released Orion and looped her in coils instead. He was cold and strong, ruthless, but not as terrible as she'd expected. He leaned over her. "You cho*ss*e not to fight me?" he asked. "Why?"

"You have our loyalty," she swore under her breath. She turned away from his sharp, feral features, but he held the side of her face and tilted it back to his.

"*Why?*" he demanded.

"Our child," she said. Her arms and legs tingled with numbness. Her head grew dizzy.

"What if I lied?" His lips brushed hers, taunting.

The words left her lips as a whisper, "You'd still have it."

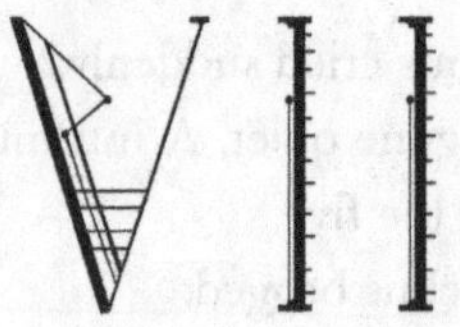

TALLIES

The RUST brand—a compass burned into the skin of RUST assassins—is also something known as a the Soul Stitch. The Hellfire used to brand the skin binds the soul to the body, so that the soul will not move on if the body is fatally injured. The leader of RUST, Cephan, can resurrect the bodies of fallen assassins, allowing their trapped souls to reanimate the bodies.
— *A History of Hierarchy* (Revised Edition)

NOVEMBER 12TH, 2106 A.D.
NORTHEAST FLORIDA
CORVUN KHLYDE

Corvun's fingers dug into the black fabric of his hoodie. He swallowed against the dryness in his mouth, and his throat stuck together, raw skin clinging to itself. He'd killed himself the night before with a single, deep slit on his wrist. He'd watched himself bleed out on his gray sheets and woke again in the morning, horrified. Just like before, he'd dreamed while he was dead—of the sandy desert and the voice that sounded like his own. Twice now, he'd woken from death. Immortal. *Immortal,* he thought, *or cursed?*

The bell rang.

Corvun flinched, but he didn't move. He sat in the very furthest, darkest corner of the dim-lit classroom. He'd been there two class periods already, and he knew that the professor knew too. He just wondered how much. Had Michael told the school Corvun was with RUST now? Warned them about the weapons Corvun carried in secret? He had a three-eighty caliber pistol tucked in his waistband and a brass knuckle switchblade in his pocket. He never wanted to hold either.

His head was bursting with pain, and he rested it against the wall.

Corvun learned to use a gun at the age of fourteen, but he'd never wanted to learn how to take a life and most of all not regularly. He'd only killed once, and it had been self-defense. A few years back, the Canes brothers held a hurricane party at an abandoned beach house. Corvun and Casper both took their fathers' nine-millimeter pistols—guns that had been issued to their fathers in their own respective times with RUST. The guns proved useful too; the party was attacked by a RUST assassin, an attempt on Corvun's own life. Corvun shot the assassin, and while the rest of the kids attending had their memories altered by the Archangels, Michael opted to let Corvun remember.

Never take a life in vain. The reminder from his father was etched in his brain, and the cut on his wrist would be just that. He'd keep a tally to ensure he'd never *not* feel the pain of taking a life. Part of him wondered if he was making excuses, if maybe he just felt sorry for himself, and maybe it was just a relief, a way to ease the pain. Even if it was temporary. But the pain came back twofold, a sickening swell of emotions, as Jayren came into the room.

"Dude!" Jayren called in his direction. He climbed the steps to Corvun's desk. "Dude, c'mon. The North Institute is having its sneak peek orientation in the auditorium in five minutes. I had us seats saved, but— Are you asleep?" Jayren jostled Corvun's shoulder.

"No," Corvun mumbled. He dragged his eyes open, but even the dim lights of the presentation hall bruised the back of his eye sockets. He grimaced.

"Oh, shit. Your *eyes*." Jayren gawked. "Where were you last night? Did you get involved with the Canes brothers again? I told you they lace their drugs—"

Corvun finally registered the solid black sunglasses Jayren wore when his vision cleared up. "Would *you* know about that?"

Jayren faltered. "Look, I had a rough night. And morning. And yeah, I might look high or *something* along those lines, but I swear to god I'm not. Lacey would kill me if I did drugs." Jayren pulled Corvun up out of his chair, and Corvun winced away from the tight grip on his wrists. He almost yelped, bit down on his tongue hard enough to taste blood, and Jayren dropped his arms. He recoiled and stared at Corvun's right wrist. His face drained of color. "Oh shit. Yesterday was your birthday. Oh my god. It wasn't— It wasn't *that* birthday, was it?"

Corvun nodded, his throat tight.

"Why didn't you—" Corvun glared, and Jayren spoke quieter, "Why didn't you tell me?"

"I didn't want to worry you."

"What are you, a fucking idiot?" Jayren bit. "Holy hell, Corvun. You— You're kidding, right? This is a joke, right? You've got to be kidding. There's no way—"

Corvun noticed the teacher eying the two of them and shushed Jayren. "Can we go somewhere else to talk about this? It's not like your sunglasses aren't suspicious, too."

Jayren nodded numbly.

Corvun followed Jayren out of the classroom. The hall was emptying, but his head still hurt when he looked at the light, so he kept his eyes on the ground and surrendered to

Jayren's lead. Every now and then, students shoved at Jayren, even shouldered Corvun, and he feared getting separated. He grabbed Jayren's hand and walked closer behind him. Corvun thought he heard Jayren hiss someone, but he couldn't be sure. Corvun thought about Jayren's sunken-in sofa and the sounds of Jayren's video games. He missed the simple days now.

Jayren threw the bathroom door open. He surveyed the perimeter then shoved the bench in front of the door. "You're with RUST?" Jayren turned to him. His voice was young and naive, and concern and panic ebbed at the corners of it.

Jayren knew the answer, so Corvun didn't reply.

Jayren's face fell.

Corvun suddenly didn't want Jayren to take off his sunglasses in fear he would see the dismay or his tears, but it was inevitable. "Are *you* okay?" Corvun managed.

"Am *I okay?* Why would you ask me if *I'm okay?* Have you looked in a mirror, Corvun? You look like you haven't slept for months, not to mention you look like you've been doped up and gone full swing Nikki Sixx."

"Are you okay?" Corvun asked again, steadier. He was proud of the glimpse of composure.

"No!" Jayren cried suddenly. "Dude, I don't know what's wrong with me. I think I got bit by a spider—or a cat or a snake, I don't know—but I'm definitely not okay. I'm turning into Spiderman!"

"Take the sunglasses off," Corvun coaxed.

"Dude, no."

Corvun stepped closer to Jayren and snatched the glasses away.

Jayren stumbled back, squinting against the blue-tinged bathroom light. He caught himself on the counter, and he stared back at Corvun.

Corvun's stomach sickened at the sight of the small black slits in the center of Jayren's pale eyes. The skin around his eyes was rubbed pink and red with irritation. Corvun turned and stumbled into a stall. He hit his knees and wrapped his arms around the toilet and puked in the bowl. His body turned inside out, bending his organs out of place. "Does your sister know?"

"Does my sister know?" Jayren shrieked. "No, man. No way. The last thing she needs is a lame, loser brother who's becoming a really fucked up Spiderman."

Corvun vomited again. "She's like you," he said.

"Why are you puking?"

"Because I hate snakes!"

"What does that have to do with anything?" Jayren demanded.

The thought twisting in his head made him sicker still. Once, when Corvun was a child, his father had him kill a snake. Corvun stepped on its skull. He assumed it was some sort of symbolic act, something to show triumph over the Devil, but now the slippery topics of angelic hierarchy and his best friend's feelings were involved. "I don't want to talk about it," Corvun said.

"You don't get to play that game anymore!" Jayren slammed the stall door against the wall and helped Corvun up. He shoved paper towels against his chest. "I'm your best friend. Quit keeping secrets."

"They're not— I'm not keepin' secrets. Every time—" Corvun sighed and ran the paper towels over his mouth. "Every time I try to explain these things, you don't believe me. You don't believe in angels, Jayren. Even if I told you *you* were one, you wouldn't believe me!"

Jayren shoved Corvun in the chest. His face pinched like a red tomato. "Maybe I would if you took me seriously."

"I *do*—"

Jayren spun and stalked towards the door.

"Stop!" Corvun called.

"Fuck off."

"Please!" Corvun jogged after Jayren and caught his shoulder. "Listen! The voices you hear? You're not crazy. I promise, okay? But if I told you you could hear angels and demons, you wouldn't believe me."

"Maybe I would!" Jayren's eyes watered. "Man, I'd believe in angels if y'all weren't dicks."

"I'm a dick, too?"

"Oh, massive," Jayren said.

Corvun offered him his sunglasses back.

Jayren snatched the glasses, slipped them on, then pushed the bench away from the door and whisked away with nothing but a sniffle left behind.

Corvun's hands grew tacky and cold with sweat. He'd guessed Jayren was a Sentinel—but Landborne or Seaborne, he hadn't even considered yet. Part of him hoped Jayren would've been Landborne, but it seemed to be turning out the other way. *Half-snake. Half-serpent.* Corvun's stomach churned again. His best friend was a Seaborne Sentinel. His best friend. He wasn't going to let that fact ruin one of the best friendships he'd ever had. He balled his hands in his hoodie sleeves and stalked after Jayren. He swung the door open only to find Jayren standing there, facing the bathroom with an indecisive look on his face.

"I'm sorry," Jayren said.

Corvun nearly threw his arms around Jayren, but he fought the urge.

Jayren yanked the sunglasses off his face and furrowed his brow in a not-very-menacing glare. "But you're still a massive dick, and I'm still mad at you."

Corvun gave up and hugged him.

Jayren sighed and put one hand on Corvun's back.

. . . .

Later that night at Corvun's house, the two of them sat cross-legged on Corvun's bed. Defeat weighed heavily on Corvun's shoulders as he picked at a hangnail on his finger. "Adapt," Corvun said to Jayren. "If you can't see where you're standin', change your scenery. If you can't win the race, cut corners and cheat until you can. Kill or be killed. That's how it is in RUST."

Jayren watched Corvun with pale green snake eyes, filled to the brim with child-like fear of the unknown.

"You understand," Corvun said.

"No, I don't," Jayren said.

"Your body does. Your eyes," Corvun motioned at his face. "You're adaptin' to survive. It's not evolution, just instinct."

Jayren looked at his lap. "Well I sure as hell hope I can keep adapting. There's no chance of either of us getting North Institute internships now. Not like I expected to get chosen anyway."

"Vena went to the presentation. I texted her. She has the information packet and she's bringin' it over."

"Great."

"Is that sarcasm?" Corvun asked.

"Kinda. We all know she's gonna get the internship."

Corvun shook his head. "She's not even interested in it. She doesn't want to write the essay. I think she's just as tired of the Archangels as I am."

Jayren scoffed. "Are you gonna try?"

"I think so, yeah."

"Why?" Jayren asked.

"It's my only chance to get away from RUST," Corvun said. A selfless sacrifice, Michael told him, could free him of the pact. Michael explained to Corvun that the time and resources North Institute would sacrifice for him would work; it was pure in intent, absolutely selfless. It'd been put in place to save *him*—years ago, for this moment.

"Ah," Jayren said.

Corvun settled back against his pillow. For the first time in his life, his bedroom felt like a safe haven, somewhere far away from everyone and everything else, a place only he and Jayren knew. The walls of the room looked like a tent, a deep, rich brown, the color of Earth and stone. Pictures he'd taken over the years and pinned to the walls were a path back to his childhood, back to innocence. He rehung a picture of Venatrix and himself more recently, and he looked over Jayren's shoulder to stare at the old, awkward selfie. He and Venatrix had been eight and twelve, and it was just before their friendship started deteriorating—each day worsened with each new bruise he collected. His hair was short in the picture, and so was hers. Her bangs and shoulder-length hair had been trimmed by his own hands. He remembered the texture of her hair still. Each strand was glossy like the wings of a crow or raven.

Jayren looked over his shoulder at the picture. "That's new," he said.

Corvun tore the bandage off his right wrist. The cool air greeted the damp, humid wound with a tacky, cold kiss.

"Would you tell me if you liked her?" Jayren asked.

"I don't. Orion likes her," Corvun said.

"Yeah, that doesn't mean you don't like her too."

"She's annoyin' and self-centered and complains too much."

Jayren swiped Corvun's phone. "Fine. Let's take a look at the texts."

Corvun glared at Jayren but didn't attempt to take his phone back; he had nothing to hide. Jayren knew his passcode and dug straight to her text string. Corvun watched him flip through the conversation, feeling a new pang in his chest at every message he reread.

'Are you asleep?' she asked.

'I can't sleep,' he said.

Venatrix sent a photoshopped image of Corvun's face on Eeyore.

'Are you okay?' she asked.

'Ben?' Venatrix again.

'Call me.' She texted again.

Venatrix made a call.

Corvun met Jayren's eyes, weakened by the burden of Venatrix's friendship, Jayren's friendship, and the friendship he wanted to pursue with Orion. Suddenly, Corvun wanted to shut them all out, move away, and never speak to them again if that meant he could spare them the awful fate ahead.

"Well that's not juicy, like at all."

"I would tell you if I liked her, and I'm tellin' you I don't."

The doorbell rang downstairs.

Jayren smiled. His eyebrows wiggled mischievously.

Corvun's muscles ached as he dragged himself out of bed. He jogged downstairs, and Jayren followed right behind him. Corvun sidestepped Cynthia at the bottom of the stairs, trying to ignore his sister's dirty glare. He opened the door to see Venatrix standing there. Venatrix's arms were tightly crossed over her chest, cutting off access to her heart. She wore a wrinkled windbreaker and her white tennis shoes and no makeup. Her eyes shifted, looking everywhere but at Corvun and Jayren.

"Seriously?" Cynthia asked.

Corvun's chest pulled tight at Cynthia's words. Cynthia had hard brown eyes and an ever-judgmental stare. Corvun found it hard to have a relationship with his sister because of this, so over the years, they'd drifted apart too. Corvun couldn't keep up with his sister's constantly changing lifestyle. He was pretty sure he smelled weed coming from her room in the past weeks.

"You can't come down for dinner and then you invite *her* over?" Cynthia asked. "You literally stopped being friends with her once you knew you'd join RUST, and now what? You're suddenly friends with her again? You've got your priorities backwards, Corvun. No wonder everyone at school thinks you're such an asshole."

Corvun couldn't move.

Even Jayren remained silent, his feet shuffling uncomfortably.

"You're really prioritizin' *her* over our family?" Cynthia asked. She scoffed when she got no response, and the sound struck Corvun like a punch to the throat.

Corvun felt so disconnected from his sister that he didn't even know how to respond. He glanced up at Venatrix.

Venatrix's eyes were wide and scared. "Can I come in?" she asked.

Corvun stepped to the side to stand between Cynthia and Venatrix. Cynthia's words made him hate himself; he never seemed to be able to make the right decisions around her. When he leaned on his family for support, he felt cold and neglected; when he leaned on his friends for support, he was called out for doing the wrong thing. His throat squeezed with frustration as Jayren led Venatrix upstairs. Corvun closed the door and turned to Cynthia.

Cynthia scoffed again, rolled her eyes, and walked away.

Corvun looked up the stairs to where Jayren and Venatrix stood. They hesitated to ascend any further without him, so Corvun made his way back to his room with them. They locked Corvun's door, cracked out a container of stacked potato chips and gummy bears, and didn't mention the encounter with Cynthia again.

"So," Venatrix started, "your eyes? Jayren?"

"Yeah, I'm Spiderman now, bitch."

"More like Medusa," Venatrix said.

"That old snake hag from Rome?" Jayren asked.

"It's Greece," Corvun said.

"Actually," Venatrix said. She looked to Corvun, holding mystery in her eyes as if they were cowboys gathered around a fire to tell ghost stories. "Medusa was a lot like a Sentinel, like you, Jay."

Corvun raised an eyebrow at Jayren.

Jayren avoided Corvun's eyes.

"We talked about it earlier. He won't believe you," Corvun said.

"Bitch, yeah I will," Jayren snapped.

Venatrix leaned forward and pinched Jayren's arm.

"Ow!"

"That's Medusa's bite! Now you're going to turn into a snake hag, too!"

"Piss off, Trixie," Jayren said with a glare.

Venatrix laughed with a wide smile.

Corvun missed that smile, her genuine smile, and he watched her laugh. "Jayren, Sentinels are guardian angels," Corvun said.

"Medusa turned people to stone. She wasn't a guardian angel," Jayren said.

"You're half right," Venatrix said. "I read about Medusa. Really, the legend is about the Deceiver Wrath. Her name is Ira. She has a serpent form—like you will—but she isn't a guardian angel. Obviously."

"He's not ready…" Corvun said.

"Hey," Jayren said. He glared at Corvun, eyes fluctuating between snake and human.

"He's a non-believer," Corvun joked with a forced half-grin in hopes of remedying his mistake. After knowing Jayren a few years, it was hard to believe he'd even hear Venatrix out about Deceivers and Sentinels. Part of him hoped he was wrong.

Much to Corvun's relief, Jayren's brow furrowed into a line on his forehead and said, "I'm not! Keep going."

Venatrix and Corvun exchanged a smile, and Venatrix told Jayren everything she knew. They talked for hours before Venatrix remembered the package she'd brought from the presentation earlier that day. She took the folded papers from her windbreaker, unfolded them, and cut the inside of her pinky on accident. She sucked on the paper cut and handed Corvun the packet. "The internship admissions essay's supposed to be about overcoming something."

Jayren picked up his phone. "I'll leave you guys to it. I should probably head home anyway."

"You can stay," Venatrix said.

Quickly, Corvun added, "Yeah, you don't have to leave. It's fine. I'd—" His voice broke, a rush of emotion pushing to break the dam in his mind. "I'd rather you stay."

"Alright, well I have to pee, so I'll be right back," Jayren said. He stood and walked out.

Corvun leaned back against the side of his bed, shaking with emotion.

Venatrix moved to sit beside him. "Do you want to talk about it now?"

Corvun's eyes flooded with tears from the deep fracture in his soul. "No," he mouthed; no sound came through. "I just thought I'd be strong enough, that I'd be ready by now."

Venatrix was silent, an unspoken promise that she would stay in the aftermath of his chaos. "Do you want to pray about it?" she asked. She glanced at his hands. "Like when we were kids?"

"That's kind of silly, don't you think?"

"No," she said. Her voice was fragile but unbreakable, an oxymoron. "C'mon."

Corvun hesitated, watched her turn and kneel beside his bed with her hands clasped like a child's. He had to mimic her, as if he'd forgotten his faith somewhere between life and death and could no longer remember the right way to pray. His back hurt, and stress ate at his mind like a disease. "I…" His breath fell from his lungs, and he had no desire to bring it back.

"Breathe," she told him softly.

"I can't do this…" His neck and ears were hot, and she pressed a hand on his shoulder. "I can't be loved like this."

"Take deep breaths, okay? Breathe in for four seconds. Hold it for four seconds. Then exhale four. Pause four more seconds, then go again. Okay? It's called square breathing. I'll do it with you." She offered her hand. He took her hand, and she squeezed it.

JAYREN OMANS

Jayren walked out into Corvun's hallway. He browsed the family photos that lined the wall and noticed Corvun's fading smile through the years. Jayren opened the bathroom door, then heard someone behind him. He turned to see Cynthia peeking out of her bedroom. He forced a smile.

"Can you help me with somethin'?" she asked.

"No," Jayren said. He stared at her, and she cleared in his vision. He watched the confusion on her face.

"I just need this dress pinned so I can sew it."

"I have to pee, sorry."

"Did Corvun tell you what you are?"

Jayren nodded.

Cynthia hesitated. "Do you know what you can do?" She offered her hand. "Come help me, and I'll show you."

Jayren wanted to slip into the bathroom and jump out the window. A chalk outline on the concrete would be better than her parents finding evidence he'd been in their daughter's bedroom. But he took her hand anyway, choosing the traitor's side. He doubted Corvun could tell him his abilities, and Cynthia showing him would probably be less painful in a lot of ways.

Jayren recalled how close he and Cynthia had been the summer before. They'd shared their first kiss together, hiding behind the biggest live oak they could find in the park. It was the best weather they'd had all summer, warm with a cool Atlantic breeze. He remembered it as if it were a movie, with bright, lively greens and flowers blooming with strong perfume. She was his first love—and he'd fallen in love with her like he'd fallen in love with so many good movie series before. Being around her gave him the same sense of adrenaline as the crack of a whip on a treasure hunt and a daring escape, or the smear of stars that looked strikingly like snow on a windshield. It'd crushed him when Cynthia and Corvun began growing apart. Part of him almost regretted growing in the opposite direction with Corvun. The awkward distance gaped between them like a canyon, and it scared him enough to stay away. He blamed it on his fear of heights, literal or metaphorical; it was the same to him. He still thought of her every time he saw a character gaze over the edge of a cliff in films. *I should have become a bridge to that gap,* he thought, *maybe then Corvun and Cynthia would still like each other.*

Cynthia's bedroom was so familiar that it put his fears to rest. It hadn't changed since he last saw it. She decorated with leftover Christmas lights and tapestries with circle-shaped patterns. Watercolor and acrylic and oil paintings hung in frames—some of which had been displayed at their public library and in contests. Everything was abstract, and the colors made Jayren dizzy. He searched for something real in the mess of spinning colors. Jayren couldn't find a single picture of Cynthia or Corvun or any other face in her room besides her own.

Cynthia took his hands, and it steadied him. She pinched his fingers at his side, gazing deep into his face. Her eyes were deep brown and amber, and it made him think of honey and sweets. "Here, hold this right here."

Jayren held the fabric tight at her waist. He swallowed hard against the proximity. It was lonelier than anything, and that surprised him. There was a disconnect between them that Jayren didn't think they could fix.

Cynthia looked down, two pins and one needle in her mouth. She fiddled with a spool, took the needle, then sewed a small knot at her right side.

"The dress is nice," Jayren squeaked. "What's it for?"

"Just for wearin'." Cynthia looked at him, and heat flushed his body. She fixed the other side of the dress. "You can let go now."

Jayren let go, a little late. His heart jumped when she lifted the dress over her head and threw it on her desk chair. "Oh, god," he muttered. He looked away, gulping down the nervousness that rose through his throat like a missile headed straight for his brain.

"You can see in the dark," she said. "Did you know that?"

Jayren squeezed his eyes shut. "Yeah. Vena said something like that."

Cynthia flipped the lights off. "Open your eyes. Let me show you."

Jayren shook his head.

Cynthia reached for the hem of his tee shirt. He wasn't sure why he helped her take it off. The fabric ruffled his hair as it came off, and he opened his eyes to darkness. After a moment, his surroundings came back slowly, shaped by black and white and gray. The canvases and frames on her walls were blank slates. Cynthia stood in the center of his vision, flaring with colors—crisp oranges and ripe reds and a pulse shooting through the canvas *she'd* become. The beat of her heart drummed on his ears.

Jayren stepped towards her, entranced. He smelled her— the mix of dull, used bedsheets, of overused perfume on her skin, dusty lavender incense, and her own body's scent—her blood and flesh. He told himself to leave, but he wanted to stay and study her too. She didn't stop him when he leaned near her face. He opened his mouth and his tongue brushed her lips, a quick flicker of black. *A snake tongue*, he realized, awestruck.

"Touch me," she whispered against his mouth. She moved his hands to her sides. "You can stimulate surfaces to smell better."

If curiosity killed the cat, god knows what this will do to me, Jayren thought as he touched her back lightly. He rubbed his hands upward. Smells, colors, feelings—it all smeared together. All Jayren could feel was instinct. He found it too easy to locate and remove the remainder of her clothes (and his). He picked her up and mounted the bed with her. His attention pinpointed on the pulse in her neck.

"You're stronger like this, too," she told him.

"Am I a vampire?" he asked.

"No," she said.

His mouth watered the longer he watched her pulse. "Are you sure?"

"Do not drink my blood," she warned. Her hand pressed against his back when he leaned in to kiss her neck, breath hitching.

Jayren tasted blood suddenly. He pulled back and felt her neck. Nothing. He touched his own mouth to find his lip bleeding. He licked his lips, only to run his tongue along four sharp teeth. His father's voice sounded in his head, *Jayren, promise me. Vow to never consume anything previously alive, and especially not still alive. Swear it to me, son.* Instantly, he was grateful for the taste of his own blood on his mouth; it stopped him from wanting hers. But that didn't stop him from twisting into Cynthia's sheets with her. He stayed there long after Venatrix went home.

CARINA BLACKROCK

"Rummy!" Carina called. She slapped her hand down on the Ace of Clubs Joshuah had just laid down on the quilt where they sat together.

Joshuah laughed.

The sun set five hours prior, and the moon that reached high into the night sky kept Carina and Joshuah company through the upstairs windows. Silky, silver light made the wood dresser by the window shine and sparked an eccentric glow on the liquor they had sitting by the bed in a swirled decanter bottle. Moonlight reflected on Joshuah's plastic playing cards.

"And that means, I am out." Carina tucked the rummy card beside the rest of her three-of-a-kind set on the bed. She laid out her hand—another set of three and a discard—and grinned up at Joshuah.

"Pirate or not, I bet you'd be an incredible gambler." Joshuah chuckled. He threw his alcohol back. "The Apocalypse, can you believe it?"

Carina scooped up her glass from the footstool and downed the liquor. "To the end of the world!" She reached for the decanter. "More."

"No!" Joshuah laughed. "You've had two glasses already."

"I have a game, *Jossh*," she said, hissing his name playfully. "Myth or legend. You tell me the stories you have heard of me, and if it is true, I take a shot."

"That sounds like a horrible idea. But…" He poured a shot into her glass. "You have a curious audience."

Carina grinned wider, and a feeling as sinister and mysterious and uncharted as a chasm on the ocean floor stretched over her.

"The *Pirate in the Red Dress* is a story of a seafarer who was captured and anointed to be a sacrifice to the Devil. Her ceremonial garment—a white robe—was stained by the blood of every demon she slaughtered in her escape," Joshuah said. He held her eyes.

Carina regretted her decision instantly. She held Joshuah's gaze like a handshake, and she swallowed the alcohol in the glass.

"No," he said in disbelief.

"I do not want to talk about that one." It was too recent, too new to her.

"That story is hundreds of years old!"

"It was a prophecy, clearly, not previously fulfilled. Next." Carina held her cup to him.

Joshuah poured another shot. "The legend that we Sentinels were told is that Calypso is a sorceress who rescues shipwrecked sailors. They say that she nurses them back to health by witchcraft. When the sailors finally make it back home, they are haunted until the end of their days, so Calypso was considered a witch. Some call you Calypso."

"Not true." She shook her head, licked her lips. "I am called Calypso because I navigated them to land so quickly, better than any lighthouse. Most of the survivors were lucky to see the light of day again, and I cannot blame their poor memory. They had been poisoned by real sea witches—swampers, demons—whatever you want to call them."

"Alright. The Hydra, or really, they call you the Red Hydra—a serpent with three tails, not a dragon with three heads. Like in Greek mythology, they say each time a tail is cut from your body, a new one will regrow. No one has seen it, though, for the amount of blood that fills the water. But each new diver and sailor claims to see three."

"They are confusing the legend with the Kraken," Carina said with a chill falling over her body. "He has many forms—some think he looks more like a giant squid, some claim the Hyrda with three heads. Since he is a Deceiver, I do not see why he could not be all of those. Besides, I only have one tail, and it is gold."

"Gold?" Joshuah raised an eyebrow.

Carina quirked her eyebrows back, glancing at the moon. "Under certain lights," she said.

"Alright, what about this one?" Joshuah started again, "There has only ever been one Phoenix. The Phoenix is a woman, a Sentinel, born only from her own ash. At the end of each Iteration, she burns by war or punishment or treason or heartache, and her ashes blow away in the wind. When the Archangels return in a new Iteration, they disrupt her ashes, and she gathers to be reborn."

Carina lifted the glass, offered a silent cheer, and swallowed the liquor. She squeezed her eyes shut as the burn raced down her throat.

"Do you remember the past lives?"

"Never," she said. "Just feelings."

"Do you remember him?"

"Who?" Carina asked, feigning disinterest.

"Carina," Joshuah said slowly. "*Corvun*. Do you remember Corvun?"

She didn't answer right away. "Just the feeling," she rasped, "like hangover."

NOVEMBER 13TH, 2106 A.D.
CORVUN KHLYDE

Corvun woke the next morning, mulling over the events of the night prior. He wondered—lying in bed with his arms and legs numb, the covers tucked tightly beneath his neck, and a dry sting in his eyes—if Jayren leaving for the bathroom had been a lame excuse to get away from Venatrix and Corvun's own emotions.

Corvun looked at the essay he'd started after Venatrix left. It was scattered across index cards like snow on his desk, frozen from the lack of her.

His alarm buzzed under his pillow. He fished for his phone and silenced the alarm. He hated waking up at six on the weekends. It was just another one of his father's ridiculous practices for readying Corvun to become a RUST killer. He wished to wake up from an all-nighter with his friends at two in the afternoon. He would've traded anything and everything to see Jayren and Venatrix passed out in sleeping bags on his floor, dozing with the sole purpose of protecting him from himself and his nightmares. Nightmares—of his future life, of the desert in his mind, of the cut he inflicted that always multiplied in his dreams to cover his arms. Nightmares of losing his friends were worse. He saw visions of himself fighting side by side with them, reaching out to save them, and the violent rip-current of life snatching them away too quickly.

Corvun's bed grew hot, an inferno covering him with sweat and sickening him with claustrophobia. He fought the thin sheet out of the noose-like shape it'd created around his neck, grabbed some clothes and dressed, and stumbled out of his room. He walked across the hall to Cynthia's room, and he stared at her door. Corvun knew she had an art gallery showing this morning. His parents never seemed to let him forget all the events Cynthia received invites for.

He knocked on the door to wake her. "Cynthia?"

No reply.

He gave her a second, knocked again.

A murmur erupted from the other side, but it wasn't Cynthia's voice.

Corvun cracked the door open and glared inside. Anger struck his heart like the reins on a war horse when he saw the mess of blond hair sleeping right beside Cynthia. He slipped in and closed the door. He could barely hold in the urge to yell at his friend, and he fought for control over the frantic beating in his chest. "*Jayren?*"

"What?" Jayren asked, drowsy.

"What the fuck are you doin'?" Corvun seethed.

He moaned, pulled Cynthia's quilt over his head.

"Get out of her bed." Corvun grabbed the cover and caught his thin arm in a fist. He yanked Jayren out of Cynthia's bed, picked each article of Jayren's clothes off the floor, and shoved them into his naked chest. "Are you out of your fuckin' mind? Get dressed."

"Dude, fuck off," Jayren muttered. His eyes were glued together, exhausted. He held his clothes to his chest with one heavy hand.

"Did you have sex with my sister?"

"What does it look like?"

"Get out."

Jayren started walking to Cynthia's bedroom door.

Corvun put a hand on his chest and pushed him back. "Put your damn clothes on. You're jumpin' out the window, you shithead. If my parents see you, we'll never be allowed within ten miles of each other. I texted them and told them you went home last night."

"Your sister's hot."

Corvun shoved Jayren towards the window. "Put your clothes on."

"God," Jayren said. He pulled his shorts on and tugged his shirt down his waist. "I have to pee."

"Prioritize next time. Call Lacey to come pick you up."

"Let me pee first."

"You'll be lucky if my parents don't see you jump off the roof. Go!"

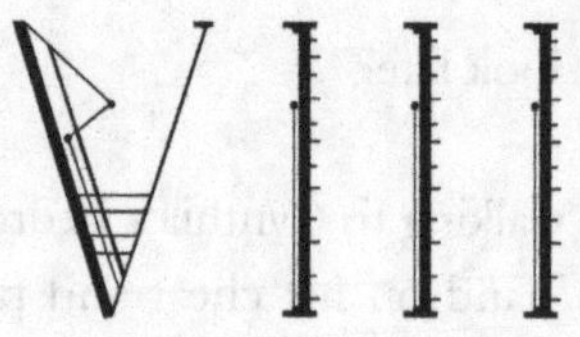

VIII

THE CHURCH'S OPPRESSION AND THE FREEDOM OF ROCK AND ROLL

A Sentinel has a halo that appears as a flame over the angel's head. The halo allows Sentinels to both understand and speak languages foreign to them. A Sentinel's halo is also used as a last resort to save the life of the soul that they guard.
— *A History of Hierarchy*

NOVEMBER 15TH, 2106 A.D.
NORTHEAST FLORIDA
JAYREN OMANS

Jayren sulked into school Monday morning with his arm in a stiff, neon red cast and a navy blue sling. *This is the new and improved walk of shame*, he told himself.

His first class was Discerning Demons—a class about recognizing and dividing demons by class—but Jayren walked in the complete opposite direction just to get away. He had his own demons to battle this morning. After the bell rang and the corridors went silent, he wandered the halls aimlessly, pushed his new, fake glasses up into his hair, and browsed the paintings covering the walls. Most were high-and-mighty illustrations of Bible stories he couldn't care less about. Jayren stopped to look at a picture of Noah's Ark. It had stark colors and an ominous cloud hanging over the sky, and the animal faces reminded him of a Chinese art style. He decided that, of all the tales from the Bible, whether true or not, he liked that one the most.

He thought Cynthia was more interesting, though. At the same time, he very well knew she'd never talk to him again. Whatever her motive, it wasn't love, friendship, or interest. Jayren rolled his eyes. Knowing her and Corvun, it was probably some elaborate scheme to undermine their friendship.

A faint piano melody that twinkled in the distance distracted Jayren from his thoughts. The way it was played reminded Jayren of a dying star that refused to let darkness consume it. Jayren knew of only one person who played that way, and he wouldn't have mistaken it in a hundred years. *That* was Orion playing, so Jayren journeyed towards the star.

Beside the band room, there was another painting that made Jayren stop and hesitate. It was *La Belle Dame Sans Merci,* which he'd written a pretty lame essay on in his Art History class. Honestly, he just liked the knight's armor and sword and back then hadn't cared much for the pretty girl. That was back then. Now, he realized the woman looked faintly similar to Ophiah, and the thought made him blush. Something from his class came back to him—something about repeating themes in art and how repeating muses are thought to be angels born into different lives. Jayren wondered, if but for a moment, if he was looking at his own past life. He shook his head. Jayren tried to take his mind off girls as he peeked through the heavy, wooden double doors of the band room. He saw Orion sitting at the piano, his face pinched with the words he sang.

Jayren had never heard a more beautiful voice, *ever*.

Orion's lyrics begged for water, for time, and for a response from his skin and bones and the longing of his heart. Jayren felt everything Orion sang, foolishly and forcibly, like it was the first voice he'd heard after years of desolate wandering alone. Jayren stepped into the room, hypnotized by the way Orion coaxed the great, black beast of an instrument into singing such a passionate melody.

Orion stopped abruptly at the creak of the door. He turned and stared up at Jayren, starstruck. Orion's fingers stumbled and destroyed the melody with a crippled fall downward. He stood, and the piano bench fell flat on the floor with a loud *smack*.

"What are you doing?" Jayren asked.

"Not singing," Orion said.

Jayren took three brisk steps toward Orion. "No, why'd you stop?" He looked at the piano. "Holy hell, that was beautiful."

"Thanks," Orion forced the word.

"Your voice is beautiful."

Orion blinked; his bashful, humble reaction confused Jayren.

"Dude, like," Jayren's mouth gaped, "You're like better than Freddie Mercury!"

"Y-You can't tell anyone you found me here!" Orion's face flushed red.

"You idiot, you're supposed to say, 'Yeah bitch, I *know* I'm good.'"

"N-*No*," Orion sounded confused and almost as if he was about to argue with Jayren.

"What I mean is that music doesn't *sound that good* anymore. You're incredible. You know Brendon Urie? Or Andy Grammar? Or what's-his-face from Fall Out Boy. You kind of sound like them."

"Swear it," Orion snapped suddenly.

"Swear what?"

"Swear that you won't tell anyone you found me here."

"Sure, okay, I swear it," Jayren said. The two boys hesitated, then Jayren helped Orion set the piano bench back up. They sat together, and Jayren turned to Orion. "So do you know any good songs?"

Orion winced. "I think—I haven't had enough sleep. You know, I really oughta go, I mean—"

"Play something!" Jayren widened his eyes at the piano.

After a small pause, Orion started hammering his fingers again. Slow at first, steady but unsure, then faster. He was one and the same with the song, as if the song was the soul and he was the body it moved. Orion sang the lyrics, and Jayren slouched in awe; Orion's shoulders pinched as he sang the treble of the first verse. Jayren lip-synced the second half of the verse with Orion, too ashamed of his nasally voice to hear it next to Orion's. "Put your fingers there," Orion said and pointed. "Do you know the song?"

"Yeah," Jayren said.

Orion instructed chords to Jayren, and warily, Jayren tried with his one good hand. The keys pricked his fingertips like ice, uncomfortable, chiming with deep, resounding pangs in his chest. It was like language, like a second tongue he'd been born with. Jayren smiled, and Orion grinned stupidly. "You've never played before," Orion guessed.

Jayren shook his head.

"Don't you think that's crazy? You can understand it like it's English." Orion bounced his thumb and pinky on two notes higher on the white keys. He continued his passionate dance across the instrument, looking at Jayren all the while.

Jayren glared at the keys. "It's not that hard. Anyone could do it."

"Most people don't know the key names. Chords are even more difficult."

Jayren hit a wrong note on purpose.

Orion laughed and shoved him with his shoulder. "It reads like language, doesn't it?" He nodded at the piano score in front of them.

Jayren adjusted the fake glasses on the top of his hair to hold a few strands back. "I mean, it's the same idea. Symbols represent a segment of thought."

"I knew you were smarter than you advertise," Orion said. "Can you read it?"

"Yeah," Jayren said, quiet and nervous. They played a little longer. Jayren felt at ease for once, like he didn't have to have walls up around Orion. He wondered if Orion would consider being friends.

After a moment, Orion asked, "What happened to your arm?"

"I jumped out of Corvun's window."

Orion laughed.

"Don't laugh at me," Jayren said with a furrowed brow and his tongue jutted up into one of his molars. He needed to change the conversation before he thought too long on the night before, so he asked, "So you can talk to the instrument?"

Orion's laugh faded. He whispered quietly, as if the two of them were soldiers ducked in a war trench, "Uh, no…" His fingers curled against the white keys with a soft melody— ammunition for the battle ahead. Jayren recalled something Ophiah had said about music being a weapon. "But I can talk to Ophiah through it."

"Ophiah can understand your music?"

"Yeah. Think of it like braille or Morse code."

"Do you want to try with me?" Jayren asked.

Orion looked at him quizzically. "I guess technically…" His thought trailed off. "Do you believe in this stuff?"

Jayren hesitated then said, "Just play something. I'll close my eyes and listen."

Orion scoffed. He picked out a melody, sharp and snappy and upbeat. It was the kind of melody that made Jayren want to jump out of his seat and dance. The melody rising from Orion's right hand sounded like syllables in conversation, and Jayren began to hear Orion's voice within the tune. He asked Jayren if he'd ask Ophiah to the winter dance, then he told Jayren that he loved the way Ophiah looked at him. He said Ophiah looked at Jayren like he was her rescue at sea, an aircraft that spotted her SOS on a deserted island. Orion thanked him, and the melody became smooth and sweet. Orion offered Jayren his serving of ice cream from lunch in gratitude.

"I'm vegan, sorry," Jayren said.

Orion beamed at Jayren. "You're not human."

"You're right. I'm an alien."

Orion elbowed Jayren, and Jayren laughed. "Sentinels are fluid in language. Rules don't apply. Have the others told you about your halo?"

Jayren shook his head. It was a lie; he was tired of hearing about it from everyone all of a sudden though. He didn't want to talk anymore, but Orion's magnetic pull kept him sitting with his palm stuck flat beneath his leg and the other useless arm pressed against his hot chest. He tried to think about something else.

"Halos look like flames. Do you remember the chapel when we learned about how the Apostles had flames above their heads? They could speak in tongues. It's the same idea. You can speak to anyone, and they'll understand. Likewise, you can understand any language like you're being spoken to in English."

"Yeah, but why?"

"Guardian angels are protectors." Orion's smile poked shy dimples in his cheeks; the freckles on his face swirled like the night sky on a screen of a planetarium. "If you were in a warzone, you'd need to communicate to get people to safety."

"Yeah, but if I'm War, how does that make sense? I'm evil, right?"

"What does that make me?" Orion shrugged.

"Badass," Jayren said. Dismay shattered his mind again. He paused a moment longer, watching Orion play with the piano, striking down their boredom one note at a time. Then he asked, "Do you consider us friends?"

Orion took a moment to answer then said, "Yeah, I think so."

"People should really look past the rumors," Jayren said, waving a hand halfheartedly. "The abuse thing and your lame ass dad, too. They're missing out. You're fun to be around. Like, you're a Class A cool kid."

"You're pretty cool, too," Orion said. "It's easier to see, now that you don't wear glasses."

"Rude," Jayren said.

Orion bit back a laugh. "I have glasses too. I just wear contacts," he said. "Do you want to sit together in Latin? You're in my class, right?"

Jayren nodded. "Yeah, sure."

ORION JUDE

"I have to go be blessed by the angels later," Orion told Jayren as they walked to Latin. He liked Jayren's company. The demons stayed quiet when Jayren stood nearby. Orion wondered if it was the same for Jayren. Surely, after having been enrolled in a school full of angels, Jayren would connect the dots—that the voices they both heard were the whispers of demons. Orion didn't understand why Jayren had such a hard time believing what was right in front of him.

"You what?" Jayren asked.

"The Archangels and all the other angels do this thing," Orion said. "Professor North leads a private sermon and prays over me and Ophiah."

"That's kinda prejudiced."

Orion stuck his folded piano score in the side of his lip while he buttoned his suit vest. He would've left it unbuttoned—the top two of his button-down as well—if it had been up to him. He felt less trapped and contained and *controlled* by the angels and their stupid rules that way. He kept his thoughts locked up though, as he had been taught to. He took the score from his mouth and ran his fingers along the crease. "I have demon blood," Orion said simply. He didn't look at Jayren.

"*You're* not the problem," Jayren said.

"You have no idea," Orion said.

"What does that mean? What have *you* ever done to anybody?" Jayren walked backwards in front of Orion. "You're beautiful, you always dress perfect, and you're talented. How can anybody call you a problem?"

"One time I lost control in art class. I—" Orion's voice tunneled back into his chest, a rabbit burrowing deep underground to hide from a wolf. "I turned all the paint in the room black. It was an accident. They suspended me for a week. When I got back, they'd removed me from art class. I'm in another study hall now."

A small crease formed between Jayren's eyebrows. "That was you? They said it was a prank."

Orion gave a wry half-smile-half-frown and nodded. "That was a cover-up story. The Archangels have this ability to change common knowledge. They do it all the time, and they've done it with past wars and events in history. In this case, they just want to keep what I've done under tight lip."

"Well," Jayren said. "They're wrong to do it."

Orion didn't disagree, but he didn't agree either. Part of him didn't mind that the Archangels covered some of his tracks. Some of his mistakes were better left unnoticed. He walked silently with Jayren for a moment.

"So, you're an artist?" Jayren asked.

"Kinda," Orion said. "I just doodle."

"What other things do you like to do?"

"I think I'd like to garden," Orion said.

"You think?" Jayren asked.

"I don't really have hobbies because I'm not allowed."

Jayren's jaw clenched, and for what seemed like the first time ever, he hesitated before he spoke. He motioned to the score in Orion's hands. "Is music a hobby for you?"

"No. It's more like studying a second language." The two boys approached their Latin classroom, and Orion held the door for Jayren. He kept his eyes on the mahogany hardwood floor, praying to be invisible. But he knew by the hush that fell over the class that everyone had stopped to look at Jayren and himself.

Jayren puffed an annoyed breath and snapped, "Y'all are supposed to be doing homework y'all *didn't do* last night. Stop staring."

Orion envied his careless confidence.

The bell rung as Jayren swore crudely at the staring students, and Orion exhaled in sheer gratefulness to the timing. He grabbed Jayren's backpack and pushed him towards the back of the class. They slung themselves into desk chairs as the professor clacked to the front of the room.

The professor scratched some precise white marks onto the chalkboard, deliberate and sharp. She instructed the students to find a partner through thin, prune-purple lips. "You will present at the end of class," she said with a voice as dry as the chalk she wrote with. She turned and finished writing the assignment.

"So do you know Latin?" Jayren asked.

"Yeah," Orion said. "You?"

"No, I usually sleep in this class."

"How do you pass?"

"I'm not, currently."

"I'll help you. Here," Orion said. "Do you know how to say 'I want to be friends with you'?"

"Nah."

"Try."

Jayren sighed. He paused, then the clunky words tumbled off his tongue in an awkward cadence.

"Close. Try again." Orion lowered his voice. "Don't think about it. Do like you did with the piano. It's just like speaking English." Orion swung his feet around to face Jayren, and he noticed uneasiness threatening Jayren's pupils. They narrowed, widened, then narrowed again.

Jayren held Orion's eyes regardless. "Okay."

Orion listened to Jayren speak slow and steady, calm but a little wary. He noticed the bob in Jayren's throat. Orion's heart began to race when he could understand Jayren's fluid Latin like it was English. In the corner of the room, the professor stilled, shuffling papers stopped, and their classmates paused what they were doing to watch the nerd anomaly.

Jayren stopped talking and looked around. His eyes darted about, and beads of sweat formed on his neck. He shielded his face with his hand and whispered, "What the hell, Rian?"

The professor stood and stared as if she'd seen a miracle. She snatched her desk phone up and dialed with woodpecker fingers. "I'd like to speak with Professor North, please."

Jayren groaned and closed his eyes.

VALENTINE NORTH

"At what point will you fear them?" Remington asked. His voice hissed like sandpaper against wood, sawing to clean and buffer the material. Despite being the Virtue of Patience, Remington paced the floor of Valentine's office. Valentine knew Remington had always considered his mind to be his greatest asset, his greatest weapon—whittling and sifting through details for days before reaching a conclusion—and he had seen the obvious signs. The Four Horsemen were forming their initial bond and growing closer to their calling. Between Corvun's initiation to RUST, Venatrix's blatant disobedience, the twins' growing restlessness, and now the Sentinel boy's oncoming change, it would happen soon.

Valentine North sat in his chair, facing the window. He did not turn. He stared out at the gray, metal city.

"They know what they are now! They have figured it out. You know this. I know this. All of us do, Val, please. If you do not make an alliance with them, they will destroy you!"

"They are still just kids," Valentine said. It was the same line he'd said for years as he watched them learn to walk, then to run, then to fight and defy their parents. Until now.

Valentine saw it in his mind's eye. He remembered visiting Michael over dinner and watching Corvun chase Venatrix down the sidewalk, both four-foot-tall children twinkling with giddy laughter. He recalled holding the twins upon their birth and being filled with the same joy he had holding children of his own—watching Orion's eyes open through tacky tears and hearing his small, tender cry for his mother. Valentine remembered how he administered Mrs. Jude a Holy Water nose spray for the twins when their sneezes spurted bouts of flames. Valentine knew that no matter how much bitterness and resentment Jayren had in his heart towards him, Valentine would still never regret the flight he took to the Midwest to meet the children. Angels had whispered about their parents, and rumors had carried over state lines. The sight of a red-eyed Jayren sitting beside his sister on the concrete step of the back porch was one he wouldn't forget. Even though Valentine had offered (open-ended) to speak with Jayren about his father's suicide, Jayren never took the offer, and Valentine expected he never would. And each time Valentine confronted Corvun over the years, he could see nothing but a child in his eyes. He refused to see past the young man's hurt and accept that he was growing into the leader he needed to be.

Remington continued, "They are becoming powerful, Valor. You would be a fool to let them continue on their reckless path."

Perhaps it was his friend's use of his God-given name, Valor, which made him suddenly feel small and not in control. Valentine had always valued Remington's counsel, but hesitation nagged at his mind today. "They cannot be tamed," Valentine said. "Whatever I do—whatever you or the others do—they will rebel. They were born with rebellion in their blood. There's no stopping them. They are a fire that must burn its course."

"They were soldiers before, trained in stature and righteousness. They have none of that now! They will become savages," Remington said. "We must intervene, put them into training under our own ranks."

Valentine turned to his friend, using his God-given name in return. "Remiel, believe me when I say I have faith in them. What if we drive them away by doing that? I have to trust this hand that's been dealt is the way they will come together, the way they find their calling."

The young, brown-haired general squared his shoulders. His styled hair came loose, and Valentine noticed the coffee stain on the general's sleeve.

"Patience, my friend," Valentine said. "Remember your virtue. I want Armageddon as much as you and all the rest. They will win this war. The end is near. Have faith. The five of them will bring Armageddon for us."

OPHIAH JUDE

Ophiah and Orion lingered at the back of the chapel. They waited, as commanded, to approach the presence of God *only* with an angel at their side. Ophiah wondered if she and her brother would be condemned further if they didn't. She wondered too: mustn't it take audacity to approach God, no matter who you were—angel or demon or human? She had it in her, she thought, that audacity. She wanted to approach God on her own. Ophiah noticed Casper and Cassie North walking towards them. Her stomach flipped uneasily, and she suddenly found interest in fixing Orion's tie. Orion watched her, a question in his eyes.

She needed coverage, a story to hide her getaway with Jayren. Casper—as her betrothed—would never approve the solace she sought in Jayren and the blind acceptance he offered her back. Ophiah whispered to Orion in Latin, "You and I went shopping on Thursday, okay?" The Latin Ophiah and Orion used with each other was bent with a slight demon dialect. Most of the angels spoke Latin, so it was her way to communicate uniquely with Orion. Some sinister part of her loved the tantalizing challenge she hung before everyone. They recognized the language but could not decipher it.

"Okay," Orion responded in kind.

"Orion, Ophiah," Casper greeted the twins. Cassie smiled beside him. Casper's voice was too pretty, his smile sinister in a way she didn't know how to discern. His blue eyes were the most sought-after blue, but they dulled in comparison to Jayren's lively, light green. Ophiah found herself comparing the similarities and differences from her soon-to-be husband and her runaway romance: Casper's blond hair was yellow like hay. He reminded her of the cherubim that decorated sky-high ceilings, with privates only covered by a fine, white cloth, and coy smiles painted on their faces. Jayren would be considered sacrilegious beside Casper, with blond hair paling from a lack of sunlight and the savage hiss on his thin lips. But only Jayren had a set of eyes she'd ever felt safe in—not judged, not cursed, not condemned, not half-demon, and not as evil as she believed herself to be.

Casper took Ophiah's left hand and kissed her ring finger.

Ophiah looked away—unintentionally meeting Cassie's gaze, then quickly looking at the ground. Sometimes Ophiah wondered if Cassie approved of her betrothal, but she was never brave enough to speak to Cassie. A dark corner in Ophiah's mind wondered if Cassie was even real or if she was simply a figment of her imagination, something she created to distract herself from how much she loathed Casper's presence.

"Where were you on Thursday? I waited for you," Casper said.

Ophiah's words bailed before they reached her tongue.

"I took her shopping," Orion said. His voice was tight, but it was a good lie. A sin. Together, they fabricated the sin. "We needed new formal attire."

Casper raised an eyebrow at Ophiah, gave a curt nod to Orion. "Let's go sit down, shall we?"

Ophiah wanted to walk beside Orion, but Casper laced his arm around her waist and rested his hand on her side. She stared ahead numbly, up to the pulpit. That was where Valentine North, the father of Casper and Cassie, would soon stand and call Ophiah and Orion up to be prayed over in front of the angels appointed as teachers and professors and assistants at the North Academy.

They filed one by one into the pew. Ophiah sat stiffly next to Casper, and Orion sat to her left. Cassie sat out of sight.

"Are you alright?" Casper asked.

Ophiah closed her eyes. Her stomach tied in a hunter's knot. She tried to focus on Jayren, on the memory of his childlike gawk and the way his eyes lit up and the small black slits in the center. She focused on the thought of his eyes.

Casper turned, put his hand on her showing leg.

Ophiah's heart jolted, and she felt Orion tense beside her. She didn't fight when Casper turned her body to him, when his hand edged up her leg and his fingers poked underneath her skirt. She'd made a scene over his advances before, and Casper had blamed her for being "tempting" and "a seductress." She hadn't been allowed to wear a skirt higher than her ankles for six months. The skirt she wore today was short enough to take the same accusation as before, so she decided not to make a scene.

Casper's mouth whispered a conversation near hers, but she couldn't make out words at all.

Demons spoke to her instead, grueling and trudging up through her barrier of constant prayer. They told her to kill Casper with her bare hands, but she folded her hands in her lap instead. She did nothing, remained still, eyes closed and holding her breath.

Casper pressed a kiss against her mouth.

With his lips on hers, she tried to convince herself that because everyone else told her this was what was best for her—that being betrothed to an Archangel heir would spare her soul from damnation—she should follow blindly. She told herself she should marry Casper—moreover, that she loved Casper—because it was simply the right thing to do. The *righteous* thing to do.

She didn't kiss him back.

"Hey," Orion said. He smacked Casper's hand off Ophiah's leg as it crept higher. "Piss off."

"Language, brother," Casper said.

In the back of her mind, Ophiah stared into Jayren's eyes. His pale, blond image slowly merged into the snake that had kept her company all her life. The snake stared at her, coiling and swirling. His movement calmed her; it was as if it were a greeting for an old friend. He didn't bare his fangs, only flicked his tongue in gentle conversation. She could understand what he said. He asked her if she wanted to go on another lunch date—subs with salt and vinegar chips and lemon soda.

"Stop touching her like that," Orion said. "Can't you see she's uncomfortable?"

Ophiah opened her eyes. She looked at the navy blue Bible tucked into the back of the pew before them. The gold-embellished title was worn away from heavy use and dirty hands. Dread set thick on Ophiah's soul. She wanted to rest her head on her brother's shoulder, but Valentine North was making his way to the stage. Valentine spoke into the microphone when he got there, loud and clear, reciting a small sermon. Near the end, he spoke of angels and demons and the prophecies surrounding them. He mentioned their calling as angels, then he said, "Join me in praying a blessing over our dear children."

Like countless times before, Ophiah and Orion rose, following the unspoken order to enter a room to the side of the stage and change into their white robes. The musky, mildew scent of the fabric hurt Ophiah's head and made her feel dirty. She followed Orion out onto the stage. She felt naked and violated, like a charm on display, as if she were just another thing the angels could use to make them feel better about themselves.

Ophiah stared out into the crowd with some sort of angry, hurting and defiance itching on her skin. She was a spectacle in front of these people, a freak. Orion took her hand and squeezed; she squeezed his hand weakly. Ophiah noticed Corvun in the back of the crowd. He sat, away from his parents, watching Ophiah and Orion fervently. Orion had recently told her that he liked Corvun, that Corvun was a nice person and that his death glare was just for show. Ophiah didn't believe it; Corvun looked like a raven waiting for them to die so he could swoop in and feast on their corpses.

Corvun lifted his phone to his ear, lips moving.

"These children are born of demon blood," Valentine said.

Ophiah wanted to cry. *Not in front of these people,* she told herself.

"We are born of angel blood, too," Orion said. His voice belted through the chapel, brash and bright like the hammering of piano keys. He needed no microphone to be just as loud—or louder—than Valentine North. "We are just as good as we are bad, but tell me why you choose to only see the bad," Orion demanded of the audience.

A tear slipped from Ophiah's eye.

Orion turned to Valentine. "Do you fear us?"

Valentine watched Orion, his lips pressed thin. Murmurs ran through the crowd. Corvun's hand lowered momentarily, his jaw slackened. He raised his phone back up and spoke quicker.

Orion continued, "Did you betroth my sister to your son to tame her?"

"She's to be married to secure her future for the Lord."

Corvun stood and walked out of the chapel.

"And me? No betrothal?" Orion asked.

"You're to walk a different path," Valentine replied.

"The wide path?" Orion challenged.

"No," Valentine said, "but a path more difficult to walk than the narrow path."

Orion's jaw tightened. "C'mon, Ophi."

Ophiah hesitated, but Orion tugged her down the stage steps in a hurry. They were the same steps where she bruised her knees praying so many times before, begging for an escape, a remedy for what she was. She broke into a run beside Orion. The change of scenery and temperature happened too quickly to register. Smears of color flashed past her and black shadows twirled in her peripheral vision. She hoped she was the only one who could see the black following them, that the rest of the church was oblivious to it. Ophiah didn't know where Orion planned to go, but she listened when he shouted, "Don't look back!"

Orion's pickup truck idled noisily across the parking lot. Jayren rolled the window down, popped his head out, and yelled. "C'mon! Hurry!" Beside Jayren, Venatrix sat gripping the steering wheel and staring past Orion and Ophiah anxiously.

Corvun stood in the truck bed, and he offered a hand to Ophiah. "Orion, help me out."

Ophiah took Corvun's forearm, Orion lifted her by the waist, and they heaved her up into the truck bed. Ophiah collapsed onto a mix of blankets of all ages. Her blood and eyes burned with adrenaline and sunlight; she panted, not quite able to make up for her lost breath.

Corvun hauled Orion up into the truck with them. He shouted, "Go!" then lost his balance and fell beside Orion as Venatrix screeched out of the parking lot.

Jayren pulled the back window open with a loud squeak. A rhythmic guitar bounced and twanged distantly on the radio. Jayren raised his right arm—which was wrapped in a bright red cast—in a thumbs-up to Corvun and Orion. His eyes flashed between the three. "Y'all good?"

Orion and Corvun both gave weak thumbs-ups in return.

Jayren winked at Ophiah, and she relaxed into the old, family heirloom quilts. Her heart still raced from the rush.

ORION JUDE

Orion's truck squeaked and bounced over the gravel road of the lost state park. Orion's hair was still wild from the fast ride over; his skin was tacky with the humidity of the sea breeze. He relaxed against the side of the bed as they drove onto grassy ground. He'd been so caught up in the escape that he didn't realize until then that his friends had essentially stolen his car. He opened his mouth, hesitated, then said, "How'd you—"

"Start your car?" Jayren asked, finishing Orion's question. (Orion figured he'd been waiting for the question for much longer than it took Orion to think about it.) Jayren turned his whole body around in the front seat. "Trixie picked the lock and hotwired it. She's a badass, dude. Even Corvun didn't know she could do that."

"I knew she could do it," Corvun said. His eyes were closed and he was smiling. "I was the one who taught her how. I just encouraged her by tellin' her I didn't think she could *still* do it."

Venatrix flipped Corvun off over her shoulder.

Corvun laughed.

"I like your truck, Rian," Venatrix said. "It's a pretty color."

"It's literally a rust bucket," Jayren said.

Venatrix pulled into a small spot between some trees and shut the engine off. "Crawl through the window," she snapped at Jayren.

"*You* crawl through the window," Jayren said.

"No, you'll look at my butt."

"Bet you want to look at *my* butt," Jayren said. "Don't deny it."

"Jayren," Corvun said, "Come on."

Jayren rolled his eyes and climbed through the back window of the truck; Venatrix followed suit.

"You could've just used the door," Ophiah said.

Jayren's head swiveled in Ophiah's direction like a compass needle pointing north. He watched her with careful, flashing yellow eyes, and he smiled wide and genuine. "Yeah, but that isn't fun. Clearly you don't know what *fun* is."

"Sure I do," Ophiah said. She bit the insides of her lips and smiled back at him. "It's riding a motorcycle with you, blindfolded."

"That wasn't fun," Jayren said. He looked around mischievously. "*Fun* is truth or dare in the middle of a forest with your friends."

"No," Corvun and Venatrix yapped.

"Okay," Orion said.

"Let's do it," Ophiah said.

"Majority wins," Jayren said with a grin.

Venatrix sighed and said, "Real quick, if you two want to change, I brought some spare clothes for you." She reached back into the front seat.

Orion glanced at the tight jeans she wore, and his heart rose in his chest.

"Rian's looking at your butt," Jayren said. "He thinks you have a nice ass."

Orion looked away, flushed. "Dude, shut up." He shoved Jayren, and Jayren laughed.

Venatrix ignored both of them. She turned around with a pile of folded clothes and glared at Jayren. She passed a small stack to Ophiah then one to Orion. "We can hold up the covers so Orion and Ophiah can change with some *privacy*."

Jayren muttered something under his breath then helped Ophiah up. He didn't look at her as he raised a cover.

Venatrix, Corvun, and Orion did the same. "Do not drop the cover, Jayren," Venatrix said.

"Or what? You'll give me a wedgie?"

"No," Venatrix said. "You'll have to answer to Rian, and he probably gives better wedgies than I do."

Jayren's eyes flickered in Orion's direction warily. "Fine, yeah, I get it."

Orion watched Jayren for any sudden movements of his hands. He wouldn't hesitate to give Jayren a wedgie if he dropped the cover on his sister, that was for sure.

"I brought you one of my jumpers," Venatrix said. "It might be kinda short, but it adjusts at the top and the waist and ankles." A pause. Ophiah dropped her white robe on the bed of the truck, and Venatrix asked, "Do you like the color?"

"Yeah," Ophiah said softly. "You can take the covers down." They lowered the covers. The jumper embellished Ophiah like the petals of a spring flower, the color of a hundred fresh lilacs. It was the prettiest thing Orion had ever seen her wear. Ophiah gave Venatrix a tight hug and whispered, "Thank you."

Venatrix's face paled. It was the first time Orion had ever seen her at a loss for words.

VENATRIX CANES

"Your turn," Venatrix said as she turned to Orion. She caught him looking at her, and it was hard to hold his steady gaze. She cleared her throat and handed him a pair of her brother's nicest jeans and a tee. "You can keep these. They'd look better on you, anyway."

Orion smiled.

Venatrix lifted the blankets with the others again, but she didn't raise them high enough to cover Orion's gaze. His eyes smiled over the top at her.

"Your face is red, Trixie."

"I'm gonna cut your tongue out, Jayren," Venatrix said.

"Okay," Orion said after he dressed. They lowered the covers, and Orion hugged Venatrix as tightly as Ophiah had. His strong arms squeezed the breath right out of her lungs, and she didn't want it back. His lips pressed against the top of her head, and she fought a quiet gasp.

"And here, North implied the twins aren't tame," Corvun said with a smirk. He quirked an eyebrow at Jayren, who snickered.

"Bet Trixie's an undercover dominatrix. She could tame anyone."

Venatrix opened her eyes and glared at Jayren. Orion released Venatrix, and they all sat in a circle in the truck bed.

"First truth or dare," Ophiah said suddenly. "Is it true? Are we the Four Horsemen? Or is it Five?"

Corvun covered his face and pulled his hand down to his chin. "If you believe the Bible, then yes. True."

"I've never heard of the Five Horsemen," Jayren argued.

"I asked Michael about it," Corvun looked around. "In Revelation, it's mentioned that Hades followed close behind Death," he said, his eyes settling on Ophiah. "Hades is the Fifth Horseman, who brings the final destruction."

Venatrix watched Ophiah's eyes water; she blinked it away, a skill she'd clearly practiced for years. Venatrix glanced around to see if anyone else noticed only to find Jayren's eyes fixed on her, too. Jayren spoke up to draw the attention away from her. "Trixie! Truth or dare!" Jayren belted.

"Truth," she said with an upward tip of her chin.

"Are you a virgin?"

"If you don't stop, I'm going to choke you with your own shoelaces," Venatrix said. She grabbed his shoe and yanked at one of his laces.

"*Yes, daddy,*" Jayren said. He thrashed his foot to get away.

"If I answer, you answer the same thing."

"Fine."

"*Fine.* Yes. And you?"

"Of course not," Jayren said.

Corvun leaned over to Venatrix and whispered, "He lost it to Cynthia." There was an edge to Corvun's voice. "Saturday morning. He broke his arm jumping out of her window."

Venatrix dropped Jayren's foot and gaped at him. Her lower lip tucked over her bottom teeth in a cheeky grin. It was the best gossip she'd heard all year.

"Enough with the dumbass questions," Jayren said.

"Truth or dare, Rian," Corvun said. He seemed just as eager to move on.

"Truth."

"Have you ever had alcohol?" Corvun asked.

"No," Orion said.

"Ophiah?"

She shook her head.

"Do you guys want to try some?" Corvun asked. He uncovered a bottle of black spiced rum from beside him.

"*Dude*," Jayren said. Shock widened his eyes.

Venatrix backhanded Corvun's arm. Bringing alcohol to an underage group was something she expected of her brothers, not Corvun. "*What* were you thinking?"

"Drinking is a sin," Orion said quickly. "So no, count me out of that. No thanks."

"Drinking isn't a sin," Ophiah said. She glanced at Venatrix. "The Bible says to be of sober mind."

"Yeah, y'all are about to get wasted on that," Jayren ran a hand through his hair.

Corvun lifted a shot glass. "No one will get drunk on one shot."

"Are you out of your mind?" Venatrix asked.

"Loosen up," Corvun told her quietly. "If you'd been in that chapel, I think you'd justify it too. And if it makes you feel better, I won't have any. Designated driver." He pointed at himself.

"I'll do it," Ophiah said.

"Hot." Jayren's snake-like pupils dilated into eager, human eyes.

Venatrix kicked his leg.

"Ow!"

Corvun broke the seal of the rum and poured Ophiah a shot. He passed her the glass.

Ophiah drank the small glass and passed it back.

"Fine," Venatrix said. "Pour me one." She was tired of being totally sober. Maybe a touch of alcohol would take the edge off her nerves and make Jayren a hair less annoying. Corvun passed the same glass to Venatrix, and she threw the shot back, wincing as she swallowed. The smooth burn made her eyes water. In a distant haze, she realized Orion was doing the same. She wondered if it was the same reason for him as it had been for her. Did the peer pressure get to him, too?

"Jayren?" Corvun asked.

"Pass."

"You're no fun," Ophiah said sweetly. She licked the rum from her lips.

"You're *wrong*," Jayren said. "Give me one."

Ophiah laughed.

Jayren leaned back and held the side of the truck as he took his shot. He handed Corvun the shot glass two feet right of his hand. Corvun chuckled, and Jayren threw the glass at Corvun's leg. "Alright, Ophiah," Jayren slurred. He pronounced her name like a British 'fire,' and she blushed. "Truth or dare."

"Dare," she said.

"Yeah, we all know what he's about to say." Venatrix puckered her lips.

Jayren stuck his tongue out at Venatrix and threw a blanket over her head. "I dare you to tell the truth."

"*Lameee,*" Orion booed.

"Do you like us? Enough to call us friends?" Jayren asked Ophiah.

Ophiah didn't shy under the attention of all the eyes on her like Venatrix expected. Instead, she glanced around and found her way back to Jayren's eyes. "Yeah, I do."

"Jayren." Corvun set the shot glass and rum aside. "Truth or dare."

"Dare, obviously."

"We all know you like her," Corvun said. "I dare you to kiss her. But," he paused, "don't get nervous and puke like you do."

The others giggled.

"What's the forfeit?"

"Kiss Rian," Venatrix said.

"I hate you," Jayren told Venatrix. "Pass on both."

"Chicken," Venatrix nagged.

"I'm not a *chicken*. She has a boyfriend. And while I can be generally careless, I'm not really looking to pick a fight with Mr. North," Jayren snapped, feigning confidence. He rubbed his neck, giving away the edge on his nerves.

"I hate him," Ophiah said suddenly. "Like, really hate him. He—Casper—he makes me sick. You'd be doing me a favor."

"Let's run away," Venatrix blurted. She was surprised by her own words, but they kept tumbling from her lips. "All of us, right now. It would fix everything." Silence followed her, and she looked to Corvun, begging him.

"It's not that easy," Corvun whispered through the quiet.

"Isn't it? Orion and Ophiah wouldn't have to deal with abuse. You wouldn't have to deal with your lame dad." Venatrix looked at Jayren. "*You'd* never feel different or alone. None of us would."

"Venatrix," Corvun said.

"Corvun, Michael bargained your *life!* And they treat Orion and Ophiah like animals! It's not fair!"

"Venatrix, stop," Corvun said firmer. "You know Mr. Jude would come after Orion and Ophiah, and I can't—" his voice turned breathy and weak. "Wherever we go, they're goin' to find us. Someone will find us and take us back home."

"*This* is home," she insisted. "Not where we sleep, or where we eat. *This* right *here* is home."

"I think I speak for all of us when I say we want to run away, too, Vena, but we can't. We have to stay, and we have to tough it out. There's a reason we're here, together. At least..." Corvun paused, "At least we don't have to go through these things alone."

Venatrix's blood pumped hard in her head, and her throat grew tight. She didn't know what else to say; she knew Corvun was right, but she was right, too. They were treated different, alienated, outcasts. She sat in silence, defeated.

"Do you think it ever gets better?" Jayren asked quietly.

"Yeah," Orion seconded the question.

Corvun didn't answer. He looked down at his hands in his lap, and he pulled his sleeve up to reveal the compass brand to the others. "No," he said finally, "but I wish it would."

CORVUN KHLYDE

There was nothing Corvun wanted more than to drop his life and run away with the other four. He saw the same look in their eyes—the fire in Venatrix's, the hollowness in Jayren's, the hope in Orion and Ophiah's. He'd sworn to himself— after coming face to face with Cephan and waking from death—that he'd protect the others by any and all means. He'd heard demons approaching ten minutes prior, and he also knew if they ran now, they'd be followed and slaughtered. They wouldn't make it to the next town.

A branch snapped in the distance.

The other four turned to look, but Corvun already had his sights locked on the spot.

"What was that?" Jayren asked in a squeak of a voice. "Did the police follow us?"

"No," Corvun said. He pulled his gun from the holster in his pants. He leaned over the edge of the truck bed and lined up the sights. "Vena, wrap the white robes around that wrench and light it on fire." He threw a lighter on the covers beside her.

Venatrix followed his instruction. The lighter flicked open with a metallic *clink*, and with a strike to the flint, the holy white robes caught fire as if they'd been drenched in gasoline. Venatrix stood behind Corvun, and the others shied behind her.

The fire doused the forest with bright light.

A black hand with long, twisting fingers recoiled from the trunk of a tree.

"Get away from the edges," Corvun ordered as he stood.

As soon as the words left his mouth, a demon clamped its hands around the side of the truck, bending the metal like rubber. It roared, loud and clattering like a runaway train or a highway car crash. The demon's eyeless face molted with restless, swirling tar that changed its shape constantly. It bared bone-white teeth. Tar dripped onto one of the blankets, searing a hole right through the light, creamsicle orange and pink fabric.

Corvun shot the demon in the head. It flung to the side, only to whip back and snarl with a wider mouth, a pit of Hellfire burning deep in its throat. Corvun fired three more rounds into the demon's molting skull. The demon vanished into a whisk of shadows, seeping down into the grass. Corvun couldn't keep breath in his lungs.

A second demon leapt from the forest and caught Orion's leg with a black talon. The talon disappeared deep into Orion's leg and dragged Orion to the edge of the truck bed. Orion screamed out in pain, only to be cut short when the demon wrapped shadowy fingers around Orion's neck. It lifted Orion.

Corvun fired his remaining bullets at the demon. It screeched—a high-pitched tone like fumes nearing explosion—and let go of Orion.

Orion winced at the skull-shattering sound.

"Ophiah, take the torch! Venatrix, get us the fuck out of here," Corvun shouted. His voice was raw and terrified. He released his magazine and reloaded the gun with his spare. Behind him, the truck door slammed. The truck engine revved to life, and Corvun dropped to his knees.

Venatrix spun the truck to face the exit.

Corvun watched the outskirts of the forest.

"There's one at the exit!" Venatrix screamed.

"Go!" Jayren screamed back. "Run him over! Fucking hell! Go, go, go!"

Orion moaned loudly.

Panicked, Corvun looked to Orion. "He's goin' to attract more of them," he told Jayren and Ophiah. He kicked the bottle of rum to Jayren and tossed him his switchblade. "Cauterize the wound. The church prayed over the robes. That fire will heal him."

"I don't know how to do that!" Jayren was hysterical. "I've only done it in video games!"

"It can't be much different," Ophiah said, panting. "I'll help you." She handed Jayren the torch and rolled Orion's jeans up.

"Hold on to something!" Venatrix called from the front.

The truck sped up and jolted. Glass cracked. A body tumbled over the top of the truck; Corvun aimed overhead as the demon toppled over them. He fired three times, and the demon vanished before it hit the ground. Corvun let out a small breath.

Orion cried out again.

"Hold him still," Ophiah told Jayren and Corvun.

"You've got this, man," Jayren said to Orion. He offered Orion a corner of a blanket to bite on.

"Take the old highway," Corvun called to Venatrix. "Go to the island."

"That's the longer route!"

"Trust me! I know a place!" Corvun struggled to hold onto Orion's arm and hold him still. Orion's yelling turned savage, as if the same type of kindling bomb inside the demons was inside Orion, too. Corvun watched three demons lunge after the truck as they spun out of the forest. "Pedal to the metal, Vena! Hurry!"

The tires ripped across concrete.

CARINA BLACKROCK

"Is that them?" Carina whispered to Corvun. They stood in the corner of the Angels' Diner by the bar, close enough that they could speak to one another without being heard.

"Yeah. Do you want to meet them?" he asked her.

The strangers who'd collapsed on the floor of Joshuah's Sanctuary had already tied anchors to Carina's heart. She felt herself sink beside them, falling too deeply, too recklessly, too *needlessly* in love with them. *You do not even know them*, she reminded herself.

Carina studied the group. A black haired girl stood to the side, rubbing sweat off her palms on her worn tee. Her eyes were glued to a set of redhead twins. The wounded twin laid on the floor, chest panting. The other twin sat on her knees beside her brother. Beside her, a lanky blond boy sat cross-legged, staring wide-eyed and horror-struck at the wrapped wound on the twin's thigh. Carina's eyes lingered on the wound, on the twins. She could smell the demon-inflicted wound; she could smell the twins' heritage, too—the ash-burn scent in their blood, a telltale sign of demon blood. There was something stronger in the twins, too, a sort of power she'd only felt around Empress Amy and Avon. "They would fear me," Carina concluded. She stole a quick glance at Corvun's right wrist, and he crossed his arms to hide it.

Corvun raised his eyebrows expectantly.

"I slaughtered a whole race of demons. Do you think the son and daughter of a demon will take that lightly?" she asked.

"They're good people. They're not their father," Corvun said. "Trust me on this one."

"Is their father a Deceiver?" she asked. She wanted to know if her hunch was right.

"Yes," Corvun said.

Carina looked to the snake-eyed boy. He lent Joshuah his good hand as Joshuah began tending to the twin brother's wound. His other arm was wrapped in a bright red cast, and the stark color of it drew her focus off the dwindling flame above his head. "And the guardian angel? His halo is dim."

"Yeah, he's," Corvun paused, breathed, "he's strugglin'. That's Jayren."

Carina looked to the black-haired girl again.

"I grew up friends with her. Venatrix." Corvun nodded in her direction. "The twins are Orion and Ophiah. The son and daughter of Kindness," Corvun said.

"Who is their father?"

Corvun paused. "Sorrow."

Carina looked back to Corvun, confused. "Do you see good in everyone?" she asked sharply. "They have demon blood, which means they were created to do the Devil's bidding."

A muscle in Corvun's jaw tightened. "Angels have the same ability to sin, to fall, and to do the *Devil's biddin'*. It's not who they are that condemns them, or anyone else. It's the choice that matters. They get to choose whether they're good or evil. Don't you think that would make them more respectable? To have a bigger obstacle to overcome and to still uphold righteousness better than the church?" Corvun asked. His hard eyes held her captive, laid a trap right before her, and waited for her to walk in.

Carina didn't speak again.

CORVUN KHLYDE

Corvun walked away from Carina, still seething. He understood Venatrix's frustration now; he'd never faced the prejudice the twins suffered until today. He tried to focus on something else, to clear his mind. He helped Joshuah lift Orion back onto his feet.

Orion gazed at Corvun, despite the heavy bags beneath his eyes. There was a fire inside him now, a match struck for adrenaline, like the first firework on a sticky summer night. He'd always crave more. That much, Corvun was sure of.

"Thanks," Orion said, breathless.

Corvun shook his head. "Don't be stupid."

"That was the most fun I've—"

"Stop," Corvun said. He and Joshuah sat Orion on the piano bench on the bar stage. "It's not happenin' ever again.

Like ever. Okay? It was too dangerous. I know better than to be out after dark. I just didn't think…"

Orion's smile was crooked, untamed and insatiable. His hair perched in a ratty tangle on the left side of his head, just above the beaded sweat on his brow. "Thank you," Orion said again, more confident. "I feel more alive than I've ever felt at those damned ceremonies."

Corvun gritted his teeth. He took his blazer off and wiped the sweat from Orion's face. He tried to brush out the knot in Orion's hair with his fingers before realizing Jayren watched him a little to the left with squinty eyes. Corvun stood up straight and fixed a hard glare on Orion. "If I had left you at that *damned ceremony*, those demons wouldn't have been able to track your scent. The prayers and Marks, they *do* somethin' you know. I should have left you there."

Orion gazed at Corvun, dumbstruck. "Then why did you break us out?"

Corvun folded his blazer. Out of the corner of his eye, he noticed Venatrix sucking hard on two fingers—her cheeks caved and her eyes rolled back—and Jayren snickering beside her. Corvun looked back to Orion to find his face and neck beet-red. "It was their idea," Corvun said with a tinge of disappointment in his voice.

"The church doesn't like us," Ophiah said from where she sat, prim and proper, on a barstool by the counter, "so why would they care to put Marks on us?"

Corvun considered Marks for a moment. They were used for many reasons by the angels and could typically only be placed by high-ranking angels. They were protections cast by angels, and Corvun guessed the church had been putting Cloaking Marks on the twins to stop demons from picking up their scent. Overall, it made it exceedingly hard to argue when outsiders described the church as "cultish." Corvun shook his head to himself.

"Who gives a fuck what the church thinks?" Jayren asked.

"Clearly not you," Venatrix said to Jayren. "I'd assume they're just trying to protect you. I just wish they wouldn't make a show of it."

Orion jumped up suddenly, climbing the piano stool and wobbling from the wound on his leg. He held his hands in fists, wide apart in a cross-like stance. "The freak shows! Look at them and their unholy filth! Pray for them, but never speak to them, or you too might burn in Hell beside them! Well, I say fuck the church!"

"Rian," Ophiah chastised softly.

"Yeah? They say we're going to Hell for listening to rock 'n roll. Do you believe that, Corvun?"

Corvun looked away, only to be caught by Venatrix's expectant eyes.

"Even you like rock n' roll, Ben," she said.

Corvun spotted Carina smiling at him from her seat on the stairs. He smiled back at her, not entirely sure as to why.

"I bet even you like rock 'n roll!" Orion pointed to Joshuah. "What's your favorite song?"

Joshuah laughed and rubbed his neck. "*Thriller*," he said with a shy grin.

"Hah!" Jayren laughed. "That's not even rock n' roll, that's Michael Jackson," he said, as if Michael Jackson were his own genre. "Rock n' roll is like *Livin' On A Prayer*."

"Yeah, but that's not even the best Bon Jovi song," Venatrix said.

"Well?" Corvun asked. Venatrix broke into song, singing a lyric from *You Give Love A Bad Name*, loudly and horribly. Corvun laughed as she skipped some lyrics she didn't know in a mumble then finished with an off-pitch rendition of the chorus. "You aren't even tryin'," Corvun told her. "*Back in Black*."

"Basic!" Jayren hollered in a low pitch. "At any rate, Taylor Swift wrote the best song of all time. I bet y'all don't even know it."

"*Holy Ground*," Venatrix said.

Jayren raised an eyebrow at Venatrix, and a smile lit up his face.

"The best thing about her," Orion added, slipping onto the piano bench. He touched the instrument, and notes twinkled out like stars filling the night sky as the sun fell asleep. A soft, galloping melody rose from the black and white keys. "She used to write every song to be stripped down to the bare bones, to be acoustic, just a guitar or piano, and just a voice."

"He knows it too!" Jayren cried.

Venatrix sang again, softer and more unsure than her first attempt. She sat on the edge of the piano bench next to Orion.

Orion glanced down at her, a smile on his face. "Here," he said. He wrapped his arm around her and shuffled her onto his lap. "Put your foot on the pedal and step down on the pre-chorus."

Venatrix nodded, grinning.

"I've heard *him* sing," Jayren said. He looked at Ophiah. "So I know you can sing. Come on."

"No," Ophiah said with a meek laugh. Her smile was forced and fake.

"Then dance with me," Jayren said.

"You can't dance," Corvun reminded him.

"Watch me." Jayren caught Ophiah's fingertips lightly and persuaded her into the middle of the room. He and Ophiah and Corvun and Joshuah moved the tables and chairs one by one to clear the floor.

Corvun could feel Carina's wary eyes as he organized the desolate dance, the peerless performance. But truthfully, he'd never felt more at home. The dim gold lights of the bar and the warm atmosphere blanketed their worry, and slowly, the horror from earlier in the day slipped away. If only for a little while. Corvun took turns dancing with Ophiah and Jayren to show them each steps to use together. He lifted Ophiah's chin when he danced with her, corrected her posture until she was confident. He let Jayren lead him as the man, biting his tongue each time Jayren stepped on his toes. He ordered them both to remove their shoes before dancing together.

They spent the next hour singing songs from the century before. Orion plucked melodies from thin air, and Jayren and Venatrix sang and sang and sang—engaging in passionate duets which often turned into competitions of who could be louder. Corvun was surprised by Jayren's steady voice, the maturity in his pitch as he sang side-by-side with Venatrix. Orion joined in here and there too, quieter, and Ophiah mouthed words into Jayren's shoulder as they danced on and off.

"Corvun!" Jayren yelled over the piano. "Do you remember when we tried out for the talent show and you learned beat boxing?"

"I have no idea what you're talkin' about," Corvun said. He busied himself unwrapping and rewrapping the compass scar on his wrist. He noticed Carina cover her laugh out of the corner of his eye, too.

"Yes you do, you dick. We learned *Bye Bye Bye*."

"Corvun, why didn't you tell me?" Joshuah asked.

"It's irrelevant and unimportant," Corvun said plainly.

"Oh no, it's not. NSYNC had five singers, and look. One, two, three, four." Jayren pointed to Venatrix, Orion, Ophiah, and himself in turn. "Five." He pointed at Corvun.

"No, Jayren," Corvun said.

"Yes, Jayren," Jayren said.

"I'm not doin' it," Corvun said.

"I'm with Corvun," Ophiah said.

"I'm in," Venatrix said with a snort of a laugh. "Let's do it."

"Majority wins." Jayren clapped with the tips of his fingers that poked out from his cast. "Lights!"

"Are you kidding?" Joshuah asked. Genuine confusion covered his expression.

"Do I look like I'm kidding?" Jayren asked.

Joshuah paused.

"No!" Jayren snapped. His wicked grin widened across his face as Joshuah dimmed the lights in the bar even more. Jayren motioned for Venatrix to come stand beside him. "They were known for their dancing."

"Really?" Venatrix asked.

"I don't know," Jayren said. "Just go with it." Corvun and Orion joined the other two, and Jayren walked them through the steps, how to stand, and how to look over their shoulders for dramatic effect. When he finished his small instruction tutorial, he asked Joshuah, "Can you put a spotlight on each of us, just one at a time?"

"Yeah," Joshuah called from behind the bar.

"You'll have to tell us how we do," Jayren said to Ophiah.

"I will," Ophiah said quietly with a rosy-pink smile.

VENATRIX CANES

Corvun's sudden, bass-driven beat box took Venatrix by surprise. Chills poked her skin, lighting her up with excitement. Jayren cued her and Orion into the song with bright, brass notes. She couldn't remember the last time she sang before tonight, but after tonight, she knew she'd never sing with anyone else. Singing had never felt *this* good, to have someone else's harmony vibrating in her chest.

Venatrix found herself turning to Jayren in jest. Their feet stomped in time with the rhythmic claps and careless swing of the dance. She held an invisible microphone in her hand, standing with her feet shoulder-width apart. Jayren turned his back and did the same, then looked over his shoulder so fiercely that Venatrix broke into laughter. Before she could catch her breath, Corvun swiped her around the waist and twirled her into a hip-hop styled shuffle. She danced with him, rubbing the lyrics into his face until he sang with her. Corvun changed the beat suddenly, and she recognized the song. It was one they'd sung together as kids, watching old movies on his small TV with a pillow fort tented over their heads. She hardly batted an eye in Jayren's direction when he chimed in to *Ghostbusters*. She realized now that Jayren had taken her place when she and Corvun had their falling out. While she used to be the one who sat with Corvun under makeshift pillowfort castles, whispering jokes with tangled hair, Jayren had slowly filled the gap she left. She could barely hold it against him.

Venatrix turned to Orion when he belted the notes louder and more passionately. He sounded something between a wiry tune of a harpsichord and an electric guitar, and her heart raced, looking at him and his own invisible microphone. The free-spirited pitch in his mouth drew her to his body like a magnet. And as soon as she put a hand on his chest—aching to feel the freedom he felt too—he grabbed her face and kissed her so deeply that her heart skipped several beats in her chest. Time slowed around him, and Venatrix wondered how long Orion's newfound audacity would last; she was a fan of it and hoped it would stay.

"One more!" Jayren yelled and proceeded to sing yet another song.

Venatrix sang the song with him, smiling so hard that her face hurt. Jayren let out a loud *"Whoop!"* when he saw she knew the song too. She marched around Orion; Jayren did the same with Corvun. Venatrix smiled at Corvun, and Corvun smirked back with the corners of his mouth. By the time the song tapered out—due to their forgetting of the lyrics and deteriorating into giggles and sloppy footsteps—Venatrix was breathless. She found Orion again and kissed him just as he'd done to her. She closed her eyes in the afterglow of the karaoke-styled clamor, and she drank in Orion's taste like cheap wine. She swore to herself she'd never apologize for loving him.

Jayren whistled between two fingers, only to receive a shove from Corvun.

Ophiah smiled and clapped, and Joshuah joined in applauding the show.

· · · · ·

When Corvun dropped Venatrix off at her front door, Venatrix said, "You gave him those old mixtapes we made." Every song they'd sung had been from the old CD they'd made together. She still had a copy of the CD—kept in a thin, clear case beside her bed. Corvun's all-caps, crooked handwriting read *THE SICKEST MIXES* across the front in shiny silver.

Corvun glanced back to the truck where Jayren cracked cheesy jokes until Orion and Ophiah turned pink with laughter. The headlights were off, but the interior lights gave the three a golden glow. "Can you blame me? It made for a good night." He smiled at Venatrix.

Venatrix smiled back, unrestrained.

"Goodnight, Vena," Corvun said.

"Are we," she started, "—are we good? I mean…"

"You mean?" Corvun prodded.

"Are we friends again? Officially?"

Corvun shrugged a shoulder then held out his fist for her.

Venatrix grinned stupidly and gave him a fist bump. She continued their childhood handshake, a high five—up high, down low, too slow—and wondered why she still missed the downward slap of his palm after all these years. She snatched his pinky in hers and said, "'Til Armageddon and after?"

"'Til Armageddon and after." He squeezed her pinky in his. He turned to head back, sticking his hand out behind him.

Venatrix lunged to smack his hand, but missed a second time. She laughed with him, smiled at his twinkling, dark eyes one more time, then shut herself inside.

CORVUN KHLYDE

Corvun pulled the Jude's truck up to their house. Silence was heavy like rain over the twins. He glanced back to find Ophiah leaning into Jayren's shoulder. Orion slouched in the corner of the truck bed, seemingly happy to stay there the whole night. Corvun killed the engine and sat in the driveway with the windows down. He drove with the windows down the whole trip due to the busted windshield and spider-web-like cracks across the glass. "We're back," he said.

"Don't make us go in there."

A subtle, dull, stabbing pain hurt Corvun's heart and reminded him of Cephan's fire poker. He looked down at his calloused hands and the bandage he'd wrapped his brand with. "The consequence will be greater if you don't," he said. The night had been too good for their own good, Corvun realized. It was a taste of the good life, a castle in the sky. But there was no castle for them, and they had no fairytale ending. They'd inherited ruins in the middle of a battlefield.

"We'll walk you up there," Jayren said. "C'mon."

Corvun got out of the driver's seat and helped the other three out of the truck bed. They trekked to the front door. Darkness surrounded the house like a prison; a dark aura fell over Corvun's eyes as he came closer. He reached out for the door handle, but the door swung open before he touched it.

The smell of rotting flesh blew away with the wind, but not before Corvun caught a whiff of it. A dead giveaway of demon blood. Corvun looked at the man standing in the doorway. He was too tall to be human, but too normal in appearance to be accused differently. Black shadows cast over his eyes, and black stubble covered his chin like dirt and blood on an animal's muzzle. He bore a healing wound over his right cheek and the bridge of his nose.

Jayren made a fist; Corvun grabbed Jayren's wrist before he could swing. Corvun's heart raced, hard and loud. He thought that when he'd see demons for the first time, he'd be ready. *I was painfully wrong,* Corvun thought. Even after a handful tonight, his nerves still kicked and buzzed at the sight of Mr. Jude. He grabbed Jayren's hand.

Mr. Jude cocked his head, and a smile crawled across his face. "Children," he addressed the twins with a voice like souring syrup. His green eyes grazed Corvun then locked on Jayren. "And," Mr. Jude drawled, "the boy who loves my daughter."

"No sir, I'm gay," Jayren said. He cleared his throat and raised his and Corvun's hand.

Corvun didn't even register Jayren's words. He was looking past Mr. Jude into the darkened house. He noticed two scythes hung above the fireplace mantle like a trophy.

Hellflame flickered below, burning white spots into Corvun's eyes.

"Why don't you come inside?" Mr. Jude instructed Orion and Ophiah.

Corvun almost took a step to follow the twins as they disappeared into the house.

Mr. Jude turned to Corvun. "Of all the demons I sent to bring my children back to me, how come you bring them? How did you protect them, *Nephilim?*" he seethed.

Jayren's hand grew hot and tacky.

Corvun fought the urge to run. He grounded himself with a glare fixed on Mr. Jude. "I know your plan to try to make them fall," Corvun said dryly. He bared his teeth in a small show of defiance. "It won't work. I'm goin' to lead them."

Mr. Jude scoffed. "They will never fight alongside you. They don't have any fight left in them. I've taken that away this Iteration, depriving them of what *you* need them for. You'd know all about that, wouldn't you, Fames?"

"We'll see," Corvun said.

JAYREN OMANS

Corvun and Jayren walked back to North Academy from the Jude's house. "In all those video games you play," Corvun started, "what weapons kill demons?"

"Silver bullets," Jayren said. Flashes of earlier in the night came back, of Corvun firing his gun, of mutilated, human-shaped creatures with long, sharp fingers. His head swam. These things weren't real; they couldn't be. They *couldn't* be. "Did we do acid?"

"Blade-type weapons," Corvun said. "What kind of *blade-type weapons* kill demons in video games?"

Jayren shook his head and stopped Corvun. "Dude, what the hell? We just got attacked by demons! *You* would know! I didn't even think they were real!"

"They are," Corvun took his cell phone out. "Vena said she and Orion are tryin' to kill Mr. Jude."

"They're trying to kill *his dad?* Dude, what the actual fuck?" Jayren shoved Corvun in the chest. His head was dizzy, and all he wanted was his bed. Horror collapsed on him. "They can't kill his dad. That's murder."

"His *dad* is one of the Deceivers, alright? He's a demon. My father struck him with a sword the night I was branded, and he has the *same* scar on his face. You saw him. Did he look human to you?"

"Bullshit!"

"Stop callin' bullshit!" Corvun yelled. "When are you finally goin' to get it, Jay? This isn't a game or a joke or fake or whatever excuse you're tryin' to make up! Fuck, what I wouldn't give to be as stupidly oblivious as you choose to be."

Jayren's stomach fell through the ground. He stood, motionless, at a loss for words. He needed sleep, an escape, to rest his bloodshot eyes. Like his recurring nightmare of his father's suicide would give him much of that. "It's not fair!" Jayren argued.

"What's not fair?" Corvun sounded exasperated.

"My dad is *dead,*" Jayren struggled to say. "And you hate yours, and Rian wants to kill his? How do you think I feel about that? I just *want* my dad back. It's not fucking *fair,* Corvun."

"Life isn't fair," Corvun said back, hard and angry. His eyes looked even darker in the middle of the night. "Don't you think I envy you, too? I wish I could dismiss everythin' like it's not real, but I'm stuck in this reality. I have to *kill* people now, Jayren. I have to shoot and kill *humans!* And the angels?

They're real to me. My dad is the Archangel Michael, damn it! How do you think that makes me feel? I can't live up to that, but that's what they all expect of me!"

Jayren shied away from Corvun's frustrated screaming. He hated the tears that welled in Corvun's eyes. Even more, Jayren wanted to throw a pillow at his face and tell him to stop crying. *We're still kids. We don't have to worry about this stuff,* he wanted to say. He knew it wasn't true. The sight of the demons—their clattering teeth and guttural hissing—scarred the back of his eyes. He couldn't unsee or unbelieve it, and he was stuck staring at his Nephilim best friend, knowing he'd never leave his side again.

Jayren made up his mind, standing in the empty parking lot with Corvun. He'd own up to all the make-believe bullshit Corvun deemed true. He made his terms. If—and only if—he was able to find and join RUST, fight alongside Corvun to protect him and Orion and Ophiah, then he would believe. Fuck the consequences.

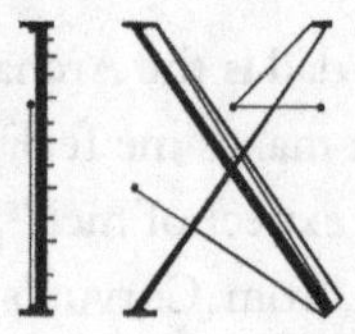

MADE IN HELL

There were five weapons forged for the Four Horsemen and Hades. Two were reforged in Hellfire. One is a bident named Scriptor de Exitium. The other is a duel-sided scythe named Scriptor de Mortem.
— A History of Hierarchy (Revised Edition)

NOVEMBER 16TH, 2106 A.D.
NORTHEAST FLORIDA
VENATRIX CANES

Venatrix sat shotgun in Orion's truck as he drove them to her house after school. The sun was hot through the windshield, even in its faraway spot in the sky. They kept the windows down, and tacky wind blew through their hair, catching stray strands against the humidity on their skin. Orion and Ophiah's blankets covered the passenger seat floor—stored for an emergency bed for the truck bed—and they smelled of pine wood and smoke. It was cozy in a way, welcoming, a home away from home. However, the cracks on the windshield proved an ominous reminder of what they'd faced two nights prior.

Orion pulled into Venatrix's driveway and cut the engine.

Venatrix's ears still rang with the sound of traffic passing, of the wind against her eardrums. She savored the sudden quiet and stared ahead at the front of her house.

"I came this far," Orion started. "Are you going to tell me your big surprise now?"

Venatrix closed her eyes and paused before she spoke. "Corvun and I used to have these wooden weapons we fought with. He texted me last night and told me to show you some basic moves."

"Like wooden swords?"

Venatrix nodded. "There's a bunch really, but my favorite was the bow and arrow. We have a scythe, too," she said. They fell quiet together, and the awkward space between them reminded her of the difference their heritage made in their lives. "Corvun saw the scythes above your fireplace. He has a theory, and I think it could work."

"Do you know what those are?" Orion faced her. "Those are Hell-forged weapons, not just scythes."

Venatrix reached for his hand, but he pulled it away. Venatrix wondered how much Orion knew about the weapons that were forged by the fires of Heaven and the flames of Hell. They were the only weapons that could cause permanent damage to angels and demons respectively. The scythes above Orion's fireplace were their best shot, whether or not Orion liked the idea of it.

Silence hung between them again like an invisible curtain.

"Are you afraid?" she asked in a whisper.

"It's not like that," he argued.

"What is it then?" Venatrix touched his fingertips carefully. This time, he didn't pull away. She brushed her hand up his arm, and he turned and gazed at her with wary eyes. He leaned closer, and Venatrix watched him blur in her line of sight until he was just colors. She closed her eyes when he pressed his lips against hers. They kissed, sweet and slow, and Venatrix tasted the bitter soda they'd shared right after school. His hands cupped her neck, and she brushed hers up under his shirt. Her fingertips touched something hard on his chest. She pinched, finding a ring at his nipple, and she quirked an eyebrow at him. "Who let you pierce your tits?"

Orion winced, gave a halfhearted laugh. "My mom. They're halos."

Venatrix raised both her eyebrows.

"I'm serious," Orion said, pulling away. "They're made of Heaven-forged metals, blessed by angels. They're supposed to keep me grounded in righteousness." He gave her a tiny smile that faltered and fell away. "Do you remember when you asked how hard he hits me?"

Venatrix nodded.

"He hits me so hard that this world—" he waved his finger in a small circle, "—breaks like glass. The fractures are red like fire. When it shatters, I can see straight into Hell, Vena. I feel like I'm burning. Everywhere I look, there are hundreds of embers falling, like these little sparks of light. And I start thinking the sparks are *that* light, you know, the light at the end of the tunnel? And just as I get close enough to touch it, it just burns. And I see it again and again and again, Vena," he whispered. "Each time I keep walking through all that fire, enduring that pain, because of that hope that I might have a chance to get out. It drives me to the brink of insanity. It's an illusion the whole time. Hopelessly hoping. I keep trying, even though deep down, I know I'm never getting out."

Venatrix didn't know what to say.

"That's how hard he hits me."

"I'm sorry." Venatrix pulled Orion into a hug. She buried her face into his neck, still at a loss for what to say to him. She held him until he hugged her back, and they stayed there until Orion pulled away. Venatrix held his face captive, forcing him to look at her. She wanted to tell him, *You can do this*. Or, *You'll banish him, and it'll all be over.* Or maybe even, *It won't be forever,* but she wasn't sure she had the grounds to say any of that to him. So instead she whispered, "C'mon," and tugged him out of the truck and up to her front door. She held his hand tight in hers as she unlocked the front door and pushed it open with her hip. "I'm home," she called to her parents.

"Dad's at the store. Mom's out back," Erin said as he walked past. He gave Orion a quick once-over with his eyes.

"I smell tainted blood," Caeleb said, close on Erin's heels. His bright eyes shone like police lights, flashing at Orion. He neared the two, and Venatrix stepped in front of Orion. "Even her perfume can't cover that up, Jude." Caeleb's lower lip jutted in a sinister jeer. His front teeth clicked as they touched.

"Fuck you," Orion snapped.

Caeleb's eyes widened, and his grin grew. "Such language! Has he tried to fuck *you* yet, Vena? Or are you still playing hard to get?"

Venatrix shoved Caeleb in the chest and shot a glare at Erin—who watched from the staircase. "Leave us alone."

"So he *hasn't*. That's a first." Erin rounded the two of them slowly, and Orion flinched like a wounded dog. "Are you sure he's even into you? Maybe he's more into boys."

"Maybe he's just halfway decent," Venatrix spat. She trembled with rage. She spun around to Erin and pushed him away from Orion. "Touch him again, and I'll cut your hands off." She glared into Erin's eyes and saw something dark there. Something was twisting him from the inside out. It was a look she'd only seen on Caeleb before. Venatrix spun back to Orion, and Orion flinched and stepped back.

He feared her, too.

She hated it.

She grabbed Orion's hand anyway and pulled him upstairs with her.

Orion slowed as they passed the hall bathroom. "Can I use the bathroom?" Orion's voice cracked. He whispered an apology. Venatrix nodded and stood by the door until he was done, afraid that her brothers would come upstairs to torment them more. She ushered Orion into her bedroom, only letting her guard down once they were safely inside with the door locked.

"Will you help me move my bed? We can stand it up so we have more room. The box with the weapons is in my closet." Venatrix bent to lift her bed. Orion hesitated, and she widened her eyes at him. "What are you waiting for?"

Orion snapped out of his daze, and together they lifted the bed to leave more space in the middle of her room. While Venatrix scooted a chair and rolled a rug away, Orion went to her closet and slid the box of wooden weapons off the top shelf and into his arms. He walked back to Venatrix, bent one knee, and rested the gray-black box on the ground. His fingers left trails in the heavy dust atop the box as he removed the lid.

Venatrix watched him, her nerves still alive and electric from their encounter with her brothers. She took a deep breath. Holding onto her frustration wouldn't do any good around Orion, and she didn't want to scare him any more. She didn't think she could take him being any more skittish than he already was.

Orion gawked at the multitude of painted, wooden weapons that tangled together inside the box. "This was your hobby as a kid?"

"Yeah, Ben and I would find pictures online and try to replicate them. Wield them, too. OneStream helped with that."

Orion picked out a whittled revolver. He lifted the wooden gun and raised his eyebrows.

Venatrix shrugged. "We had a lot of time."

"This is professional woodworking, not a hobby."

"I mean, Michael helped us with some of them." Venatrix knelt. "The gun was for aim and a steady trigger finger. We used a fake bullet casing on the nose of the gun and pulled the trigger. It helps with sharp shooting." She put a hollowed, cylinder-shaped nut in Orion's palm.

Orion looked at her, but his face was empty. He reminded her of paintings she'd seen in art museums. He was so beautiful, the details of his face so carefully carved, but he looked hollow. Distant, or maybe just unreachable.

Venatrix took a stick from the box along with two scythe blades. She secured the two makeshift blades to either end of the stick, pointing opposite directions, then she stood. "Here," she said and offered Orion the double-ended scythe.

Orion shook his head.

"What?" Venatrix asked.

"I don't want to be Death," Orion said. His eyes fell.

"We don't always get what we want," Venatrix said, firmer than she anticipated, "but if you learn how to wield this, you might get something you want. To protect Ophiah? And yourself?" She ducked into his line of sight and raised her eyebrows. "I'm not asking you to be Death right now. I'm asking you to learn to wield this so you can banish this fucker that abuses you."

Orion hesitated then took the scythe from her.

"I read about us," Venatrix said. She picked a dagger from the box for herself. She backed up, held one hand open and ready, and flipped the dagger backwards in her other hand. "You have the ability to banish demons with your scythe. But first, you gotta know how to use it."

Orion tested the weapon's weight and steadied it in his hand.

"Spin it," she said.

Orion spun one hand over the other.

Venatrix lunged through his slow motion and swiped the blunt edge of her dagger at his shoulder.

"Ouch!"

"Faster." She smiled.

Orion obeyed. He dodged her second lunge. He spun the scythe to his side then jabbed the point on the top of the blade in her direction. He tried an over-the-head slash, but Venatrix slipped past it. She ducked under the staff and closed the space between them. She poked the dagger on his chin.

"Tristan won't show you mercy," she said.

"If he's the leader of the Deceivers, do you really think I can banish him?"

"You can and you will. I'll teach you every day until you're ready," she offered.

Orion nodded. "How am I going to banish him with a scythe?"

"With the cross," she said with a small grin. "Again."

Orion stepped back into the give-and-take, swiveling combat with her. He swiped her skin with the scythe a few times; she caught him with clever strikes to his underarms, ankles, and back. He hissed in frustration when she doubled her attacks. Her heart raced as he picked up on his weapon's movement. Their frantic shuffle heated the room with humid sweat. Orion hooked a blanket on the tip of his scythe, slung it onto the floor, then tripped her with a second swipe of his blade. She collided with the ground with a loud *thwump*. Orion stepped towards her and pressed the blade under her chin. Venatrix stared up at his wild, forest-green eyes and glistening skin. Venatrix hadn't even noticed his clever disarm; her dagger laid two feet out of reach. Adrenaline numbed her fingertips.

Orion's eyes fogged with black.

"Help me up," she told Orion. Her voice shook.

His lips curled in the start of a snarl.

"*Orion*," she begged.

Venatrix's phone buzzed with a soft piano melody of *Für Elise*, and Orion sucked in a sharp breath. His eyes blurred with black tears. The tears fell, dripping from his chin and staining his shirt. His bottom lip quivered. He dropped the wooden scythe suddenly. "God save me," he whispered. He whisked out of her room.

Venatrix panted, stood, and scampered after him, chased him down the stairs. She jogged barefoot down the carpet as fast as she could but couldn't keep up.

"Oh, Vena!" her mother chimed from somewhere by the kitchen. "Is this—"

Orion flung the front door open.

Venatrix jumped into the darkness behind him. "Wait!" she yelled.

Orion whipped around so fast that she stumbled back. "Stop! Don't follow me!" He bared his teeth as he spoke, and she faltered, dumbstruck. His green eyes had gone black again in the dim evening. The light from her family's porch shed an eerie, pale glow on his skin.

Her momentary hesitation gave him another head start. He walked further away, and she started after him. Hands grabbed her, stopped her. Her parents spoke reassuring things to her, but she struggled against them with a heavy weight in her chest. Panic kicked against her bones. "Rian, wait! Come back!" Confusion blurred her mind. *Where is he going? What happened?* Everything was fine; he was improving. What changed? *What happened?*

Orion's engine roared to life.

. . . .

Venatrix's heart didn't slow down. It pattered long into the night, replaying every moment, every move. She couldn't define reality from her dreams; she walked the line of both with flashes of their duel in her mind's eye. In her dreams, his eyes were all black and his scythe, silver.

Cold brushed her neck.

She jolted out of bed. Her covers were damp from sweat from her neck and back and legs.

It was hard to swallow.

There was tapping somewhere.

She looked to her window, expecting Orion to be back on her rooftop.

There was only rain.

ORION JUDE

From his bedroom window, resting on his side with an aching pain in his spine, Orion thought of her.

NOVEMBER 17TH, 2106 A.D.
NORTHEAST FLORIDA
OPHIAH JUDE

The classroom bustled with nonchalant banter, small talk about upcoming tests and assignments, the off comment about North Institute's upcoming internship, and the clicks of pens and pencils scribbling away at last-minute assignments. It smelled of permanent marker and dry-erase marker, clogging Ophiah's nose as she sat numbly in her seat. Salty snot ran down her upper lip.

Ophiah glared down at the light-pink, four-cornered fold-out fortune teller. Four crude renditions of Satanic symbols blemished the top, drawn in red pen. The words inside labeled her: slut, whore, Lilith, little succubus, demon, Made In Hell.

Her heart pounded in her head; her eyes filled with hot, blotchy tears. She wondered if anyone watched her sit and stare through the aching blur in her mind.

A tear fell on her off-white suit jacket and stained the pale fabric with black. She stood and rushed from the classroom. A subtle breeze of laughter and jeers sounded behind her like wind chimes—angelic and pure and bright. *Some angels,* Ophiah thought. *Some angels. It's always going to be this way,* she convinced herself as she disappeared down the long, empty halls. She found solace in the school's garden. Ophiah sat tucked away between the roots of an ancient live oak and beneath the lonely shade of the Spanish moss. Sunlight floated down like flakes of pure gold. She dug her hands into the moist, warm dirt around her. She picked out old, broken oyster shells and breathed in the scent of wild magnolias. And she stayed.

Ophiah reminded herself: *Feel it. Feel everything. Feel the emotions you feel shame for: hatred, anger, envy. Then let it all go and breathe.* She recited verses, prayed with her eyes wide open. She hated her life. Emotion welled in her chest, and she wished she could turn to stone right where she was. She'd rather be a wishing well. At least that way, she could collect pennies and dimes and the hopes of hopeless romantics, and she would find company in their solitary glimmer from underwater. She wished to reflect the sun like that.

A little later, after clouds blanketed the sun, Ophiah left the empty garden and made her way to the locker room. With her eyes downcast, she pulled fingers through her hair and the tangles there, the resurrection ferns that the wind had relocated to new homes in her hair. She listened to the conversations in the locker room, which smelled overwhelmingly of soap and shampoo, of softener sheets and tacky bubble gum. Ophiah didn't smell a trace of sweat from the gym class before.

One of the girls standing at the wall-long mirror sprayed perfume over her shoulder, straight into Ophiah's face. "Take a shower," Krista said to Ophiah. "You smell like dirt."

Ophiah coughed and kept walking.

Krista's voice carried, following after Ophiah like the smell of her overused perfume. "Oh my god, I slept with Caeleb this weekend. He's so hot."

Ophiah shot a glare back in her direction. *As if that's something to brag about,* she thought.

"You slept with your boyfriend, right? God, I remember that! Casper North slept with *you*, and you threw a bitchy fit about it." Krista painted her lips pastel pink to match the gold highlighter and smoky eyeshadow she'd used. She smiled coyly into the mirror back at Ophiah, a quirky side-smirk with narrowed eyes. "You should appreciate something good when it happens to you," Krista said out loud. Her eyes added a silent, *Burn in Hell.*

The mirror before Krista shattered suddenly, as if a fist had smashed the glass.

Nothing touched it save for Ophiah's glare.

The girls standing around Ophiah screamed. One by one, they ran past her, and Ophiah welcomed their shoves and shouts as they fled.

Krista's face had changed; worry creased her seamless foundation.

Ophiah glanced at Krista's forehead, at the grown-out roots of her dyed hair. There was a Mark there, like some sort of see-through weather forecast, a brand or a tattoo that indicated her last day alive. Ophiah had always been able to see the Marks on everyone, always hoped her eyes were tricking her or the demons were teasing her. She started to

understand, to accept it. "You have no idea what's coming for you," Ophiah said slowly. She met Krista's eyes again, and Krista backed away and turned and ran.

The locker room stood still.

Ophiah looked at her shattered reflection. Eight different eyes peered back at her like a spider in a deadly web. The image haunted her, twisting and unsettling. She'd never felt like she'd seen her real reflection before now. The distorted image—her black-lined eyes with demons at the brim, ready to possess her mind—looked the way she felt.

Jayren busted through the door of the girls' locker room, and Venatrix stumbled in behind him. They stared, wide-eyed. Jayren ran to her first, and he held her shoulders firmly. "Are you okay? What happened?" he demanded. "What did they say to you?"

Ophiah's eyes darkened. She smelled blood, felt a trickle on her upper lip. She turned to Jayren, helpless. It was debilitating, the passionate surrender she wanted to offer him. She'd give him anything he asked.

"Get her some paper towels," Jayren said to Venatrix. He guided Ophiah towards a bench.

Demons whispered coiling words to Ophiah, demanding the strength from her legs, and she stumbled. Her calves gave way under her weight. Jayren caught her under the knees and rushed the rest of the way to the bench. He laid her down, resting her legs to his side and holding her shoulders in his lap.

He wants to kiss you. He wants to love you so badly, the demons said in unison, a multitude of whirling voices.

Ophiah couldn't move. The room was dark now, painted in shades of gray from the black that clouded her eyes.

Look at his eyes, Hades.

"Look at me," Jayren whispered. He cradled Ophiah's head, wiping away the blood on her nose and lips with stiff paper towels. "You're alright. You're okay. Look at me."

Ophiah squinted through the blackness. Slowly, she focused on Jayren's face. His hair fell around his face, soft and clean and airy for a change. His face was red with panic and embarrassment. His eyes cut through the black in her soul and opened the time and place in her mind where she stared into those same eyes—*his* eyes—every night, lonely and scared. She wasn't scared anymore. The sore ache in her throat sputtered into a heave.

"You're okay," Jayren said again. "See, Ophi?" He brought her close to his chest, and she blinked the shadowy ink out of her eyes. Ophiah grabbed his shirt. Her ear pressed against his heart, and she listened to the worried drumming. The rhythm quieted the murmuring of the demons. She wanted him to say her name again.

"H-How did you do that?" Venatrix asked, breathless.

"She's not evil." Jayren's chest rumbled against Ophiah's ear, and she went slack against him in surrender. "Neither is Rian. The others don't get it. No one does! I can hear those demons when they talk to her," he said firmly. "I can hear what they say to her, to Rian too, okay? No more lies, Trixie. I get it. The voices I hear are angels and demons. I'm not crazy, and neither are Ophi or Rian."

Ophiah's tears bled hot on Jayren's shirt. She shut her eyes tight and breathed in the smell of day-old cologne. She imagined he'd grabbed the shirt off his floor before running out the door. He smelled a little like plants, too, and she wondered if he'd spilled soy milk on his shirt or spent the afternoon beneath the trees and Spanish moss like she had. A hint of a smile teased her face, and she asked, "You believe in angels and demons now?"

Jayren's face paled when he looked at her. A small dimple in his chin gave away his fear. He nodded, nostrils flaring. Ophiah pulled herself up into his arms again, and he held onto her so fervently she was convinced he'd never let go. Her fingertips dug into his shirt, and she wondered if he could feel the slamming of her heart pressed against his chest. The light from his halo flared above them like a silent explosion, the start of a war. It warmed her.

VENATRIX CANES

Venatrix had never seen such conviction, such devotion in two eyes before. She stared at where Jayren peeked over Ophiah's crooked shoulder. His wide, green eyes reflected the chaotic dance of the flame above his head. It doused the room red—even in her own vision—and her heart beat in her throat.

Breathe, she begged him silently.

Jayren squeezed his eyes shut and slipped quietly into the space he held Ophiah in.

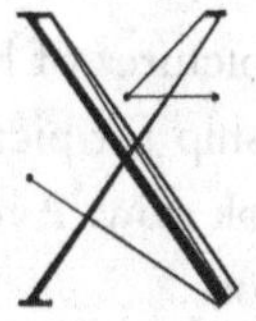

MEMORIES OF ASH AND FIRE

Prophets are not the only ones who can see the future. Sometimes, angels are given prophetic dreams, too.
— *A History of Hierarchy*

NO RECORDED DATE
CARINA BLACKROCK

Carina watched the sun set from underwater. She loved the sight—the deep, rich reds and pinks. *Pink skies at morning, sailors take warning. Pink skies at night, sailors' delight.* She recalled the rhyme that kept her seafaring a little easier to predict. The sun dipped beneath the surface, soaking the water with crimson.

She remembered the times she'd done this before. She'd beg Leroy for the twenty minutes between the sun first touching the water and the final sight of the sun above sea level. No matter how they argued, he always gave in, and she always gave him a monstrous hug before leaping into the ocean.

Carina thought of Leroy as the sun sank deeper—of his leathery, cherry-wood skin and the gold beads he kept at the end of each dry, gray braid in his hair. She wished to see him before his fall. Would he have looked different? Carina wondered if he had any pictures of himself from before. She would've searched their ship for pictures if it hadn't sunk. It was too dangerous to look now. Avon would be waiting for her as soon as she left shore.

A violent current washed over her skin as if her thoughts triggered a rush of cold water. It felt as if something swam past her, and she turned to look, finding nothing but red-orange rays piercing through the sea. She twisted again, and a giant sea creature swam in front of the sun. He opened his mouth and swallowed the distant ball of fire whole. Long, saber-tooth fangs closed on the sun.

Carina's body numbed with adrenaline and paralyzing fear. The water choked her lungs suddenly, and she needed oxygen to breathe. She raced upwards as the dragon swam wide laps around her. She couldn't swim fast enough.

Avon's movement pulsed through the water like the beat of a war drum. He slithered through the water, nearing Carina with ease.

Her hands hit the surface, but she didn't break into the atmosphere. Her heart jerked in her chest. She pounded her hands against the waves. Her fists boomed in the thick, slow water. She screamed, but no sound came out.

Teeth punctured the end of her tail, jerking her away from the surface.

Carina yelled again, soundless. The teeth stung like venom and fire, even after they'd released her. Carina wound into herself, coiling her bleeding tail around her in a pathetic excuse for armor. She peered out into the water to find Avon swimming towards her, his jaw gaping open. She closed her eyes, and she waited.

The clamp of Avon's teeth threw Carina down onto the hard ground. Water fell around her like rain. The clattering sound jumped into life, sparking into a building fire. The walls around her burned. Carina looked up, threw her hair back. Sweat covered her like the ocean had.

The building around her began falling piece by piece into ash.

Carina lifted herself into a crouch. She heard shouts in the distance. She heard Orion calling, "Corvun!" His voice faded into the snapping blaze.

Carina ran after the sound, shielding her face with her arm. Sparks and embers sizzled spot-scars onto her skin.

"Get him down!" Corvun's voice echoed from the opposite direction. "Get him down!" His shouting became hysterical.

A beam fell from the roof, and Carina ducked away. When she stood, she saw the silhouette of four people in the distance. She recognized Corvun's stature, and she watched him clasp hands around Orion's face.

"You can do this," Corvun said. "Just don't look back. Promise me. *Promise me.*"

Orion nodded.

Carina saw Venatrix and Jayren huddled beside the two men. The smoky vision faded as the four rushed through the chaos.

Carina tried to follow them, but the roof fell from the house. She looked up into the black sky, but it held no stars for her to study or guide herself with. She spun, looking for an exit. She spotted a door within a sprint's distance, and she ran with all the strength she had left in her. Carina threw herself at the door. The wood creaked. Again. She stepped back and shoved her shoulder into the exit again.

She collapsed into the empty night.

Carina lifted her face to breathe in clear air. Before her, she saw familiar black, double monk strap dress shoes pointed in her direction.

"Azrael," Cephan called her.

Carina got to her feet, lost her balance, and fell backwards.

When she fell, she woke.

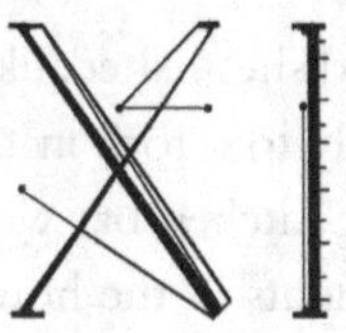

THE ROAD TO RUST (IS PAVED WITH GOOD INTENTIONS)

The Abyss is on a plane between the Earth and Hell. It has no sun, no moon, and no stars.
— *A History of Hierarchy (Revised Edition)*

DECEMBER 11TH, 2106 A.D.
NORTHEAST FLORIDA
JAYREN OMANS

Jayren's bones ached with stress. He was strewn over the whole sofa, and Lacey pushed his foot off the headrest of the couch as she passed.

"Don't act like a slob," she told him.

"I am a slob," Jayren said. "Haven't you seen me?"

Lacey didn't reply. She clanged some dishes in the kitchen. Water spurted and hissed in the steel sink.

"I've been thinking about joining RUST," he said. He wondered if she could hear him. He wanted her to care, wanted her to drop everything and ask what had gotten into his head, to ask if he was okay and sit down and just be his sister for once.

Lacey paused. The dishes halted, like a clamor of armored soldiers coming abruptly to a fork in the road. Jayren sat up and looked through the kitchen bar window. Her rose blond hair reflected the dim lights in the house. It looked an awful lot like a helmet worn to battle if you asked Jayren, and he wasn't getting through. Lacey resumed washing the dishes in the sink.

Jayren sighed and collapsed back onto the couch. He glanced at the muted TV. The forecast for that week moved across the screen. Jayren always kept a wary eye on the weather. The northeast corner of Florida had been getting more and more snow over the past century, and Jayren hated snow enough to move further south. But he was stuck here, living with Lacey, who was respectively stuck under Professor North's sponsorship. It was the highlight of Jayren's week if they got a forecast with no chance of snow at all. Snow littered this forecast like shreds of craft paper in a classroom, all over the place and totally unwanted.

The program paused, and the commercials flitted through slides of the FBI's most wanted (mostly RUST), the assassins with the highest bounties on their heads, and the missing persons who RUST was suspected of being guilty for. (That was most missing persons, so Jayren wondered why they even needed to put that on the screen.) The phone number at the bottom of the TV requested any information—and compensation for information received. But giving up that information was nearly as dangerous as the assassins themselves. RUST had eyes and ears and influence everywhere. They hijacked phone lines, so the chance of RUST hearing someone give up information was as good as a target on a forehead. Personally, Jayren couldn't believe the government was so hellbent on catching an organization that was as elusive as a shadow. RUST was like some sort of unstoppable freak of nature, collectively. Something about being that untouchable appealed to Jayren. He bet no one would try to break his glasses if he was with RUST.

Knowing someone probably had eyes on keyword searches, Jayren picked up his phone and searched "RUST."

Your move, he thought.

DECEMBER 11TH, 2106 A.D.
THE ABYSS
CORVUN KHLYDE

In the month he was in the Abyss, Corvun learned quickly how RUST operated. RUST existed in the Abyss, a plane between Earth and Hell, and it was always dark. There were rows of warehouses that served as housing, similar to a subdivision of cookie-cutter houses. Corvun—because he was an unpartnered assassin with no team—did not have his own warehouse. Corvun was free to come and go from the Abyss. He had the option to live in a community dorm reserved for assassins from the States or to stay any place that might've offered him shelter back on Earth. There weren't many. Michael, at the very least, understood what Corvun faced, but his stepmother didn't take to it lightly. Cynthia, of course, could no longer stand the sight of him. Corvun opted to stay in the men's dormitory in the Abyss most of his time, save for going to school and struggling through the remainder of his education.

The dormitory was cruel, reminiscent of a military operation set up in the depths of a mildewed, water-damaged factory. White beds stood in rows, mirroring the design of the warehouses. The sheets were prickly and brittle and smelled strong of bleach and sweat. The dorms had no privacy. If someone slept naked, everyone knew about it. Corvun resorted to sleeping dressed, atop his cot, somewhere in the center of a field of strangers' beds. The community shower was the last place Corvun would be found, so he splashed his face with water at rest stops back on Earth. Michael let him shower if he showed up looking miserable enough.

The men's dorm was downstairs, and a set of hanging metal stairs led back to the main floor. The men passed the women's (upstairs) dormitory on the way out of the warehouse. Corvun was sure that was the women's favorite part of their day—getting catcalled by vulgar men who smelled like black coffee, whiskey, and cigars. Corvun never looked at the women. But sometimes, the women were just as bad as the men, smelling of hard liquors and cigarettes and sex. Corvun avoided those women as much as possible after his first time being groped by one.

The Abyss outside the States' dormitory was just as bleak and shady. A little ways off from the dorm, there was a gated estate that lurked further in the shadows. Down that same direction, rugged stores and leaning buildings spotted the side of the gravel like roadkill. The first time Corvun wandered down that path in hopes of finding some sort of food or snack, black-clad characters offered him illegal street drugs or war-class weapons. One man who sat haunched just inside an alley baited Corvun with dirt on Heaven's Army. He'd given Corvun one bloodshot glance and smiled so sinisterly with teeth like broken plates that Corvun's hair stood on end. He never went back that way, besides to go to the Archives.

The Archives were where all assassins were required to report to in order to pick or be assigned missions. Corvun wasn't really required to go yet since he didn't need the income. Michael still gave Corvun enough funds to support himself. Once Michael stopped, Corvun would find himself walking through those massive, metal double doors in deprivation and starvation. It—*killing*—would be his last resort to even feed himself.

The only thing that got Corvun through any of it was the mornings he escaped to sit on the beach back on Earth and listen to the ocean. Sometimes he slept on the beach. Secretly, he wanted to wake to Carina glaring down at him. Even her dagger at his throat would make him feel more alive than he felt now.

Sometimes Jayren chanced sitting with him on the beach, too. They didn't talk as much anymore, but Corvun let him know how grateful he was by bringing Jayren bags of vegan gummy bears. With each passing visit, Jayren ate less and less of the bears until finally he didn't open the package at all.

"Those are your favorite," Corvun said.

"Yeah, not anymore."

Corvun looked at Jayren.

"Ever tried dried pineapple? Damn good shit," Jayren said.

"I'll make a note for next time," Corvun said.

Jayren's silence told Corvun they might not have too many more next times.

DECEMBER 17TH, 2106 A.D.
NORTHEAST FLORIDA
VENATRIX CANES

Venatrix watched the back of Orion's head from across the room. His hair changed as winter approached. Blond highlights streaked his hair, as if he'd been to a salon recently, but his hair looked unusually unkept, not as if it'd been carefully styled or dyed. Orion looked as if he was letting himself slip. Orion reached into his bag which was slumped at the foot of his desk, and Venatrix noticed a blond streak that grew adjacent to the arch of his eyebrow. The hair shone blond from the root to the tip of his long hair. They resembled something of horns, and Venatrix started to wonder if—rather than a stylistic choice—his hair had grown that way naturally. She studied him absently. Never mind the history assignment on her desk.

Orion's head tipped backwards in her direction, but he didn't look at her. He looked at her shoes.

Venatrix almost threw a pencil at his face.

He hadn't talked to her in a month.

Then again, she hadn't tried to talk to him either. She took to sitting behind him like a hawk in the classes they shared so she could ward off any bullies before they even got to him. Venatrix's phone buzzed on her desk, and she glanced down at her screen. From the corner of her eye, she noticed Orion's dark eyes looking up at her face. She didn't look at him. She stared—not really reading, just staring—at Corvun's text, willing herself to *not* look at Orion.

'I think I have a final draft for my internship essay. Will you look at it tonight? I emailed it to you.'

Venatrix texted him a quick 'Sure,' then looked at Orion.

He was turned around again, scribbling notes.

She sighed and her back caved against her seat. She watched the three-dot icon on her screen bounce as Corvun typed up a response.

'Did Orion ask you to the dance yet?'

'Did anyone ask you to the dance yet? Why are you asking me this?'

Venatrix bit her cheek angrily. She thought about Orion again, wondering what he'd look like with his hair combed and nicely dressed in a button-down shirt or a classy vest. One thought led to the next, and she realized she missed the taste of his lips. She also remembered that the wooden scythe had gone missing from her bedroom the week following their short training session. Her frustration rekindled.

'He told me he wants to ask you, but he thinks you'll say no.'

Venatrix glared at her phone.

'And he asked me if I'd see how you were feelin' about it.'

She could hear Corvun's exasperated tone through her phone. He was tired, Venatrix knew. Corvun had been missing days at school left and right, showing up with bloodstains on his jeans, new scars and bruises, looking like the kind of trouble her brothers asked for. No one dared to even look at Corvun these days. The dark welts beneath Corvun's eyes might've warded others off, but Venatrix just wanted to hug him. He didn't let her close enough anymore. He'd become the physical manifestation of a walking shadow. She couldn't believe he still tried to invest in the four of them as friends.

'Let's talk after class,' she texted

Corvun didn't reply.

The bell blared like a siren dooming the area with oncoming, severe weather or the telltale sign of an air raid. She gathered her things into her arms and ventured towards the hall. From the doorway where she stood, she saw her brothers smoking a joint down the hallway. One of Venatrix's teachers, Mr. Barstad, was quick to scold both boys and demand their exit. Caeleb dropped the joint at the teacher's feet and stepped on it. He rubbed it into the mosaic masterpiece on the floor then spit. Venatrix watched the fury in Mr. Barstad's eyes; the teacher could do nothing but stand and watch.

Her brothers sauntered out the nearest exit as Mr. Barstad knelt and cleaned the mess.

Venatrix's chest burned with embarrassment. She weaved through the mindless student traffic and knelt beside her teacher. "Let me help you," she said. She took a napkin from her duffle bag and unfolded it. She wiped up the spit and brushed the remainder of her brother's marijuana into her napkin.

"Thank you, Miss Canes." Mr. Barstad's eyes remained downcast. The wrinkles around his lips—wrinkles from smiling so constantly through his career as North Academy's chemistry professor—hung a little lifeless. He slid his fingers over the sides of his mouth in concern. "Vena, I'm worried about your brothers." They stood. Mr. Barstad took the napkin from Venatrix and tossed it in the trash.

"Seems everyone 'round here is more concerned about me."

"You only cut your hair. Besides, it's grown now. Look at you, you're looking like a young woman these days."

Venatrix glanced at the exit her brothers had used.

Mr. Barstad did too. "They've been showing signs of rebellion to the Archangels' lineage. I worry they've sold secrets or compromised the Archangels' plans," he said. "I would advise you to steer clear of as much as you can."

Venatrix's heart ached in her chest. Part of her wanted to save them. The other half already knew they were a lost cause.

CORVUN KHLYDE

Corvun called Venatrix on their break, and they agreed to skip their next class to meet on the baseball field. Corvun found a perch underneath the shadows of the awning. He watched for Venatrix. Little bugs of insecurity gnawed at his heart, biting and pinching him with doubt that she still wanted to see him at all. But she showed, with her steel gray windbreaker and nineteen-eighties style red, blue, and yellow duffle bag. She marched to the stands and glared up at him. Her eyes were so loud. That blue—that now shone brighter than the graying skies—yelled at him for lurking where miscreants and misfits swapped dirty secrets. She clamored up into the metal seats, and Corvun couldn't stop his mind from considering her own survival rate in a place like the Abyss. If she thought boys slobbered over themselves in a private academy, she'd lose her stomach to what advances Corvun had dealt with himself.

Venatrix stopped short of the shadows and dropped her duffle bag on one of the white-gray benches. "I'm not sitting up there. You look like you're doing drugs. Like you're still doing them right now."

Corvun sighed and stood. He lumbered down a few awkward steps then plopped onto the bench beside her bag. "Better?"

Venatrix sat next to him.

"Orion won't shut up about you."

"Orion won't talk to me."

Corvun chuckled. "Unlike me, he didn't grow up swallowin' your venom. He's terrified to talk to you."

Venatrix didn't speak.

"He's in love with you."

"Everybody is in love with me," Venatrix said.

"I'm serious, Vena. He's…" Corvun paused. "He doesn't *want* anythin' from you. He just wants to be with you. You should hear him. Before he and Ophiah head home, he always says somethin' nice about what you wore that day, even if you blew in lookin' like a wreck. That mornin' you picked that ugly pimple open? He thought that damn band-aid on your jaw looked cute."

Venatrix didn't say anything. She slouched back between the benches and stretched out her legs. She crossed her arms tightly.

Corvun mimicked her pouting.

Venatrix glared at him. "What are you doing? You look ridiculous."

"You should see yourself." He laughed quietly.

She laughed too.

Their laughter disappeared with the rest of the sunlight.

"How are you?" she asked.

"Just okay," he said. "You?"

"Just okay."

Corvun pulled his sleeves over his hands. His hood warmed his neck.

"Have you…"

Have you killed anyone? Corvun knew it's what she wanted to ask, she just didn't want to finish the sentence. Corvun couldn't swallow. "No, not since I joined." He wanted to leave suddenly, but her nimble hand on his arm stopped him. He rolled his head to the side, facing away from her so she wouldn't see him cry.

"You can talk to me if you want."

"I know," was all he said.

VENATRIX CANES

At the end of the day, Venatrix stood before Caeleb's black and silver car. She glanced down the street. A ring of a storm cloud haloed the sky. She could walk to the bus stop, risk the rain and lightning in exchange for the mental abuse her brothers would give. She wanted nothing to do with them, to never be associated with them again, and the thought of changing her name crossed her mind. *One day*, she promised herself. She slipped into the back seat, feeling the subtle effects of her brothers' persuasion; she'd hesitated one moment too long. She thought about the last name she wanted to take for herself: Major. When she was little, she'd learned from her parents that most of the Archangels looked to the stars when picking their names and the names of their children. Her last name Canes had come from the constellation *Canis Major*. She'd thought to take Major instead as a curt nod to her family but a name of her own.

Erin turned around in the passenger seat, pulling her from her thoughts. To her surprise, he didn't say anything to her, only offered her a joint.

She didn't reply. Her stomach jerked inside her when Caeleb left the parking lot. She looked out the window. She'd be stuck with them until they all got home.

"Don't say I didn't offer," Erin said. He lit the end of the joint and smoked it himself.

"Can you roll down the window?" Venatrix asked Caeleb as the bittersweet smoke clouded her vision. Her eyes and throat burned, and her thoughts slowed.

They laughed in past tense. It registered too late for her to care.

Even with the edge taken off her awareness, she felt as alert as ever. Her heart jittered; she slumped back in her seat and hugged her bag to her chest. It felt as if she was on a road trip, lulled in and out of consciousness by the swaying of the suspension, breathing in the distant massacre of a skunk. *But road trips don't make you stop thinking,* Venatrix thought. She didn't know how long she sat in the car, eyes closed, with her shirt tented over her nose. It was longer than it took to get home, or at least, that's how it felt. Time slowed, her muscles atrophied. She no longer felt strong or agile or in control. She felt like a dead body, zip-tied and bagged up and slung in the back seat. She didn't know where they were taking her, but when she opened her eyes, it was dark outside.

Her brothers were speaking, and she listened.

"…the weapon he had looked like…" they muttered, in and out, "…you know, the Archangels."

"No one knows who Cephan is."

"That's not true. The Archangels know. You know how I know?"

Erin grunted.

"…he told me. He's an Heir…"

"How is that…" Their voices faded.

Venatrix stared into the dark forest ahead, framed in the dash and her brothers' dark silhouettes, and wondered what all the headlights saw. Something moved ahead. She should've been scared, she thought, but instead she was amused. She thought the movement was funny, like a human was trying to act like a bloodhound. The shadow disappeared for a few minutes. It came back, walked right up to the car, and stood before it.

Her brothers stopped talking.

Venatrix looked at the person for what felt like an eternity. It was a familiar stature, lean and long and lanky. She could smell her own breath under the hem of her shirt until she didn't, until she stopped breathing. Until she realized it was *Orion* standing just ahead of her brother's car.

"Lock the doors," Erin said.

Venatrix looked at her door. She pulled the lock and opened the door.

"Are you crazy?" Caeleb shouted back at her. "He's possessed! Don't you see his eyes?"

She tumbled out, unable to keep her balance. She propped herself up on her forearms, and humid dew soaked her knees and thigh. From her spot on the damp grass, she studied Orion.

His eyes were dark, black, and empty.

"Leave her!"

Orion turned to her brothers. The forest filled with a deadly ticking sound. Caeleb's windshield busted suddenly, and inside, both brothers screamed. Caeleb threw the car in reverse and squealed away. Slowly, Orion's attention turned back to her. He moved terribly slow, as if he were underwater. She felt like she was underwater, too, just looking at him. *You're supposed to be scared,* she tried to remind herself. She couldn't form words to say. She breathed in the clean air, but she couldn't pick herself off the ground. She stared at Orion, and he looked at her with a blank expression and a nosebleed. She wanted to clean his face off and hold him, just like Jayren had done with Ophiah.

Orion walked towards her.

She forced herself to her knees as he crouched beside her.

"You're stoned," he struggled to say. His words were the hissing sound of fire being doused with water. "Did they do this to you?"

Venatrix nodded. She wrapped her arms around his neck.

They stayed there on their knees, holding one another for a while. Hot, thick tears smeared between them, and when Orion spoke, his voice was young and soft. "Why didn't you run," he murmured, "…from me?"

Venatrix looked up at his face. The blackness in his eyes washed out with his tears, streaking his face with black. She wiped it away with her thumbs. "I would never run from you."

Orion held her tighter. He lifted her off the ground, and Venatrix felt small and safe, as if she'd just been wrapped up in a childhood blanket. She felt at home, and that was a first.

"Where are we going?" she asked.

"My truck is at the trail up ahead. I'll drive you home."

"Are you okay?" she asked finally. "Why were you out here alone?"

"I was practicing," he said. "I did it, Vena. I learned how to banish demons. I did it with your wooden scythe."

"What?"

"It's not the weapon. It doesn't have to be Hell-forged," he said hastily. "It's *me*. I'm the one with the ability to open portals to Hell."

Venatrix's mind was still hazy. She thought, *What if he opens up a portal right here and now? Could he do it with just his mind? Would he take me too, to show me what it looks like?* Part of her wanted to know what Hell looked like, but she considered all these questions might be better asked sober. Instead, she asked, "Are you ready to banish Tristan?"

"No," Orion said.

"Why not?"

"It's," he swallowed, "not just as easy as that. I fought some imps, a few demons like the ones that followed us in the forest that night. They all come at me at once, and little demons like that, I can take them on. But Tristan…"

"What if it were one-on-one?" Venatrix asked. She rested her head on his shoulder and gazed at his face in the moonlight. "Maybe we could pray over the house, Mark it in some way, that way you're guaranteed a one-on-one fight. Do you think you could do it that way?"

"Maybe," he said. "Maybe."

Venatrix tucked her chin into her chest, rested in his arms. *Maybe,* she replayed his voice. *Maybe. Maybe. Maybe.* Orion's heartbeat was a steady drum by her ear; his breath hummed a lullaby. She slipped into sleep, rocked by the gentle, swaying rhythm of his steps. She slept for a long time.

· · · ·

Venatrix woke later in her bed, if only briefly. Darkness cloaked the sky, and Orion's smell (which was that of the Earth, of sweat and dried, crusted blood) clung to her like he'd been sleeping in her bed all night. She rolled over, expecting him to be there.

He wasn't, but a small tuft of flowers was.

Venatrix reached for the flowers with a heavy arm. The flowers were forget-me-nots, and the silver-white moonlight drenched them where they lay beside her. She touched the dainty sprout, thinking she'd never seen anything so pretty.

JAYREN OMANS

Jayren exhaled, even and thin. His breath billowed in steam clouds that reminded him of pictures he'd seen of paper mills and factories that ran long before World War III. He thought about the war, too, and how things might have been different if things hadn't happened the way they did.

He didn't trust all the stories he heard about the war, but it didn't matter. Somehow, the abandoned place where he stood had come to be, and his five-pound history book gave him a semi-sensible timeline to justify how it'd gotten there. This factory stood at the edge of the city, just close enough to get to and just far enough away to be abandoned.

Jayren's reflection glanced back at him through the frost-laced fractures on the glass window in the metal door he approached. He pushed open the stairwell door and trudged up the steep, concrete steps that smelled of damp rain and standing water. He tugged his coat tight around his body. A few down feathers poked him. He didn't usually use the coat—which was a hand-me-down from his father and one of the few things he brought with him from Indiana—but tonight it was all he needed.

As he climbed the flights of stairs, he thought. He'd done his research, every minute of everything he needed to know. Joining RUST *must* be a willing decision, and there is no escape from the life. From your initiation forward, you are a slave, branded. After searching for this information, he'd been extended his own personal invite. He'd accepted, and a cab was at his house just before dark. Now here he was, with spit too cold to swallow lodged in his throat and his veins icing over. Still, all Jayren could think about was Corvun and Orion and Ophiah and how much they needed his help. Jayren put his shoulder into the door at the end of the final flight. And on the top of the abandoned building, his knees locked up.

Jayren, alone on the rooftop, wandered to the edge. He heard the ocean in the distance. The sky was dark and starless, and he stared at the empty street below and the little white flakes that twirled like ash after a bombing.

"I have been waiting for you for a very long time," Cephan's words curled with the snow. "You're here to join RUST."

Jayren turned slowly, fear numbing his body.

Cephan's image soaked into his mind like blood staining a white rag. Cephan radiated power like a nuclear base. His sleek, killer suit was polished and pressed in all the right spots. Cephan's light eyes pinched into an eager, hungry smirk, flicking momentarily to Jayren's neck and the thrumming pulse there.

Jayren tucked his nose underneath his dad's old scarf and breathed in the faded smell of Venatrix's perfume. "Yeah," Jayren responded simply, "I want to join RUST."

Corvun was going to kill him. If Cephan didn't kill him first.

"Do you know what you're in for, boy?" Cephan's white eyes cut into him.

Something in the darkness, an invisible wrap of a noose, tightened around Jayren's neck. His vision blurred. He glared into the distance, fighting the dampness that chilled his eyes.

"Yeah, but I got a condition for ya, man. I'm Corvun Khlyde's partner. No fucking exceptions."

Cephan scoffed. "You're as dumb as they say."

Jayren's jaw snapped into the groove of his molars.

"Come with me," Cephan said. He extended his hand, and the sharp tip of a white compass poked from beneath his sleeve.

This is for Corvun and Rian and Ophi, Jayren told himself. He glared at Cephan's hand, reached out and took the tight, cruel handshake. *No one will ever touch me again,* Jayren swore. He would find a way to become so powerful, so invincible, that no one could ever hurt him or his friends again.

"Wait 'til your friends learn of this choice, Mr. Omans. They may not think so highly of your decision."

Could Cephan read his mind? He wouldn't be surprised, frankly. His head hurt. His hand hurt, too; his bones scraped together under his skin.

Darkness whirled around Cephan, and he pulled Jayren through a black void.

Jayren's thoughts tore at the seams. His eyes felt glued shut as the thick, black, watery atmosphere burned his skin and lungs. His bones rubbed wrong inside him, his muscles ripped and healed, only to be shredded by exhaustion again. Shadows ate at his skin with a wet heat like a fever, using him up inch by inch until he couldn't move. He wondered if this was what Ophiah and Orion felt, and Jayren wondered if he'd been better off if he'd just jumped from the building's roof to his death.

The time in between was foggy, as if his memory was paint water and he'd stuck a finger in it and swirled until nothing was quite coherent. There was darkness, a lot of black. Little spots of light winked in his vision, there and gone again. There was a metal chair, the taste of copper at the back of his throat.

A pressure on his throat, too. He touched a stiff, braided rope that twisted around his neck, tighter and tighter, until all the chaos around him spun into nothingness.

Voices made up the entirety of existence.

Jayren could hear them—the demons more than the angels—engaging in battles. Their cries were the fall of a wounded soldier, and their warfare was the shaking of the ground beneath bombs and grenades. The demons smeared in black, like spilled ink on a page, wiped away in a failed remedy. The angels dropped like white rain, splashing and jumping with vitality. The white blotted out the black smears, but it never ended. It blended together into gray.

Jayren's vision turned gray, too. Heat flushed him as he tried to open his eyes. He touched his face, only to find that his eyes were already open. He felt smooth, hardened scars on his face around his eyes. He looked around at the gray.

Mars, the war to end all wars. Mars, the demons chanted. *Choose our side, Mars. The greatest warrior would become even greater! Come with us, come with us!*

A black fang caught his arm.

Jayren snapped towards the shadow, but it smeared away, leaving no path to follow. Jayren winced, holding the wound. Heat welled from the deep sever. He fought his scarf off his neck and tied it tightly around the bleeding cut.

Do not listen to the demons, a soft voice whispered.

"Dad?" Jayren spun in search of the familiar voice. He looked up into the grayness.

A vision of white eyes looked into his, then a hot breeze whipped it away.

Sentinel! The only Horseman with no wings! A demon teased. *They will not wait on you, but we will. We will.*

They need you to protect them, his father's voice again.

"Dad!" Jayren cried out.

Your father isn't here. He abandoned you, a serpentine voice coiled between his feet and snatched his ankle in a tight grip. *Kin of the Devil!*

Jayren slung the black shadow loose and stomped on the makeshift snake. In his fists, two thin, white-light swords manifested. His lungs ached, full of hot air. Sweat caked the back of his neck, and his shirt stuck to his chest like a plaster mold. Ahead of him, the gray sheen split in half.

Massive, clawed hands ripped the gray apart, and a dragon blacker than night slithered through the tear. First its muzzle pried through, then its long, bear-like neck. The Deceiver flopped like black tar, slapping foot by foot down into the gray.

Jayren didn't need to be told the name of the Deceiver because he could feel its effect. The desperation, the lost cause, the flicker of hurt longing for hope. It was Tristan, the Deceiver Sorrow, Orion and Ophiah's father. That ache pierced his chest and pinned him wide open. He couldn't help but imagine Orion and Ophiah climbing inside his chest and curling up against his heart as if he were a fire to keep them warm.

Jayren's white-light swords manifested into white gold.

Tristan twisted and reared his head. His throat rumbled with a deep growl, and the sound caused Jayren to start to really *see.* Tristan's jaw dropped into an evil, beckoning bellow, a roar that plucked colors into existence, falling like fruit cut from a tree and left to rot. Jayren saw the colors: the light brown of his mother's eyes, the blue and green flannels his father wore. He noticed the gray-blue jeans that hung in his father's closet after his suicide, and he watched the blond of his sister's sun-bleached hair turn orange from her sudden reclusiveness once they moved south. The sound of his family at fall festivals or singing carols at Christmas was yellow like joy, like a sunflower blooming at the edge of summer. When Tristan's howl drew to a close, the yellow died out, a crumpled, decaying brown.

Tristan's long canines locked together, crossing over his face like a barred mask, and the colors washed away, turning back to a diluted gray. *I will kill your friends,* Tristan promised. His words filled the air as the color had, striking Jayren with bright, sour tones. *You will watch me destroy them.*

Jayren spun one of the weightless swords in his hand.

Tristan's sharp, spiked nose twisted towards him. Black ink peeled away into the air around him, turning it dark gray. *You cannot stop me.*

"No," Jayren agreed, slow and calm. "Not yet." He begged his voice not to fracture into broken sobs. "But one day, I will."

DECEMBER 17TH, 2106 A.D.
THE ABYSS
CORVUN KHLYDE

"You have a new partner. Meet him at the graveyard." Cephan had said simply that and no more. Corvun mulled over the words. Over and over and over. He stalked to the graveyard at the edge of the warehouse division of the Abyss.

It was open and dark, like everything else. Blackness filled in the voids like the white of a paper filled in the background of a coloring page. Tombstones stood there, though they bore no etching. People didn't die here in the Abyss. They got shot in the head, and then they came back. *And then they came back,* Corvun thought dreadfully. Corvun's stomach twisted up in a spring-trap of nerves. How *did* they come back? *How did they come back?*

He narrowed his eyes, glared across the bed of empty gravestones. The murky smell of the graveyard reminded him of a real one, where decaying bodies returned to the Earth. The thought tied Corvun's stomach into a sudden slipknot. He didn't think it was too far-fetched for a man who scarred angels with Hellfire to reverse the process of life and death. Corvun scoured his eyes over sleek marble. He stopped on one, a weeping angel with an overhanging arm, which had been severed at the elbow. A name sunk into the stone the angel stood on, as if an invisible signet ring was pressing the words into wax. It read: *Jayren Lyall Omans, March 2nd, 2089 – December 17th, 2106.*

"No, no, no," Corvun rushed over, fell on his knees before the grave. He pressed his fingers against the cold stone, trying to rub away the etching, hoping it might just be his imagination, the darkness, or the shadows playing with him. He read the words over and over and over. He scrambled back on the dirt, his black pants caked with the damp brown dirt, and he sank his fingers into the ground. He dug. Venatrix's text tone whistled in his pocket, but it sounded so far away. Corvun grabbed fistfuls of dirt from the divot he made. His eyes blurred. *You need a shovel,* he told himself.

He stood, and his knees seized up, and he lost his balance. He fell, he waited, then he stood again. He wiped the sweat from his forehead and neck, smearing himself with the dirt on his hands.

This isn't happenin', he thought bitterly. *You won't find a shovel. You won't.*

Corvun knelt again, and he dug harder, deeper, longer. The fabric of his shirt plastered to his skin, and he thought he smelled rain in the distance. It wasn't possible here, Corvun knew, but he had to hope for something. If it wasn't Jayren's living body buried six feet down, it had to be rain. *I'm goin' to go insane. I'm goin' insane.*

"Corvun!" a muffled shout, deeper down.

A wave of sickness rushed over Corvun. It felt as if someone had thrown a rotting burlap sack over his head and choked him with the string.

"Help me! Oh, god! *Corvun! Please!*"

"Hold on," Corvun shouted. He hoped to sound strong and sure, but he sounded young and helpless. "Hold on, please."

He dug for an hour.

As he brushed the final layers of soil from the wooden casket, Corvun heard nails on the wood. Jayren cried inside, sobbing with muffled, staccato notes. It was the same way Jayren woke during their overnighters, sputtering on tears he shed over nightmares of his father's death. He sounded just as scared, just as terrified. If not more.

"Listen to me, Jay," Corvun steadied his voice. His throat tightened. "Move to your left. I'm goin' to use a knife, alright?"

Jayren shuffled in the box.

Corvun grabbed his knife from his belt and flipped it open. He stabbed through the left side of the casket, wedged it in. Wood beams snapped and loosened. The smell of blood soaked the damp wood. Jayren's quaking sobs turned into frightened yelps. Corvun pried at the casket until there was enough leverage to pull the wood away with his bare hands. He reached into the dark hollow and took Jayren by the forearms.

Jayren tumbled out of the casket with lanky, awkward bones. His skeleton collapsed into Corvun, and Corvun hugged Jayren so fiercely that Jayren whimpered. He hugged back with wet, tacky fingers on the back of Corvun's neck.

The smell of copper hit Corvun full force. *Blood,* he realized. Jayren was covered in his own blood.

"Are you okay?" Corvun asked. A more appropriate question would have been: *What the hell are you doin' here? Why are you in a casket in a graveyard in the Abyss? How did you get here? Why would you do this?* Corvun couldn't start to understand what compelled Jayren to sell his life like this; he didn't know why or how it had happened. Still, the moment simmered down to only one question. He asked again, softer, "Are you okay?"

Jayren shook his head.

"Can you walk?"

Jayren hesitated. "Maybe," a weak answer. He nodded. "Yeah."

"Let's walk to a warehouse," Corvun said. "I'll help you."

Jayren tried to stand. His ankle twisted, and raw fingers dug into Corvun's shoulder. "I—I can't," he managed, then he cried.

"Then I'll carry you." Corvun didn't wait for Jayren's permission, nor did he comply when Jayren uttered an unconvincing refusal. He picked Jayren up and trudged his way out of the deadly slope he'd dug to save his friend. His legs were taut with pain. He glanced back at the scattered piles of dirt that resembled tiny burial mounds. Remnants of their past had been buried in Jayren's unearthing: their happiness, their sanity, their childhood, their innocence.

Jayren's head slumped into Corvun.

Corvun turned and carried Jayren to the edge of the warehouses. He journeyed into the uniform rows, trying to weave a pattern no one would be able to follow. He didn't know exactly how it worked—having a partner—but he had to hope he'd have some sort of sixth sense to track down Jayren if he couldn't find his own way back to the warehouse. Corvun learned very quickly that bullies existed in the Abyss too, and they loitered on the outskirts, patrolled the stagnant streets looking for an easy kill. Once Corvun lost sight of the graveyard and wandered for a few minutes, Corvun chose a warehouse. He kicked the door open, and the metal creaked and slammed on the opposite wall. Jayren flinched in his arms. He carried Jayren to the far corner, being careful to find a spot out of the light cast by the eerie lamps outside. Shadows always granted some sort of safety here.

Corvun knelt and laid Jayren down against the wall. He wrestled his own shirt off, sawed the sleeves free with his pocketknife, then covered Jayren with the remainder. He cut the sleeves into careful strips, sitting across from Jayren. He tried not to notice how Jayren looked, how he slumped, lopsided against the wall like a forgotten toy doll. His knobby, thin legs bent in awkward directions. Corvun couldn't stop thinking about how he still sort of looked dead. He paused, swallowed hard. "Give me your hand," he said.

Jayren's eyes were swollen and pink. He didn't move, just looked at Corvun numbly.

Emotion strangled Corvun. He reached out and took Jayren's hand. He opened his small, metal canteen and washed Jayren's hands as best he could. Jayren's hands were blistered, with splinters lodged in the fingertips and fingernails bent back. Where Jayren's nails had chipped and broken, there were sharp, jagged edges left cutting into his pink skin. The nail on Jayren's right pinky finger was mostly gone, and Corvun fought back another wave of aching nausea. Gently, Corvun wrapped each of Jayren's limp digits with shreds of his tee shirt sleeves.

"Am I dead? I'm dead, I know it," Jayren spoke, dry and breathy. "I saw a dragon. Dragons aren't real."

Back to this again? Corvun thought. *After everything happening right now?* Corvun sank against the wall beside him, and the two sat in silence for a long time. "I'll have to get supplies," Corvun said finally. "I have to get a clean bowl to soak your hands in, alcohol to clean them, food and water. You need clothes."

"I want to go home," Jayren's voice popped with emotion.

"This is your home now," Corvun said slowly. He got to one knee and one foot, ready to stand. He put one hand on Jayren's shoulder to calm him.

"Don't leave," Jayren begged. "Jusst," he struggled, "sstay. I-I'm sso sscared. Pleasse."

INTERLUDE III

THE ESCAPE

The constellation of Orion was chosen for the Horseman and Authority of Death, Mori. Mori will be a great and renowned fighter throughout all of his lives. His constellation was chosen to shine brighter than those around it.
— *A History of Hierarchy*

438 A.D.
ROME
SERPENS

Five gladiators remained.

From up above the sandy rink, a voice boomed, saying, "It's a fight to the death." The audience murmured. "Only one can survive. Only one can reclaim their freedom." The arena clattered with Roman soldiers, who lined the high observation decks. They all drew a bow and arrow.

Serpens looked around at the others warily. He didn't trust someone not to make a reckless move. Corvus had very little allegiance to anything. Venatici, Serpens guessed, wouldn't have the skill to win a fight against any of them. His only threat was if Orion made a sacrifice to save Ophiuchus and her child. They all eyed each other, and Serpens wondered how many of the others were running through the same kinds of thoughts in their heads.

Yet, no one made a move to kill another.

The Roman soldiers readied their arrows.

"Can we shoot them down?" Venatici asked slowly.

The tension changed. Serpens smelled that change in the atmosphere, a revaluation, a shift from fear to fight or flight. Their best bet was together, and Serpens would put money on all the others thinking the same thing. So he responded, "It would be suicide." Corvus stripped a nearby, slain gladiator of his shorts and tossed them to Serpens. Serpens dressed in the garment, wondering if his eyes had changed back to human eyes or if they were still snake-like slits.

"Orion, Venatici, Serpens," Corvus called quickly, "pick up bows and every loose arrow you can find." He took an arrow from his own quiver, nocked it, and pulled the string of his bow tight. "Ophiuchus, can you make us a way out?"

"Yes," she said.

Orion took up three arrows into this string, balanced the wood on his thumb, then breathed deep. He exhaled a fine spray of fire, lighting the tips of the bundled arrows.

Serpens's eyes locked on Orion. He saw the gland beneath his tongue lay flat and disappear behind Orion's crooked grin. Orion winked at Serpens, grinned even wider at Corvus.

Corvus lifted his bow and arrow. "Stay alive," he said. "That's an order."

ORION

Orion's throat pulsed with the tangy, metallic aftertaste of fire in his lungs. "Stay behind me," he told Venatici. He listened to her shaking breaths. "Hold that bow high, and aim behind the guards. Aim to shoot through them." Orion pulled his arrows back, his muscles burning in protest from his earlier stab wounds. His arrows *whisked* up into the audience, and the onlookers scattered with a frantic cry of, "*Fire! Fire!*" Orion glanced over his shoulder at Venatrici, watched her shoot one arrow. The military commander fell from the highest post. The side of Orion's mouth tugged upward. His stomach filled with the liquor of her scent, her sweat, and her raw ambition. "Again," he said.

They stood back to back, calling warnings to one another as trouble came their way. Orion kicked arrows to her, and Venatici swiveled and plucked each arrow from the ground as if it were a dance she grew up learning. She offered each tip to him, which he lit with the wild flame from under his tongue. They dodged and ducked away from each arrow the Roman soldiers rained down on them.

Venatici cried out suddenly, her hand finding Orion's waist and holding tight.

Orion spun around to her, and she steadied herself on him. An arrow protruded from deep in her thigh.

"Release the lions!" a guard shouted.

No, no, no, no, Orion thought.

"Get it out," she cried.

"No time," he said. He put one hand over her thigh and snapped the wood with his other hand. He hoisted Venatici up into his arms. Two arrows lodged deep in the ground right by Orion's feet. He panted, backing away from the center of the arena.

"Orion!" Corvus called.

Orion spun.

A lion prowled towards him; Corvus stood in the distance beyond it. He readied an arrow, piercing the lion in the back haunch. The beast flinched and twisted, bearing long fangs at

Corvus. Corvus loosed two more arrows at the cat—one to the head and one to the throat. "Come on!" Corvus yelled at Orion and Venatici.

Orion raced towards Corvus, and Venatici held tight to his neck. Corvus shot down three guards in three quick draws. The remaining Roman soldiers fled the fire Orion and Venatici started in the stands. Orion breathed in relief. Now they only had the lions to worry about. He spotted Serpens and Ophiuchus at the exit gate. Ophiuchus touched the heavy bolt barring the door with blackened hands, and Serpens defended her from the lions as she worked, his sword slashing in wide circles.

Orion watched Serpens as he and Corvus ran. Serpens's attacks were short and precise, fast and lethal. He cut down two lions, countering the animals' attacks as if he'd been raised in a pride. A third lion lunged at him, and he drew a knife from his belt, striking the lion's ribcage and throwing the beast aside.

"Hurry!" Ophiuchus screamed. She shoved the charred bolt aside, and the lock turned to ash. She and Serpens hauled the heavy gate open.

Dust and heat stung Orion's eyes. Sand kicked up from his sandals and burned hot needle-points in his calves. Corvus made it to the door before Orion, turned, and shot more arrows behind Orion.

Orion heard the lion's thudding paws, the growls and whimpers. When he reached the gate, he lowered Venatici, ushered her into Ophiuchus's arms, then turned and exhaled flames. The fire created a burning border between the lions and themselves, and Orion helped Corvus and Serpens drag the door shut.

SERPENS

Serpens slinked around the empty corridors, sensing the distance. There were no heat markers in his vision, meaning there were no bodies lurking in the tunnels close by, and he couldn't hear anything but the echoes of their own voices. Venatici whimpered and yelped as Corvus and Orion tied her leg and removed the arrow lodged in her thigh. Her cries bounced down the brick halls and disappeared into the flame-lit distance. Serpens kept watch. "We don't have much time," he reasoned. "News will spread, and there will be eyes all over the streets."

Corvus stood and met Serpens where he kept watch. "I know someone," he said. "She'll be at the docks. She owes me a favor. If we can get there, we're in the clear."

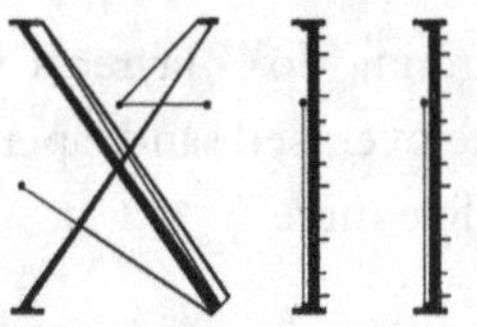

STELLA MARIS

RUST assassins have the ability to move in shadows. It is a power granted to them by the Black Magic that holds RUST together. They can use this ability to warp in and out of different planes, effectively traveling to the Abyss and back. They can also use it in combat.
— A History of Hierarchy (Revised Edition)

DECEMBER 18TH, 2106 A.D.
NORTHEAST FLORIDA
CORVUN KHLYDE

Corvun brought Jayren back to Earth, relocating them from the Abyss to Corvun's bedroom floor. As soon as they had their bearings, Corvun shoved his Glass phone towards Jayren and insisted he call Lacey. "Tell her you're stayin' here for the weekend," he said. Corvun gave Jayren new clothes to wear, got him a glass of water and a protein bar, and after all was said and done, they sat together in silence.

"She's not going to let me live there anymore," Jayren concluded.

"She won't," Corvun agreed. He thought of how his own father (who had brought the consequence of RUST on Corvun) barely let him live at home anymore, either. His father had said it was necessary, that it would help Corvun become who he was meant to be, but Corvun knew his stepmother had some say in the matter, too. Corvun scoffed.

"What are we gonna do?" Jayren's voice was frail and worn and ripping like overused sandpaper.

"We're goin' to live there."

"*There?*"

"Yeah," Corvun said.

They were quiet a while longer.

"I'm goin' to go see someone. I want you to stay here until I'm back, okay?"

"Yeah, man. No problem."

Corvun heard the fear and terror in Jayren's voice; he wouldn't leave Corvun's small nine-by-nine room because it was safe. It might've even proved safer than Jayren's own bedroom. Lacey, after being taken under Valentine North's wing, adopted the same hellbent mentality of the Archangels to take down RUST. It was some sort of lifelong feud. Valentine North and the Archangels may have had a large role to play in the North Institute, but it was mostly for show in the humans' eyes. They needed the power and influence to go against RUST publicly, the resources to move against the dark, underground power. North Institute was respected; North Institute and RUST were mortal enemies. Corvun had been offered some sort of gracious immunity for being Michael's son, but he wasn't sure that extended to Jayren if he was found out. Corvun crouched in front of Jayren and held his face. "Listen," he said. "Lie down and get some rest. Act like you're asleep if my parents come in and hide your wrist. And stay here," he annunciated the last words, hard and stern.

"*Yessir,*" Jayren managed.

Corvun helped him up into his bed.

. . . .

The sun didn't warm the cold. High noon was as bad as an exam Corvun hadn't prepared for. It seemed no amount of prepping had him ready for anything happening in his life these days. He thought about his draft for his North Institute internship as he walked down Centre Street. He didn't feel ready for the presentation he'd have to give for that either. The prompt had been to write about a overcoming a hardship, and Corvun had written about RUST. Venatrix was exceptionally proud of what he wrote, and even though he hadn't once mentioned RUST, she'd connected the dots. She always did.

Corvun slipped into the Angels' Diner. The gold handle was icy to the touch, but it gave way to the warmer bar. A few humans lingered around the tables, speaking softly to one another. A couple sat by the window with just their fingertips touching. Steaming, hot drinks and breathy laughter mingled between them. The young man had a lipstick smear on his jaw, near his ear. Corvun kept looking, kept browsing, trying to act as if he was only people watching even though his eyes searched for Carina. When Corvun turned to Joshuah at the bar, Joshuah was already looking at him. Corvun stepped over to the counter and sat stiffly. "Anythin' with spiced rum," he said, slow and careful. They both knew that they couldn't speak freely about angels or demons or anything in between with humans in the bar, so their exchange was distant and cordial.

Joshuah mixed Corvun a drink on the rocks and slid the glass across the slick, glossy counter.

Corvun grabbed Joshuah's wrist before he could pull back. "Where is she?" he asked quietly.

"She told me not to say."

"Did she know I would come today?"

"Somehow." Joshuah sounded nervous. He rubbed his neck; his breath swallowed his words. "Man, I don't know how she knows. It's a sixth sense."

"I need her help." Corvun's voice cracked. He shook his head, trying to dismiss the strange things Joshuah said. He couldn't feign the confidence he'd perfected over the past year, let alone think straight enough to follow what Joshuah was saying. "Where is she? *Please*."

"She's headed to the docks," Joshuah said. He spoke so quietly that it made Corvun wonder if someone else was trying to listen in. "She left just a couple minutes before you got here."

CARINA BLACKROCK

Carina wrapped Leroy's massive leather coat around her. The fabric was coarse and dry and three times too big for her. It smelled of salt, sweat, old worn leather, and fleetingly of an expensive cologne she'd scraped up her savings to buy Leroy for his fiftieth birthday. She'd purchased the cologne from an overseas merchant on one of their routine mail stops, bartering the remaining amount with a pearl necklace of her own. She remembered how Leroy had joked about all the ladies he'd woo at port, about how he was *finally* a gentleman. Carina felt small without her old friend.

And she felt followed.

Just as Leroy's coat smelled like her memories of him, the Deceivers smelled of their sins. Leroy had taught her this too, and she knew Sloth and Greed best. She'd heard rumors of the others. Lust smelled of a gentleman's bar, thick with smoke and perfume and skin and sex. Envy smelled like poison, sour and stinging and eating away at the heart. Sloth was that of a lavender and chamomile bath too good to leave. Greed smelled like gold. Gold, silver, precious metals, and nickel and copper, too; of a coin being rubbed between two fingers.

A harsh breeze blew down the street, whipping Carina's hair around her face. She struggled to fight it all back behind her ears. Clouds raced across the sky, blowing that very scent her way. She smelled money, smelled power. She smelled Avon.

She shouldn't have smelled him, though. Leroy told Carina many times that Avon, the Kraken, was bound to the sea by Marks laid by the Archangels themselves. Avon should have been unable to leave the sea, but Carina smelled him close by, only yards away.

Carina spun, searching the horizon. The quaint downtown street looked the same as it had since her arrival. Trees grew slow and languid, and green weeds pushed through weakened concrete. Paint chipped off brick buildings here and there. Old murals faded into dusty cream, mauve, and stale brown. Up above, Carina spotted a crow sitting atop a building. The bird watched her. It was unmatched in size. That was the giveaway: The crow was bigger, stronger, more lethal. Built to slaughter. Carina had grown up fearing shadowy appearances like these because RUST assassins could take the form of anything black—a crow or any array of birds, a dog or a wolf, a cat or rodent. Anything considered bad luck. The crow ruffled its feathers, and shadows cascaded downward, another telltale sign. It blinked and looked past her.

Between the two buildings to her left, there was a creaking groan. It reminded Carina of the mast breaking on Leroy's ship.

She jerked in the direction of the sound.

Clouds covered the sun. A chill covered her skin.

If something hid there between the brick buildings, she couldn't see it. Carina knew Deceivers could make themselves invisible to angels, to demons, to mortal humans. In that form, they manipulated things around them by means of demonic power only. On other occasions, Deceivers would take human form to be seen and interact in the human world. Carina had experienced Sloth that way, and she had seen proof of Sorrow's presence in the material world in Orion and Ophiah's existence. That the children of a Deceiver walked the Earth meant that a Deceiver had taken human form to conceive and raise the twins. Carina wondered if their rich, warm features were true to who they were or if they used a slight of eye—deception—to hide their true nature.

Carina glanced back at the crow with a queasy feeling in her stomach, only to find it'd abandoned its perch. She closed her eyes, breathed deep, and kept walking towards the marina. If she could get to the water, she'd be able to fight better, to run if she needed to.

Shadows clotted her vision suddenly. Gentle hands wrapped around her arms and backed her into a different alley. When the black cleared, she glared into big, dark, puppy-dog eyes.

"Quiet," Corvun whispered in his shadowy mist. He stood very, very close to her. He wore a simple outfit, black head-to-toe, and he looked deadly. Only RUST assassins wore black in this day and age. It was a signature look the assassins adopted, and no one wanted to even risk being associated with the group. Over time, black clothes went out of style. Corvun didn't seem to mind flaunting his status to anyone who might spot him. His uncombed brown hair reminded her he was still young and irresponsible. Liquor tinged his breath. She studied the brown freckles that poked his skin. It looked as if someone dipped their fingers in chocolate and flicked it at his face. Carina wondered what he tasted like, if his lips were soft and sweet like chocolate too, or if they tasted like the leftovers of his liquor.

Corvun looked to the street.

Carina followed his gaze.

Avon sauntered the sidewalk, throwing a black and gold cane in a wide circle around him to rest it on his shoulder. He wore a monocle and carried a pipe tight between his lips. He didn't look like the pirate that attacked her at sea, but his demeanor was the same. Carina knew Avon couldn't sense her or locate her unless her greed got the better of her, but part of her wondered if Avon *did* know that she and Corvun stood quietly together, if he was only taunting the inevitable.

"Fitting name, Corvus," Carina teased under her breath. She needed to get him away from her; she'd been trained against feeling greed, and he hadn't.

Corvun glared at her. His eyes held such intensity: fire and ice, passion and hatred, the knowledge to save a life and the ability to take one. His eyes were not necessarily pretty. They were deep and dark and worn in. The bags beneath them painted his face with tired colors, purple and blue bruises from the lack of rest. His lips pressed thin, and he whisked away with the wind when it gusted again. His presence was nothing more than inky shadows dragging away in the direction he had gone. Towards Avon.

Carina ran in the opposite direction. God save his soul if Corvun wanted to face a Deceiver with abilities vastly beyond his own. Carina would rather save what she had left of hers. But a *snap* and *crack* of a gunshot rooted Carina's feet to the ground. Her heart beat in her throat. She spun. In the distance on the street, Corvun stamped his foot hard on a wooden plank of a broken crate. Something shiny flipped into the air, and Avon's eyes followed. Avon's appearance changed, a heavy leather coat swinging around his ankles. Teeth bared in his snarl as he glared at the coin in the sky. Corvun unholstered a sleek, fifty-caliber gun and fired twice. The bullets ripped through Avon's figure, streaking out behind him like skipping stones on a lake. Darkness followed the bullets like the ripple effect of water.

Corvun caught the coin in a fist, stepped closer, and jammed the gun against Avon's forehead. Avon vanished a second later, cackling like the pirate Carina knew him to be. "Reckless boy," Avon's voice echoed. "I smell your sin. You want power. Let me give it to you."

Carina saw Corvun's hesitation. She hesitated too, then whistled between two fingers, sharp and angry. Corvun's attention turned to her in a split second. He took off running, his weight collapsing into black, sulking shadows that pulled in her direction. The awkward, inhuman slingshot movement unnerved her, reminding her of her own time in RUST. Her breath hitched when he stood only inches from her.

"What is this?" Corvun asked in a brash snap. He held a coin in her line of vision.

"How did you get that?" Carina had put the coin on a chain that morning, tucked into her shirt. She reddened at the thought of him noticing the coin and swiping it without her realizing. Carina tried to snatch the Sacajawea dollar from him.

Corvun moved too fast, slipping the coin out of her reach. "Why do you have it?"

"Give it *back*."

"This is blood money," Corvun said. He flashed the coin at her again. "My father once sold a life for a dollar coin. He said it was one of his partners in RUST, that it was an attempt at a plan to free him from the RUST pact." Corvun's eyes searched hers. He swore under his breath. "He had a coat like that. I've seen pictures of his partner wearin' that coat."

He was close again, so close Carina could smell his sweat and stale blood on his hands. She shoved him away.

Something snapped in the distance again. Her chest rattled with a frenzy. "We need to leave this place. Avon is going to come back and kill us both."

"We need to talk," Corvun said. He retained his calm, bewildering Carina.

How is he calm? That demon will slaughter him. Carina looked out of the alley then back to Corvun; he gazed down at her, searching for something he wanted, something she had.

"Let's make a deal," Corvun said.

Heavy steps clunked closer. The sound bounced around the hazy afternoon, and Carina couldn't pinpoint the source.

"I can take you somewhere to protect you, to hide you," Corvun said.

"I do not need your protection."

Corvun seemed amused. "In return I need you to keep a friend of mine safe. Jayren gave himself to RUST." Corvun watched her, and she saw a threat of tears in his eyes. Carina wondered if he would fall apart in front of her. She scoffed; he couldn't cry to get what he wanted, not from her. Still, a hook snagged her heart and reeled her in. Maybe it was Corvun; maybe it was the thought of the harmless guardian angel boy turning himself into a killer. Even if she didn't know Jayren, she understood what he was doing. Sentinels were so much more effective as warriors. "Cephan buried Jayren alive," Corvun continued. "He's traumatized, Stella."

The world slowed around Carina. Corvun's eyes held her steady. "Stella?" she demanded an explanation for the name.

"The name I'm choosin' to call you." He sounded so sure, as if he'd picked her lock not with a key but with the knowledge he'd pieced together for himself. "I promise I won't ask about your other names. They don't matter to me. Whoever you were before, that's your secret. You have my word. But I need your help," he begged.

"Okay." She wasn't sure why she agreed, but in that moment, it was easy to hand him her heart. Corvun lifted her into his arms, and shadows swirled around both of them. Carina wrapped her arms around Corvun's neck as he warped them to the Abyss.

. . . .

Carina stood in the warehouse, her nerves still buzzing. Corvun left hours ago to retrieve supplies to make the warehouse livable. Carina swept the area, wiped down the windows, and checked on Jayren every now and then. Now—having done everything she could for the old skeleton of a building—she paced back and forth in front of Jayren.

Jayren sat on the floor with his knees tucked beneath his chin and his hands wrapped around a red blanket. The pink irritation around his features made her throat hurt. She didn't pity. She couldn't *feel* pity. But she assumed if there was such a feeling for her, it might be what she felt now, that thread-thin adrenaline that kept her upright with her knees locked and her senses on high alert. Carina hesitated, stopped pacing. Jayren didn't bother to acknowledge her, even in their good two or three hours stuck together. She wanted to speak to him, but she didn't know how. She took a step over, and his eyes snapped up to her.

"My name is Stella," she said calmly, as if she were trying to coax an abused animal. She knelt to show him she meant no harm.

"Your name is Carina," he said to her. "Corvun can call you whatever pet name he likes. He told me your name is Carina." There was something deeply sarcastic and bitter about Jayren's voice. The dry edge of his words warned her against coming any closer mentally or physically.

Still, she asked, "Can I sit beside you?"

"No." Jayren nodded at the space before him. "But you can sit there."

Carina sat cross-legged where she knelt, feeling the tacky, dirty concrete under her palms.

"He told me you have a lot of names."

"This is not an interrogation," Carina said.

"Yes it is," Jayren said. He sounded so sure of himself.

Carina laughed, bright and loud, startling Jayren. "Alright, fine. What is that blanket?" she asked.

Jayren's eyes and nostrils flared. The dim halo above his head flashed brighter. His lips worked for words, but nothing came. His pale green eyes slitted, fixing her with a serpentine glare. Carina almost expected him to spit venom at her, but he sat, stone-still and calculating.

"You are Mars," Carina said slowly. She saw it now—how his halo was red, not white or yellow fire like all the other Sentinels she'd met. Something clicked together in his eyes, some sort of recognition of the name. Confusion blurred over it.

"Mars?"

"Your God-given name," Carina said. "It is Latin for war."

"Yeah, that's what they say," Jayren said. He didn't sound so sure anymore, now that Carina had turned his game back on him. "Who are you?"

It was Carina's turn to double back inwardly. She'd never been asked that question, only been accused of the lore and legend of her names. She wanted to burn her names to ashes, to take a new one—maybe the one Corvun offered her—and become something more than her rumors. Jayren offered her that chance, but she wasn't sure what to tell him. *It would only be fair to give him your God-given name in exchange for his*, she thought to herself. Aloud, she said, "Corvun told me you do not believe."

Jayren rolled his eyes. His face paled like a rosy paintbrush in a cup of water. He looked away and rested his head against the wall.

"You are tired of hearing that?" she guessed.

"Yeah." He wrapped his hands in the red fabric again.

"Well, you can choose if you want to believe me after you hear what I have to say," she said. She watched him turn back to her. "I am like you, a Sentinel. But there are only two like us. We are the most powerful in our rank of angels."

"You make it sound so epic. I still get zits. How old are you anyway?"

She wasn't quite sure. She knew she'd been a young child—perhaps a toddler—when Valentine and Michael were enlisted in RUST. But she didn't age the same as humans, that much she was sure of. She had always been painfully aware of everything happening, always carried her memories, even the ones from the very beginning. She didn't have a good answer for Jayren, so she gave him the first number she thought of. "Twenty-seven."

"So you're a cougar," Jayren said.

"What?"

"Nothing. You don't look like you're thirty."

"I said twenty-seven," Carina said stiffly. This boy did have a way of getting under one's skin. Fitting, she thought, for who he is.

"That's pretty vague."

"If I tell you the truth, you cannot tell Corvun. He will regret bringing me here."

Jayren offered his swollen, meagerly wrapped pinky finger.

Carina watched in frustrated confusion. She couldn't decide if the gesture was offensive or not. She'd never seen Leroy do anything but lift a middle finger, never a pinky.

Jayren gave her the biggest eye roll she'd ever witnessed. She'd seen demons give her a half-hearted eyes-to-the-corner, but Jayren's eyes disappeared beneath his eyelids. "Pinky promise. It means I won't tell him, okay? Like, cross my heart, hope to die, ride or die. Y'know?"

"No," she said.

"Okay," Jayren said. He shifted, crawled over to sit cross-legged right in front of her. "It means that I promise. Genuinely promise, with no intention to lie to you." He looked at her with a very intense gaze, something more mature than she expected from him. She wondered if Corvun lied about him not believing. Jayren offered his pinky again. "I *promise* I won't tell Corvun. This stays between us."

Carina raised her hand.

"Make a fist. Hold the pinky," Jayren said.

She followed his instructions.

Jayren smiled with the corner of his mouth. He grabbed her pinky with his with a youthful vigor.

"My God-given name is Azrael," she introduced herself. "I am the Angel of Death."

· · · ·

They talked until Corvun returned. Jayren asked wide-eyed, eager questions about the Bermuda Triangle, about the demons there, and about Carina's seafaring trips with Leroy to distant lands. Carina wasn't convinced Jayren would keep the secrets from Corvun, but she prayed he would. She wasn't sure that Corvun would trust her after he learned her true identity. His father, Michael, hadn't, but rather watched her with faraway fascination. It made her feel alien; Jayren made her feel more human than she ever had.

Corvun returned in a whisk of black, holding two dufflebags. His switchblade gaze pierced through where she and Jayren sat—huddled together, swapping hurried stories—and Carina felt his cold down to her bones. This life was sucking the warmth from Corvun.

Carina and Jayren stood to greet him.

Corvun offered Carina the bags then turned to the door. He pulled his fingerless, leather glove off and pressed his palm to a simple glass panel to the right of the warehouse door. The building lit up with pale lights.

"Can people see through the windows?" Jayren asked warily.

"No." Corvun didn't turn. "It's a mind-link. I can control the warehouse with Black Magic. Cephan grants all the assassins Black Magic to do things like this… On the outside, it looks abandoned like it did when we first got here. But it's locked. No one's gettin' in. It's safe." Corvun stayed still, his gloved hand clenched around his other empty glove. He blinked away tears with a bob in his throat, and Carina noticed it all. Corvun had to know it himself, that he was slipping away. It seemed, Carina assumed, that all the Archangels and Deceivers and other authorities knew that the Horsemen had potential for great evil if not trained right. Why else would Cephan bargain for Corvun's life? They were a piece of a bigger puzzle. Finally, Corvun asked, "Did he behave?"

"Did you tell him I am his babysitter?" Carina asked, crossing her arms.

"Jayren, this is your babysitter, Carina," Corvun called over Carina's head.

"Thanks, mom! Dad's a better babysitter than you."

Corvun gave Jayren a loving glare, and Carina fought a laugh. "Here," Corvun said with a hint of a smile. "I got some first aid supplies." Corvun gave Carina clean bandages, a bucket of water and salt, and a small scrub. They went back to Jayren and set the supplies down.

Carina sat in front of Jayren again, but he shrank away at the sight of the white bucket and scrub. He hid his hands, and Carina reached out to rest a hand on his knee. "It will feel better afterwards. Your hands will become infected if we do not clean them. Please," Carina said. She lifted her hand, held it open for him. "I will be gentle."

"It's her or me," Corvun said.

Jayren glanced at Corvun then gave Carina his hand. Tears dripped from his eyes as she dipped his hands into the salt water and scrubbed at his chipped and torn nails. Her eyes welled too, a poison swimming at the top of her stomach. His fingers bled from the reopened wounds. Corvun changed the water five times for each hand. Dirt flaked from Jayren's skin little by little, like dirty snow falling from the sky. His knuckles turned splotchy and pink, and his face was red by the time she finished. She wrapped his hands, and he watched her with eyes that were so thin, so scared, that his narrow pupils smeared away in his tears.

"We will take care of you," Carina promised.

Jayren took his hands from her. His bandages blossomed with red.

DECEMBER 18TH, 2106 A.D.
THE ABYSS
JAYREN OMANS

Jayren carried himself up the stairs of the warehouse. He hurt in ways he didn't know he could. His fingers were stiff with cotton tucked between them. He felt as though a really powerful, robotic spider had woven him into a web of barbed wire and stretched his limbs to their limits. The spider had venom, too, that ripped little marks in his memory with the same painful, metallic aftertaste. He couldn't remember bits and pieces of the past few days. His body gave out frequently. The same as now. He lost his footing on the stairs, knees bending at awkward angles.

Carina, who walked behind him, caught him. Her arms held him like Mother Nature. She picked him off the metal stairs with arms like tree branches and carried him the rest of the way up to the dorm—or maybe to Heaven. Did it matter? It didn't make sense. She wasn't as big as he was, so he must've lost weight or *she* must've been superhuman strong. He tried to wrap his mind around it, but by the time she laid him on a white cot, the sharp tang of metal seared deep into his brain. Lying flat on his back, he suddenly couldn't recall how he got there at all.

Carina pulled a cover over him.

"Do we have a bath?" Jayren asked. "I feel so gross."

Carina said something distant. Her words sounded like the mist in a mountain range. There, but silent.

"I'm gonna puke," Jayren said as nausea overtook him.

Carina moved quickly and held a trash can beside his bed.

He leaned over and dry heaved. His chest hurt. The gagging squeezed his chest so tightly he couldn't catch his breath. He didn't puke. Nothing came up, in fact. He just tasted stomach acid in the back of his mouth.

"Corvun!" Carina yelled.

Jayren's head hurt. "Holy hell," he swore.

"Turn off the light," Corvun said.

The room went black.

"Is he okay?" Carina asked.

"Am I okay?" Jayren echoed.

"He's just started changin'," Corvun said to Carina.

"Changing?" Jayren asked. Corvun said something faint—something about "his angelic form"—that Jayren couldn't make out. Jayren looked from Corvun to Carina, and they flashed in neon color. Behind Corvun's figure, two massive, white-hot wings tucked calmly behind his shoulders. They were huge. The size of the wings was Corvun's body mass multiplied by four or five times. The wings didn't fit in the room, either; they went straight through the ceiling and walls. *That's because they're not real,* Jayren told himself.

Jayren heaved over the trash can again.

Corvun walked to Jayren and knelt. The white mass behind him billowed to combat gravity, like a cat flailing its tail to stay upright on a fence.

Jayren could make out Corvun's face between the purples and reds and pinks that swirled over his skin. The hard, grayscale surface (that pulsed with color like seismic waves) gave depth to his figure. Jayren reached past Corvun's shoulder and grabbed for a handful of feathers. Corvun smelled like rum and like his car—an old, navy candle fragrance, Jayren's flat soda from their favorite burger joint, leather, and rubber. Jayren would give anything to be back in Corvun's car, all the windows down and the sunroof open, speeding down twisting roads and rapping together as loud as they could. They lived to annoy; now the memory just annoyed him.

Corvun watched Jayren's outstretched hand.

"I'm delusional," Jayren decided when he couldn't feel any of the feathers behind Corvun.

"You are not delusional… Corvun, he sees your wings. It is an ability of his, as a Sentinel."

Corvun stiffened.

"I can't touch your wings, Corv," Jayren slurred.

Corvun pushed Jayren back down into the bed gently. He pulled a blanket up to Jayren's shoulders, and Jayren realized he was cold. Goosebumps pricked his arms and legs, and even the coarse, over-bleached white blanket was welcome. He watched Corvun and Carina exchange a few more bubbling words. By the time their communication reached him, it was in a language he couldn't decipher. The two floated away, and Jayren sank to the bottom of the ocean floor. His body wouldn't move, so he closed his eyes. He breathed in thick, watery oxygen until darkness finally wrapped around him.

CORVUN KHLYDE

Corvun watched Carina from the doorway of the community shower. She was dressed in his clothes—a black tee and gym shorts—and she worked through her newly washed hair with a toothed comb. The comb snagged on her tangled, curly hair. Corvun wondered if she missed the sea-breeze in her hair, if she still wanted to be on the water. He didn't have the guts to ask her about her seafaring. She didn't belong here; she looked out of place. She shone brightly, and the dull, gray room around her resembled more of a milk carton than the grand vanity Corvun thought she would appreciate. She showed no aversion to the room, though, and he wondered if he had her all wrong.

Carina's gold eyes flashed at him from the mirror. "Like what you see?"

Corvun looked away, finding the empty shower stalls much more interesting.

"Stella," she said. "Where did you get that name?"

"It's Latin for star," he said.

Carina laid the comb down and turned to him. "So you study Latin, too. I thought Leroy was mad when he said all angels knew the language."

Corvun was suddenly very aware of the nervous heat spreading to the tips of his fingers and toes. "I just… I wouldn't know how to thank you for helpin' me look after Jayren. I just figured, since you hated all your other names…"

"Just say thank you." Carina's eyes burned into his, smoldering into yellow embers. They glowed, unnerving him, reminding him just how feral she was. Lithe muscles flexed beneath her speckled skin as she walked to him, and her cat-like eyes sized him up. She tucked her strawberry blond hair behind her ear, challenging him to speak.

Corvun felt unworthy in her presence. Still, he whispered, "Thank you."

Carina smiled with her teeth.

. . . .

The following week was quiet, muffled with thin layers of snow on Earth and recovering hearts buried in the Abyss. Jayren stayed in bed, and Carina tended to him with hot apple cider and warm washcloths to his forehead. Corvun skipped the winter dance at North Academy to look after Jayren, though Jayren asked about the dance multiple times. "Who did Ophiah go with? Who did Orion go with? Did Orion ever ask Venatrix?" Jayren dozed through Corvun's short answers of, "I don't know. I'll have to ask. They haven't said."

Corvun learned from Venatrix that she had not gone. Orion never asked her, and she hadn't seen him at school in the days leading up to the dance. Ophiah was absent those days, too. Venatrix assumed things were going downhill at home for both the twins. When Corvun gave Jayren the answers, he left the last part out.

Christmas was a flicker of light that came and went like a short-wicked candle.

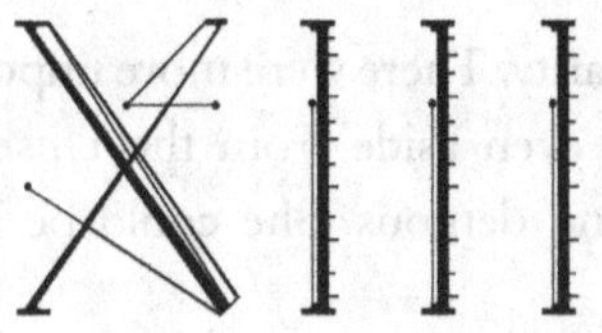

THE ARCHIVES

Marks are protections cast by angels, much like spells or enchantments.
Marks come in many different forms. A couple of examples of Marks
are Binding Marks, which suppress the affected's power, and Cloaking
Marks, which hide one's true nature from being detected. Cloaking
Marks can also be used on locations…
— *A History of Hierarchy*

DECEMBER 31ST, 2106
NORTHEAST FLORIDA
VENATRIX CANES

Venatrix snuck out just before dark. She managed to contact Orion over the winter break by tucking a folded note in the seal of his window. She found a reply three days later in the arms of the plant just below. They'd agreed to meet at the library for an all-nighter to catch up and do some more research. It was risky, sure, but so was what was happening at Orion's house. She brought with her a few hair ties—one in a small bob of a ponytail, one on her wrist—several bobby pins stuck strategically in her hair, and a glass dagger (stolen from her mother's vanity). It was all stashed in anticipation of what she would need to do tonight.

The Earthy scent of moist wood and forest undergrowth soaked into her skin. She loved the outdoors when she was little. Then came the standards, the makeup, the boys, the pressure of popularity. There were more important things, she realized, possibly even aside from the Unseen Wars waged between angels and demons. She could be happy. *That* was important.

Thunder groaned in the distance, seconding her thoughts.

The sun slipped through the twisting branches of live oaks and dripping Spanish moss. She thought about how much she missed Orion as she picked her way through the forest between her house and the library. The dirt was soft and fertile between her toes. Bushes snagged at her pajamas, and she pushed them away with the low-hanging vines that brushed at her hair.

Orion met her by the back door of the library, speckled with leaves, tiny fibers of moss on his jeans, and a resurrection fern perched on his shoulder. He had a black eye and a welting, purple and green bruise on his left arm.

Venatrix ran to him and threw her arms around his middle. She held him as tightly as she could. "Hey," she whispered.

"Hey," he whispered. The setting sun dappled his damaged skin with gold. "We don't have a lot of time. We should get inside," he said. "Do they have alarms?"

"No," Venatrix said. Orion picked her arms off him, and reluctantly she pulled two bobby pins from her hair. She approached the back door, bending the black metal pieces into the tools she needed. She picked the lock quickly, swiveling the bobby pins back and forth to align the lock.

Behind her, Orion said, "I missed you." She didn't have to see his smile. He made the whole forest quiver with excitement. She glanced over her shoulder to find him standing there with his arms crossed loosely over his chest and a meek smile. It was a bright smile—brighter than any full-blooded angel's smile—and it existed in spite of all he'd been through. Venatrix loved that smile. She stood in awe of him.

"C'mon," she whispered, tilting her head towards the open door. Orion neared her, and he cast a warm, soothing shadow over her as they slipped in together. She closed the door, and he rested his hand on top of hers. She blushed, gazing up at his green eyes and cheeky smirk. "Did your mom ever tell you about the Angels' Archive?" she asked.

"No," Orion said.

"The Archive keeps books about angel history. Every library has access to it since angels are everywhere. It's not in the actual floor plan, but there's a portal." Venatrix took his hand and snuck across the hollow library to the stairs. They rounded the spiral, metal staircase to reach the overhanging second floor.

"How does that work?" Orion asked.

"The same way they cover up the past and do anything else. Prayers and Marks."

Orion's eyes twinkled curiously in the dark, and Venatrix tugged him towards a maintenance door. "It's in there?" he asked. She nodded, then he said, "Anyone can go in there."

"Try," she challenged.

He grabbed the handle and twisted. A closet full of brooms and mops, books for a clearance sale, and cobwebbed walls gaped back at them. "Those books?"

Venatrix laughed and closed the door. She took her mother's glass blade out and cut a shallow slice in her palm. She reached for the handle again, twisted, then opened the door. A shadowy hall revealed itself on the other side.

Orion said nothing. He stepped into the hall after her and closed the door.

Venatrix found a light string and pulled. A single bulb switched on. The hall wasn't as big as it first seemed. It was more of a sort of attic with a low ceiling, dense with old books and the smell of paper and pages. She wandered down a side row, running her fingers over the spines of the books at eye level. Dust caked her fingertips.

Orion appeared at the end of the row she'd tucked herself into. She smiled at him. He glowed a rich gold color in the dim yellow light, like a statue in a museum. The low lights highlighted the royal arches in his face, drenched him in liquid-gold armor. She took a book off the shelf and blew dust at him playfully. He sparkled in the pale glitter. Orion stalked to her and scooped her up suddenly, and Venatrix dropped her book on the musky wooden floor. Orion held her up against the wall, his lips brushing hers.

"We're supposed to be studying," she whispered against his mouth.

"If he drags me to Hell, I want to be able to say I loved you with my whole heart," he said.

Venatrix's voice failed her. She fell into his lips when he kissed her. He kissed her like she was oxygen, and she dug her fingers into his shoulders, feeling his flex beneath her hands, his chest against hers. Her pajamas slipped ajar, but he didn't touch the skin they exposed. He didn't move his mouth from hers. "You won't fail," Venatrix sputtered when she caught her breath. Her heart thundered. "You can't."

Orion hugged her, swift and tight, catching her off guard. He squeezed her, threatening to never let go. "I'm scared that I will," Orion said, his words muffled in her top.

Venatrix lifted his face in his hands and kissed him again. "I love you," she said, staring at his yellow-green eyes. She'd never said those words to a boy before.

"I love you," he whispered back.

. . . .

Venatrix and Orion sat on the floor of the Angels' Archive long into the night, books open and around their legs and ankles in the shape of a crown. They flipped through pages, outlining things with a blunt, four-inch pencil they found on the floor. They worked alone and they worked together, calling out each other's names when they found something relevant. Venatrix touched him frequently—when she would reach across him or in front of her—to keep her balance. Each time Orion watched her, enchanted. But they didn't kiss again. They searched until they found every last tidbit of information on any sort of immunity Orion could use for himself, any prayer or song or Mark to protect his soul. They recited the facts until they memorized them. They worked 'til Orion's alarm—set to mark sunrise—beeped a monotone melody.

Venatrix tore a page from one of the music books.

"What are you doing?" Orion craned his neck.

"Don't look!" Venatrix smiled. She pulled her knees to her chest to obscure his vision as she scribbled a note on the score. She folded it up into a neat square then handed it to him. She pulled back before he could pluck it from her fingers. "Promise me something."

"Anything," he said.

"Don't read it until after you banish Tristan."

"Okay," he said. "I promise."

Venatrix handed him the folded page and gave him a tight-lipped smile.

JANUARY 1ST, 2107 A.D.

NORTHEAST FLORIDA

OPHIAH JUDE

Ophiah sat with Casper in the coffee shop. Early morning light drenched the table they sat at, and Ophiah drummed her fingers across the golden-glossy surface. She tried to make the most of it, sitting across from someone she dreaded so deeply. She tried to tell herself, over and over, that he was *good* for her, that her mother meant the best with the betrothal.

Casper answered a phone call with a beaming voice and his curly blond hair bouncing in excitement.

Ophiah could have shoved pencils in her ears. She would have enjoyed the coffee shop otherwise, she thought. It smelled sweet and slow, like carefully stirred coffee in the morning. Painted canvases hung a quiet quilt of feelings on the walls, colors of deep purple and royal blue and splashes of yellow. Casper brought her here because she requested it. It was a new local spot that offered vegan options. Ophiah hadn't told Casper that she was trying a vegan diet because Jayren was vegan. She turned her head and gazed out the glass box of a window. The sun's reflections left burn marks in her sight. She was thankful she couldn't see Casper or much else when she turned back to thank the waitress for their food.

Casper ended his call and reached across the table to caress her wrist.

Suddenly, she wasn't hungry.

"I was just speaking to Kadhi," Casper said, as if Ophiah hadn't witnessed the whole phone call. "You remember him, right?"

Of course, she thought. *You only know one person who tolerates you. Only one person likes you. Everyone else thinks you're god-awful.* Her chest hurt.

"Father hired him about a decade back, I believe," Casper continued. "He's ex-RUST, but he's the hardest worker father has. He just got a promotion!" Casper sounded really happy, but he always sounded happy. In fact, Ophiah was sure he hadn't seen a single day of hardship in his life, and the thought twisted her stomach again and again.

Casper's palm rested warmly on the back of her hand.

It made her think of the night he pressured her into sleeping with him. Most times, she tried not to think about it. It complicated the simplicity Casper wanted. He'd forgiven her. *He'd* forgiven *her,* but she did not forgive him. She wanted to drag him to Hell. She felt his hands pulling the skin of her legs again, and she slipped her hand away and tucked it in her lap.

Her new phone rang in her purse. (Valentine North replaced her phone for the sake of keeping her prescriptions up to date.) A small mercy. She looked at the caller. Orion— an even greater mercy. Hope flickered in her heart; Orion was always her salvation. He was always there, always called, always stepped in, as if he had a sixth sense in line with her emotions. He always knew when she needed him. Ophiah answered the phone, and Orion let her speak first. He always let her speak first. "Oh, hi Mom," she started. She forced a lump down her throat, swallowing hard. "Yeah, Casper took me out. I'm sorry, I thought I got all my chores done before I left. I'll see if Orion can give me a ride home."

Casper cocked his head.

"Yeah, I know. I'm sorry. Love you, too, Mom."

"Love you, too," Orion echoed.

Ophiah's heart swelled with gratitude. She hung up the phone and redialed Orion before Casper could say anything. "Hey Ri," she said, tossing her hair over her shoulder to feign confidence. Orion was quiet on the other side again. "Where are you? I was wondering if I could get a ride home. I forgot some chores this morning, and Mom wants me to come home and finish them."

"I'll be there in five," Orion said.

Ophiah believed him. If it were up to Orion, Ophiah would never be alone with Casper. For that, she owed him the world. She thanked her brother, ended the call, then slipped her Glass phone back into her purse. The world around her came back into focus—the people in the café who flipped papery stories between their fingers, who texted or tapped on phones and laptops, sipping coffee and murmuring small conversations. Finally, she said to Casper, "Orion is coming to pick me up."

Casper nodded, his prior excitement sliding from his face. "Let me walk you out?"

She nodded, too.

They stood, and he pulled her close, leaving a kiss on her lips. He kissed her longer than she wanted, and she became bored with his selfish indulgence. For once, she wanted to eat alone and satisfy herself. To Hell with gluttony. Maybe that's why she wasn't left to her own devices. Maybe the Archangels knew she would lean into the temptation around her. Maybe that wasn't all bad. When Casper's lips parted from hers, she looked at them. They were wet and pink. He kept his face shaved, but she still noticed the nicks and scratches from his razor on his neck when she stood close to him. Up close, he was still human too, in a way. At fault. Imperfect. Like her.

Casper guided Ophiah from the café after leaving a twenty with the untouched coffee and muffins. They walked out to the parking lot, and Ophiah couldn't help but notice Casper's new, electric white sedan parked close to the building. Due to wide-spread poverty, most people drove old gas cars manufactured before World War III which had later been converted to electric; because of the North's legacy, Casper was born into money. The North Institute had cured cancer, and Valentine North and his family were doused with understated stardom from it. Though in a rebellious contrast to her family, Cassie turned it all down. She always shopped secondhand shorts and flannels and modified them all to fit right. Her car was a small, gold sports car made before the war. Each time it broke down, her parents offered to buy her a car. Cassie kindly turned down the offers and instead requested the tools to fix her car in her driveway.

Still, nothing compared to Orion's teal blue truck. Relief rushed over her as it screeched into the parking lot. *That* was home, a fortress made of sheet metal and blankets. Fleetingly, she wondered if Cassie could help fix Orion's broken windshield. Ophiah wiggled her way out of Casper's arms.

"Call me tonight," Casper said. It sounded more like a demand than a request. "I love you."

Ophiah didn't reply. She swung around the front of the truck and spun into the shotgun seat beside her brother, slinging her purse onto the car floor. "You're up early," Ophiah noted. She noticed he was missing his favorite blazer, too, which he wore almost every day. It was his comfort item, she knew, that easily hid his tattoos and the frequent bruises up and down his arms. "Where's your sweater?"

Orion floored it. The tires screamed, hot and angry, as he rescued her from the dragon in disguise. She could feel her twin's anxiety and fear in the air around them. Something was off. Orion flaunted the sleeve tattoos on his arms like armor.

"Are you okay?" Ophiah asked.

"Yeah," Orion shook the question off. "I forgot my sweater at the library."

"When were you at the library?" she asked. They never kept secrets or lied to each other.

Orion didn't answer.

CORVUN KHLYDE

Slowly, Michael weaned Corvun off any source of aid. Corvun saw it coming for miles. His relationship with his stepmother had always been strained, despite her soft spoken, wise demeanor, but now she argued the side that Corvun needed to be out of the house. Being affiliated with RUST worried Corvun's stepmother that it would attract more of the assassins to their home, maybe even put a target on their heads to strike a nerve with Corvun. Even Michael couldn't argue that, having seen it all firsthand. Corvun was told to say his goodbyes, so he tried. He sat with his father at the dining room table and asked about his real mother, asked what side she would take. Michael—with heavy eyes downcast and a hand over his chin—told Corvun his mother would have fought to her dying breath to break the RUST pact for him.

"She knew," Michael said slowly. "She knew what I signed away when I signed that blood contract." He closed his eyes and shook his head. "We wanted you so badly, Corvun. Even nineteen years to have you… Every day was Heaven on Earth."

"Why sign the contract if you knew what I'd have to go through?" Corvun asked. He fought a rising scold, the ache to yell at his father and show him exactly how much damage the contract had caused him and his relationships with his friends.

Michael sighed, heavy and slow. "Valentine swore to me we'd work to break the pact. We both managed it before. We thought we could get you out. Besides, Cephan had us pinned. Either I signed the contract to get out and have you, or you never would have been born. This Iteration would have been for nothing without you." A pause. "And worst case scenario, if we can't, you'll learn things there that will help you grow into your role as one of the Horsemen. It will try you, son, in every way possible, but it will ready you, too. Cephan thinks he is in control. You *must* prove him wrong."

Corvun didn't ask any more questions. Instead, he wondered if his father had said all of that to his mother before he signed the contract. His father didn't seem to be the kind to ask permission, but rather, to ask forgiveness. Corvun didn't remember his mother, but he wished he did. She'd died in childbirth while delivering Cynthia. Michael had always considered it a miracle, Corvun's birth. He told Corvun that night, too, that human women couldn't bear the children of Archangels easily. It had taken all eight Archangels praying over her to save her life from complications in the first pregnancy. The second pregnancy was never meant to happen.

That was the last time Corvun stayed at the house.

He tried to say goodbye to Cynthia the next morning, but she didn't open her bedroom door, and instead, he just uttered a quiet, "See ya."

. . . . .

Corvun avoided the RUST Archives as long as he could, until every last penny his father gave him was gone. He knew ramen noodles and oatmeal wouldn't give him the strength to maintain the kind of lifestyle he faced now.

Corvun stared at the large double doors of the Archives building. Bolts and nuts lined the beams barring the door, as if it were a map outlining some elaborate battlefield. The door stood there like a grand exhibit, a tale of history of how RUST came to be and undermined life as humans knew it. The handles of the Archives offered themselves in a slim, grooved arch. Corvun reached out, and he glared at the brand on his wrist. Cruel would never be enough to describe the feeling. Every new greeting would not be "Hello, my name is," but rather, "I am a weapon, I am owned by a tyrant, and I am most likely here to kill you." Corvun recoiled at the thought, stumbled to the side of the building where he lost every ounce in his stomach. He dry heaved until his vision dimmed to black and returned in splotches of dots. Wincing, he could smell the bitter acid mixing with the mud as his vomit splashed on the ground.

When he finally regained his balance and his head, wiped his face, and loped back to the door, a woman held the door for him. He didn't have the nerve to look at her or thank her; he only noticed that her black boots were splattered with blood.

Inside, long rows filed down the hall, filled with books and folders. At the very front stood a desk that was lit by green-glass accents and a gold piano lamp overhanging the slanted surface. No one was at the desk. Corvun walked to it, swallowing hard against the bitterness that still swelled in the back of his mouth. He glanced around. The assassins there weren't interested in him. They had their backs turned and noses deep in the files they read. Corvun looked down at the slanted mahogany desk. Shadows seeped down from the narrow drawers that lined the very top of the desk, and they rippled into a paper for Corvun to read. Black ink curled cursive letters onto the paper.

Corvun Khlyde,

Again, what an honor to have such a renowned warrior under my command. It is good to see you've finally found your way to your calling. Take your time browsing. Find someone who suits your liking. I have found in my many years of the business that assassins take to one way or another in methods of killing. For example, some prefer to make a clear shot while others would rather use their hands. Find your style. It is an art. I make no rules in your missions besides that the target is eliminated and that you leave no tracks behind.

Cephan

Corvun looked up, but his vision went blurry with dizziness. He folded the paper up and walked slowly to the first shelf. The manila folders slashed at his fingertips like little razored tongues as he ran his fingers over them. One bit a papercut into his thumb as he slid the file out. He opened the folder and looked at the typed mission. His stomach turned again. A night had been detailed in writing, with names and locations and targets. A couple on a blind date for New Year's. His hands shook, and he dropped the file. Little red drops of blood fell into the open folder, and his stomach growled in an angry protest inside him.

He wondered how long he could go without food.

He wondered how long Jayren and Carina could survive on scraps.

He knelt slowly, his strength and willpower seeping out of him. He gathered the papers, accidentally smearing his blood in streaks along the white-cream folder. He tried to clean it off. The disaster was bigger.

He took the folder with him when he left.

. . . .

Corvun heaved a duffle bag onto the center island counter in the main dorm room. The dormitories consisted of one main room—a joint living room and kitchen—and four small bedrooms. The walls were painted white and had a rough texture to them, as if an angry student had layered white-out over all his notes again and again, refusing to believe what was there. Carina stood in the middle of the pale scene, stunning

Corvun's tired eyes like a spotlight. She wore a low-cut tank-top and a pair of loose, flowy sweatpants with ties strung with red and gold beads. She was the only thing there worth looking at.

Corvun unpacked a few boxes of oatmeal.

"Are those for you?" Carina asked.

"They're for Jayren." Corvun removed a bottle of hurricane-proof rum. "And this one is for you, a gift from Joshuah."

"What did you bring for yourself?"

Corvun grabbed water bottles from the bag and showed Carina. He turned his back to her, not wanting to engage in that conversation.

"You starve yourself," Carina said plainly.

Corvun hesitated then said, "I haven't been able to eat anythin' for weeks." What food he had tried to eat always came back up shortly after. His stomach acid chewed holes in his stomach that only water could ease. It worked less and less as the days dragged on. Corvun wrestled his leather jacket off and laid it over the duffle bag on the counter. Air chilled the moist, tender skin of two new cuts on his arms. He severed the skin barely an hour ago while reciting the names of his first two victims. He couldn't stop thinking about them. He kept seeing their mouths slightly ajar with a leak of blood, their eyes so empty shortly after they'd been dancing with the sparks of new love. Corvun replaced that light in their eyes with terror, with nothingness. Two gunshots. His heart pumped in overtime; spots clouded his vision, and he braced himself on the counter.

"You scar your arms?" Carina asked.

Corvun unpacked a smaller box on the counter, removing granola bars and a few apples. He reached to grab the glasses on the counter, and Carina's hand stopped him.

She held his arm, not too far from the self-inflicted cuts. "The scars?" she asked again.

"Lives I've taken. I don't want to forget how to feel," Corvun whispered. He looked at her nimble fingers and nothing else. He wondered if it was a mistake to bring her here.

Carina was silent.

Corvun pulled his arm loose and sat at the counter. He held his head in his hands, his stomach and head spinning on an axis around Carina. "I'm not ready for this," he said slowly, under his breath. "I'm scared for Jayren. I don't know what to do."

Carina sat beside him. "Let me help you." She rested her hand on his arm again, lighter. "I can help you."

Corvun nodded numbly. What was there to lose? He didn't trust her, but Jayren had taken to her, so he assumed that must be a good sign. But something inside him, perhaps instinct, wanted to surrender to her. He'd fought the feeling, but only so far.

Carina poured Corvun a glass of water and said, "For your stomach."

"Thank you," he said.

They sat for some time. Carina cooked a pot of oatmeal, and Corvun nibbled at a small bowl of it. She spoke about her time in Hell's Alley, telling him about the dancers there, the Deceiver of Sloth—Empress Amy—who ruled the island, and how Carina escaped with Leroy. Corvun asked her about Leroy, and she told him little facts about her friend. She lost her headstrong demeanor when she spoke about him; her sideways smirk didn't show. "Leroy was a Sentinel, too. He protected me. He was a Fallen. He fell when your father tried to save him from the RUST pact."

"I'm sorry," Corvun said.

Carina gazed at him with pretty, golden human eyes. "In our travels, I heard a saying. It was something like… 'Some time ago, our ancestors were wronged. Someone hurt them, and they hurt others in retaliation. Pain has been passed down like a family heirloom. Every generation, the same hurt. They hurt you. You will continue the pain to the next generation. Heal the heartache. Stop the legacy. Your ancestors will thank you.'"

"I don't think that works for us."

"If you have a family, it will."

"Do you think you'll have a family?" Corvun couldn't hold her eyes when he asked. He wanted a family for the very reason she put a finger on. He wanted a son, to be a better father than his was, to give the world to his child. Only, he didn't expect the world to last that long. "I mean," he paused, "because we're damned."

"We are not damned," Carina said. "I think I would like to have a family one day." She put the used dishes in the sink. "But for today, I think I would like a dance."

Corvun raised an eyebrow at her. "You dance?"

"I had to pass time in Hell's Alley one way or another," Carina said with a small smile.

"I can use the warehouse as a trainin' simulation," Corvun said, "to create obstacle courses I think up. I'm sure I could make it look like a studio."

"It is a good distraction," Carina offered. "You can consider it training, too."

"To stay in shape?" Corvun cocked an eyebrow. Carina nodded, and Corvun nodded too. "I might steal that idea."

"Well?" Carina said. She held her hand out for Corvun, and he took it. She led him out of the dorm and downstairs to the warehouse floor. Slowly, according to Corvun's thoughts and vision, the warehouse changed. The floor was paneled with wood, and mirrors lined the walls. He followed her out into the middle of the floor. He stopped, held her wrist lightly, pulled her back. She spun into his arms, and he grinned a little. Carina melted like caramel in his arms, a sweet-tooth smile on her lips as she closed her eyes. Corvun ran his hand down her back, and she curved into his palm.

"Samba?" he asked.

"Do you know it too?"

Corvun nodded. Whatever guard she held up, Corvun could feel it fall quietly like a theater curtain dropping from the rafters. Her velvet skin formed in his hands, and he gave in to the rich luster of it. He guided her in a couple, low, slow steps. She warmed up to him like the sunrise, blushing in a sky of pink. Her breath crashed like the shoreline. Corvun was used to dancing with Venatrix. While Venatrix was a force, she was stiff and strict and formed. She knew the rules only to break them, and she broke them like the crack of a shattering mirror. She was terrifyingly good, and boys feared dancing beside her. Carina was different. Carina moved like nature itself, bending in the wind but never breaking. Her fingers were the brush of ivy, her lips the beckoning of a thorned rose. She fluttered in and out of his arms, fingertips tracing the inside of his palm. Her hair spiraled around her face. She strutted back to him slow and languid, as if she knew exactly the power she wielded.

When their bodies met again, she whispered, "I know you."

Corvun knew the feeling, too, but he didn't speak. She felt familiar, like they were one and the same. They mirrored each other's movements perfectly. He was the shadow and she was the sun, with eyes like glowing embers. He rolled her between his hands as if he was testing the weight of a weapon. She was small, a little frail, but sinewy and strong. He felt the muscles lurking under her freckled skin.

Corvun let Carina lead the dance.

VENATRIX CANES

"Canis Major," Orion said to Venatrix. "The greater dog."

They sat on her roof looking at the stars. She didn't respond to him, just pondered the thought of Orion seeking out the constellation that she would name herself after.

"That's the bitch that followed the hunter Orion," he said.

Venatrix elbowed him, laughter teasing her face. "You piece of shit," she said. "I picked it before I knew you. Canes comes from Canis. I wanted to keep my family name in a way, but still make a name for myself."

Orion reached into his pocket. He pulled out a small vine, woven together into a perfect circle. Tied onto a gentle perch on the top sat a forget-me-not flower.

Venatrix's throat tightened. "What is that?"

Orion smiled at her. He held the makeshift ring for Venatrix to admire. Even in the blurry distance behind the brown-and-blue Earth-woven ring, Venatrix could see his sad eyes. "It's a promise ring."

"Rian, we're just kids."

"Kids? We're Conquest and Death."

Venatrix gently pushed his hand down, but he wrapped hers up in his bigger one.

"It's not like after high school—after this is all over— we'll go back to how it was before. We are never going to go back to being strangers. I'm in *love* with you."

"Ask me again after you banish Tristan," Venatrix said. She wondered if banishing the demon had become a crutch— an excuse for her to push Orion away. Truth was, she was scared out of her mind to be in love. She didn't like her emotions being tied up in someone else's hands.

"I don't want to think about that right now," Orion said.

"What if he kills you?" she asked. The power in her voice startled her, rattling tears into her eyes.

"That's why I want you to have something to remember me by," he said. He offered her the ring again. "And if he doesn't, I'll buy you another one. I mean it, Vena. I want you and everything that comes with you."

Venatrix shoved Orion's shoulder playfully, reaching out and plucking the ring from his finger to examine it closer. She found herself sinking into his armpit, and his cheek rested on her head. "You made this?" she asked. The vine was strong, made of a thick, wood-like plant. The flower knotted on the top would wilt overnight, so he'd made it just for this moment. Venatrix glanced up at him. "Would you take my name? Major?"

He smiled. "I would."

"Orion Major." She smirked, smug. Her skin turned hot on her chest. "It feels funny not sticking a guy's name on mine for once."

Orion kissed her temple. "You can give me an answer afterward."

She nodded. The darkness leaned in to consume them as the night grew deeper and older. *Keep shining for me*, she thought as she closed her eyes. It was the note she wrote to Orion, scribbled at the bottom of her favorite musical score. She wondered if he'd uphold the promise.

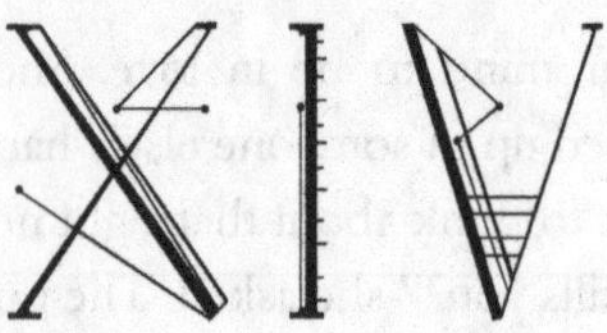

IF THE STORIES ARE TRUE, WE'RE SCREWED

With their power of persuasion, the Archangels have the ability to alter collective memories. This must be done as a group, with all eight Archangels present. This is done to ensure that certain recurrences through history—such as the reiterated lives of the Four Horsemen—are not noticed by mortal humans. They create new stories and legends to mask the truth and protect their plans.
— A History of Hierarchy

JANUARY 21ST, 2107 A.D.
THE ABYSS
JAYREN OMANS

Jayren sized up Corvun where he stood in front of him, hands wrapped and balled into fists. Jayren pulled at the fabric on his own hand and adjusted the tight spot between his thumb and forefinger. They stood together on the warehouse training floor, and Corvun had planned their first training session. "Can we do this another time?" Jayren asked. He still wasn't feeling great. His eyes stung, and he could barely see straight. Corvun's image wobbled like a reflection in a shaky mirror.

Corvun raised his hands, open and cupped. "No. You've got to learn. You have no idea where to start."

Jayren eyed his hands.

"Punch," Corvun said.

Jayren balled his fists warily.

Corvun's quick movement cut through the space between them; he snatched Jayren's wrist. "See what I mean? You'll break your damn finger." Corvun unwound his fist and plucked his thumb from under his fingers. He pushed Jayren's digit up against his first and second fingers.

"Sorry," Jayren said. He felt pretty dumb. He should have guessed that one. Corvun's cold eyes just made him feel smaller and dumber.

"*Punch*," Corvun said again.

Jayren lashed out, striking the side of Corvun's right hand. "Weak."

Jayren furrowed his brow. He hit harder.

"Did you even know what you were gettin' into?" Corvun asked. "Put your hands up."

Jayren mirrored Corvun's previous stance.

Corvun hit his palm dead on, and the impact cracked the center of his hand. Something popped. Jayren shuffled back when Corvun tried to punch again. "What are you doin'? I'm just showin' you—"

"Dude," Jayren rasped. His throat was tight in his neck. "Give me a minute."

Corvun ran his hands through his hair, pulled on it. He gave an exasperated sigh. "Did you think you'd just show up and not have to fight? Not have to kill? What did you think this would be?"

Not my best friend punching me, Jayren thought. He couldn't speak. Fear popped again and again in his chest, like twigs snapping under tires.

"Well?" Corvun demanded.

"I didn't want you to be alone," Jayren managed in a hoarse whisper.

Corvun's eyes didn't show any gratefulness for their friendship or Jayren's sacrifice, only a hard, slick, black surface that Jayren couldn't see into anymore. "You're more of an idiot than I thought."

Jayren shoved Corvun in the chest as hard as he could, but his weight was shadowed by Corvun's entire stature, and Corvun didn't move a muscle. (Jayren hadn't gained back the weight he lost since joining RUST yet, but Corvun had always been bigger anyway.) So Jayren made a fist and swung at Corvun's jaw instead.

Corvun deflected the punch.

"Dickhead!" Jayren said.

"Obvious move." Corvun backed up. "Try it again."

"No, you'll just knock me off again."

Corvun held his arms out to the sides. "Free hit. But take the offer before I change my mind."

Jayren narrowed his eyes and wiped his sweaty palms on his pants. "I don't want to be a bully."

"Offer expired." Corvun dropped his arms. He took two steps then swung his leg over and around Jayren's shoulders. Jayren fell, hands slapping the concrete. Corvun grabbed his head and twisted his neck back. "You're not a bully. I'm the bully. You're just savin' your own skin."

Jayren grimaced and smacked Corvun's hand, hoping he would get the idea that he wasn't into it.

Corvun let up.

Jayren glared at his ankles and grabbed one. He yanked as hard as he could.

Corvun tripped and fell.

"You asshole, just teach me the basics." Jayren glared harder at Corvun.

"I tried! You wouldn't punch!" Emotion peeked through the fractures in Corvun's voice. He pushed himself up off his elbows and glared back.

"I'm scared!" Jayren yelled.

Corvun was panting, and his chest collapsed. His eyes got wider, but they got duller too. He hesitated for a good minute then said, "Me too, Jay."

They sat for a while. Jayren watched Corvun rub his face, unwrap his bruised hands, then wrap them back up. Then Corvun sat still. Jayren kept watching.

"It doesn't get better, does it?" Jayren asked.

Corvun shook his head. He stood.

When Corvun walked to him, Jayren didn't shy away. He took the hand Corvun offered him. His compass brand burned beneath where Corvun had carefully wrapped gauze over it to cover the sore wound. Jayren stood face-to-face with his friend, but words were parasites on his tongue. They just stayed there, sucking his wits out of his only good muscle.

"Let's try again, alright?" Corvun said.

Jayren nodded. He tried not to flinch under Corvun's steady, molding hands. He worked Jayren into a fighting stance, starting with making good fists. He kept thinking about all the dangerous things Corvun knew all the years they'd been friends but never let on about.

"Look. Watch me, okay? When you punch—" he pushed his fist forward and twisted his leg and hip forward with it, "use your whole body. You'll build muscle over time, but if you just—" Corvun stood stiffly and jutted his fist forward. "You won't channel any power. Try it." He patted his chest. "You won't hurt me."

Jayren slugged him, but Corvun barely moved.

Corvun paused before he said, "Okay, *good*," the words as hard to remove as if he was pulling molars from his mouth. "Again, but use your body like I showed you." They repeated the process over and over until a sweat broke on Jayren's neck. Once his right arm went wobbly, Corvun told him to start with his left.

"Good," Corvun said, eyes slightly wide. "You have strength in your left arm."

"Yeah, from breaking my right." Jayren punched Corvun's sparring hands. "Where's my cast anyway?" In all the chaos, Jayren hadn't immediately noticed—when Corvun pulled him from the coffin—that his cast was gone. As if being buck naked in a coffin wasn't enough, he also had to deal with the embarrassment of his more-responsible friend dragging his naked ass out and nursing him back to health. It was enough to make him want to coil up and cringe to death. His cast was gone, and his arm was totally healed. His braces had mysteriously vanished, too. Now—nearly two weeks later— Jayren had enough clarity to think about the events.

"You technically have a new body," Corvun said. His eyes flickered away from Jayren. "Cephan—he heals the mortal flesh and restitches the soul. That's why the compass brand is called the Soul Stitch. It keeps your soul from leavin' this world, from movin' on. Kind of like a staple."

Jayren would've asked for a better explanation if he didn't still feel like shit.

"You have minor healin' abilities now, too." Corvun showed Jayren how to deflect a punch, then he threw one of his own.

Jayren ducked. "What?"

"You can heal non-fatal wounds. So if I break your arm and don't sever your artery," Corvun motioned to his previously broken arm, "you can mend bones like nothin' happened."

"How?" Jayren paused.

Corvun shook his head. "That's for another day. C'mon. Let's keep goin'."

NORTHEAST FLORIDA
ORION JUDE

Orion gazed at Venatrix. She wore tight, spandex shorts, and her fair knees sank into the dirt at the edge of his house. Her fingers were caked with Earth. Her hair pasted to her neck with sweat, and she wiped the back of her hand across her forehead. She left a smear of black on her face like warpaint. She grinned at him.

Orion held his burning bush sprout absently.

"Stop staring," she teased.

The sun got hotter on Orion's back, and he stared down at the hole he'd dug with his bare hands. He rested the plant there and scooped dirt back around the roots. Sweat tickled his back and sides in serpentine streaks. They'd planted shrubbery and flowers all the way around the perimeter of Orion's house for two solid hours after getting back from school. The air was cooling off with the coming evening, but it didn't quite relieve the powerful sun.

The front door opened. That froze Orion's blood. His head snapped in the direction of the noise. They'd worked around the back of the house first, hoping to be discreet and avoid his parents. Now, his mother stepped out holding two glasses of water. Her brown hair billowed around her face with playful blond highlights from her own time gardening around the lawn. (Orion was always astounded at the amount of care and patience and kindness she could pour into her vegetable garden in their backyard.) His mother's face pinched into a mousy, curious smile. "Hey kiddos," she said. Her voice was small and sad, like the flicker of a flashlight in a police search for a missing child. It faded quickly. "Water?"

Venatrix stood, smiling. She took the glass from his mother. "Thanks, Missy."

Orion stood and followed suit. He accidentally smudged her small, frail hand with dirt in the process and apologized immediately. He couldn't apologize enough, in fact, and he kept talking until she hushed his sorrys and pressed a fervent kiss to his forehead. Orion always felt huge and clumsy next to his mom, like a lion trying to catch a mouse under a paw, but whenever she touched him, he stilled.

"The plants look wonderful," she said. She paused, then under her breath whispered, "But you didn't pray over them, did you?"

"Of course they did," Mr. Jude said from the front door. The dim orange lights inside the house silhouetted him. He crossed his arms. When Tristan looked to Venatrix, Orion felt a flare of energy in his heart, adrenaline pumping in his bloodstream.

Venatrix smiled a raw, savage smile. "You'll get what's coming for you."

Before Orion could move, Mr. Jude caught Venatrix by her school blouse and yanked her to him, baring fangs. "Only someone as reckless as you would assume this could hold me," he seethed down at her. He released her and backhanded her with a loud *crack*. She twisted downward like a broken table, limbs slack. Her glass of water shattered on the sidewalk.

Orion bolted to her, catching her head before it hit the concrete. He dragged her dead weight up into his arms. He glared up at the demon who stared down with pits for eyes and a flicker of fire on his tongue. Orion's mother sobbed, a shivering hand over her mouth. Orion's mind raced through a thousand words he didn't understand, but only three words slipped from his trembling lips: "I'll kill you!"

"You cannot kill me, son," Tristan said. "But I can kill her and your other friends, and I can kill you."

Orion hugged Venatrix's still body to his chest. Her breaths were tiny on his shirt, and he remembered why he hadn't made friends before. *This* is what he was afraid of, what he feared most. He was a danger to any friends he made. He regretted that night he knocked on her window. "Burn in Hell," he spat. "I *will* make you burn in Hell."

JAYREN OMANS

What if this is all true? Jayren thought from Venatrix's hospital bedside. Horror pooled in his stomach. The room was dark, the curtains drawn to blot out the blood-red sunset. Corvun stood stiffly beside Jayren. Neither of the boys had words. The blackening bruise on Venatrix's face silenced them. Jayren didn't think a normal man could hit a girl hard enough to put her straight into a coma.

Orion and his mother sat next to Venatrix's immobile body, and North and Michael stood solemnly with Venatrix's parents. "She'll recover," Professor North said.

What if it's all true? Jayren thought again. *If it's all true…*

THE ABYSS
CARINA BLACKROCK

Carina watched Corvun. He unloaded twelve rounds into a target, hitting the bullseye all but once. He released the magazine, tossed it aside with a clatter, then slammed another one into the handle of his pistol. It snapped with a metallic *click-clack*. He released the slide and aimed the gun again.

Chills pricked Carina's skin. From her perch on the warehouse steps that led to the dorms, she said, "Something is bothering you."

"Vena." He got off three bullets. "She's in the hospital in a coma." His mouth worked like his trigger. Corvun fired the last bullets so fast it startled her. He threw the gun at the target, and the paper shuddered, crumpled in a jagged, backward flip. Corvun rubbed the sweat through his hair, slicking his hair back and out of his face. He must have torn up more than twenty targets; Carina lost count after a handful. The papers were scattered across the floor like fall leaves, dead and abandoned.

"What happened to her?"

Corvun laughed tightly, heartlessly. "Orion's father hit her. He hit her temple. At first, they thought she was just unconscious, but they couldn't wake her. If that isn't bad enough, my sister is missin'. My father spoke with me last night about it. No trace, no evidence, just vanished like she'd never existed in the first place."

The news paralyzed Carina. *Why go after his family if they already have him?* she wondered. She understood Venatrix being targeted, but why Corvun's sister?

Corvun turned to her. His eyes were so hollow that it was almost as if someone had carved two holes out of his face like a jack-o-lantern. "You know, my parents tried to ask me if I had anythin' to do with it. We didn't get along, but I didn't want to kill her, for fuck's sake!" Corvun stripped a dagger from his belt, spun, and chucked the blade at his last target. The paper severed, clean and straight, and his dagger clattered across the floor.

Carina flinched.

He took a deep breath, but it didn't seem to calm him any. Corvun walked to Carina and sat on the step beside her. His legs were so long that they arched over the step where her own feet rested.

After a pause, Carina said, "Let me help you look for your sister."

Corvun picked at the dirt on his hands, and Carina noticed his nails needed trimming. He stood and grabbed a broom and started sweeping up shell casings. "We won't find her," he said.

"Maybe not, but there is no chance if we do not look."

"Okay." Corvun paused. He manifested another broom from shadows, propped against the stair railing where she sat. He didn't turn, didn't look at her or ask her to help, just continued with his work.

Carina took the broom in her hand and joined him. She could feel his hurt sizzling in the air like lightning. It made the hairs on her arms stand on end. She worked with him, sweeping the metal shells into the corner. She met him there. He stood very still, like a statue amidst a storm. His eyes dripped with water. Carina propped her broom against the wall and touched his face. His skin tore into a sob at her touch, and he placed a hand over hers. Carina felt her heart bend backwards inside her, aching and snapping tendons inside her chest.

She coaxed him upstairs, convinced him to take it easy, to let her take care of him for the night. She sat him on his bed and knelt before him. With a white bucket in his lap, Carina washed his purple and blue hands and left them to soak. He didn't speak to her as she groomed his neglected wounds and bruises. He watched her with deep, dark eyes that reminded her of the trenches at the bottom of the sea. She took a small blade from his side table, dipped the metal into the water beside his hands and stood. She tilted his chin up and shaved the stubble from his neck.

Corvun turned to stone. His pulse vanished beneath his skin, invisible.

"I will not hurt you," she reassured him.

"There's nothin' like showin' your neck to someone who could," he said.

Carina shrugged and gave him a small smile. "What use would you be to me dead?"

"What use to you am I alive?"

"Purpose," she said.

"What does that mean?"

"I could win your war single-handedly, Crow. That is not why I'm here. I am here to guard you," she said, "and the others."

"Is that why they tried to kill you in Hell's Alley?"

Carina quirked an eyebrow at him, and his eyes swiveled up in her direction. He closed them again when she stroked his neck to brush away his shavings.

"Do you think they're tryin' to stop us before…"

"Before you become something powerful? Yes," she said.

Corvun took a tight, deep breath.

Carina nicked his neck by accident, and he flinched and hissed. "Hold still," she told him. She grabbed a rag and dabbed the blood from his neck. He laughed, the ball in his throat bouncing; she considered nicking him again. "Stop laughing, you pathetic thing. You are nothing but a child in a man's body."

Corvun laughed more. "I'm nineteen. Did you expect a hero?"

Carina caught his chin between her fingers and tilted his face to hers. "I expect a little obedience while I tend to your negligence, boy." She paused. "I never told you what happened in Hell's Alley."

"Jayren did."

Carina's heart skipped a beat. "Did he say anything else?"

Corvun opened his eyes and gazed at her.

"Just curious what I need to fill you in on," Carina said. "Did he mention anything about angels and demons?"

"No, you know him. It was aliens."

Carina allowed herself to relax, to laugh a little. She listened to Corvun retell Jayren's telling of her time in Hell's Alley in a playful high-pitched voice and animated expressions on his otherwise deadpan features. She smiled watching him; Corvun was digging a hole in her chest, softening the frozen soil with his warm hands where he planted Jayren and himself. They'd bloom for her, but they were wiry like weeds. She'd never be able to dig their roots out now.

JANUARY 22ND, 2107 A.D.
NORTHEAST FLORIDA
JAYREN OMANS

Jayren thought about Ophiah. He thought about her a lot these days, actually. As Corvun and Jayren walked into the Angels' Diner that afternoon, Jayren thought about the sharp peaks of her cupid's bow and the shy look she always had in her eyes. Joshuah called to Corvun, and Jayren stepped away to let them talk one-on-one. He walked slowly around the perimeter of the empty tavern to look at the pictures on the walls and to be alone with his thoughts. His curiosity moved slowly from Ophiah to the photos. Most were old, some were snatched right out of the wild west. He stopped at a wanted poster. The edges of the golden paper were charred black, but the eyes of the outlaws in the banner still burned.

"Corvun?" Jayren said over his shoulder. He glanced back to see Corvun and Joshuah deep in conversation. He looked back to the picture and squinted his eyes. His pulse pumped in his head. *What if it's all true?* The voice in his head echoed again.

The outlaws were four, the photo taken at gunpoint. They stood in the middle of a dust-covered road, and sand billowed in little clouds in the corners and distance. The similarity struck Jayren a little *too* closely. There was no way to look at their leader—a peg-legged, dark-haired killer with his pistol held facing the heavens—and not think of Corvun. He had the same eyes. Another man, tall and built like a god, held two matching pistols forward like the arms of a smiling clock, telling the remaining time of his opposer. A woman stood beside him, knife and gun held together before her. Her short hair hung like a boy's, choppy and savage around her strong jaw and vicious smile. Jayren's eyes fell on the last of the four, a man with his hat tipped too low to see his eyes. A single braid fell from beneath the cowboy's hat, and his hands hovered above two guns at either side of his hips.

'*And that,*' he could hear Venatrix's voice, coy and snarky all at once, '*was the only time they came close to catching us!*' It was the perfect cowboy-campfire story.

Jayren knew little about the process of taking pictures so long ago, but he recalled it took some outrageous amount of time like twenty-four hours. He slipped his Glass phone out and did a quick search. He noted the time: fifteen minutes was average. Jayren looked back to the picture and noticed a ghost-like blur that wasn't present in the other photos around the bar. The camera hadn't had enough time to fully capture the image. *Probably before they escaped,* Jayren thought. His hair stood on end.

"Corvun!" Jayren said again, forcing volume into his voice.

The other two stopped talking.

"When was this picture taken?"

"In the nineteenth century," Joshuah said.

"Were we alive in the nineteenth century?" his voice choked short. "Corvun?"

Corvun walked over and snatched the framed photo off the wall. "Why did you hang this?" he demanded of Joshuah.

"It's a great picture! It's honestly the best I've got. You guys—"

Corvun stalked back to Joshuah, but he swayed in Jayren's vision. Jayren's head swam, and he slumped into a chair. He listened to Joshuah's frantic muttering. *No way.* In a squeak, Jayren asked, "What did they call themselves?"

"Theatre of War," Corvun said, "but they were more widely known as Armageddon or the Apocalypse."

Jayren rubbed his face with both his hands. *Cowboys. I even had the same braid…*

"This picture is supposed to be *lost*," Corvun hissed at Joshuah. "The Archangels would have you burn this."

"Are all the others…" Jayren looked around at the brown-and-tan pictures.

"Angels, or humans that angels protected in their lifetimes," Joshuah confirmed.

Corvun sighed.

"There were angels in the wild west," Jayren echoed. "What did they do? The wild west was a killing spree."

"You surprised you were a part of it? There are other avenging angels, too. Haven't y'all met one recently?" Joshuah asked.

Corvun slammed a fist on the bar counter. "Stop it. Get rid of this."

"What am I supposed to do with it?" Joshuah bit back.

"Burn it," Corvun said.

"I want it," Jayren said.

"Can I give it to him?" Joshuah asked.

"No. Absolutely not."

"Carina would let me have it." Jayren rolled his eyes. He stood and walked around the right side of the bar where more of the medieval artifacts hung, in frames plated in gold. His sights locked on a lion with ruby-stud eyes on the end of a sword speared through a stone. "Excalibur," Jayren guessed.

"The one and only!"

"Can I…" Jayren stepped up to the base of the stone. He put his hands on the hilt of the sword, and they fit perfectly in the worn grooves there.

He held his breath. He pulled.

Nothing happened.

"Excalibur," Joshuah said, "is known to the angels as the Sword of the Sentinels, Ferro."

"So you're telling me King Arthur was an angel, too?"

Corvun winced.

"The legend is backwards," Joshuah explained. "You can thank the Archangels. They covered up each of your past lives so people wouldn't notice your returns. The sword was never drawn from the stone, hence it's still stuck there. That sword belonged to the greatest warrior of its time. It belonged to *you*. You drove it into the stone in your final battle, right as you took your last breath. No Sentinel has been able to draw it since," the words rolled out of Joshuah's mouth like a skipping stone on a lake made of glass. He was really good at talking fast, Jayren realized, and he got the whole story in before Corvun could stop him.

A shadow covered Corvun's already dull expression, and Jayren shot him the most pissed off glare he could manage. "I want that fucking picture," Jayren said.

THE ABYSS
CORVUN KHLYDE

"When were you gonna tell me the Archangels lie to us, huh?" Jayren demanded once they returned to the warehouse. "How many lives have we lived before this?"

"You know, maybe I'd be more willin' to tell you these things if you didn't shut me down," Corvun said. "You don't believe in this stuff, remember!"

"How many times?"

"I don't know," Corvun said bluntly. Each word fell like stones pummeling down in a landslide. The ground slipped from beneath Corvun's feet, moving his foundation.

"What do you mean you don't know?" Jayren dug deeper at the ground under him. "For fuck's sake, you acted like you know all about that picture! We were a band of cowboys? Why wouldn't you tell me that? What about Excalibur?" Jayren balled his hands into fists, ready to throw.

"Let's go downstairs," Corvun offered, "blow off some steam."

Jayren didn't protest, only said, "I'm gonna whoop your ass, Corv," as he shoved past.

Carina caught Corvun's arm before he could follow Jayren out of the dorm room. He'd barely noticed her when they'd come back, but she'd watched their heated exchange from the small kitchenette with a shallow glass of rum in hand. Her hand squeezing his muscle reminded him of his pulse, of the blood pumping through his veins, fueled by his frustration at Jayren. He was angry at Jayren. He was angry at Jayren *more often than not*, he realized. He breathed slowly, counting to four.

"Talk to him again," Carina eyed Jayren, "after whatever it is you boys are going to do."

"Paintball," Corvun told her.

"Paintball," she tested the word. Her brows furrowed. "Sorry?"

"Come watch," Corvun said tiredly. He stole a glance at the microwave clock. Green letters read 7:38 P.M. It was just the beginning of their day, but he wanted to sleep now.

"Has he shot a gun yet?" Carina asked.

"No," Corvun said. "He needs time." Corvun turned and exited the dorm room, out onto the metal walk overhanging the warehouse space below. His footsteps rattled on the grated, fence-like floor. He jogged down the stairs after Jayren, manifesting a simple obstacle course of items for them to use in training. From a table that rolled up to the end of the metal staircase, he grabbed two pistol-styled guns. He tossed one to Jayren. "Pretend it has bullets," Corvun said.

Jayren tried to catch the gun with open palms, didn't get a good grip, and it clattered to the ground.

"Pick it up."

"Does it have bullets?" Jayren's eyes flashed at Corvun like a lighthouse, wary of a storm he might lure in, or worse, who might blow in with that storm.

"Paintballs. Don't worry about reloadin' either." Corvun leveled his gun at Jayren's forehead and pulled the trigger. A paintball flung outward and exploded against his forehead. It burst into bright red, like a tomato on a bad stand-up comedian. Corvun chuckled.

"Hey!" Jayren smeared the paint out of his eyes with his arm. He ducked below the second shot. He aimed at Corvun, and a paintball *whooshed* past Corvun's ear and popped on the metal railing behind him.

"Watch it!" Carina called.

Corvun turned to see her just a few feet from where the paint splashed like fruit in a food fight. She grinned and sat a step higher. Something stung Corvun's shoulder, and he whipped around and glared at Jayren with a hasty grin.

"Got you," Jayren said, rather monotone.

"Did you use the sights?"

"No. It was a stroke of luck, honestly," Jayren admitted.

"Hold the gun up, and line up those three dots." Corvun watched Jayren over the nose of his own gun. Jayren tried to mirror Corvun's pose, but his feet were side by side beneath him and his arms bent. Corvun shook his head, lowered his gun, and walked over to stand side-by-side with his friend. "Stand with your feet shoulder-width apart, shoulders back. Arms straight." Corvun leveled his sights again and showed Jayren how to stand; Jayren studied Corvun's pose and mimicked him. "Real guns have a kick to them, so get in the habit of holdin' your arms straight."

"Did you bang her yet?" Jayren eyed Corvun.

"What?" Corvun snapped.

Jayren raised his eyebrows. "Have you *seen* how she looks at you?"

"Shoot her." Corvun's face burned. "Aim and shoot. Right now."

Jayren smirked stupidly. With all the convincing he needed, he aimed at Carina, and her eyes flamed with anger.

"Boy!" she stood, warning him not to shoot.

"You're takin' too long! Hurry!" Corvun found himself laughing. "Hurry! She's spotted us! She's comin' this way!"

Carina stalked down the stairs. "Corvun, I want a gun."

"Shoot!"

"She won't quit moving!" Jayren pulled the trigger. The paintball exploded past her thigh.

Carina was on them before they could move. She disarmed Corvun with a quick upward shove to his gun and a swift *crack* to his nose. Corvun doubled back; he hadn't expected her to punch him, but he should have. Corvun held his nose as the pain seeped into his cheekbones to mingle with a rising blush.

"Go stand over there, Crow."

Corvun obeyed Carina's order, and Jayren snickered. He turned to see Carina showing Jayren new techniques. He didn't think he'd find it attractive—Carina with her hands wrapped tightly around the grip of a gun—but he couldn't shake the betraying signs from his face. A paintball nailed him in the crotch, and he winced.

"*Dude.*" Jayren laughed. "Protect the goods."

One at a time, Carina called out body parts on Corvun for Jayren to shoot at. Corvun cupped his hands around his groin, grimaced through the stings of paintballs smacking against his shoulders, belly button, and left knee cap. They exploded as they hit him, leaving him a colorful mess of dripping paint.

"Good," Carina said to Jayren.

Corvun reached out one hand for his gun, but his other hand stayed. "Give me my gun," he said.

She shot his cupped hand with terrifying accuracy, and Corvun tensed.

"Pirate," Corvun scolded.

"Assassin," Carina sang. She shot his throat, cutting his next words short. "Let me train the boy. You go get some rest."

"You're gonna need a serious shower first," Jayren said with a snicker.

· · · ·

Corvun rubbed his hair with a white towel then looked into the bathroom mirror. He was free of color finally—back to his near-black-and-white self, save for the purple bags beneath his eyes. He stood alone in the bathroom, and he savored the quiet. The bathroom was more of a locker room, really, huge and tiled with white and pale blue from the floor to the ceiling. The floor tapered to a shared drain in the middle of the room. Three dividing walls stood between four shower stalls, each of which had its own toilet just to the left of each metal showerhead. There wasn't much privacy—no curtains, no doors. Things like that were a luxury. The mirror, which filled the entirety of the sink wall, reflected back the shower stalls and obliterated any real sense of privacy. *But,* he thought sourly, *that's RUST.* It was still better than the community showers.

The mirror fogged with a soft blur. Corvun's shower had been hot and long and refreshing. He grabbed his change of clothes from the sink counter and wrestled the sweatpants over his tacky, wet skin. The exhaustion in his muscles convinced him to pass on the shirt. He wadded his towel up and tossed it into a metal laundry basket that looked more like a trash can. He walked out of the bathroom, back to the overhang. The metal beneath his bare feet was cool and hard. He went to his left, back to the dorm.

He'd almost put his hand on the doorknob when he heard loud, friendly chatter and laughter. He pressed his ear to the wood and listened instead of going inside.

"He's not mean. He *acts* mean. Shit! You should hear what Trixie says about him."

"Venatrix?"

"Yeah." Jayren cackled. "She says he has a heart of gold. High praise, coming from her."

Carina laughed with a chiming, staccato laugh.

Corvun grinned. He paused, listened to their ongoing conversation, and waited for the topic to change before he decided to walk in. He'd never witnessed Jayren open up to anyone, but Carina had an authority about her that demanded respect and—from Jayren it seemed—loyalty and friendship.

Kinship. Carina and Jayren perched on towels on the sofa like abstract art pieces, eyes gleaming with mischief and colors spilling over them like Heaven had a fight over who should wear the most wild shades Earth had to offer.

"Golden smile, Crow," Carina said. She had a light blue spatter on her jaw. She'd used her finger to streak the excess paint horizontally across her nose like vibrant warpaint. Jayren had done the same with red, using a full handprint that covered his right cheek and forehead.

"Do you want to shower?" Corvun asked Carina with a small chuckle.

She stood and walked to him, doubling back when Jayren reached to grab the towel that stuck to her backside with painty plaster. She laughed again, showing her teeth. "That would be nice."

Corvun went to his room and retrieved an extra shirt and a pair of sweatpants then offered them to Carina. He took a clean, folded towel that was on the end of his bed and handed that to her, too. "Here."

Carina's gaze trailed up from his extended hands. Her eyes hesitated against his bare chest, danced upward to admire him in a way Corvun had never experienced. Her fiery eyes bore into his. "Jayren doesn't stay angry at you very long," she observed.

"There are worse things than findin' out you've been a cowboy in your past life. Watch. He'll want to know about it. He's fightin' an anger that originated from somethin' else. His backlash is aimed at anythin' he can find to be upset about."

"Do you think he believes yet?"

"Y'know I can hear you, right?" Jayren shouted from the other side of the thin wall.

"I think he does," Corvun whispered. "At least, he's on the verge of it. He wouldn't argue if someone told him Excalibur was his sword."

Carina's face rounded into a cheeky smile. "Thank you," she said, patting the clothes and towel, "for this."

Corvun nodded at her, a faint smile pulling at his lips.

JANUARY 23ND, 2107 A.D.
NORTHEAST FLORIDA
OPHIAH JUDE

Ophiah and Casper walked side by side through the long halls of the North Tower, which stood on the north side of the city. The skyscraper was the headquarters for North Institute, where Valentine North kept his affairs in order. It had become a beacon to the city after Valentine North's family was awarded the key to the city. Fading afternoon light struck the windows in pale blue. Another storm front charged the sky like a second wave of war. Ophiah's dress heels clacked a rhythmic chant, a clash of swords beating shields in that very war. She kept Casper's stride easily; she met his impressive height with her heels. And she got the eyes, not him. She was stunning. She wasn't happy about it either. Casper had been the one to pick out her dress. "Wear that one," he'd told her. "It matches the color of your lips. It complements your features." But it was an inch too short, and she busied herself every next minute by touching the backs of her legs and tugging the skirt down.

"Is this what the essay is for?" Ophiah asked.

"The essay?" Casper asked. "Oh, you mean the internship letter. Yes."

Ophiah sighed, running her hands over the thin, expensive material again. Some designer brand she didn't care about, some silky material she hated. It felt much too showy for her. Ophiah coiled her hair on her hand like a snake wrapping itself around its prey. She shot a death glare at anyone who dared to look down her legs.

"Come on," Casper said with a hand slinking around her hip. "You look fine. Quit fooling with your hair."

She opened her clutch to keep her hands busy. She thought that if she didn't, she might not be able to stop herself from strangling Casper. Her wallet was empty save for her ID, bank card, and a few dollar bills. Casper told her the clutch would look good with her outfit. He was better at being feminine than she was.

The hall of the North Tower stretched on like some Roman conqueror's palace. Tall, marble pillars separated the huge, glass windows from one another. They walked the floor where all the business with Casper's family took place. The halls and conference rooms smelled faintly of burning coffee, of bagels, and of perfume suited for the heavens. Conversation buzzed as they walked past, as if they walked straight into a blooming garden, alive with pollinating life. She didn't look at the people around her; she would've preferred to go sit in a real garden, watching real honey bees bumble about their business rather than gawk at the designer, cocktail dresses that mocked the vibrancy of life.

Casper pressed a hand to the small of Ophiah's back and led her into an office. She would've rather had him not touch her at all.

Valentine North sat at the end of a gold-swirled marble table. He spoke pleasantly with some of his workers, among which was a doctor with short white hair named Ralph Bennett. He was her own psychiatric doctor, and of all the angels that worked for Valentine North, Ophiah guessed she probably liked Dr. Bennett the most. He wore circular, thin-rimmed glasses that gave his blue eyes a potent effect, like the combination of alcohol and medication, and had a deliberate way about him. He looked over to where she and Casper stood and smiled with sparkling, wrinkled eyes.

"Casper, brother!" Dr. Bennett said.

"Dr. Bennett!" Casper chimed. They walked to one another and embraced.

Dr. Bennett turned and smiled at Ophiah, greeted her with a press of his cheek to hers and a squeak of a kiss beside her ear. "Darling Jude," he said. He held her shoulders and looked her face over. Her frame relaxed in his hold; he didn't look lower than the sparkling earrings dangling at her neck.

Casper walked off to greet Valentine.

Ophiah watched him, briefly wondering how Casper and his father could be so vastly different. Valentine was kind; he gave her and Orion special attention. He took time with Ophiah in therapy, gave her home remedies and medications she could take in and out of school. Dr. Bennett had aided Valentine with the dosages.

"How's the medication?" the doctor asked, as if he could see the thoughts swimming in her eyes.

"They make me sleepy," she admitted. *Still,* she thought, *better than burning in my own skin.*

"I'll send over a new dosage to Valentine tomorrow. Sound good?" She nodded, and Dr. Bennett continued, "And your mother? How is she? I haven't seen her in so long…"

"She's alright," Ophiah said. She wondered what it must be like for the Archangels. Many of them were close, but her mother—the Virtue of Kindness—had been separated from her family in a sense. Ophiah didn't think she could survive without Orion like that, at least, not for very long.

"Come sit," Valentine said. A shadow fell over the room as a storm cloud blew over the sun. Aside from Ophiah,

Casper, Dr. Bennett, and Valentine, Michael and Gabrielle were also in the room. Michael and Gabrielle stood off a little ways—Michael at the window, surveying the distance, and Gabrielle surveying the room. They drew nearer at Valentine's command, and once they were all seated, Valentine started. "Do you know why animals sense storms before they arrive? Even before they show on a radar?"

Casper yawned. Ophiah was sure he'd heard these same questions a hundred times, but Valentine was looking at Ophiah. So quietly she said, "Because they are inhabited by spirits." She thought of Jayren. "They are Lesser Sentinels."

Valentine's gold-brown eyes peered into her.

She continued, wavering but louder. "The storms are Unseen Wars waged on humanity. Angels and demons battle in the storms."

"Good," Valentine praised her. "Casper, what is the lightning?"

Ophiah answered before him. "It's the hand of God reaching for fallen warriors." She found her voice finally. Rain pattered against the window, a mock applaud of her knowledge. Lightning struck nearby, a white whip of light seizing something on the ground. Bellowing thunder rattled the cups on the marble table.

"And what about Armageddon?"

"We won't live to see it. Our time here will be over," Casper said.

"Corvun talks about Armageddon all the fucking time," Jayren said through the phone. Ophiah had called him just to listen to him talk. She told him she'd had a bad day, and he didn't ask any questions. He began yapping like a smaller dog trying to impress the likes of a titan of a hound. He was munching on chips, smacking his lips through the phone as he

said, *"Oh god, what was it… Oh! Something like—it's a codename for us. Y'know, the Four Horsemen."*

"Do you believe that?"

Jayren paused then ignored her question. His voice grew solemn. "It's, uh, a test of sorts. I guess he said we use it as a codename for our battle, but it's not really the canon Armageddon."

"Canon?"

"Yeah, y'know, happens in the books."

Ophiah laughed.

"So it's like, if we win this trial, phase-one Armageddon," he hesitated, "then we bring the real Battle of Armageddon."

"Like the Apocalypse."

"Yeah," His voice hushed. "Like the fucking end of the world."

"Which Armageddon?" Ophiah asked.

Valentine's eyes twinkled. "I ask these questions in search of a new CEO. We will provide training, but we need someone who is passionate about our cause, who can see the bigger picture at play, and dwell in God's wisdom. Our current CEO, General Direlight, is stepping down from his role—once we are able to fill it—to spend more time in our military field. So," he hesitated. "I want to offer the mentoring, and ultimately the position, to one of you."

Ophiah's heart jumped in her chest, as if she'd hit a curb driving out of a parking lot when she'd been sure she was in the clear. This was too ordinary of a setting, and it'd taken her by surprise. They'd met with Valentine like this many times, often just for lunch. Ophiah furrowed her brow, but Valentine North dipped his head in a small bow; he was a lion, and he was showing respect to her as if she were his equal.

"Father," Casper said. "She is unstable. How could you trust her with something like that?" Ophiah should have expected his response. Casper swatted her down like a domesticated cat knocking a vase from the highest shelf, and she shattered. "*I* am your son. Surely, I should be considered first. Of course, she could be my assistant, help me. But lead us as a company?"

Ophiah remained silent. In Casper's outburst, she could do nothing but stare at her cold hands. *Submit. Lie down. Don't fight it.* Voices, over and over. Her mouth watered, and anger rose hot on her shoulders. Embarrassment, despair. It didn't matter; her emotions weren't allowed. She looked up, choking down her hopes and dreams and pride. *So the last shall be first, and the first last. For many are called, but few are chosen,* she repeated the verse. Over and over until the moment passed. Until it was all over.

She moved numbly, as if something else controlled her body, stood, and walked out. Everything was a blur, a haze of tears and fury, as she made her way out of the steel tower. She had the shock factor, a few-second lead. She got to the lobby before the whispers caught up to her.

"Ophiah!" Casper called. He chased her out of the building.

"I don't want to talk to you!" Her voice tore out of control. He was right; she didn't belong among the angels. She was too much chaos, too much hurt and pain spinning like a tornado out of control. Wind licked her hair up into her face as she ran. The moist, rain-drenched roads soaked the air with the smell of lake and oil.

Casper stopped at the door of the North Tower.

Ophiah spun and glared at him.

The tower behind Casper glowed with neon blue accents, and most office windows were blacked out at this hour. Dusk lurked in the reflections. "What do you want me to do?" he asked. Dismay and confusion crept through his voice, and she hated it.

"Maybe *pay attention* to me for once. Act like you care about me. Maybe then you'd know what to do, what I *want*."

"I thought this was what you wanted," Casper waved his hand at the North Tower, "to be in the family business."

"To be your assistant? And *you*, CEO? Get off your high horse, Casper." She yanked her heels off one at a time, then chucked one at Casper's face. He ducked. The second heel shattered the window behind him. "Jayren knows."

"*Jayren!*" Casper said with an airy laugh. "Is that what you want? Jayren? To be with him and that group of misfits?"

"You make them sound inhuman," Ophiah hissed. She bared her teeth, and it turned into a smile. "Call them what they are," Ophiah dared him.

"The Four Horsemen," Casper said flatly. "You will never be a part of them, even if it's what you *want*, Ophi. You don't belong with them."

"At least they love me."

"I love you!" Casper said.

"They understand me!" she shouted back.

Casper looked around at the streets, as if he expected some assassin to creep up and slaughter them. It was the reason the streets cleared after dark. After dark, the assassins came out to do the Devil's dirty work. *He should be afraid of what stands right in front of him*, Ophiah thought. She smiled because it was what she was told to do. She smiled because they taught her to stitch the pain up inside, to never let it show. But her eyes ripped him apart, worse than any assassin would. She was taught to hate her blood for what was in it, but it was power, too. The lights of the North Tower flickered in and out. Their hum dulled, gasped, then roared back to life.

Casper stared back at her. "Demon," he spat.

"There it is," she whispered. "They see the angel."

"They won't be there for you when you need it," Casper challenged. "Let me prove it. Call them. They won't answer."

Ophiah froze, captive in Casper's cold eyes. She would. She weighed her options. She wanted Jayren to be the answer, but he wasn't. Even her own brother was tied up with watching Venatrix. She didn't doubt he would answer, but calling Orion wouldn't win her points with Casper. It was Corvun. Somehow, that's how it would work. If she wanted an answer, no matter how bitter or brutally honest, she would get it from Corvun. And in the end, it was Corvun who had told her she was Hades, the one who followed the Four Horsemen. She clutched her phone in her fist and dialed Corvun's contact (which Jayren had punched into her phone with sticky, sugar-and-salt-covered fingers on their lunch dates for "emergencies"). Silently, she thanked Jayren.

"Hello?" Corvun answered.

"Corvun," she said.

Casper's eyes hardened.

Ophiah straightened her spine. "I need a ride home. It's—"

"Ophiah," he said her name like a stranger. "I can't. We don't—"

"Dude!" Jayren hollered, faint in the distance. He ran his mouth, "Goddamn, gimme that phone. Ophi?"

Her heart stuttered. His voice sounded as warm as an embrace in stolen, sacred moments together. "It's an emergency," she said slowly.

"We'll figure it out. Where are you? We'll be there. Give us five minutes."

THE ABYSS
CORVUN KHLYDE

Corvun snatched his phone out of Jayren's hand. "What do you expect me to do?" he snapped.

"God, I don't know. *Save her*," Jayren snapped back.

"Take your motorcycle," Carina said from where she sat on the couch with one of Jayren's comic books in her hands. The cowboy picture from the Angels' Diner laid beside her on the red cushion.

Corvun nodded slowly. His motorcycle was downstairs in the warehouse; he would do what he could.

"She's at the North Tower," Jayren said darkly, "with Assper."

NORTHEAST FLORIDA
OPHIAH JUDE

"Well?" Casper asked. "Where's your knight in shining armor and his daring rescue?"

"Right here," Corvun said in a dry voice behind her.

Ophiah whipped around, hair standing on end. Corvun looked the part—not so much of the knight but of the assassins that crept around in the night. He wore leather that shone like black metal, reflecting eerie traces of the North Tower's lights. He was nearly invisible in the growing darkness. Behind him, a glinting metal beast.

"Fames!" Valentine North shouted as he busted through the massive double doors of the tower. The wind whipped around him, flapping the unbuttoned suit-jacket into sharp wings beside his hips. His hair flung back like a mane, and Corvun stared wide-eyed at the ruling Archangel.

Corvun grabbed Ophiah's wrist lightly. "Let's go."

Ophiah nodded to Corvun. He straddled his bike, and she did too, latching onto him as tightly as she could. The last thing she saw was Casper and his father running down the marble stairs towards her before her surroundings turned into inky black streaks all around her. She wasn't accustomed to this kind of speed, but she welcomed it. Wind tugged at her hair; instead of looking to see where she was, she tucked her face into Corvun's back. She almost wished it wouldn't end— the free feeling of the ground moving effortlessly beneath them, the world spinning like a coin—but it did, too soon.

Corvun's body stiffened, a jerking impact as he braked just a little too soon. "We're here," he said to her.

Ophiah opened her eyes to see the long driveway of her house. Shadows stood sentinel around it; she saw a Mark shining subtly over newly planted shrubbery. It hovered over her house like a giant blowing bubble, translucent and rainbow, wavering like water in the night. Carina and Jayren sat on the step of the porch, but they were nothing but shadows too.

Jayren stood first, Carina close behind him. They walked to meet halfway, but Jayren shuffled right up to her, halting just short of catapulting into a hug. On the slant of the driveway, he matched her height. And even in the dark, she could still see the way his eyes admired every inch of her face. But he didn't touch her, and he didn't say her name. Everything she wanted was right there, still out of reach. He asked her if she was okay, and she nodded. That was the end.

THE ABYSS
JAYREN OMANS

Corvun manifested a fire in the warehouse that night. Jayren thought it was a clever illusion on Corvun's behalf, totally equipped with the smells and sounds. The oak wood snapped and seasoned the air with scents of Earth and smoke. The illusion had been created around a small candle so that they could roast vegan marshmallows while Carina, Corvun, and Jayren sat together. In the distance of the warehouse, the illustration faded, and Jayren could see the black, empty windows that peered back into the Abyss. He prayed no one could see in. (He didn't know if he believed Corvun about no one being able to see in.)

"They can't," Corvun confirmed out loud, "see in. We're safe."

"Hey Corv," Jayren said. His face felt warm in the orange glow of the fire. In fact, his cheeks were so hot he could almost smell his flesh burning. He thought it smelled like fried fish for some reason. He shook the thought away. "Wanna tell a cowboy campfire story? Theatre of War, eh?"

Corvun scoffed. "You don't remember it. I don't remember it. I assure you Orion and Vena wouldn't either."

"Theatre of War, hm?" Carina's brow arched mischievously. "You speak of the outlaws."

"But somehow *she* does?" Jayren threw a cracker at Corvun then made himself a s'more. The vegan marshmallow (which Corvun had so politely searched high and low for) sweltered and swelled in the fire, blistering with crispy black. His mouth watered.

"They were demon hunters," Carina said. Light danced across her face, casting long, insidious shadows in the deep ravines of her eyes and coy features.

Corvun sputtered on a swallow of his whiskey.

Carina whipped in Corvun's direction. "Do you doubt me? They hunted forces of evil—witches, vampires, werewolves—in the wild west!"

Corvun leaned away. He licked an expression of distaste across his lips. "Fables," he said. "Campfire stories for settin's like these."

"Legends." Carina gazed deep into Jayren's wide eyes. He munched his s'mores and twisted his finger around the marshmallow that melted into messy strings around his hands. Carina continued, grinning with her teeth, "Their gunslinger was the most deathly accurate of their time. They called him Snake Eyes. Do you know why?"

"He had snake eyes," Corvun guessed, even and bored.

"Because he had the eyes of a snake," Carina disregarded Corvun, "and he was faster than the strike of a black mamba. Even more lethal. He could take down five men in two seconds. All of this, blindfolded!"

Jayren gaped. The corners of his lips stuck together.

"They say he liked to blindfold his girls, too," Carina said, leaning forward and winking.

Jayren snorted when he laughed. He thought of blindfolding Ophiah, and his face turned red between bouts of laughter. He needed to change the subject. "What about the others? What about the peg-leg guy?"

"He was their leader, lost his leg to the demons," Carina said. Her eyes wandered to Corvun; she gave him a knowing look that Jayren couldn't quite put his finger on. "They tried to drag him to Hell. Luckily, his band's loyalty saved him. The Grim Reaper took his leg with the swing of an axe. Saved him from death—or should I say—Death *himself* saved their leader. They used a lasso as a tourniquet and cauterized the wound, camped out until he could carry his own weight again. In other words, he was as good as a corpse without his men."

"How do you know all of this?" Corvun asked. The curiosity in his voice took Jayren by surprise. Corvun pursed his lips and shifted where he sat, eying Carina.

"Joshuah told me."

"Figures."

Jayren shoved Corvun. "It's a good story."

"What other stories did Joshuah tell you?" Corvun asked, and Carina laughed.

Jayren watched Carina watch Corvun like a hawk as she told him more stories. The tension between them was too tight, like a guitar string tuned to the brink of snapping. Jayren thought briefly of the nights he'd sit with Corvun while he tuned his old acoustic guitar. Jayren would always cackle when Corvun snapped the strings too quickly then began spewing a stream of profanity that embarrassed even Jayren.

Still, Carina's eyes cut into Corvun with a hunger that Jayren knew all too well; she wanted love. She craved his love. The way she looked at him, the lower lids of her eyes adjusting in the firelight to focus, undividedly, on him. It proved to Jayren more than anything that they'd been lovers in a past life.

Jayren wondered if he and Ophiah had been lovers in a past life, too.

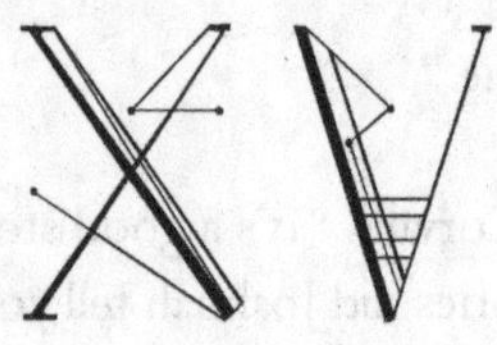

THE START OF WAR

Every angel has a God-given name. Their God-given name speaks directly to their soul, to who each angel is at their core. In their human forms, they recognize the name. Once an angel has come into their full power, they will know the name as their own.
— *A History of Hierarchy*

JANUARY 24TH, 2107 A.D.
THE ABYSS
JAYREN OMANS

"What do you see?" a voice—much like his own—asked Jayren. "*Listen.*"

Jayren turned, swimming through his movements in the nothingness around him. He heard cries, distorted and bellowing, the hiss and fizzle and whine of bombs speeding through the air. He heard bullets rupturing bone. Explosions, death, pain. War.

The scene inked around him, dropping like blood in water. He stood in a narrow hall, and the walls were drenched black with sorrow. Men slumped against the sides, others stumbled backwards, spattering with a red mist. Shrapnel ricocheted, lodging itself in arms and legs, arteries, and any exposed flesh. Men dropped like flies around Jayren, subject to wicked heat. His throat squeezed.

"What do you see?" the voice asked again.

Jayren watched a man kneel beside his wounded friend. In a flash, his throat ripped open and burst with red. Red, everywhere. *Thump,* as the man hit the ground. The friend's eyes widened with terror. Heart-wrenching yelling stabbed the atmosphere—again and again. Until it didn't; until a bullet lodged in the temple, spraying the wall with red.

Jayren closed his eyes.

"What do you *ssee?*" the voice hissed.

"War," Jayren sputtered into the chaos.

"I can't hear you!"

"War! Dammit! War!" he sobbed. Fear rattled his chest.

"Look at me," the voice growled from down the hall.

Jayren winced. He peeked into the mass, grotesque bloodshed and violence. The lights flickered and swayed. On and off, on and off. On—and there stood a man, a crude, jarring reflection of himself. Jayren's heart stopped. He could feel it, the lack of pulse, Death's hand taking hold of it.

Off.

On—and the war raged on.

Off. On and off, quicker. Jolting, sparking.

On—and Jayren stared down the man. He wore a thick, bloodied blindfold. He smiled a thin-lipped, coiling grin. His fingers curled around the fabric and slid it down to reveal white, empty eyes. He cocked a scarred eyebrow. "Like what you *ssee?*"

Jayren's legs threatened to give. He caught himself with one hand on the wall. "No," Jayren said, shaking his head. Then he begged, "No, no, *please.* Make it stop."

Off. A hesitation. Then on again.

Ophiah stood in the once bloodied hall, now empty and quiet. No trace of blood. No trace of combat. She tilted her head at him curiously. Jayren's heart burned at the sight of the sharp bow in her lip and the smooth curves that adorned her.

Her hair slipped like water over her shoulders, and Jayren eyed her hourglass figure and wondered what it would be like to hold her.

"War isn't always what it seems, is it?"

Off and on—the lights went—off and on.

Jayren was left looking at himself again.

"The battle you wage in your heart," the blind man said. "You see?"

Off and on. Jayren stared down the next image—one of his father dangling from the ceiling. He fell, scrambled back, panting as his heartbeat returned. *Thu-thump, thu-thump*. Faster, until it was all he could hear.

His father's face was empty of emotion, red, swelled, and cold. His father's open eyes just looked. Looked, not at a future or at his wife or kids. Looked. It meant nothing. He wore the same outfit, plucked from history: a green and orange flannel and pale jeans with a slit straight across the left knee. The hot summer afternoons when he used to kneel on that knee to wipe childish tears from Jayren's face were distant memories now. His father's body was as limp as a wet rag, his life and soul seeping ever-slowly out of him.

Jayren was screaming. He was small again, nothing but a boy tripping and stumbling over basement steps. He sounded nothing more than the cries he'd cried then, ripping from his throat, making his throat raw flesh, glass and gravel. He was desperate, helpless. A prisoner to the war inside him.

CARINA BLACKROCK

Carina woke, ripped from sleep by a sharp cry splitting through the quiet dorm. Her chest heaved as she tried to settle her initial shock. She hoisted herself up out of Corvun's cot, and stared across the dark room. She recounted the night before—the fire, the stories, helping Jayren into bed then following Corvun to his. They sat on his bed for hours, only inches apart and swapping slow gazes that made Carina's ears turn warm. Carina helped Corvun with new ideas of how to locate his sister. Eventually, he kissed her forehead, told her to sleep, then vanished in black smoke. He didn't say where he went or when he'd be back, but the kiss he left on her skin left a phantom ache in her chest.

Another scream clawed through her ears, distorting into a broken sob as it faded. Carina's heart pounded. She suddenly remembered a pain that caused the same unsolicited cries from her lungs. The pain returned, throbbing inside her ribcage and the bones of her legs. She pushed the covers aside and flicked the lights on. She stumbled through the empty dorm as another loud plea sounded from Jayren's room. She hurried to Jayren's room—didn't knock—and cracked the door open to find him writhing in pain and strung across the room.

Her heart constricted at the sight of him.

His torso blushed an angry pink in irritation, dotted with light purple bruises and red lines where he scratched at his skin in horror and denial. A curling, reptilian tail was where his legs should have been. The body of a snake filled the floor of the small room. His new skin gleamed a sickly pale color, and it was covered in light, iridescent scales that fluttered restlessly. Like feathers. Crescents of bright red blood laced each scale with fine lines. The muscles and untrained power beneath his skin tensed and flexed and cringed with every breath he took. Carina's eyes followed the trail of him to where his arms covered his head. He muffled his face in the covers of his cot, but it did nothing to mute his screams. Her chest tightened as he sobbed again; his shaking body refused to settle. "Jayren," she whispered.

Jayren's face snapped up in surprise. Agony trained his features pale white. His eyes were ringed with red irritation, surrounded by tears that made her own eyes sore. When she pushed the door open and stepped inside, his whole body recoiled in one quick, snappy movement. He dragged his new tail up onto himself, coils upon coils, in the corner of the room. His bare chest and face shone with damp sweat; he clutched his arms with white-knuckled hands.

Carina held out her hand as she approached him slowly. "It is okay," she said. "It is just me." She took one step nearer.

His skin still flickered, scales still fluttering. Carina could feel the ghost of it on her own skin. "W-Where…"

"There is no need to speak," Carina said and hushed him. She sat on the edge of his cold, damp bunk and watched him unwind slowly, unfolding until his long tail flopped back across the floor and relaxed. She could still see the pain coursing through him—a wavering distortion to the atmosphere around him—like electricity racing through thick power lines. His body moved against his will, twitching and twisting, and Carina listened to Jayren's hiss and gasp at every involuntary flinch.

"Where *iss* he—agh—gah," Jayren's voice contorted unnaturally, spiraling out of his mouth like a windstorm. "Where *iss Corvuss?*"

"I do not know." She jumped when Jayren's tail brushed her bare foot; he flinched back, too. "Come here, Jayren. Lay down and rest." She sat back on his bed, crossing her legs. Reluctance clutched Jayren, but slowly he inched towards her. He rested on the bed, lowering his chest and head into her lap. Another wince pained his colorless features. Carina's heart

pulled tight at the way Jayren's tacky arms wrapped around her suddenly. "Do you remember what I told you? What we are?" she asked.

"Can you— *H-Hass* it felt like *thiss* for you before?" His sharp speech was cool against her leg.

"My first time," she said. She touched his head. Cold sweat. He didn't draw away this time, so she stroked her fingers through his soaked hair. "It does not feel like this forever."

"How many *timess?*"

"Maybe twice." She rubbed her thumb over his neck, where his hair stood on end. Jayren struggled to form words. His teeth gritted loud enough for Carina to hear, squeaking and grinding. The longer she stayed, the calmer he became.

"Do you understand what you are?" Carina asked.

"A *monsster*," Jayren hissed.

"An angel," she corrected.

"How can an angel look like *thiss?* I'm *hideouss.*"

Carina's heart hurt again, but his feelings weren't unknown to her. She remembered her own confusion and fear and horror of her first changing. She wished she would have had comfort in that time, but Leroy was a distant mentor in her upbringing and did no such thing. So she flattened her hand against Jayren's smooth, scaled skin and didn't pull away when he shied beneath her touch. "You are not hideous."

"I look like the rope he *ussed* to kill *himsself.*"

"Who?"

"My dad," Jayren said. He curled onto her lap and stilled finally, wrapped around her as if she was a childhood memory.

Carina felt her pulse pumping in her chest, her wrist, her neck—pricking with pins and needles as a foreign feeling set in. She wasn't sure what to say to him, how to comfort him quite right. She wrapped her arms around Jayren's head and cradled him to her chest. She wouldn't let him go, she decided. Not in her lifetime. She would lay her life down for his if that was what was asked of her.

CORVUN KHLYDE

Corvun returned to the dorm that evening. After spending the day in sunlight, he had more energy than he anticipated, but his nocturnal lifestyle still nagged at his body, making his muscles weak with fatigue. He expected Carina and Jayren to already be awake, swapping stories again, but there was no sound in the white dorm. He decided to wait, lying on the couch, until Carina and Jayren woke up. They'd been up late by their means, after all, and Corvun didn't want to disturb either of them—especially not Carina. He thought he'd have a much harder time keeping his thoughts in line after seeing her fast asleep in his bed, anyway. Corvun sank into the sofa, and he thought for a long time. He thought about what his parents told him on his brief visit earlier that afternoon—that they were pregnant. In the moment, Corvun lashed out, accusing them of trying to replace Cynthia and himself. He accused Michael of trying to kill their stepmother. He hated how the words sounded as they left his mouth, but he didn't take them back. He wouldn't. His relationship with his family was fractured before; now it was broken, gone. He tried to convince himself he didn't miss it.

Twenty minutes later, Jayren stumbled out on wary fawn feet. He wore a tee and boxers, and his face was flushed red. Eyes slitted in fear, his knees wobbled uncertainly. He stumbled to the kitchen and fell on the way.

Corvun jumped up and ran to him. He helped him stand. "Are you alright? What happened?"

Jayren's throat bobbed. A tendon pulled taut at the surface of his neck. He shook his head. "Can you ask her?" His voice was so weak. Dry. Crumbling. He'd been crying again, Corvun guessed. Jayren wheezed and dry heaved.

Corvun dragged Jayren to the counter by his underarms, where Jayren lost his s'mores and whiskey to the stainless steel sink. His spine lurched, muscles went rigid, then he fell slack and passed out in Corvun's arms.

Carina rushed out a moment later.

"Clean the sink," Corvun told her. He picked Jayren up and carried him back to his bed. Water hissed into the disposal. "And bring a bucket."

"Please?"

"Please!"

Jayren was as pale as his white cot.

Corvun held Jayren's face, and his heart pounded hard in his chest. "Is he okay?"

Carina set a trash can on the floor next to Jayren's pillow. "He had his first changing," she said.

Corvun swallowed and nodded. That made sense.

"He will be alright. I was sick like this when I had mine. He will bounce back. He just needs time. Let him sleep for now."

· · · ·

Two nights later, Corvun sat in a chair across from Jayren. Jayren stared ahead with wide, green eyes and flushed, rosy skin. He actually looked healthier than Corvun had ever seen him. Attentiveness filled his face, and a strong angle carved his jaw. His cheekbones were higher now, too. If this had been the "angel puberty" Jayren was waiting on, it hit him like a car crash. It looked elegant on him, and *that* was deceiving.

"You're checking me out," Jayren said. His voice rang smooth and clear.

Corvun shrugged. "Open up."

Jayren opened his mouth. His breath was sharp and tangy like the smell of metal.

"Remind me to get you some mouthwash," Corvun said, wincing back.

"Nhugh," Jayren responded.

Carina scooted a chair up beside Corvun's. She handed him a butter knife. "Here. He will have an extreme reaction to blood for the next few weeks." She used another kitchen knife to cut a small nick in her palm.

Jayren's eyes slitted to eager, carnivorous eyes. They snapped in the direction of Carina's hand. Corvun caught his jaw between his thumb and forefinger. Jayren's canines were twice the length of the average human canines now, and his first molar protruded more too. As he opened his mouth, two venom glands protruded forward and laid flush against his fangs.

"Holy shit," Corvun muttered.

"Ehh-th et khuuhl?"

"What?"

"Is it cool?" Carina translated for Jayren.

"Stop tryin' to talk." Corvun pried at Jayren's mouth. He wedged the butter knife behind Jayren's venom glands and pressed. The soft, gum-like flesh spat black venom into Jayren's mouth, but Jayren didn't seem to notice. Corvun and Carina stared as the black coated Jayren's mouth in a sheen that oozed with the bitter smell of death.

"That must be why they compared him to the black mamba," Carina said. "They have black mouths."

"Whh-uuht?"

"Stop," Corvun said again. They leaned closer. "How poisonous do you think it is? Black mamba venom can kill a human in about thirty minutes after a bite."

Carina looked at him, her eyes pondering his knowledge.

"I liked snakes growin' up," Corvun mumbled, staring numbly into Jayren's wet mouth, "until I had to kill one. Michael said it was a survival technique. If you ask me, he was tryin' to really push that verse—crushin' the serpent's head and all that."

"Well," Carina said, "for him, I would say after biting someone, they would last only a few minutes." She shook her head then pointed. "Push on those glands again. See? The amount he ejects is based on pressure. So hypothetically, if he bit down harder, more venom would push into the wound. I would give a victim one to five minutes based on the strength of the bite."

Jayren's mouth continued to darken.

"Look." Carina pointed again, this time at his tongue.

It was elongated like taffy stretched across two metal bars. Doused in black venom, it jutted out and forked at Corvun's hand. "Yuuhh taayhet lyyhke guuhn hoowdeurr."

Corvun released Jayren's face and stared at him, exasperated.

"You *tasste* like gun powder *iss* what I *ssaid*," his voice spiraled awkwardly around his protruding fangs. "I *ssound badasss*."

"You sound like a middle schooler with braces," Corvun said.

"No, I'm *passt* that *phasse*."

"Clearly not."

"He needs to learn his abilities," Carina said, "and he *must* learn to control the urge to consume blood."

"Can I go *ssee* Ophi?"

"No," Corvun and Carina said in unison.

Jayren rolled his eyes.

Corvun hesitated then spoke slowly, "Although, I did agree to meet Rian to see Vena," Corvun said. "Ophiah might be there. It would be a good test to see how he does," he said to Carina, and then to Jayren, "I'm sure you'll need supervision until you can control yourself. You had poor impulse control before this."

Carina raised an eyebrow at Jayren, but Jayren only shrugged.

JANUARY 26TH, 2107 A.D.
NORTHEAST FLORIDA
OPHIAH JUDE

Ophiah stood behind Orion's shoulder, observing the scene before her. They all stood around Venatrix's bedside—Corvun and Jayren, Orion and herself. Valentine had left the room only moments before to let them have time with Venatrix in her unconscious state. With them, she felt more at home than she ever had. The room smelled like the plastic from Venatrix's saline IV drip, the distant sweat of Corvun, and the intoxicating body spray Jayren wore. He'd changed since she last saw him, and his eyes kept locking with hers. A blush grasped her skin like the heat of a fire, and Ophiah wondered if Jayren could smell her embarrassment like she could smell his cologne.

Orion took a chair and sat against Venatrix's bedside. He took her hand, held it, and rested his chin on the side of the bed frame. Ophiah swallowed hard, her nerves electric in her brother's absence. She'd always been his shadow, but now she stood outside it.

"Will she be okay?" Ophiah asked. It drew her the attention she secretly craved. She flourished in the flames eating at her skin when the boys looked at her. She wanted to burn with them, she realized, to have a voice in their madness and solace in their quiet moments after the fire. But Valentine and Casper would never allow it.

Ophiah never had a good look at Corvun before now since they only ever knew each other as friends of friends. She thought he looked a little terrifying, with a stark nose and wide-set, black eyebrows that were permanently sharpened by worry and despair. His face was hollowed more than the photos she'd seen of him before, and his cheekbones rose out of slightly sunken cheeks. He was a skeleton with friends kind enough to drape him with a costume so it wouldn't be Halloween every day for him.

Even Jayren looked different, his narrow face a little fuller. His features appeared more deadly in the low, orange light, as if now he had every right to shed his nerdy, school-boy act to reveal the killer hiding inside him. His bones were harsh with strong edges, but his eyes were pink and puffy as if from a lingering infection. His green eyes darted over her figure, hesitating when he found a spot he liked. His eyes grazed her cleavage, and she pulled her blazer shut. When he paused over her throat, her stomach wrung violently. His deliberate gaze held her with such intensity that she felt like a mouse in a snake's coils. A bead of sweat ran down her spine.

Corvun dug a heel into Jayren's foot, and he snapped out of the trance. With one hand wrapped around Jayren's arm, he whispered, "If you don't cut it out, I'll drag you out of here. Do you know what I had to bribe North with to let us on the property?"

"Your soul?" Jayren asked dryly.

By the look of Corvun's thin, pressed lips, he didn't take the joke lightly.

"What if she doesn't wake up?" Orion asked. His voice was but a murmur, so unsure.

"She has to," Corvun said.

"But what if she doesn't?" Orion's voice cracked.

"Then you go through with the plan to banish Tristan."

"Won't it be pointless?" Jayren asked. "If Conquest is out of the picture, winning the Battle wouldn't matter. You said we all had to make it out alive. The times before—" Jayren didn't sound so sure either.

At least he's trying, Ophiah thought.

"When one of us died before, it was always an auto-fail. Game over," Jayren said. Dismay hung in the air, but he continued, "If she doesn't wake up, banishing y'all's demon father or whatever, the Battle—all of it. None of it even counts, right?"

"We can still fall in this lifetime." Corvun glared at Venatrix's impassive face. The dark pits of Corvun's eyes jumped up to Ophiah, and she almost doubled back at the vigor in his expression. "Tristan is the Deceivers' leader. Without him, they won't be as organized. We have to keep that risk—the risk of fallin'—to a minimum. If we fall in one lifetime, we're Fallen forever. But we can still hope and pray for Vena to wake up. Pray over her until she does. Bedside. Every day." An order. "Jayren and I won't be able to. I bribed North with the location of an ongoin' commission. They'll catch the RUST assassins, but if we do that too many more times, it'll get suspicious. It has to be you two."

Orion shifted.

Ophiah's chest filled with disbelief and somehow—hope. "They call our prayers invalid. They say God doesn't hear the offspring of demons."

"Yeah, well *they* lie to you," Corvun said. His voice seemed to raise the temperature in the close-quarters inferno. "You are still Angelborne. You get the choice—to be good or evil— not them."

"Okay," Ophiah whispered. His lack of doubt in her was startling.

"Pray for her," Corvun begged. "Please. Here. Every night. *Make* it count."

"We will," Ophiah said.

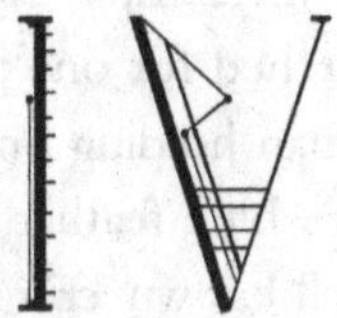

INTERLUDE IV

THE WAGER

438 A.D.
ROME
CORVUS

The sun scorched Corvus's skin as he ushered Serpens, Venatici, and the twins down narrow market alleyways. He avoided the routes the guards patrolled, sidestepped the slaves and spies he knew of. He guided their escape by the map etched into his veins. The smell of freshly baked bread grabbed his attention for a split second, and he considered what he was leaving behind: security and the known. He shook the thought away, kept a steady hand on Venatici's back to keep her in line. She glared at him, and he gave her a warning look in return. He still had his bloodied dagger in his belt, and he wouldn't hesitate to stop her from running if he needed to.

The maze of buildings opened to the docks finally, leaving the five of them subject to the sun. The wet wood beneath their feet gave little relief. The air smelled of salt and of drunks who gambled through their trips. Sailors wandered, some waited, and Corvus searched for one pirate in particular. He spotted her, a lean woman holding one hip in her hand and flagged by the expensive blue feather in her hair. It marked her as a dangerous, well-known criminal. *Only criminals help criminals*, he reminded himself.

"Corvus," Orion said. He tossed a bag of chiming coins.

The shock nearly caused Corvus to miss the catch. He didn't ask where Orion got the bag. It didn't matter. He peeked inside, surprised by the wide array of gold coins, different shapes and sizes from many years prior. He gave Orion a curt nod and led the others to the pirate at the end of the dock. "Serpens," he said. He tossed the bag of coins back to his friend then motioned for the others to stay where they were.

The pirate drew her sword, slow and nonchalant, aiming the tip at Corvus as if it were a hand to take and kiss. Corvus stood at a distance, and she admired his face, tilting it up to her with the edge of her blade. She glanced over his shoulder to his followers. Suddenly, she stepped close to Corvus, dug her sword between his feet, and hissed eagerly. "I've already heard the *rumorss*. You're too late. I'd get more money to sell your head than to help you, my dear crow."

"News doesn't travel that fast." He leaned closer to her.

"The birds tell me," she said with a smile. Her lips neared his.

"It'd only be a hunch."

"It's the kind of trouble you get into."

"I need out of here," he said.

"How desperate are you?" Her golden eyes flashed at him, yellow only for a moment. She stepped away. "Hold the bag over my ship. We'll make a bet."

Corvus turned to Serpens, and Serpens tossed a different bag back. Corvus obeyed the woman, extending his arm and holding the bag over her deck.

"If it's precious gems, I'll let you board. If it's gold, I'll sell your heads for more." She shot a glance at the others.

Corvus held his stance.

The pirate caught the edge of the bag with her sword and sliced through the mesh fabric. Rubies fell onto her top deck, and her eyes flashed again. The look vanished, like a ghost being banished from her body. She stepped off her boardwalk, offering it to the others. "Come aboard. Where to?" she asked.

Corvus waved to the others.

Serpens boarded last, winking at the pirate and tossing her another, smaller bag of gold.

She glared at Corvus.

"You of all people, Carina, should know not to make bets with snakes." Corvus raised his eyebrows. "Get us as far away as you can."

VENATICI

Venatici kept close behind Orion as they descended into the ship. She didn't dare leave his side after the faithfulness he'd shown her in the arena. Beside him, she felt safe. Still, she struggled to keep up with his easy stride and his dismissal of what had just ensued. "Where did you get that gold?" she demanded. "What about the rubies? How did Serpens know she would want rubies?"

"Swiping from purses of dames is a petty crime. Easy as hell. And pirates are easy to predict." Orion grinned at her.

"My sister and I stole the passage and more. Serpens was in on it. Corvus tipped us off before we left the arena—that Carina would want money but that rubies would win any bet with her. We didn't have time to explain."

Venatici's head hurt.

Orion smiled, his hair disheveled and falling in his face. The bandage wrapped around his arm and chest was bloodied and sweat-soaked. He grabbed her arms. "We are free! Don't you understand?"

"From this day on, we will have a bounty on our heads," Venatici said. "We will never be free."

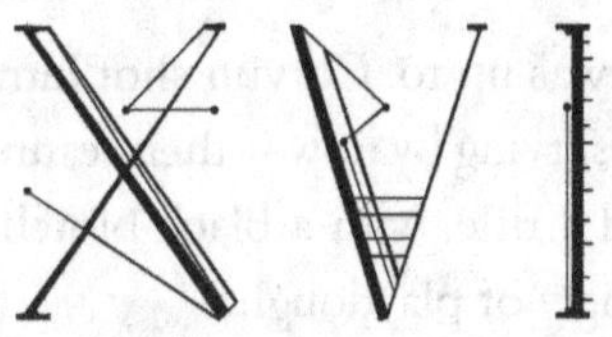

DEATHBENDERS, DANGERS, AND THE UNHEARD PRAYERS OF THE FAITHFUL

*RUST assassins are given the name "Deathbenders" after their ability
to die and come back to life.*
— *A History of Hierarchy (Revised Edition)*

JANUARY 28TH, 2107 A.D.
THE ABYSS
JAYREN OMANS

Jayren dreamed about Ophiah for days after seeing her at the hospital. He dreamed about her skin, the smell of her blood, and the horror in her eyes when he looked at her. He tried to shake the dreams, tried to stay awake as long as possible until they caught up to him with fingers made of darkness. Often he sat with Carina, who tested his patience eternally by cutting her hand to train his bloodlust. Other times, Jayren watched Corvun train.

Corvun had a file laid out on a desk downstairs on the training floor when Jayren ventured downstairs that night to see what Corvun was up to. Corvun shot him a glance—used to his frequent observing by now—then resumed cleaning two guns, a pistol and a rifle, with a black-blotched, yellow cloth that smelled strongly of playdough.

Jayren wandered up and read the folder. He wasn't sure what he imagined the shock or horror to be when he first encountered a mission file, but it didn't hit him quite as hard as he expected. A subtle sinking feeling thrummed through his pulse, then it vanished. "So," he cleared his throat, "are we— are we doing this one?"

"You're not."

"You are?" Jayren asked. "Alone?"

Corvun glanced at him. "Are you ready to kill someone?"

Jayren shook his head. He watched Corvun fold the cloth and put it aside then piece together the guns as if he was rehearsing his nighttime routine. He finished the rifle, puzzled the handgun together, racked it, then *snapped* the trigger once. Jayren flinched. He didn't know what he expected. The magazine was still unloaded on the desk.

"Do you want to train?" Corvun asked Jayren.

Jayren nodded.

"Let's go over the basics again." Corvun motioned at the chair for Jayren to sit. "Recap."

Jayren sat down. He looked at the open, scattered file.

Corvun sat on the side of the table. "RUST is like a game. You take these…missions, objectives, tasks…and complete them. They're to be completed with the utmost precision, no error, no fault, no tracks left behind. Kill the targets. There's no alternative. Kill the targets, and you get paid."

"How much?"

"Not enough," Corvun's voice was wry. He put a small, fabric pouch on the desk. "If you think you'll fail a mission, you take a suicide pill. Cephan will bring you back to life, upon death. It's like a game over, like a restart. If there's any doubt at all that you'll fail… It's easier to kamikaze out. If you fail the mission, leave an error or mistake or someone catches on to you—Cephan will take it up with you personally. He'll kill you, and he won't bring you back. Understand?"

Jayren nodded. "How does he…uh, y'know…*pick them?*"

Corvun fell silent. Then he started, "Say you believe in angels and demons."

"Okay," Jayren said. He left the door to his mind open just a little.

"Michael told me it has to do with Biblical lore," Corvun started. "There's a verse that says, 'Anyone who hates another brother or sister is really a murderer at heart.' Those hateful thoughts are responsible for the creation of the mission files. The hated get a target on their head."

"Wouldn't that mean that just about anyone can be found in the files?"

Corvun nodded. "As long as the hate resides in someone's heart, the object of that hate continues to be a target."

"God, that makes you look at it a different way, huh?"

"No kiddin'." Corvun ran a hand through his hair. "The missions will change based on time and circumstance, too. We have a lot at our disposal, though, so completin' a mission with precision isn't as hard as it sounds." Corvun stood and took a few steps back. He waved his hand. "Compare this warehouse to your backpack, like in a video game. You can call and send to it directly. When you're on Earth—" he paused, held his hands up, "if you are without defense, anythin' here in our storage is at your immediate beck and call."

Jayren watched as the handgun wavered like a sandy shadow on the desk. The stray bullets beside the magazine dissolved into black, dusty ash and swept into the magazine. Then, the gun and the magazine both sifted away. They reappeared—with a lingering trail of black fog—in Corvun's hand. Corvun smacked the magazine into the gun, spun on his heel, and unloaded it into a target suspended five yards away. Jayren turned rigid-stiff in his seat. The banging of the gun rang in his ears. Shells *clinged*—near soundless—on the warehouse floor.

"So it's kinda how the paintballs worked?"

"Exactly. It works the same with real guns. We have to keep our stock up to summon ammo. We can't summon anythin' we don't have." Corvun laid the empty gun back on the desk. The slide was kicked back, and the barrel jutted up at an awkward angle. "We have a similar ability with travel. We have the freedom to come and go directly from the Abyss to Earth and back again. It's like teleportin', but we can't teleport to different places—from one Earth location to another Earth location."

"So we can go from the Abyss to the island, but not from the island to Jacksonville?"

"Yes. With RUST, we're given Black Magic. Deathbenders—which is what we RUST assassins are called—can do things that are typically abilities reserved for Archangels, and even some of the Powers in Heaven." Corvun stopped abruptly, muttering something hasty about the Archangel lineage, then continued. "We can move the anatomical structure of your body with your thoughts." His voice warbled. He shifted away in grainy blackness that pulled across the room. He reappeared in his fullness, waiting for Jayren's response.

"That's trippy as fuck." Jayren said. He should have been more creeped out, but after everything he'd seen, weird was his new normal. "But, I've never seen an Archangel do *that*. I'm pretty sure I'd remember it if I did."

"Doubtful, even if you did, with the frequency they alter memories. Besides, abilities like this would take the Archangels decades on decades to master; they have to access a higher state of being and translate that into the human vessels they're in. Michael explained it to me once. Even he can't do it outside of RUST. But I think that's what Cephan wants us to believe—that it's Black Magic. Maybe the Devil did grant him that—powers that shouldn't belong outside of Heaven—but think of it this way: What if someone was free of RUST and realized it wasn't Black Magic, just the brilliance of the angels? If North and his men came after Cephan with these abilities, they might have a chance."

"Corv, that's crazy. It doesn't really make sense."

"Faith—"

"Faith is a lie for the hopeless," Jayren bit back.

"Trust me on this one, Jayren."

NORTHEAST FLORIDA
CORVUN KHLYDE

The commission was clean and simple, in fact, too much so. Corvun swept into the old house on the breeze, through a crack in the window. He glanced around at the old canvas paintings that soaked up the smell of magnolia soap and citrus-and-evergreen candles. Cross-stitch artwork hung in colored, wooden frames, and white doilies were stained with brown drops from coffee and tea. Corvun couldn't see very well for the heavy, patterned curtains that draped the house in darkness. All of a sudden, he wasn't sure if he trusted his own ability or his own judgment. He thought, upon choosing the mission, that it would be clean and quick and there would be no emotions involved. Perhaps he could even consider it a mercy kill, for the woman to die at his hands rather than the hands of her terminal disease. He wondered how she was chosen for the files—if it was a stranger or a family member who felt burdened by her presence. He hated the thought— that someone could think that, that she was left with no one to defend her and no adequate way to defend herself. *Maybe if they hadn't outlawed guns, she'd have a fighting chance,* Corvun thought bitterly.

He stepped into the woman's room. She was a lump on the bed, still and in a bundle of awkward joints and knotty skin. Emotion lodged in his throat. He paused, and his foot landed on a board that creaked and moaned, voicing the very pain and protest in his own mind.

"Boy, I've already heard you. I know how the wind blows when it carries your kind," the woman rasped.

Corvun whispered in return, "Then you know why I'm here."

"Well, then, get it over with."

"Can I fix you something? Tea—maybe?" Corvun struggled with the words. His blood was static in his veins, a live wire, sizzling with regret.

The woman gave a short, staccato laugh. "Assassin or no?"

"Assassin. Bad at it."

"So be it." The woman struggled with her covers, and Corvun was all too aware of the weight of his gun in his holster. He helped the woman unwrap herself from the cocoon of down blankets and held her arms until she was sure of her own feet. He helped her into the living room, where she pointed to a lamp. He lit the room, then left to make her a tea in the kitchen. "The box on the left of the sink," she told him before he walked out.

He brought her back a steaming cup of tea then sat stiffly across from her.

The woman looked at him with eyes set in folds of wrinkles. Corvun wondered if the wrinkles came from years of laughter, and he envied her. That wouldn't be the life he led. "You are not what I expected," the woman said with narrowed eyes.

Corvun realized he didn't ever know his grandmother on his mother's side—not his birth mother or stepmother. His father, Michael, didn't have a grandmother because he'd come to Earth—not been born—as all the Archangels had done. Jealousy burned in Corvun's heart. He envied people who had something like *this*, too. Something normal. He wondered who he was taking it from, and his eyes welled with tears.

She reached out and touched his hand, but he flinched back. "An assassin who cries," she said with a lifted brow.

"Trust me, I didn't want the job."

The woman sipped her tea with a bit of a slurp. The lines around her lips pursed. "This tea is wonderful. These days, I can't seem to make it right. Always break the bag one way or another, and the leaves get out. Tsk. But this… Thank you."

Corvun thought about his suicide pill, wondered what it would taste like. They sat in silence, and Corvun's eyes stung in the dim golden light. He rubbed his face, trying to think of any way out, but he'd just gone through this with Jayren too. There was no alternative.

The woman finished her tea and set her cup on a doily. She hummed a small tune, eyed the gun at his hip, then folded her hands in her lap. "Let's get this over with."

Corvun cleared his throat. "I want to talk—before." His father's voice haunted the back of his head—"*Never take a life in vain.*"—and this was all Corvun could think to do. To find this information and commit it to memory: "I want to know your name."

Her eyebrows raised, and her pale eyes glistened in the low light. "My name is Lara Walker."

Corvun looked down to his hands. The pain in them seemed to grow to life. It became a cruel handshake from the Devil himself, breaking each joint inside his skin. Reluctance spread with the pain. "Your birthday," he said.

"Oh, we don't keep track of those things by my age."

"Please," Corvun said. His throat was almost too tight to speak.

"I think it was coming…in December. December fifth."

December had passed, Corvun thought bitterly. *Doesn't anyone celebrate with her?* Corvun wondered. So he memorized her image instead: the gentle amber glow on her yellowing hair and the old knit sweater she wore with blue-green sequins sewn into the shoulders. "Tell me your favorite memory."

"Oh, I have many of those. *Those* start adding up," she said with a chuckle. "I used to visit the beach when I could walk better. I'd be out there for hours. I'd feed the birds, and all the youngins would gripe. Thought that because I fed the songbirds, the seagulls would get the wrong idea."

Kill her, Cephan's voice echoed deep in his mind.

Corvun's brow cinched. He tried to control his voice as he whispered his next words, "Confess your sins." When he drew his gun and stood, she looked up at him with a distant expression.

"To whom?"

That was all he needed to hear to remember her forever.

"Jesus Christ, the son of the God who created the universe. He was born blameless and never sinned so that he could take on the sins of humanity when he died on the cross," Corvun said the words he'd recited before coming. He hoped he wouldn't have to. His voice gave way when he whispered,

"Accept this, that he died for you. Accept him as your savior, please."

Lara's eyes searched his.

Corvun swallowed hard, but emotion threatened to wreck him like a hurricane unleashed. His fingers almost gave, almost turned to sand and whipped away in the wind. He almost apologized to her, almost said something else. Anything else. Words bit at his tongue like salt. The storm inside him built up its power.

The trigger was cool, but the snap of the gun cracked his mind open again.

He wondered if it ever wouldn't.

His ears rang.

The graveyard in the Abyss, Corvun learned, was also a burial place for victims. It went on for miles beyond what he'd seen. It was why no one ever found the bodies of RUST victims. He forced himself to look at Lara, forced himself to scar his mind with the deep, dark red on her sweater. He wished her away—her suddenly vague and unoccupied eyes, the small gape of her lips. She vanished in black, like ink seeping down into the couch, down, down, down…

He glared at the mess of blood. The storm in his head raged louder. He wanted to wreck the room, to tear the quilt from the back of the couch, upturn the coffee table, and hear her tea cup shatter on the floor. He could've taken every frame off the wall and flung it across the room, could've smashed every lamp, could've broken everything.

But the only thing he did was alter the vision of the couch. A trick of the Archangels.

The blood unstained from the couch, at least, to the human eye. It picked away like water washed from the atmosphere. It dissolved, and so did the smell.

THE ABYSS
CARINA BLACKROCK

When Carina saw the new cut on Corvun's skin, she forced him into her arms. He shattered there, like a million droplets of rain. She pleaded with him, tended to the tears on his face, ushered him to his room where she sat close to him in the dark. She cleaned his wrist and wrapped the wound, and she whispered to him with her lips pressed to his shoulder and his face.

He told her he didn't want to do this.

She told him she knew.

They were together like that for hours.

Corvun struggled to heal himself. Between his healing powers as an Archangel and the healing abilities he had from RUST, he should've been able to. Corvun weighed as much as a headstone, leaning into her. His sorrow was heavy, and his exhaustion laced him with dead weight. Carina combated the weight, nested into his side like a crutch. Carina held his inflicted arm and ran her fingertips lightly around his open wounds. He'd had them for weeks, and they hadn't healed, and she knew better than believing any lie he came up with.

He needed protecting.

A fire struck in her soul again. She thought of Leroy and the passion *he* held in his eyes. He had been hellbent on protecting her. Did he know? Did Leroy know his old RUST partner would conceive the son that *she* was made to protect? Or was it just the hand of God at work?

Carina glanced at the irritated compass brand on Corvun's wrist. She lifted his hand and kissed his palm.

He woke at the gesture in quiet, reclusive shock. He began untangling the mess that was their bodies.

"Stop," she said. "Stay here. It is okay."

Corvun stilled and sank back into her. "What if—" his voice was raw, "—Jay…"

"Jayren went to see his sister. We are alone."

Corvun's head tilted towards her, and his nose buried into her hair.

She felt a tear fall into one of the curves in her ear. "Stay here," she whispered.

His body quaked with a silent sob.

"Breathe, Corvun."

· · · · ·

When Corvun finally pieced himself back together, slid off the bed and out of the room, Carina followed him. She leaned against his doorframe while he filled a glass of water. "Corvun," she started, "your arms… We need to talk about it."

"What's there to talk about?" he asked. He coughed lightly on his water.

"Why do they not heal?" she asked. She wanted to hear his reason.

"I try. It's—" he paused, fabricating syllables and willing them into words, "—not easy." He looked away from her. The absence of his dark, powerful eyes made her feel as if she'd just been unearthed from a grave, that he was the Earth and she'd been buried far beneath him. He looked back at her, and his gaze smothered her in darkness again. "The guilt I carry…"

She could feel it. Easily. "Let it die," she told him. "They are dead, and you will kill many more." Corvun tried to turn away from her, but she grabbed his arm to stop him. "Leave your guilt in the ground with them. It is where it belongs, for someone like you. Focus on what you have."

"What do I have?" Corvun asked.

"Jayren," she said. She raised her eyebrows. "*Me.*"

Corvun glanced at her lips, then quickly looked away.

"Jayren can help you carry this burden. Let me show you something," she said. She led him downstairs to the mock range he set up there. She took a gun from the table to the right of the stairs, slipped a loaded magazine into the weapon. She shot one bullet, and a hole *snapped* through the paper, dead on the bullseye. She looked at Corvun, who maintained his heavy silence. "Blindfold me then spin me."

Still showing little emotion, Corvun manifested a strip of black fabric in his hands. He walked up behind her and tied it over her eyes like a blindfold. With her other senses heightened, her skin warmed with the touch of his rough hands. He spun her three times in the darkness. "Again," she said, and he entertained her.

Carina's nostrils flared. In a heartbeat, her surroundings came back to her in a flash of grayscale. She saw the target as a blank piece of paper, closer than the flat, blank walls far behind it. She saw her previous bullet hole. She aimed and unloaded five more bullets through the same hole. After the ringing in her ears subsided, she heard Corvun's heart race in his chest. "Jayren can do this. His echolocation abilities will allow him to. Teach him." She turned to Corvun; his figure seared her sight with a white-hot holy glow. "He will be able to take commissions with you so that you are not alone."

Corvun tugged the blindfold down off her face. "What are you?" he asked.

She looked at his mouth as he spoke. She smiled. "If I told you, you would not look at me the same way you do now."

"What way is that?"

"Like you want to study me."

He cocked an eyebrow.

"You can if you would like to." She stepped closer to him.

He put a hand on her face carefully, then cradled it with both his hands. He leaned in, drank her in slowly, with wet lips on hers. He tasted like the bitter twist of stomach acid. She kissed him, only as deeply as he allowed her to. They stood very still as it happened, with only their hands touching each other's necks and faces. She closed her eyes and savored his slowness, his insatiable interest in her.

NORTHEAST FLORIDA
ORION JUDE

Orion braced his feet evenly apart beneath his shoulders, his hands a balanced distance on the wooden post of his stolen scythe. He glanced around the clearing. Sunlight bristled through the leaves. Icy humidity and dampness licked at the blades of grass around his ankles, at Orion's neck. Winter birds chirped in the branches above, which were dressed by fragments of lace-like Spanish moss. Salt seasoned the air. He could smell critters dashing through the undergrowth, hear the wind *wishing* through the trees, the snap of the twigs…

That snap reminded him of the night he played truth and dare with his friends in the bed of his truck.

It was enough to trigger a response. Black seeped into his eyes. He let it take him, just a little. He fought better when he gave in. *Just a little.* The inky swirl revealed the demon's movement in more clarity; Orion realized this after his time training in the forest like this alone.

With newfound power laden around his neck, Orion fell into step with the light weight of the wooden scythe. It was like a dance. He spun on his heel to stare down the pitch-black, swirling, tar-skinned creature.

It spoke like a flame, words curling and coiling like fire through a path of gasoline. *Child of darkness, come with us. We can make you strong. You are so strong.*

"You should be scared of me," Orion told it. He lifted the wooden weapon, and the demon flinched back. It surprised Orion the first time a demon had this response. After all, the scythe was just wooden. It made him wonder then: Was he *himself* the true source of power? Shadows flipped and twirled off the demon's neck as the edge of the wood neared it. Orion grinned, recalling his own sharpening of the makeshift blade. Perhaps *that* gave it its power—Orion's care and touch. He came to terms with this revelation, quietly, confidently. He *was* a different breed. He could kill demons. He could kill angels. He was vengeance. Anger slithered into his tendons, pulling him tight with a harrowing need to rip through the demon opposing him.

Son of Sorrow, you could rule us! Rule us, it begged. Bone-yellow teeth clacked in its attempted smile. *Come with us, Son of Sorrow,* it hissed, outstretched a hand. *Rule with us.*

Orion spun the scythe, severed the demon's hand. The wooden blade sliced right through the blackness of the shifting entity before him. Its limb fell like a rotted apple to the ground, where it ruined a patch of green grass with decay. Hellfire sizzled in its blood. The demon screeched, but it was just ringing in Orion's ears. He wondered if that's what the ringing in his ears had always been: demons crying when they came too close. To his mother, to his sister, to the angelic power flowing through his own veins.

Orion shoved the wood into the blackness of the demon's throat.

Its face contorted, offered him another twisted, putrid smile. *Spare me, kin of my kin. Do not kill me! Banish me!*

"Burn in Hell," Orion spat. He yanked the staff of the scythe, cutting through the wet, gurgling neck of the demon. It foamed with dark, cherry-red blood then flopped to its side, limp and lifeless. The twirling of the demon's shadow fell still, and the tar of its body spilled across the ground. It created a pool of rot and decay and death in its wake.

Orion glanced off to the left where he'd made a small, shoddy sundial. No matter how many hours he spent out here, it was never enough to sate the fear in his blood.

Time was ticking.

JAYREN OMANS

Jayren found that warping in and out of the Abyss was easier than he expected. It reminded him a lot of tapping through an video game menu to select his location, just like Corvun explained. Jayren appeared at the corner of his house's street. He stood facing the direction of the house, stomach churning. He walked, hands in his pockets. Night spread over the Earth like the wings of a massive bat, and moonlight peeked through the thin, membrane clouds above.

When he reached the front door, he noticed the lights were still on behind the blinds. He stared at the door for a few minutes, wondering if he should bother knocking at all. Lacey hadn't even texted him to ask where he was, where he'd been for the past few weeks. Maybe she believed all the passive-aggressive comments he made about joining RUST. Maybe Professor North told her, since he knew. Lacey's silence made it pretty obvious to Jayren she wanted nothing to do with him anymore.

Jayren looked at the door for a while longer. He reminisced on the days he and Corvun came running back in sudden torrential downpours, pounding on the door with slick, shaking fists. As soon as Lacey would open the door, open her mouth to scold them, Corvun and Jayren would skip and sputter, squish and splash through the front door, drop most of their clothes (keeping only their underwear on), then dash back to Jayren's room to find a change of new, warm outfits. Despite all her angry glares, she still always picked up their clothes, tossed them in the dryer, and left them blankets and hot chocolate near the TV.

She had her own, cold-shouldered way of showing she cared about him.

Jayren wasn't convinced this was the same.

He couldn't work up the courage to knock, so he faded into a trickle of darkness that pulled him back underground.

JANUARY 29TH, 2107 A.D.
NORTHEAST FLORIDA
ORION JUDE

"Why do you want to go back to school on a Saturday?" Jayren asked. Orion watched him lounge back in the passenger seat of his truck. His feet were propped against the dash, and his toes left small smears on the windshield.

Orion drove, white knuckled. "I don't have a piano at home." *And it's the best way for me to pray,* he thought. He was worried. His training wasn't advancing as fast as he hoped, and Venatrix wasn't waking either. He didn't know if he could go up against Tristan without her encouragement, without her crystal blue eyes cheering him on. Orion realized Jayren was staring at him. Orion glanced over, then looked away just as quickly. He swung into a parking space at the recreation center. His head was spinning, his heart danced with a dizzying flutter. Orion cut the engine. "I've done this every day," he told Jayren. "Ophi too."

Jayren looked down at his hands.

"What's wrong?" Orion asked. He rolled the windows up, and the two boys sat in silence.

Breath flared out of Jayren's chest. "What *isn't* wrong?"

Orion rested his head back against his seat. He felt that.

Jayren looked out the window. He took a minute before he spoke, but time passed like the inevitable slip of the sun beyond the horizon, and no one liked to be alone in the dark these days. "I wasn't really a fan of Trixie off the bat, but I didn't want anything bad to happen to her. And Ophi, y'know. We weren't really talking before, but now she doesn't talk to me at all. I guess because of RUST. And just everything else."

"If you don't want to talk about it…"

"Killing people," Jayren choked on the words. "I mean, I haven't yet. I know Corvun has, and I know how it hurts him. We both know *I'll* have to. I haven't seen my sister in like a month either. She won't even talk to me."

Orion sat silently. He listened as Jayren sniffled weakly, as snot gurgled in his sinuses, listened to the tender ruffling of fabric.

Jayren pulled on his long sleeves to wipe tears from his face. "It's like—I wish I could've had a better relationship with my sister. I feel so *alienated* from her. I just fuck everything up. God. And when I was little… *Fuck*. I didn't know until after Mr. North let me read a file about it. I guess my dad was a Sentinel like me," Jayren said.

Orion's heart skipped a beat in his chest. It was the first time he'd heard Jayren use that word in reference to himself.

He continued, "He, uh… He was a nurse in a psych ward. He fell in love with one of his patients while treating her. He cured her, and everyone was amazed. Or at least, that's what it looked like. He um…" Jayren used his pointer finger to make a twisty motion by his temple, "…scared off the demons. Like you and Ophi say I do. Well, they got married and had Lacey and me. I guess the demons got to Dad."

The heaviness in Jayren's face broke Orion's heart, and Orion looked away.

"He hung himself. I found him," Jayren said. "I always thought that was the worst part, finding him. But really, I think the worst part of it all is that when he died, my mom went insane again. She was screaming on the kitchen floor. Not in shock. Delusional. She was saying things about eyes and voices, screaming, *'They're back! They're back!'*" Jayren cleared his throat. "My sister called nine-one-one. Mr. North was in town. He showed up with the police and ambulance. They shipped Mom to a ward down here, and Lacey and I got put in foster care. Lacey's old enough now, so we live alone. Lived. Past tense. God."

"I'm sorry," Orion said.

"I just honestly thought that at some point, telling this story would get easier."

"If there's anything I can do…"

Jayren shook his head. "C'mon. At least this will get my mind off of it."

Orion nodded. Jayren slipped his flip-flops on, and Orion led Jayren out into the cold and across the parking lot to the wide, squat building that was the recreation center. Bitter wind cozied up to Orion's neck, curling wicked fingers around his ears. Winter's spirit leaned in to kiss his lips with fangs made of ice. He found it hard to speak. Somehow, he managed. "Thank you for trusting me with all that. Those things are tough to share," he said as they walked.

Jayren didn't speak, just rubbed his nose. Steam puffed from a single nostril as one side stayed flat in the cold.

Orion held the door for Jayren. A warm blast of air rushed over his face. They made their way to the theater stage, where the grand piano sat in the corner, tucked behind a thick, red velvet curtain. A few students practiced ballet around them, and Orion reminisced about the first time he'd met Jayren. They walked over, and Orion slouched onto the bench. He motioned for Jayren to sit beside him. "Do you want to help me?" The keys were cool on his fingertips as he began to play, and the porcelain-fragile touch reminded him of how it felt to touch Venatrix, too.

"Help you what?" Jayren looked at the piano.

"Pray for Vena."

"Oh, man, I'm not really a pianist."

"It's got nothing to do with whether you can play well or not. God still wants to hear from you." Orion glanced at where Jayren stood beside the bench again. "I know you don't want to act like any of it is real, but when you were talking in the car… You believe it, don't you?"

"That's," Jayren swallowed, "…not it. Can we just not talk about it?"

"Sure," Orion said.

Jayren sat beside Orion.

Orion stroked the keys in a downward motion, lulling a melody out with the beckoning move of his hand. He let the melody grow then fade then twinkle back into existence. "It's still a prayer," he told Jayren, "just in a different language."

Jayren nodded. He watched.

Orion let go of the melodies and harmonies, and they blended together on their own, hammering away at the pain in his heart. He reached over with his foot and lowered the sustain pedal. Jayren let out a short breath beside him, craned his fingers over the higher keys. He curled his fingertips. Then he jumped in with Orion, and his notes sputtered out in disarray. Something sloppy, but real and genuine. He hit so many wrong notes, but the right notes he found struck the air like a killing blow of a sword. Orion watched several shadows recoil from the room in awe; he hadn't even noticed them before. Anger hissed through Jayren's teeth as he picked up the passionate tempo of his cluttering notes. Orion heard his pain, his heartache, his anger. The raw discord was a spur in Orion's stomach, but he'd never heard anything so honest, so true to the way Jayren lived.

"You make me look bad," Jayren said.

"Don't compare yourself to me. This is for Vena," Orion said.

Vigor leaped into Jayren's fingers.

They played until frustrated tears overwhelmed Jayren, until Orion burned out with fire on his skin and righteous anger in his chest. Orion's joints ached. Jayren sniffled. They sat together, staring down at the vast, endless array of possibilities the piano offered. They didn't speak. Their lungs had set fire with the breathtaking effort they poured into the piano like gasoline. The fire dwindled, but they lingered in its warmth.

JAYREN OMANS

Whatever warmth and kinship Jayren found with Orion wore off by that night. Jayren stood at his old house again, staring at the front door. A chill spread through Jayren's blood. He couldn't feel his nose, the arches of his ears, or the tips of his fingers. Forget his feet. He pulled his dad's scarf close around his face. He could still smell Venatrix on it, even though it had been months since she took it, and her scent should've been too faint for him to smell by now. But he could smell her even better, he realized. Her scent was that of rosemary and lemon and earl gray tea. He could smell her sweat and breath lingering on the fabric, too.

All of a sudden, he was overwhelmed with new smells from the inside of his house as the door swung open. Lacey stood there. Her frame was upright, tight, and stern, and she fixed him with a bitter, sour glare. Jayren thought she might say something, chastise or scold or tell him off or *something*. But she just stood and glared—or stared, maybe—with green eyes distant and slitted in sheer horror.

Jayren looked at her eyes real good. They were snake eyes, for sure, which meant she'd hidden her true nature—and his—from him. Or maybe he'd just refused to accept what he saw until he'd seen it on himself. He wondered if his eyes narrowed too as he took her in. "Lacey—"

She started to close the door.

Jayren stepped closer. He could smell the dinner she was cooking. It was just one meal.

She slammed the door.

"Why did you even open the damn door?" Jayren yelled at the burgundy wood.

"Go away," she yelled.

"I just want to talk." Jayren rested a hand on the door, where frost bit at his palm. He leaned in and pressed his ear to the door. He listened to her breathe from the other side of the wood; for the first time, he realized she could probably hear him breathing, too. He stayed there, listened to her chest choke into a sob. He stayed there until he couldn't handle the cold on the side of his face. Fear, shame, guilt—it all formed an icy layer over his mind. He couldn't feel the fire that so often sat forefront in his soul. He'd done it—joined RUST to be with Corvun, so that no one could ever pick on him again, so he could protect Orion and Ophiah—but at what cost? He lost the last of his blood family that he actually had.

The door stayed closed.

"I'm sorry," Jayren whispered finally.

The porch light flicked off.

Jayren closed his eyes and returned to the warehouse. He stayed in his room with the door locked for the rest of the night.

He grieved the cost.

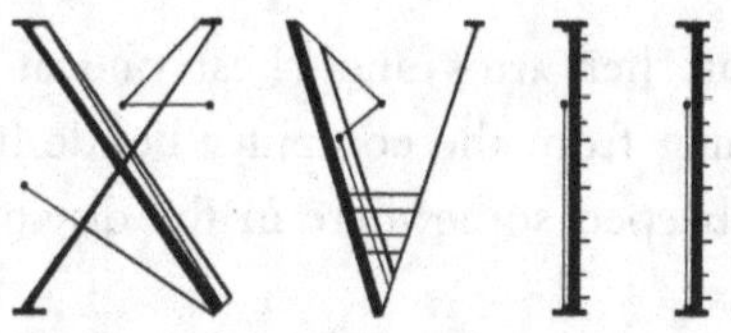

WILDFLOWERS IN THE
WAKE OF A STORM

The Mediating Grounds consist of a plane between Heaven and Earth, where both angels and demons can report to the Spokesperson for the Lord.
— A History of Hierarchy

JANUARY 30TH, 2107 A.D.
NORTHEAST FLORIDA
VENATRIX CANES

Venatrix bolted upwards. She was soaked with cold sweat.

A monitor beeped beside her, drowning out the fading shouting in her dream. The dream had gone forever—on and on—the voices swirling in a whirlwind of nonsense. All in darkness. All she remembered was a broken voice shouting, "I will make you burn in Hell!" On and on, over and over. *Burn in Hell! Burn in Hell!*

Venatrix focused on the beeping.

Slowly, the room came around too. The room was washed in warm, orange night lights. Two empty chairs sat to the left. A window closed its eyes just beyond. Cleaner soaked the floor with the smell of citrus chemicals. The more she focused on the room, the more the voices in her ringing ears faded. She sat. Wiry snakes leeched onto her skin, and she peeled each sticker off her arms and chest one at a time. The beeping—coming from the computer beside her—flatlined, and an alarm beeped somewhere in the distance. The door *clicked* open next.

Professor North stepped inside. Venatrix caught a glimpse of her parents on the other side before he closed it behind him.

"Where's Rian?" she asked.

Professor North didn't speak right away. The lion of a man sulked to her with heavy steps. He took her face in his hands, examined something there. He pressed a thumb into a surprisingly tender spot on her cheekbone.

Venatrix flinched away.

"Do you remember what happened?"

Venatrix drew a blank. She studied North's golden-brown eyes. She thought harder as she did so. She remembered the smell of Orion's dirty shirt, the sharp scent of sweat. She shook her head. "Is he dead?"

"No. Orion is very much alive," North said. He sat beside her, causing a divot on the hospital bed and making Venatrix feel like a kid on an inflatable trampoline. "Nice touch with the gardening, Venatrix. It seems you two did your homework on Marks. Tristan is contained inside that house, and no demons can get in. As long as Orion maintains the health of the plants, the Shielding Mark remains."

Venatrix stared at the royal blue of her hospital socks as her headmaster spoke. Thoughts crept back into her mind like little bugs nesting on new grounds. Had Orion tried to face Tristan yet? Was he doing that now? What if she could help him? What if he *would* die without her help? She didn't let the emotion reach her face. North would stop her if she tried to intervene. It was better if he didn't know the thought even crossed her mind. So evenly, she asked, "How long have I been out?"

"Nine days," he said.

"Did he visit?"

"Every day." Professor North nodded to a little vase with hand-picked wildflowers. Blue forget-me-nots dotted the bundle. "There is something else I need to tell you, Venatrix. It's about your brothers."

Venatrix stared blankly at Orion's wildflower bouquet. Her pulse thumped hot in her ears.

"Your brothers compromised us. We don't know everything yet," he said. Quiet, thoughtful, calm. "They've been in interrogation for three days."

JANUARY 31ST, 2107 A.D.
NORTHEAST FLORIDA
JAYREN OMANS

"Venatrix is awake," Corvun said briskly. Jayren struggled to match his friend's pace as he stalked down the school halls on Monday morning. Corvun took a commission the night before, slept for only half an hour before waking to the news. Jayren watched Corvun defy crippling nausea and fatigue, clean blood from under his fingernails, and cover a self-inflicted wound on his wrist before whisking both of them from the Abyss. Venatrix woke Sunday, Corvun told him as they walked, just after a sermon Valentine North gave at the North Academy. Corvun had been there. *Carina* had been there. The thought chilled Jayren.

Jayren stopped walking. He stood in the middle of the gold-plated hall, staring after Corvun. "Did Carina have something to do with her waking up?"

Corvun stopped and turned. "What are you talkin' about?"

"Nothing," Jayren said hurriedly. Still, the correlation nagged at him; the Angel of Death was present to spare someone from death. It made sense to him, and it made him cold with realization at the same time. And again, he thought, *What if it's all true?* He shook the thought off then jogged to catch up. "Where are we going?"

"To see Vena." Corvun eyed him. He rounded the next corner, which left the pair of them in the nurses' wing of the North Academy. A woman with a clean, graphite-gray uniform bent beside Venatrix. Venatrix sat in a wheelchair, nodding lightly to the instructions the woman gave. The nurse looked at the boys then said, "Don't let those boys wheel you anywhere either lest they run you into a wall, my dear girl."

"I'd rather stick her in a corner with the brakes on," Jayren said. The nurse shot him a glare that sent needles scratching down his back. She smelled like gauze and bandaid packing, and Jayren was already ready to leave. Venatrix wheeled herself away from the nurse and towards Jayren. Trying to suppress the haunting memories he'd made in his own time in hospitals, he asked Venatrix, "Are you limp or something?"

Venatrix glared. "Just a little weak, dipshit."

"Missed you, Trixie."

Her glare turned to a grin.

"Vena," Corvun said. Her eyes were kinder to him, and they softened when he knelt before her. Despite this, she leaned away when he cupped her face. "Hold still."

"Dude, you're not her dad. Stop touching her." Jayren kicked Corvun's thigh.

"*Ben*," she muttered, cheeks pinched in his palms. "Stop. *Shtop*. Gerroff!"

Corvun held her tightly, adjusting her face to the light of the window. Corvun examined where the bruise had been. Her skin was ivory again, glowing and sleepy. Her hands wrestled with his wrists, slipped, and flattened against his nose.

"Dude, *back off*." Jayren yanked Corvun's hands off Venatrix.

"It's gone," Corvun said.

"It was just a bruise. No cuts, no scars." Venatrix watched Corvun warily. "No permanent damage."

"I beg to differ," Corvun muttered.

"Where's Rian?" Venatrix asked. "North wouldn't tell me."

As if right on cue, Orion's long, flat Converse pattered down the hall, slapping loudly at the entrance to the nurses' wing. His wide eyes shone at them, and he smiled so brightly that Jayren thought for a moment that he needed sunglasses to witness Orion's joyous beam. He exhaled shortly, and Venatrix sucked in air too, her chest rising like a bird puffing her chest for her mate. Orion called Corvun's name, though, and Corvun's eyes widened. Jayren noticed the same subtle shock in Venatrix's face. Orion's eyes gleamed, shifting between the two. They settled on Venatrix's mouth, and he licked his lips. "Corvun—you're going to miss it! Come on! The presentation for the internship!"

Corvun darted after Orion.

"Shit! Jayren cried. He grabbed hold of Venatrix's wheelchair, teetered her forward, and took off.

"Hurry!" Orion encouraged. He stole a glance behind him, and Corvun did too. Jayren and Venatrix laughed as if they inhaled helium, giggling high-pitched, airy noises that snorted like the puttering noise of a deflating balloon. Jayren jerked the wheelchair back into a wheelie, and they all ran faster.

"Stop running!" a teacher shouted after them as they sped past halls and classroom doors.

"Catch us if you can, bitches!" Jayren shouted, louder. He blew a raspberry with his tongue, and Venatrix shrieked something about the spit he left in her hair. They arrived in the auditorium, panting and damp with sticky skin. Gaining a few stares, the four clamored into a back row to listen.

VENATRIX CANES

The auditorium was dark with spotlights pointing to the stage. Deep red velvet curtains hung behind the podium, where a girl named Gracie finished her essay. "A single instrument in an orchestra cannot create a chord alone, just as a singer in a choir cannot sing a harmony by oneself. I overcame my struggle of creating music when I came to the realization that I cannot do it by myself. Success is not accomplished alone. A successful person succeeds with the support of those around him or her. I overcame by surrounding myself with people who will help me get to the end of my score." Her voice trembled, but she drew calm when her final words came out. The crowd clapped vivaciously for the soft-spoken girl.

"When are you up?" Jayren asked Corvun.

Venatrix leaned over to hear.

"After her," Corvun said. He nodded to where Krista, Caeleb's latest girlfriend, took the stage. White lights heated the stage, and the air warmed with anticipation again. The crowd quieted, stilled.

"Breathe," Krista said. She counted.

She counted to four, and Venatrix's blood ran cold. Her heart kicked in her chest, stomach collapsing. Numbness spread through her, breaking any excitement Gracie had left with her speech. Venatrix gave Krista a few lines, waited to see if she knew this essay by heart from all the nights she'd studied it for Corvun. Venatrix's throat squeezed shut as Krista recited Corvun's essay line for line.

How? she wondered in horror. She tried to piece together the event.

Then it hit her out of nowhere.

Valentine's voice. *Your brothers compromised us.*

She'd spent plenty of time away from home recently. And she knew her brothers to snoop through her room before, especially Caeleb. She didn't put it past him to find a draft of Corvun's essay there, to pass it to Krista, and let her submit the work as her own. By the time Venatrix put it together, Corvun was already hurrying away. She couldn't speak or call after him; she was still and paralyzed in her wheelchair. She was stuck listening to her brother's girlfriend read an essay Corvun had poured his heart into. Venatrix glared up to the stage, where the brunette read lazily, carelessly, with lowered lids. She spoke with the sides of her mouth, and it drove Venatrix mad. Venatrix clenched the arm grips of her wheelchair, knuckles aching with pressure. She threw her arms into her wheels and spun off squeaking after Corvun.

Corvun disappeared down the back right hall. She could smell faint traces of the cologne he wore trailing behind him. It reminded her of the fragrance he had in his old economy car. She thought of the midnight drive they took back when Corvun just got his learners permit, how he snuck her out and they drove deep down town roads long abandoned. That night, he told her so many stories while they stargazed. He told her, with tears in his eyes, about the snake his father made him kill that day. He told her that he never wanted to kill again.

That was years ago.

Jayren stalked past Venatrix, vanishing in the hall ahead of her, and Orion grabbed the back of her wheelchair and pushed her after the others.

Salty tears slipped down her face and into her lips. She scratched her face dry with her blouse, leaving pink blotchy skin in its wake. "Corvun!" she shouted. *Did he put it together, too?* She was so mad at herself, she could barely see straight. She knew the weight of this essay. This was a plan that the Archangels had put in motion to save his life from RUST. She cried louder, "Corvun!"

Corvun stopped, his shoulders stiff. He didn't turn to the other three.

Jayren stood halfway between herself and Corvun, but even he didn't dare take another step. "We'll figure something out," Jayren said. "We can talk to them, right? The teachers?"

"After all the trouble we've been in this year? Do you really think they'll believe *us?* Krista is a straight-A student, and I can hardly keep a C these days. No," Corvun said.

So this is it, Venatrix thought. This sealed their fate. Corvun was trapped in RUST. Jayren was there with him. Corvun was a killer now, and he could be nothing more than that in this life. Jayren would become a killer, too, because of how dearly he cared for Corvun. There was no reversal in sight, no redemption. This fire burned to the end, and they were halfway in. Venatrix wondered if she'd seen the start of it in past lives. Did it always start with that deep-cut heartache in Corvun's eyes?

"Together," she blurted.

Corvun watched her, emotion painting his face.

"We'll figure something out, *together*," she said. "You don't have to do this alone."

VALENTINE NORTH

Valentine and Gabrielle stood in a second-floor observation room that overlooked the auditorium and the presentations underway. Valentine watched the stage where Krista finished her speech. He looked then to the three empty chairs and the missing wheelchair at the back of the crowd. He'd watched Corvun stalk from the room. He didn't blame the boy, either. Valentine exhaled, guilt heavy on his chest. Perhaps he could side with Corvun in the argument that the essay had been plagiarized. Valentine knew it to be true, after all. He could see through what happened easily, like a sixth sense; Krista's sin and insincerity were written all over her. Valentine could pick Corvun to spare his life. But if he did, Jayren would have been left in RUST alone. Valentine considered that maybe solely for this reason, he was grateful for the turn of events; he didn't want to think what Jayren would become on his own in RUST either. *Some sacrifices must be made,* he thought, and he could not ignore the repercussions of saving Corvun blindly. If word of a plagiarized essay came up, Valentine decided, he would rule in Krista's favor for the sake of Jayren's alignment. *Jayren cannot fall,* Valentine reasoned with himself. *Too many times before, the others have followed in Jayren's fate, in his footsteps.*

It didn't ease the guilt much at all.

It wouldn't sit well with the Seven. Remington already presented Valentine with the logic, the ranks Corvun could rise to under RUST's control. Even Michael fought for Corvun's case with a fevered, heated argument. The son of Heaven's greatest warrior now rested in the hands of the Devil.

"Valor," Gabrielle said.

"Belle," Valentine replied to his wife.

Gabrielle touched the small of Valentine's back. The action was so kind and small that he knew instantly that something had changed. He turned to her, and she peered up at him with blue eyes. Her eyes swam with righteous anger from Heaven itself. "Come with me."

Valentine thought briefly about how his own wife had saved him from the RUST pact, years before. After a search mission gone sideways, Michael had sought out someone to heal Valentine's then broken wings. Not to anyone's surprise, Michael found Dr. Bennett and his nurse, Gabrielle. Gabrielle had spent day and night at Valentine's bedside, pouring her heart and soul into his every need. By the time he was healed, his pact was broken, too. He and Michael had both hoped they could do something like this for Corvun. In theory, it would've worked. In theory.

Valentine followed his wife from the auditorium. The crowd cheered behind him only until the world itself closed and folded away as he walked with Gabrielle into the Mediating Grounds. This was a place for the supernatural. It was a mid-plane between Earth and Heaven where all angels and demons could report to God. The mid-plane rolled out in whites and bright scenery far in the distance, the Earth somewhere behind, and Hell lurking in the shadows.

The Spokesperson for the Lord stood between two, great white pillars. His skin was the color of opal, his eyes and mouth agape and shining with bright light. When he spoke, it sounded like thunder, "This you know: that the sons of Suriel and Raquel have compromised a battle on the coast. They warned the demons of the attack. One hundred and eighteen angels fell in battle, and the Deceiver Greed made it to shore. Greed has not walked the Earth for two thousand years. The Lord's armies have kept him offshore."

Valentine heard this from Remington and Michael, who had been in the battle, but to hear it now made it more concrete, more final.

"You have heard they are to be tried by the church for justice," the Spokesperson continued. "And now the Lord has another command for you. When Caeleb and Erin are ruled guilty of treason, place Venatrix in RUST. She will be a double-agent for you."

Valentine closed his eyes. *So this is what changed.* "I fear for Venatrix. She fears losing her friends. I fear she will lose her faith."

The Spokesperson sighed, a sound like howling wind. The ground shifted, and something bolted from the shrubbery behind them. Eyes of young angels and demons alike peered from behind pillars in the distance. The Mediating Grounds watched. Sworn to temporary peace and waiting to report their own news, all onlookers bore down at the two bowing Archangels and the Spokesperson.

"Venatrix still follows the Lord's commands in her heart," the Spokesperson said. "The Horsemen will be united in their path. Set the girl on their path now so that what is to come can be."

"What of Orion?" Gabrielle asked. "He will attempt to banish the Deceiver Sorrow."

"And if he dies?" Valentine added hastily. "Will there be yet another Iteration? We ache for Armageddon." He spoke for the Seven. He—like all the other Archangels—grew impatient for the Final Battle through every Iteration they endeavored. Time moved differently in human bodies, and they watched the rise and fall of humanity over many different eras. They had their hand in wars for His Divine Plan, and they watched the five children grow into their power to fight each lifetime. Valentine fought beside the Horsemen, and each time they fought, they were slaughtered. Mars always fell first by a violent, merciless death. The others died fighting to avenge him.

"Be patient, Valor. Orion must face the sin inside himself. He will turn to the Lord," the Spokesperson said, "and the Lord will not fail him."

JANUARY 31ST, 2107 A.D.
THE ABYSS
CARINA BLACKROCK

Carina looked at the dorm while Corvun and Jayren were away. She browsed Jayren's meager belongings, some sun-paled postcards with poems about Spanish moss and lighthouses. Each was sent to his mother and stamped with "return to sender" in red. His small, waist-high dresser was scattered with a few blunt pencils. His gun was there too, unloaded with a plastic, orange chip in the barrel to keep it open. The gun was a three-eighty caliber gun, with ambidextrous safeties. Bullets littered the wood surface like lead tears. The metal wastebasket beside his dresser held a rainstorm of pencil shavings, like leaves stripped off trees from high velocity gusts. It made Carina wonder if he had a journal stashed away somewhere, too.

She noticed—as she picked Jayren's dirty clothes off the floor—a bottle of painkillers at his bedside. It gaped like a hungry mouth. The lid was nowhere in sight. Carina saw his old prescription glasses there too, folded beside the pill bottle. One lens was shattered, and the nose, hinge, and earpiece were wrapped with medical tape. She found a laundry basket in the spare room. She dropped Jayren's clothes into it. She found Corvun's dirty clothes folded on the floor in the corner of his room. She added them to the basket, too.

Corvun's room chilled Carina's blood. His type of clean was clinical and calculated. He was inhumanly organized. Corvun's desk and dresser were clean and clear. Across his made, white cot, he'd laid five guns. Two semi-automatic rifles, one sniper, a fifty caliber gun, and a three-eighty caliber gun. She touched each black steel weapon with the tips of her fingers. The weapons seared her vision, like tarnish on gold. They were bars of a prison, laid out in cruel mockery. He was an executioner, and he knew it. He was the filth of royalty, the weapon the Archangels used for their dirty work.

There had to be a way to stop him from walking this path. She wanted to save him.

She eyed the sniper.

Walk away. Walk away, you fool, she said to herself. But here she was, on the same cursed ground as Cephan. Her fingers itched for that trigger, for revenge. Perhaps, even, by killing Cephan she could free Corvun of his fate too. *You do not know how to use that,* she told herself. Then she considered it couldn't be too hard. She'd seen Corvun hit targets with ease using it.

And she could do it. Usually, it took Heaven or Hell-forged weapons to kill Fallen angels or demons, but Carina had been a weapon made by God himself. She could kill any angel or demon with any weapon at her disposal; she had no need to seek out special means to kill. All she needed was herself.

Carina convinced herself. She thought of Corvun. Even though she did not quite know him in this life yet, this was the life he carved out of necessity and spite. He had no escape. He was a breed of savagery with the ability to cut a maimed limb from his body if need be; she guessed this could mean amputating people from his life just as clean and easy. His only disadvantage was that his emotions bled all over the place. His room reeked of that kind of loneliness and the cold, hard world that had greeted him with a heartless embrace. Corvun would break his neck pulling back from that embrace.

Carina made up her mind. She snatched the sniper from the bed, and the strap flopped at her thigh in a clumsy, useless manner. She fiddled with the stock of the gun until she found the magazine flush in the black metal. It was loaded.

She took the rifle downstairs and fired two practice rounds to familiarize herself with the weapon. She much preferred the precision of a knife, and she reveled at the thought of slitting Cephan's throat and feeling his life bleed dry on her hands. But she knew Cephan could bring her to her knees with the snap of his fingers. Cephan would slaughter her, given the chance.

She wondered how Jayren would act if that happened; the boy had taken a liking to her. She guessed Corvun already had some sort of revenge flowing in his veins. Those boys were a dangerous mix of chemicals, the kind that promised destruction on a catastrophic level. She would hate to be a catalyst prematurely.

Carina slinked to the door, gathered her breath into her chest. She clutched the sniper rifle and waited. *You single-handedly won a war. You single-handedly destroyed a city. You single-handedly wiped out Hell's Alley,* she whispered in her mind. But she did not feel brave. She did not feel strong or powerful. And that had been under different conditions, a war God had called her to, not a war she waged on her own.

Her back hit the wall.

Shrieking clawed through her ears. Hissing. Crying. The sound of glass shattering. The sound of demons dying all around her. The wet slop of the human forms, the human hosts that the demons corrupted, as she cut through them. One hundred, two hundred. She sheathed a sword through the neck of a child, and its eyes hissed with Hellflame.

Three hundred.

She whorled around in a frantic defense, cutting down the closest of the demons circling her.

Four hundred.

Sweat plastered her hair to the back of her neck.

Five hundred. Six hundred.

She was stained with blood that burned her skin, slowly, like tar licking with the heat of smoldering embers.

One thousand demons she'd slain, but now she could not shake the fear or dread. She did not walk on holy ground here. Even though Hell's Alley had been cursed ground, she had been on Earth. This place—the Abyss—was a gateway to Hell. She walked along a demon's path here, where angels were rare or Fallen. She longed to wield a sword on the ground of free will again.

When she regained her head and twisted the handle of the warehouse, the building grew dark and damp and distant. It looked like any other warehouse in the endless rows of killer hideouts. Corvun's illusion faded, and Carina left the door cracked. She trusted her ability to track down the scent of Corvun and Jayren, but she didn't know if she could get back in without them. She turned out to the Abyss and the artificial light. Even Corvun's fake, illusion of light had been kinder and safer. Shadows flickered on the ground as blackness clinked at the lights like beetles in the night. Beetles did not exist here.

Carina searched the warehouses with deft steps, found a metal fire escape around the side. She jogged upward as quickly and quietly as she could.

"Were you and your sister close?" Carina walked beside Corvun. They explored the streets downtown in the city, disguised as a couple on

an ice cream date. Corvun went out of his way to take her to the vegan gelato ice cream place Jayren liked best.

Corvun laughed when she smeared ice cream on her nose from diving into the delicious, creamy dessert. She tried to wipe it away, and he helped her. Finally, he said, "No. I don't remember ever being close to her." They sat together and people watched as they ate. Carina told Corvun she could pick up scents off people, that his sister would likely smell a lot like him. There was a chance they might catch a lead. Corvun was unconvinced. He'd said there had to be better ways to look for her than this as he gazed out over bustling streets.

Carina licked the cold ice in her hands. The chilly air filled her mouth, and brain freeze forced her eyes shut. If anything, it was nice to get away from the Abyss for a while.

Corvun chuckled again. "Never had something this cold?"

"Hell's Alley is hotter than Florida, and I promise you they do not have gelato," she said. She opened her eyes to find Corvun staring so intensely into her face that she forgot the cold. Heat washed over her neck and chest. His eyes dripped down to her lips, where she sucked ice cream away. She wanted him to kiss her. "You will find her," Carina said to him. "You just have to keep looking."

"I know," he said. He turned away.

And he had kept looking, every spare moment he had. He flew over the city, patrolled the streets by foot, strapped in guns and knives. She was in awe of his loyalty to his family, a family that had turned its back on him.

Carina wondered if his loyalty extended to his found family the way Leroy had been loyal to her. Would Corvun search for her if she were found and taken by Cephan or Avon? She could only hope—that she was not on her own, that the boys were loyal to her as she swore she would be to them.

She tasted the atmosphere when she reached the rooftop. She picked up the scent of holy blood. Of Cephan. Did Corvun know Cephan was one of the Fallen? Or was that another secret that the Archangels kept to themselves? With the smell of Cephan's tainted blood, a waft of tarnished, tangy coins filled her nose. Her heart leapt into her throat.

Carina stared into the scope of the gun. She saw them then; Cephan and Avon sauntered side by side, engaged in a low, quiet conversation. Cephan wore a plain, sleek three-piece suit, and blood stained his dress shoes. Avon wore an untied tunic and brown pants that ruffled in many folds above his boots. She watched, her finger on the trigger. The gun's recoil would cause too much of a delay. She could take one of them out, but not both. She'd seen Corvun take his time to re-aim this style of gun, and it would allow for retaliation from Cephan or Avon or both. Both men could rip her apart like a doll in a shark's jaw. She wouldn't stand a chance.

A gold compass gleamed in Avon's extended hand. The needle spun like a hurricane with no end. As Cephan and Avon whispered, pacing the maze of warehouses, the needle danced differently. Avon hesitated, and he glanced in Carina's direction.

She slumped down against the side of the roof, sniper rifle pressed across her lap. She held her breath.

After a moment, Carina peeked over the top of the warehouse. On the broken concrete-gravel road, the compass sat abandoned and pointing.

It betrayed her location.

No, she begged. *No. No!* She sank back and closed her eyes. *They will check the warehouse first. But they will check the roof too.* She cursed and stayed low as she crawled to the fire escape. Peering over, she saw the two men lingering just below. They spoke slow and tantalizing. Did they know where she was?

Carina glared across to Corvun's warehouse. It was two rows over. She estimated the distance. She could jump rooftops if she ran fast enough. She would have to leave the gun. She placed it on the roof silently. Standing, she tested the strength in her knees, her weight, and her balance between the balls of her feet. She inhaled, exhaled. She tried Corvun's breathing exercise. She thought of the rooftops in Hell's Alley. This was easier, closer. This was so much simpler than thieving from demons and running with bags of jangling coins and riches—only to be caught and scolded by Empress Amy at the end of her breathless race.

So similar. So easy, she told herself.

She ran, and she leapt through the air. Her toes hit the roof first, and she kept her momentum through the next jump. The third jump, she misjudged. She hovered—thanks to her halo—which bridged her discrepancy. The effect of her halo was as if there was a canopy over her, or like the fire in a hot air balloon. She could not fly with wings like other angels could, but it granted her small aid. It granted her *enough* aid. Her feet collided with the roof, and she lost her balance and fell. She skidded across the roof of Corvun's warehouse, laughing in hysterics. Insanity. She tasted salt.

No time. No time for tears. Get up, she urged.

She clawed her way to the fire escape of his warehouse. Metal shuddered beneath her feet. She climbed through the window and onto the overhang that looked over the warehouse floor. She passed the first door on her left—the showers—and slipped inside the second door to the dorm. Before she closed it, she watched a hand reach out to the entrance door below and push it open. *She* left that open invite. Now she wondered if Cephan and Avon would have been able to get in had she closed the front door behind her.

Carina retreated into the dorm, then into Corvun's room. She hit the floor, sliding beneath the white cot and all the way against the wall. She didn't breathe.

Then she heard Avon. He walked up the stairs, rattling them like a beast. The shake and quiver of his coats and his deep, throaty growl. He smelled thick of the ocean as he stepped into the dorm.

"What is it?" Cephan asked. His voice was exasperated. "If she were here, I assure you I would have found her."

"The boy's scent covers her up. But she's here, I can smell her. You cannot tell the difference with your inferior nose, *angel*," Avon spat. "They smell alike, Corvun and Carina. They chase the riches of the heart. But the boy does not reek of holy, righteous *death*."

Cephan stepped into Corvun's room, and Carina covered her mouth. She stared through blurry eyes at Cephan's bloody dress shoes. She squeezed her eyes shut. She wondered if Avon could feel her pulse.

"I want her, Cephan. I will destroy her," Avon's voice was wicked, the push and pull of the tide and the roar of the waves and the hiss of the ocean spray. "She took everything from us. You swore! You swore that we could contain her. She killed them all!"

"I told you to take precautions." One of Cephan's shoes pointed in Carina's direction, the other out towards the dorm room. Cephan was stopping Avon from entering the room. They knew. *They knew she was there.* "She is no Archangel, no Nephilim, no average Sentinel. The Angel of Death requires more *delicate* attention," Cephan said carefully. He picked the words as if he were plucking precious gems from a crown. He plucked the remaining hours from her life.

Just as he'd done to Leroy.

JANUARY 31ST, 2107 A.D.
NORTHEAST FLORIDA
VENATRIX CANES

Venatrix stepped inside her house later that night. She left the wheelchair with the nurse and tested her legs, walking home from school alone at dusk. Dark be damned. At least now she knew she had two friends who could call the night a friend, too. Permanently. Everything was silent. Venatrix stepped out of her shoes and noticed a dim light in the kitchen. Licking her lips, she smelled stale dinner in the air. She heard her mother and father talking there, too. "Mom? Dad?" she called.

"Come sit down, darling," her mother said.

She approached slowly.

Her parents sat with drawn expressions, eyes tired and hollowed like burned candles. "What's going on?"

"Sit down," her father said. She obeyed. His voice was coarse. "It's your brothers, Venatrix. They…" His voice was gone. His short black hair had cowlicks she hadn't noticed before where white sprouted at the roots. His light blue eyes were faded, too.

Even her mother looked different, wiry, unkempt and exhausted. Her eyes bore more wrinkles without makeup. "We've taught you for years about the Unseen Wars," her mother said. "Your brothers interfered with one of those battles. They told the others—the demons," she struggled to say, "of a planned defense. The other side doubled their offense. Our ranks were decimated because of the information your brothers gave away."

Venatrix's head swam. She didn't understand how her brothers could tell secrets to invisible forces. True, she knew about the Unseen Wars. They were battles fought by angels and demons in the sky, most often during storms. Visible storm fronts were often the front lines of a war. These Unseen Wars had tangible outcomes, too. When the angels won, it was often a victory for the people, for justice. When the demons won, it was the death of liberty and freedom. She wondered what this outcome was.

Her father seemed to sense her question. "The defense was to keep a Deceiver—who we bound to the sea for centuries—trapped. We lost this battle, and now Greed is loose on Earth," he said. "You've been studying the Deceivers lately, haven't you?"

Is that an accusation? Venatrix wondered, taken aback. Her research spent the last few weeks all over her bed, and in the wake of her coma, she was sure her parents had happened upon it. Her jaw hung and she stumbled clumsily around her words. "I-I was just reading up," she said. Maybe if they didn't believe her, she could show them her notes about banishing Tristan. "That book on my bed— It was just for fun. I-I thought it was cool."

"Vena," her mother said. She rested a hand on Venatrix's trembling wrist. "The church wants to try your brothers, not you. But you have been summoned for questioning."

"No." Venatrix stood. "That's outrageous. You don't think I had any part of that, do you?"

"Venatrix, it's just so that you can state a side," her father raised his voice.

"Isn't my word to you enough?" Venatrix glared at her parents. "I'm nothing like them!"

"You have a bad habit of lying, and you've been out of line," her father said. He stood, and he towered over her. "You will appear at that trial. Refusing to appear before God's council is as good as the treason your brothers have been accused of. You will be there."

Venatrix's face pinched with sour emotion. She wanted to scream. Instead, she turned on her heels and fled to her room. She threw her bedroom door open and glared into the dark sanctuary. She flicked a few lights on and plugged in her Christmas lights. Gold doused her room, and she heard the annoying grumble of thunder in the distance. She recalled Orion climbing through her window in the middle of a storm, months ago. She wondered if *that* had been the storm all this time—the storm her brothers betrayed. Did the storm change everything? She longed for the innocence and naivety that her new friendship with Orion offered at that time, so long gone now. Venatrix crumpled atop her bed. Her eyes felt like dry marbles in her head; she didn't have the effort or willpower to cry. Instead, she turned over and dozed off in thoughts of Orion and Jayren and Corvun and a black storm brewing over the heart of the city.

JANUARY 31ST, 2107 A.D.

THE ABYSS

CORVUN KHLYDE

Corvun and Jayren got back to the dorm after dark. Corvun's head was still spinning from the outcome of the ceremony, and hatred pulled at the loose ends of the night. But as Corvun walked into the living area of the dorm, his stomach hit the floor.

He stared at Cephan and Avon. The demons stood there in the middle of the room.

"What's this?" Corvun asked. By the look on Cephan's hawkish face, Corvun knew he had chosen the wrong words. He couldn't ease the bitterness that burned his throat. He was told his warehouse was exclusive; he thought Carina was safe here. He'd been told no one could get in—not even Cephan—

if the door was closed. Rage worked his mouth at the sight of Avon's feral grin.

Cephan checked a pocket watch, motioning for Avon to walk past him and out of the dorm. The Deceiver snarled in Corvun and Jayren's direction as he lumbered past, and chills spread over Corvun's skin. Jayren touched Corvun's back, and only then did Corvun realize his consciousness was fleeting.

Cephan fixed his tie. "Pest control," he said simply. He raised an eyebrow at Corvun, a challenge.

Corvun cleared his throat. His heart wasn't beating, he thought. His face paled. "Of course," he said.

Jayren remained silent as a shadow.

Cephan walked past Corvun. Corvun waited for him to exit the dorm, then followed him to the overhang. He watched Avon and Cephan exit; Cephan shot one more glance in Corvun's direction, a wry grin on his thin lips. The door closed, and Corvun's lights buzzed back to life. The quiet hum of white noise returned.

"Carina?" Jayren called. His voice cut like it did post-nightmare. Boyish, small, scared. "Carina!"

Corvun stalked back into the dorm. His heart trampled his chest. "Look everywhere," he whispered to Jayren. They searched the bathroom, the spare rooms. Carina only gave herself away with a sniffle that Corvun could've mistaken for the vents. He stood beside his bed, his heart wrenching inside him. Four guns barred his bed with black. His sniper rifle was missing. A small sniffle again, then a quaking sob. Corvun fell to his knees. Corvun waved Jayren off with a gentle nod when Jayren looked into the room. Corvun put one hand flat on the ground then laid on the floor. He stared at the ceiling.

She cried, and he listened. Her sobs tugged on his soul hard enough to shake tears from his horror-struck trance. He turned to look at her. Carina's face was splotchy and red, a deep bruise in the dark of his cot. She was curled into herself, quivering with fear. She looked so simple and plain in her fetal position, in hiding. She reminded Corvun of a jaguar cub, tucked away from a bigger predator. She seemed so dangerous all this time, but here she was. She flinched when he stretched an arm to her.

"It's me," he reassured her.

"Prove it," she rasped. "Greed takes many faces."

Corvun hesitated. "When I met you, I knew you by other names. But the first name I called you was Stella. Stella is Latin for star," he said. "All of my closest friends are named after stars, and if you are what the legends say you are, you'll be our guidin' light, our North Star in the night."

Carina's fingertips grazed his.

"I wanted to kiss you that first time we met, when you knocked me on my back in Josh's bar."

"They know I am here," Carina whispered, changing the course of the conversation. "They will kill me. They will make you kill me, Corvun."

"I won't let them," Corvun said uselessly. He knew exactly how stupid he sounded. What chance did he stand against Cephan, let alone any of the Deceivers?

Carina's fingers traced the inside of his open palm. Her eyes were distant, looking at something beyond him. She tried to draw her hand away, but Corvun closed his around it. Her breath hitched, and her eyes flickered back to his. When he pulled her, she neared him. He helped her from under the bed, and she sat close to him. Carina grabbed his face, leaving him no time to gasp for air before she pulled him under into a deep kiss. He swallowed the taste of her, the salty tears and the lingering flavor of rum on her soft lips. He brushed her hair away, tucking it behind her ears. She opened her mouth to his, and he explored her as if she was the ocean and he was a desert traveler given his first glimpse of the wonders of the world. She was flush against his body when Jayren stepped through the door again.

Corvun pulled away, panting, and looked at Jayren's accusing eyes.

Carina laughed brokenly into Corvun's collarbone.

"That's quite the *glad you're safe*, Romeo," Jayren said. "Did you ask her if she's okay?"

Corvun licked his wet lips, pressed them together, then shook his head.

"Carina, are you alright?" Jayren asked.

Carina nodded, resting her head against Corvun's chest. "Thank you," she said to them.

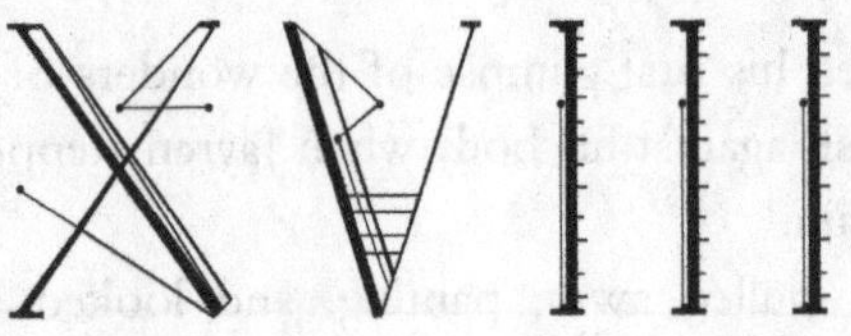

BANISHING SORROW

*Though Latin is a popular choice of language for angels, both angels
and demons have their own languages, too. Both languages stem from
the Old Tongue spoken by God, Heaven, and thus, Adam and Eve.
The Angelic and Demonic variations of the Old Tongue cannot be
understood by opposite parties. Though if one should be born of both an
angel and a demon, there is a chance that a Halfbreed could understand
both. It is more likely that a Halfbreed would understand one instead of
both; more research is needed to confirm theories.*
— A History of Hierarchy

JANUARY 31TH, 2107 A.D.
NORTHEAST FLORIDA
ORION JUDE

Orion stared at the scythes above the fireplace while he sat at
the dinner table with his family. The chandelier above their
table was made of antlers of Landborne Sentinels that Tristan
hunted and slaughtered for game; he never failed to remind
them when they looked too long. Hellflame flickered in the
mouth of the hearth below, ever-burning and casting
grotesque orange and amber pillars across the living room
floor.

Silverware gleamed in Orion's hands. The dining room
was too dark, and light only reflected on one other thing in the

room. The Hellforged weapons. Orion's eyes darted back to the scythes.

His mother seemed to notice. She stroked the back of his hand. "Orion, honey, can you fetch some more water?"

Orion nodded. The dry chicken in his mouth was too bland, too hard to swallow. He forced it down, nearly choking, as he scooted his chair back and stood. He glanced at Ophiah. Her hair was still damp with the smell of lilac shampoo. Orion's eyes found Tristan next, who glared back. Orion walked to the fridge and brought back a pitcher of water. Holy Water, even against his own prior scrutiny. He knew it could have no effect and only warrant Tristan's wrath, but Orion was out of options. He was desperate. He was almost so desperate that he could taste his sorrow and despair. He wondered if Tristan could taste that, too.

As if to answer, Tristan gave a small smile that showed his teeth.

Orion—much to his own surprise—smiled back. Despite his fear, he felt strong for the first time in his whole life. He knew his body, his ability, his weapon. He stayed standing, reminding himself of his own power and authority, and he poured his mother a glass of water. He stayed standing to show Tristan that he was on a higher level of power. It was a threat, a challenge. "Would you like some," Orion chewed out the words, "*father?*"

Ophiah froze.

"A peace offering," Orion forced. His words were carefully chosen to show he knew the brief history that landed Ophiah and himself in the very situation he stood in now.

Tristan shook his head, offering his glass all the same. Orion poured the water, and it sloshed brightly in the cup. "If you think Holy Water can do anything to me, you are a fool," Tristan said. He lifted the clear glass to his lips, swallowed the water down through cheeks of untrimmed scruff. The scar on his face twisted as he smiled at Orion. "If your mother had the audacity to pour me a glass, it might do some damage, but she is kind and weak."

Orion set the pitcher down. A collected calm covered him.

Tristan grabbed the back of Ophiah's hair, lifting her out of her chair.

Ophiah struggled, reached behind her head for his hand.

"Even your sister has more faith than you. She could have poisoned me with Holy Water. But you? You can't even decide if you're good or evil."

"Put her down," Orion demanded in a hot breath. "Now."

Tristan grinned in a way that pulled his lips too far across his face. His eyes grew dark, and so did his silhouette. Orion had seen him turn this way before, and he knew the reason. Usually, the sorrow of his mother was the cause. Her grief over the situation fed Tristan's power and made him turn into a monster like this. This was worse, more menacing. His eyes burned like two smoldering embers in his dark face. Orion wondered if Tristan fed off the sorrow of him and his sister, too.

Panic controlled Orion's body—a numbing pulse, pins and needles in the back of his neck, chills that raked like claws down his spine. Chaos rose from some place deep inside him, something he'd sealed under lock and key and countless chains. Something powerful, beneath all of that, rattled the metal cage inside him.

"Ri," Ophiah managed. She winced, clawing at Tristan's hand as he lifted her from the ground.

"Holy Water won't stop me from breaking her neck," Tristan said with a click of his tongue. His bare hand was big enough to crush the bones of Ophiah's neck, Orion realized in horror.

"I command you—in the name of the Lord—to put her down," Orion spoke through his teeth. He hit the ground with both knees. "*Please*," he begged.

At first, Tristan's face lifted with amusement. Then he realized the intent of his final word.

Orion did not beg Tristan. He begged Heaven to hear him, for God to reach a hand down. The chains inside him cracked open. Metal crinkled back like paper. A spirit from the depths of Hell prowled out, and it had the power of Heaven instilled in its blood. Orion shivered as he felt that spirit fill his body. It fit perfectly, as if it had always been ready to use Orion like a second skin.

Ophiah's eyes grew wide.

Orion could not see the smoke fall from his own lips, but he could smell it. He tasted the blood that trickled down his upper lip and onto his tongue. He reached out and called for the weapons that hung on the wall like a trophy. The scythes rattled.

Tristan released Ophiah. She scrambled back to her mother in shaking fits.

The scythes snapped from their place, and Orion stood to meet them as they flew into his hands. He twisted the weapons, weighing the metal and meeting the two blunt ends in a flash of brilliant white. Heaven's light, like a strike of lightning, seared the weapons together with a white-hot glow that lingered on the metal. Power buzzed in his nerves, wild and rampant. Orion spat blood at his father's feet. "I can't kill you," he struggled to say. Demons tried to hold his tongue, but he was stronger. "But I can send you back to Hell."

Tristan straightened.

The weight of the scythe in Orion's hands was so balanced that he had a hard time telling the weapon apart from his own bones and body. It whispered through his being, '*Chaos, chaos, chaos,*' like a war chant or a rhythmic, twisted hallelujah that swelled deep in the church of his body. '*Kill him, kill him, kill him!*' it shrieked, and it set Orion's nerves on edge. In harmony, it sang, '*Bless us, Son of Kindness. Separate his bones. Send him to Hell.*'

It was like a fever dream, staring down the gruesome half-man, half-beast hybrid before him. Tristan bared sabertooth fangs and had hands made to slaughter—elongated with talons that could rip his stomach open and spill his insides across the floor. The claws had nowhere to retract to. Black, thorn-like ridges grew from his dark hair, as if he were a lion made of pure onyx. His skin was flecked with black, too. Ash-like scales fluttered over his skin as Tristan took on the beastly form. His eyes of ember blotted Orion's vision, leaving blind spots as if he looked at the sun itself.

'*He fears you, Son of Heaven! He knows you are powerful,*' another voice pulsed through the metal, into his skin and bones. He clutched the post of the scythe. He bent his knees, readying himself. Orion became painfully aware of his mother and sister as he swung the scythe in its first full circle. The *slink* of metal through the atmosphere sent the two women shrinking back in fear. The noise was cruel and merciless and cold. He managed a glance at them. His mother held Ophiah where they cowered on the kitchen floor, and Ophiah held her ears. Her eyes stared into nothingness, filled with black. Blood stained her nose, and sobs shook her body like the glass that rattled on the dinner table.

The silent, lurking beast inside Orion ripped through something else. Orion wondered if it was ripping through the blessings and prayers the church administered to Ophiah and himself. That *thing* inside him severed whatever held it back, and its power shot through his veins like adrenaline. A *snap* cracked through his back, and tingling filled the bruises Tristan left on Orion in his last beating. Orion straightened too, and he leveled the scythe with the Earth, both hands gripping the handle. "Go to Hell," Orion said, "and don't come back."

Tristan smiled through thick, reptilian lips that coiled like a snake deep into the muzzle of his face. Shadows billowed like smoke from his body and swished across the floor. He dropped to four legs, prowling like a lion made of shadows and ember, more a dragon now than human or demon. He swung a tail across the living room, wiping out furniture and clearing an arena for the two of them. Tristan crept forward, his eyes darting in the direction of Orion's mother and Ophiah.

Orion stepped forward. He thought he should've been horrified to see his father turn into something so evil-looking, so primal and feral, but he guessed that deep down, he always knew his father's true form was wicked. He swung the scythe in a circle, swiping the blade through Tristan's ridged tail. The scythe left a deep sear that glowed like white-hot fire in his leathery skin.

Tristan roared in pain, coiled his tail around Orion's legs, and threw him across the room.

Orion collided with the wall, and frames and pictures shuttered and collapsed on the floor with him. *Get up*, Orion begged himself.

Tristan was on him again, now in the form of a man. Tristan wrapped a hand around Orion's neck and lifted him to the wall.

Orion clawed at the demon's hands, and he bared his teeth. He fought for fragmented breath. Claws pierced the wall behind him, and Orion's eyes threatened to roll back.

A glass shattered on the back of Tristan's head.

Orion sank to the floor. Behind Tristan, he spotted Ophiah holding another glass of Holy Water, ready to throw it like a grenade. "No!" Orion shouted at her. "Stop!"

Tristan spun.

Orion pleaded desperately with the atmosphere, the invisible angels and demons both, to wrap around Ophiah and throw her back down on the floor beside their mother. He didn't understand what compelled him to do it; it just felt like instinct. The invisible presence around her body obeyed, and Ophiah folded back to where she was before. Orion leapt to his feet, grabbed his scythe, and delivered three consecutive swings. He kicked Tristan, and it sent the demon stumbling back. *End this*, he begged himself. *End this. End the suffering. Banish him. Save them.* Orion breathed hard. He threw himself forward, into a twisting dance that ached through his bones. Two attacks, and two dodges.

"You will never win," Tristan said. "Even if you do—what use would it be? You will still burn in Hell with me."

Inwardly, Orion begged God to forgive that side of him—the cruel hatred, the cowardice, the hopeless sorrow that coiled deep, deep inside his heart. He wanted to become unbreakable and bulletproof. He wanted to come into his calling, to become Death himself. He would fight beside the others.

In death, he thought, there is always a new beginning. Always something new. In Tristan's death—in his banishing—his mother and sister would begin a new life. That's what he fought for. He reminded himself of that.

Orion lunged back into a spearing attack. The point atop the scythe pierced Tristan's side. Orion grinned, baring his teeth. He sliced the second blade on the underside of Tristan's arm as he dodged.

Tristan dashed forward, caught Orion's wrist before he could slam the weapon down over the demon's neck. Orion strained against the strength of the bigger man. His heart sank when Tristan smiled and drove a dagger into his side.

Orion doubled over in pain. The cold, hard blade intruded his body, viciously demanding attention. His blood warmed his side as he gasped.

Ophiah cried out behind him.

"They did this to you. Your mother. Your sister. Those other three *delinquents*. Some delusion they placed in your mind told you that *you* could defeat me. Who was it first? Was it Victoria?"

Orion wondered what he could possibly mean by Victoria. Orion didn't know anyone by that name. He kicked Tristan in the stomach as hard as he could. Blood slicked Orion's side as the dagger withdrew. *I will fight beside them*, Orion reminded himself of his goal. He would fight on the side of good. One day. He took two wide swings at Tristan. The third lash cut through Tristan's bicep. The wound leaked black blood.

Tristan hissed and struck Orion again, this time on the face.

Burning pain slashed through his right cheek.

"A little something to remember me by," Tristan said with a nasty smirk.

He knows he's going to lose, Orion realized suddenly. That was enough to fuel his fire. Blood raced down his right cheek.

They engaged in the duel again. More ruthless, more wild than before. They countered and swung and twisted through the chaotic battle-dance, neither one ahead of the other. Tristan struck with fists too big and too hard to be made of bone and flesh. His dagger left an afterburn of red in the air. The silver of Orion's scythe clashed against it. The fire in the pit behind them snapped and cheered. Sweat matted Orion's hair to his neck; his wounds clotted and stopped bleeding. He still stank of the metallic stains on his body and his own exhaustion.

He led the fight as much as the scythe did. The weapon weighed and judged and executed the fight. Orion became the weapon the scythe used, the entity to wield the power it could not wield for itself. Orion surrendered to it, the dramatic push and pull of the silver blades. Like a body dancing beside his own, it tossed him in and out of movement, bending him around obstacles and danger, rushing through dives and swings and throws of the blade.

Still, Orion took hits. Each battering of Tristan's fists sent Orion reeling back. Another knock to the face hit him like rocks falling from a cliff. His mouth dry, he spat blood and a tooth to the ground. Orion prayed to Heaven and Hell, and the world around him came to his aid like the rush of a storm on the coast. The angels and demons that swam around their ankles slowed Tristan's movements and gave Orion the small mercy of an advantage.

Orion spun in a fast, seamless movement. First, another dodge. Then an offense that severed deep into Tristan's thighs. He cut the demon's muscles to the bone. The phantom feeling of his scythe grazing hard bone reverberated through his hands and arms and down to his own legs. Tristan fell to his knees. *Every knee shall bow,* Orion thought smugly.

Tristan glared up at Orion, still carved with a heartless smile. Blood gushed from his legs, making a mess of dark red and black on the floor around him.

"In the name of the Father, the Son, and the Holy Spirit," Orion recited. He sliced his scythe down through the air, and rays of gold light split the atmosphere. Blackness and the ashy smell of Hellfire shot through the open void. "I command you to return to Hell," Orion said. The words were hard in his mouth, like stone on his teeth and gravel in his throat.

Slowly, Orion rounded Tristan where he knelt, immobile, at Orion's mercy. Orion kicked Tristan's back, and Tristan lurched forward. Tristan chipped like a broken, stained glass window. Each piece dissolved slowly, pulling towards the rip in reality. Once the dust of Tristan's human body was sucked completely into the void, Orion summoned his remaining strength to heave his double-sided scythe up and cut a short sever across the gash. It closed the portal in the shape of a crude, searing cross that faded in the moments after.

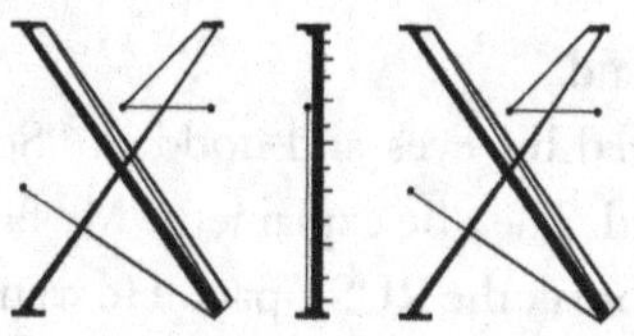

AFTER

If an angel commits treason against Heaven, the Eight Archangels will put the angel on trial. The Archangels are permitted to use their power of persuasion to compel the angel to tell the whole truth of their treason.
— *A History of Hierarchy*

FEBRUARY 1ST, 2107 A.D.
THE ABYSS
CARINA BLACKROCK

Carina walked into Corvun's room before she retired that night. Corvun, who was already shirtless, glanced up at her. He returned to his job of propping his guns against the wall and placing his pistol on his bedside table. "I want to thank you again," Carina said.

"No need, really." His eyes looked at her bare legs.

She shifted on her heels.

His eyes grazed their way up to her face. Hesitance filled them, but so did longing.

She sucked her bottom lip into her mouth.

Finally, he said, "I can't."

"You do not want to," she corrected.

He breathed into his hand, looking away. He sat then did not move from his place at the edge of his bed. His rough hands rubbed over his face and through his hair. "Is it true that all RUST assassins are sterile?"

"Yes," she said.

Corvun closed his eyes and nodded. "So my father told the truth," he said. Then he explained, "My father made a deal with Cephan to break the RUST pact. He wanted a family, but the cost was his firstborn's life in return."

"I am sorry," Carina said.

Corvun's eyes lifted to hers, his brows pointing to her face.

She wondered if he would ever make the same deal. She touched his lips with her fingertips, and warmth spread up her arms. She lifted his face. He touched her legs behind the knees. Even in the bedroom, it seemed, he still held onto his killer tendencies; he threatened to pull her balance from under her. Heat throbbed between her legs.

She pressed one knee into his bed, breathed into his mouth. He held her steady—a vise-like grip on his hesitance— kissed her slow at first, then crashed into her. His teeth clacked against hers, and she moaned into his lips. Before she could get both knees on the bed, Corvun pulled her underwear off. She shed her shirt, and Corvun kissed her chest and her stomach, holding her hips all the while. Carina turned to gold in his hands, a blushing fire of amber and tarnish and rose. His kisses lingered above the scars that blemished her skin. His tongue tasted the jutting bone of her hip, closing into a wet kiss.

He pulled her legs out and spun her onto his bed. Her heart rushed to her head and took control of her brain in that same moment. She rubbed her hands over his arms. She'd become too dizzy to know how he got undressed. She didn't care. He wrapped his arms around her, and he made love to her in a way she swore she'd known before.

"If I say that I've loved you all my life," he said, his voice heavy and slick, "would you think I'm crazy?"

Carina shook her head. She grabbed a fistful of his hair, and his hand found tufts of sheets beside her shoulder. His other stayed on her hip.

They laid together after they'd had a greedy fill of each other, and he kept her close. He held her like the night sky cradled the sea. She held onto him like he was her own life incarnate. "I know you," she whispered into his chest. The twin bed was too small to be comfortable unless they stayed tangled up in each other. "It's the way you taste."

Corvun's chest smelled hot like the leak of cologne and the embarrassment of the intimacy they shared. He still breathed hard through the beat of his racing heart.

"You taste like power," she said, "like hunger."

NORTHEAST FLORIDA
VENATRIX CANES

Venatrix dreamed of Orion. She dreamed of his black eyes and the smears of blood below his nose. She held his face as it twisted in pain, as his teeth gnashed against themselves. She kissed his forehead. He smelled of blood and cinnamon and potting soil. She held his head against her chest, and the blood from his nose and tears from his eyes dripped down her collarbone.

He trembled, spasming with movements she didn't understand. Something else lurked just beneath his skin, and it fought to take control of him.

THE ABYSS
JAYREN OMANS

Jayren dreamed of Indiana. He looked up into the gray sky. To Jayren's right, endless fields stretched on. Trees littered the horizon. To his left, a property was fenced with barbed wire, and beyond, stacked with stained silos. The stains looked like red blood on thick, concrete pillars. Jayren always imagined this was where vampires kept blood stores from their harvest. Now, the thought didn't seem too far-fetched.

His thoughts clouded the dream, and it fragmented like light refracting through water. Thunder rumbled and rain misted his vision. He saw his grandmother crouching before him, handing him a teddy bear. He read her lips, *I made this for you*. The memory of her voice was deleted, removed, replaced. Jayren's eyes welled.

Without warning, his skin ripped. The pain was that of a teddy bear being torn at the seams. He suffered a fatal wound, and teddy bear surgeons pulled him back together with a thread made of barbed wire.

The metal fence twisted into the park where he last saw his teddy bear. He'd sat in that park on the foot of the slide, talking to his bear. His name was Black Bear, dubbed that day. They talked about the aliens who conquered space. When his father called for lunch, Jayren left Black Bear with a promise. "I'll be back," Jayren said. He and his family left suddenly that day, right after lunch, to visit his grandmother in the hospital. She passed away shortly after they arrived. When they returned later to retrieve his friend, Black Bear wasn't there.

Sharp, ripping pain poked through Jayren's legs, and he cried out through the dream.

. . . .

Sleep shattered around Jayren like glass. His skin felt elastic, and it tore him open. The pain of bones breaking and reshaping inside his lower half tied tension around his joints and neck. His tail bound his legs and wrapped him in muscles he had no control over. He arched off the bed, a scream shredding his throat. He clawed his chest, and the little daggers of his broken nails cut through his skin. He scratched at his waist. Panic swung blows to his stomach. The tail attached to his body moved against his will. It coiled, rubbing raw against itself. The feel of scales hissing backwards against each other felt like pulling a hangnail back or catching a scab on a sweater. Sharp, acute pain.

"*Oh, god, no!*" Jayren belted. The sound of his muscles on the floor was the slap of corpses hitting the ground. His tail wrapped his bedside table, and the wood crunched in his hold. He snapped it. Something inside him wanted to test its strength. The animalistic instinct broke the table down into splinters and fragments of wood. Bones. All he thought of was the snapping and crunching of bones.

Carina burst through his door. "Jayren," she said. Corvun stepped in beside her, but his face paled and he disappeared a second later.

Jayren sobbed. Oxygen coursed through him, but never enough to warm his blood. Screaming distracted him, eased the mental pain a little. He cried for the loss of his father. He cried for the loss of his innocence, of his childhood. Hysteria wrapped him up in a second skin of scales and cold blood.

But then, nothing. His screams rang in his ears, hollow and furious. He screamed louder, ever louder, but no one could hear. He felt it down to his bones—no one could hear the anguish, the loneliness, the heartbreak, the fear.

Carina went away. In the distance, she and Corvun shouted.

Jayren could hardly hear above the blood thumping against his ears like a kick drum.

Carina came back to his room. "Come here, child," she said softly. She extended her arms for him. "I will carry you, okay? I will take you to the showers. We made you a bath. Water will soothe the pain."

She didn't have to ask twice. Jayren wrapped his arms around her neck, and she looped her arms under his back and his bleeding growth of a tail. She held him so kindly that Jayren did not feel like a monster in her arms. She called for Corvun, and Corvun stepped into Jayren's room with his sleeves rolled up and water dripping from his forearms. But Corvun looked at Jayren's tail as if he were just that: a monster. Something inhuman and wild and gross. Jayren twisted away from his friend.

"Pick up his tail. He is too heavy for me to carry alone," Carina said.

Corvun stepped closer to Jayren's tail, but Jayren hissed at him. Jayren's vision blurred, and he noticed the billowy, predatory wings glowing behind Corvun. Jayren slashed his tail underneath Corvun's feet. Corvun fell to the ground with a loud crash. His head banged against Jayren's dresser knobs, and he shouted Jayren's name.

"It is his instincts," Carina said quickly. "He sees your wings. Some birds are scavengers. They will eat snakes if the snake is wounded. He thinks you will hurt him."

"That doesn't help," Corvun argued.

"Try to understand," she said, "for his sake."

Corvun's eyes fixed on Jayren's. "I don't want to hurt you," he said slowly.

Jayren felt hot tears on his face. His tail wrapped around Corvun's core in a tight knot. "You're the *reasson* I'm here," Jayren struggled to get the words out of his mouth. His tongue narrowed in his mouth. "*Thiss iss* your fault."

"Listen to me." Corvun winced. His fingers pushed against Jayren's thick tail. His thigh and knee popped under the pressure. "This was always goin' to happen. This. Your changin'. With or without RUST."

Jayren loosened his hold, but he stayed wound around Corvun. He glared at his friend. Expectant, waiting. He needed an answer that would make sense. Pain flickered through his skin, and he blinked at the agony.

"The first time your eyes changed, that was the onset of your transformation. It's just shitty timin' that it happened here. I'm sorry that we got mixed up in this. I'm sorry," he repeated. "And I'm sorry I've been an ass. I didn't know how else to warn you. I didn't think you'd believe…"

Jayren's stomach filled with nerves when Corvun stroked a hand down his scales the right way. He did it absent, lost in thought, just a gesture as he spoke, as if he were wiping their past clean off the table. Jayren's eyes rolled back. Jayren guessed this was what pet snakes felt when their owners touched them right. His eyes grew heavy with a weight he couldn't lift back up.

"The scales hurt you," Corvun realized, his voice boyish and young. He looked at Jayren's reptilian body. "Do you like how that feels?"

Jayren nodded and nuzzled down into Carina's neck. She had been tense, Jayren noticed, after she relaxed suddenly at the gesture.

"Let's get him into the bath."

Carina nodded.

Corvun stood, letting the loops of Jayren's tail fall around him. This time, Jayren did not fight him as he picked up the excess length of his snake-like body. Jayren fought nausea as the two carried him to the bathroom. Carina nudged the door open with her foot, and steam greeted them like a sloppy kiss. Carina and Corvun stepped down into the bathroom. Three feet of water stood just past the steps. The lapping splashes calmed Jayren's mind, and he held onto his friends' arms as they lowered him into the water. His tail slapped into the shallow bath in a fleshy, wet sound. Jayren sank into the hot water, and his muscles started to unwind.

Corvun sat on the steps with his feet in the water, and Carina sat in the water beside Jayren.

CORVUN KHLYDE

Corvun rubbed his face. He listened as Jayren's breath steadied into a normal rate.

Jayren swished his tail in the water.

Carina spoke to Jayren quietly, and they sounded like home. The whistle on their voices, the little *plonks* of their hands in the water as they talked. Corvun lost himself in the sound of them. Carina told Jayren how to control his tail, how to move it correctly. Jayren slapped the water loudly and sent water spraying up into Corvun's face.

"Hey!" Corvun snapped.

Jayren laughed. Weak, but sure as hell.

Corvun couldn't help but laugh with him.

"Is that a hickey?" Jayren narrowed his eyes.

Corvun put a hand to his neck and rubbed nonchalantly. At the mention of the blood bruise, he felt Carina's mouth on his skin again. He cleared his throat. "What?"

Jayren snickered. "I get it," he said. "You're still angry at me for getting lucky before you."

Carina splashed Jayren. "Stop it."

Jayren grinned at Corvun; his face was wild and raw and tired like a newborn animal. Red ringed his eyes with irritation. His lips were dry, and they split when he smiled wide.

Corvun and Carina exchanged a glance. Corvun knew Jayren would abuse his inability to conceive once he knew. He'd find out eventually, but now was too soon. Corvun didn't know if he could listen to Jayren talk about all the girls he had the opportunity to sleep with, given the chance. Carina dipped her chin, as if she understood the look in Corvun's eyes.

Jayren sloshed his tail around in the water again. He looked down at the lower half of his body that had become so alien and foreign. Corvun looked too, finding that all the blood from the ripping and tearing skin had washed away. Even the torn flesh—that reminded Corvun of popped, white bubble gum—dissolved in the water. Scales covered Jayren's body. They shone, iridescent and fluttering with colorful, silvery hues. Corvun thought the shape and color of Jayren's scales almost resembled feathers from wings.

"How long do you think I am?" he asked.

"Seventeen feet, at least," Corvun said.

"Twenty-one," Carina said.

"Bet," Jayren said.

"Sorry?"

"Make a bet," Jayren said again. He grinned even wider at Corvun. "Then measure me."

"I change my guess—" Corvun started. Jayren wound his tail around Corvun's shoulders so quickly that Corvun could do nothing but hold his breath before Jayren dunked him face-first into the water. Corvun heaved Jayren's heavy tail off his back and flung his head out of the water. He rubbed the stinging water out of his eyes and gasped for air. "Fuck you," he said.

Jayren just laughed.

"Male Sentinels range in the twenties," Carina said.

"What about chick Sentinels?" Jayren asked. "Bet she's longer." He wiggled his eyebrows, and Corvun sent a spray of water at Jayren.

"Fifteen feet," Carina said. "Females range in the teens."

"Holy shit, so wait—"

Corvun glared at Jayren. He worried Jayren would say something else wildly offensive, but Jayren's face was lighting up like Christmas Eve in a little town. Corvun's anger faded quickly, and he reveled in the glowing conversation the two drove into, as if the words they spoke were decorations in a local park.

"You said you're a Sentinel. But you're like—" Jayren leaned forward. "Are you like a mermaid?"

Carina laughed. "I guess you could say that. There are two breeds of Sentinels," she explained. "There are the Seaborne Sentinels, like you and I. We take the lower form of a snake or a sea-dwelling creature. The other breed is the Landborne Sentinels, like Joshuah," Carina said as she looked to Corvun.

Cotton filled Corvun's stomach. He realized he'd been surrounded by guardian angels all his life. More, over time. He wondered if the Archangels ordered it, or if he attracted them like magnets.

"Joshuah is the type that usually takes the lower form of land-dwelling creatures. His form mimics a stag," Carina said.

"What about me?" Jayren asked.

"You are shaped after a black mamba," Carina said.

"And you?"

"A tiger shark," she said.

"Nuh uh," Jayren said.

Carina shrugged. She leaned forward dramatically. "I have the teeth of one, too."

Jayren raised an eyebrow at Corvun. "I thought I saw teeth marks in that hickey." He leaned back, stretching his arms across the doorway step. He rested his head back and flashed a toothy grin at Corvun. Cockiness exuded from him as he grew into his own instincts. His serpentine features gave him a monstrous smile.

CARINA BLACKROCK

When Corvun left the showers to get towels and a change of clothes for everyone, Jayren took the chance to ask a question. "If you're the Angel of Death," Jayren said, "then shouldn't you be powerful enough to face off with Greed? And Cephan, too?"

"I have to come into my power before I can stand against them." Carina looked at her hands. Whatever miracle took place in Hell's Alley was the work of God. She knew all of them—Corvun, Jayren, Venatrix, and the twins—would have untethered amounts of power once they came into it. One day, they *would* be strong enough to defy Cephan and all the Deceivers. "I do not have my full powers in this life yet," she said.

FEBRUARY 2ND, 2107 A.D.
NORTHEAST FLORIDA
VENATRIX CANES

Valentine North reserved the entire courthouse so that it was empty. As far as humans were concerned, there was a pipe leak and a maintenance team was fixing the issue. Venatrix sat with her brothers in the courtroom, and she took in her surroundings. The ceilings were high here, and the domed ceiling was lined with burnished wood. Valentine North stood where the judge would on any other day. Two Archangels were at his sides, and the others sat to the left of them in a jury.

Valentine called for everyone's attention, ordered a moment of silence in respect to the Holy One, and then told the Archangels to take a seat.

Venatrix dared to let her eyes wander a little more.

Professor North looked as almighty as ever, his hair brushed back and not a wrinkle in his silver-gold suit. No time for the traditional judge's robe; Venatrix wondered if North thought it a silly human trend more than anything. To his right sat his advisor and wife, Gabrielle. She wore her hair in a bun styled slightly to the left. It cascaded with feathery blonde hair. Around her neck she wore a set of red reading glasses, and in her hand she held a silver pen.

To the left of Valentine was Michael. His pen rested beside a notepad, like a sword and a shield. Michael watched her with the same judgmental eyes that scoured her like Corvun's black eyes did. She felt utterly useless as his father gripped her in a gaze of power and purpose and dignity. *So that's where Corvun got it.*

Venatrix turned.

The Archangels which she was familiar with sat at the front of the jury. Her own parents were there. And to Venatrix's surprise—Missy, too, had made it to the event. Venatrix's throat tightened. She wanted to think about Orion, but she distracted herself by moving on. In the next row back, Venatrix recognized Lynx's dad, General Direlight. He always had his hand in Valentine's operations, from what Venatrix understood, but she didn't see much of him. General Direlight's face was passive and young but discerning and judging at the same time. His gaze made Venatrix feel like a war map, some sort of soon-to-be military execution that would put her in the middle of the playing field.

Beside the general, a doctor sat with curious eyes. Venatrix didn't know him, so she studied him the way he studied her. She wondered if he had arrived on Earth first when all the Archangels came down to take on their human lives. The doctor was older but with a young spirit like the others. His silvery blue eyes twinkled like a doctor's scope. He rubbed his chin with a thin, bony hand then he adjusted the bow tie at his neck and leaned back as if he made a diagnosis on her right then and there.

Venatrix glared at Valentine.

I am Conquest, she wanted to say. *You have no right to keep me here like a child. I am as powerful as any of you.* But her tongue held still, chained by fear and uncertainty.

"Caeleb Canes, Erin Canes," North addressed her brothers. "You have been accused of treason against the Most High."

Venatrix's blood turned cold. An eerie chill fell over the room like a blanket of new snow in the dead of night.

"Do you know the consequence?"

"Yes, Valor," Erin replied.

Caeleb just scoffed.

Valor was the name they were required to address North by in this trial. It was his God-given name. Venatrix wondered about the repercussions of Caeleb dismissing him with a snort of his nose. The consequences had high stakes; the consequences were falling. Venatrix had thought her brothers might already be Fallen, but it seemed—by the state of the trial—that because of their ranks as Archangel Heir—they were being shown mercy and given a second chance, a choice. Venatrix maintained absolute silence. Her time in this trial would come, she assumed, and if not, she would walk out unscathed. She strained her neck against the tight white blouse that wrapped around her pulse like frost.

"The Deceiver Greed was bound to the sea. Were you aware that the battle along the shore—which your betrayal affected—was a defense to keep the demon bound to the ocean?" North asked. His voice sent violent ripples of goosebumps down her arms and back. It was the closest she'd ever heard North to being truly furious.

"Yes, Valor," Erin said.

"Yes, Valor," Caeleb echoed, quieter. "We were asked to interfere for that reason."

Venatrix glanced at her brother. She was shocked Caeleb added information of his own accord. Valentine North clicked his tongue, bringing her attention directly back to him. He held her eyes there. She didn't try to fight the invisible command.

"Venatrix Canes," North addressed her, holding her in his steady gold eyes. The lines on his face showed just enough. It gave the appearance of wisdom—something the angels were oh so fond of. Those wrinkles had seen wonders, earthquakes and devastation; they were also the worry she and her three new friends burdened him with. She wondered: if she called North out on caring for the Four Horsemen so deeply, would he acknowledge it with the same reverence he regarded the Seven Archangels?

North turned to Venatrix. "Had you known of any of these operations: the defense strategy, the purpose of the battle, or the betrayal?"

"No, Valor," she said. Then, in hindsight, she remembered: Mr. Barstad, the day her brothers hot-boxed the car, her parents' concern. Had she guessed there was something happening but dismissed it? Or was she simply too busy with Orion to even give it a second thought? She couldn't even answer for herself. Did her brothers gang up on her again like they had at the parties? Used their ability to alter memories to make sure Venatrix thought nothing more of it? She'd sworn she wouldn't let anyone control her like that again, yet here she was. She felt sick.

North glanced at the jury. He leaned back into his chair and began presenting the facts. Every now and then, Michael input facts of the battle, too. Apparently, he fought in the battle himself. Venatrix couldn't move, and her hands on the desk turned cold and sticky. Did Corvun know her brothers put his father at risk? She swallowed the nausea rising in her throat. She wanted to go home.

Home would never be the same.

"Caeleb, Erin," North said. "Who asked this betrayal of you?"

Erin didn't speak.

Caeleb did. "Cephan," he said.

"Did he ask anything else of you?"

"He asked us to strip our sister of her confidence and to break Jayren's glasses in order to make him fail his classes. He asked for Corvun Khlyde's internship essay, too. He asked us to persuade someone to plagiarize it. We were to do all that we could to undermine the Four Horsemen," Caeleb said, monotone.

Whispers rose, and even Michael shifted in his seat.

"What did he offer you in return?" North asked. His voice did not change from steady, calm, knowing.

"Immortality," Caeleb said, and Erin hung his head.

Gabrielle paled, her hand folding back into her lap. Her complexion turned ghost-like. Beside her, Valentine also lost color. He withdrew his hands, too. Gabrielle glanced under the podium then looked up at Valentine. He kept his eyes trained forward, hard and scolding on Caeleb.

"Would you sell your eternity in the Lord's presence for the little time immortality will grant you here?"

The little time, Venatrix reflected. So it seemed Valentine and the Seven deemed this the last Iteration. The Archangels expected her and Jayren and Corvun and Orion to come into their power as the Four Horsemen, to win their war. Venatrix felt her blood drain, like hosing hopscotch chalk off a sidewalk. *How do you know?* She wanted to ask. *How do you know for sure?*

"The jury will not take part in this trial," North announced suddenly. "I alone will decide your sentence. Repent, and I will offer you a second chance. You will become dormant for a time, and we will wake you when we see fit."

For Armageddon, Venatrix thought. *They'll wake my brothers for Armageddon.*

"Or," North said, "honoring your instilled free will, we will allow you to leave. Doing so would be to turn your back on God's will. You know full well that should you leave and follow that path, your crime will cost you your eternal soul." He was still pale.

Caeleb and Erin both bowed their heads in prayer and submission. They took the first option.

Michael stood, and another silence fell. "Valor, if I may?"

North glanced at him, nodded.

"The humans will know this: the brothers will be publicly involved in a drug bust. The house was broken into, and the family killed. They will be off the radar. Caeleb and Erin will serve their sentence. Samuel and Rachael will work directly with us in the North Institute." Michael's voice edged around anticipation and impatience. He looked to Valentine.

"And Miss Canes," Valentine sighed and added, "You will become a double agent for us, inside RUST."

No.

Her parents stood from their seats, and even the doctor behind them protested. Her brothers lifted their heads to look at her. Venatrix stared back at Valentine, begging him with her eyes alone. She craved attention, but this was too much. Every breath in the room whirled around her like a tornado.

"Listen to me," Michael commanded of everyone. And they silenced. "This is Valor's order, one he was given by the

Spokesperson. I second this motion. Jayren and my son," his voice actually faltered, "have already been branded. We cannot alter their path. That much is clear. So we set her into theirs. They will protect her. Have you not seen it?" He glared at the room, daring someone to object to the friendship which bonded like welded metal in the past months. Michael's hands slackened at his side.

General Direlight spoke, "She will be slaughtered. She has never fought…like *they* do. The assassins… If they get a hold of her…"

"The three will learn to fight. I will tell Corvun of the plan. He will not let any harm come to her. I can *promise* you that much." Michael turned to Valentine next. "Armageddon will never come if they do not grow into their callin' together. It will just mean another Iteration. One after the other. We have to try. What is the worst that could happen?"

"They could fall," Valentine said evenly. "They will be in Cephan's hands, and we know the Deceivers will stop at nothing. The stakes will be high."

Venatrix couldn't continue to sit and say nothing. She wouldn't take it, being talked about like this. Besides, the nagging thought of Orion came back when she realized Missy had not done so much as breathe during the whole conversation. "Where is Orion?" Venatrix asked aloud.

The room hushed again. Valentine and Michael looked to Missy, who shook her head.

"I don't know," Missy said.

Venatrix's head spun.

"Did he survive?"

Did he survive banishing that wicked, powerful demon? A Deceiver?

"Yes," Missy whispered. There was pride in her voice, in her son. "He opened the Gate to Hell. My daughter and I were knocked unconscious right after. When we woke, Tristan and Orion were gone."

A sickness swam at the top of Venatrix's stomach. What if Orion was dragged to Hell too?

"If Orion can open the Gate to Hell, then we can assume he is growing into his power already. We must assume he can take care of himself for now. The three will look for him once they have safely established a team."

So that's it. That's all there is, Venatrix thought. She wanted to fight, to tell them to search Heaven and Hell for Orion *now*. Her hands balled at her sides. But she could not fight this sentence. *For now. Just for now. Just for now,* she decided. She would make it through. Her friends would be at her side. They would protect her. She repeated the lines. Over and over.

She didn't believe any of it.

OPHIAH JUDE

Ophiah packed her last box. All of Orion's belongings were packed next to hers like plant bulbs nested into new dirt beds. Ophiah packed Orion's memory so deep in the grooves of her mind that he was like flower seeds in the cracks of pavement. He wasn't really gone, and he never would be. Not to her. She reminded herself of this again and again.

She sighed, and her room echoed the sound back to her.

"Are you ready, honey?"

"Just a minute," she called to her mother.

A spring breeze blew through the open windows. Today was the first day they'd open all the windows. It was the first week without Tristan. The thick scent of freshly cut grass and thriving plants all around the house filled her lungs. She closed the last box, wiping a trail of sweat beside her ear. She pulled her hair back into a ponytail and she wondered if she'd cut it all off to memorialize the change of season in her own life.

Orion isn't gone, she reminded herself yet again. She felt him tucked away in the corner of her mind. Dormant, like a flower waiting to bloom at the edge of summer. Perennials always came back; they were too determined not to. It was just like Orion's everlasting joy. It always came back, too. She'd see him again.

Ophiah closed her eyes and prayed. A simple "thank you" wasn't enough to express her gratitude for the power God granted Orion. She had prayed endlessly, unceasingly, as the darkness fell on the house only a handful of nights before.

She couldn't stay here. She breathed in all the memories, all the abuse held over her head like a weapon, the nightmares and sicknesses that kept her restless for years. She hadn't had a nightmare in the few nights in between. If she had, they were distant. Fading. She stood. She was happy to leave. Peace settled into her heart as if the room to breathe, the room to grow was the gentle watering of a plant, and moisture seeped into her soil and skin and nurtured her dry heart.

Exhale.

Ophiah helped her mother remove the curtains. The house appeared so much smaller with nothing in it. No darkness, no closeness, no memories. She promised herself she would make new memories in her new place.

Her mother kissed her head. "Casper is coming over in a few."

Ophiah avoided her mother's eyes. *New memories. This is a new start.* Ophiah walked outside and stood in the driveway, staring up into the sky until Casper pulled up. She glared at him, and he hesitated to get out of his car. *If Orion faced Tristan, the least I can do is face Casper,* she told herself.

Casper put his hand on the silver side of his father's convertible.

"Don't," Ophiah said. Her voice sounded bright, tall, and proud. She'd grown into something brilliant. She bloomed in the sunlight, holding every ounce of power that her old tee (which was smeared with dirt and dust and sweat stains) and jean shorts had to offer. *This is me. This is who I am. I make the calls in my life.* She was a force of nature, she decided, and she would blossom for Casper to watch but never to touch again.

"Excuse me?"

"It's over," she said. "I'm done. We're done."

Casper's brow furrowed. Shadows cast dirty brown colors into his blond hair. Even if he was an Archangel Heir, he was no better than she was, no cleaner, no more holy or righteous.

She redefined herself, right then and there.

"Leave, Casper," she said. Her voice didn't shake. The breeze whispered through her ponytail, stroking her neck and caressing chills into her skin. She embraced the feeling. She embraced the words: "I don't want to see you now or ever."

"You'll regret it."

"No, I won't," she told him.

Maybe the moment was as fleeting as the clouds drifting over the sun. Maybe she'd find herself tangled in another bad situation with him. But she swore she would never stay there long.

Her heart belonged elsewhere.

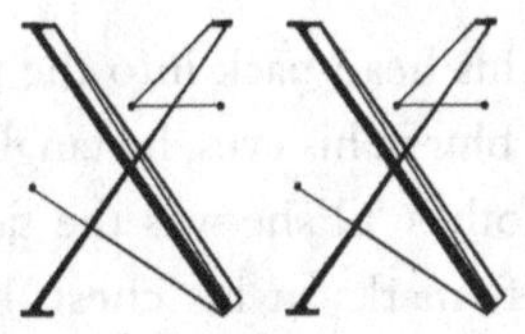

TO MAKE AN ANGEL FALL

All angels and demons have some healing abilities. The only thing that can permanently scar an angel or demon is a Heaven-forged or Hell-forged weapon. Heaven-forged and Hell-forged metals nullify the restorative abilities of angels and demons.
— A History of Hierarchy

FEBRUARY 2ND, 2107 A.D.
THE ABYSS
CORVUN KHLYDE

Corvun took Carina to bed with one arm wrapped around her waist and the other hand grasping a bottle of rum. They'd taken shots together—Carina at four and Corvun hardly managing two. Carina tasted strong, too. It was all he could think of. They hit the bed, and he wondered where the rum had gone until he watched Carina take a heavy swig straight from the bottle.

He didn't know what to say to her. He reveled in the red-hot blush on her face which covered her like a pink sunrise. He wondered if it was the rum making her blush. He wondered if he looked the same. He leaned up into her mouth as she set the bottle on the floor beside his bed.

Corvun rested his head back into the pillow as she sank into his lips. With a blur in his eyes, he tangled into her, ripped and tore at their clothes 'til she was the tide and he was the shore. Her nails left marks in his chest, but her touch was fleeting, and it washed away in her heavy breaths. She would be different in an hour, tomorrow, and forever after that. She was never steady, he'd learned, and though he held her close to his body like this, he knew he could never keep her there.

Carina cried out, and Jayren kicked the thin wall separating them. "Shut up! God! Ew!" Jayren yelled, muffled. Carina put her hand on Corvun's neck. She didn't stop a second moan; neither did Jayren.

. . . .

Corvun woke with a start. He tousled with his memory in his half-awake state, and the emptiness on his cot beside him chilled his skin. He ripped out of bed and dressed quickly, standing, stalking, stumbling, searching… Liquor still clouded his mind. He found Jayren in the kitchen. He gripped Jayren's shoulders. "Where is she?" he demanded.

"She's not with you? She never left your room…" Jayren's brow furrowed. The confusion there deepened, worsened. He sank into horror. "She said Cephan knew she was here."

Corvun released Jayren. He twisted himself into a void of blackness, tearing through the dark atmosphere of the Abyss until he heard a distant chuckle. It was Cephan, deep in the pit of the plane between Earth and Hell. Corvun pinpointed the sound. His shadows fanned apart, blasting away from his body. The black dust settled into nothing. Corvun stood facing Cephan and Carina.

The first thing he noticed was Carina. She was naked and kneeling at a gleaming metal whipping post. Shackles cuffed her hands. Her eyes widened, snot shining at her nose. Tears left little paths of light on her bruised face. She sobbed at the sight of him, and her eyes twisted into puffy red knots. "No," she moaned. "Corvun, *no*." She begged him to leave. *They will make you kill me, Corvun*, her words looped in his mind, a skipping record that haunted this waking nightmare.

In the box-like room, Cephan stood amidst a treasury of lethal, ancient weapons. Cephan's cane leaned against the wall in the far corner. Cephan smiled. In his hand, he held a whip— one just as vile as the gnarled, twisted blades that barred the walls. The black leather dangled with nine tails, each tied around metal stars. Cephan's white-toothed smile beamed in the dark. He rolled his sleeves back, and his thin lips curled back with them. "You made it just in time. Let me give a demonstration, Corvun, of how I'll have you kill her." Cephan raised his arm.

No, Corvun breathed.

The whip slashed through the air, striking Carina's bare back.

She buckled, yelling out into the stuffy room. Her body convulsed, quaking with muscles that could not aid her escape. She rattled against the post, and her hands turned purple and blue where she pulled at the shackles.

"You will deliver forty lashes," Cephan ordered. "Perhaps, if you go easy on her, she might survive it."

"No," Corvun begged. "*No*, please don't make me do this."

"Fine." Cephan raised the whip without hesitation and threw his arm back down. He separated Carina's skin with those metal-tipped tails. "I'll do it."

Carina screamed again and again and again. Three more terrible lashes shredded through the damp, tacky air.

It brought Corvun to his knees. "Stop. Stop, *please*. I'll do anythin'!" Corvun pleaded. He couldn't bear to watch Carina's face break any more, couldn't stand the sight of blood on her dry lips or her lithe muscles tensing beneath her sweating skin. Her voice was embers on a fire—no longer flame. Dwindling, fading. Her screams crackled out and wasted away in between her breath, falling to ash against his eardrum.

'*Fight him. Fight him, Corvun,*' Jayren pleaded from the back of Corvun's mind. It sounded as if Jayren was speaking inside Corvun's own head. Corvun didn't question the sudden connection or how Jayren could know what Corvun saw before his eyes. Images of an escape plan flashed from Jayren's mind to Corvun's. '*Save her. We're not letting her die like this, dammit.*'

Corvun stood. Tears fled his eyes.

Carina stared back, her mouth ajar from screaming. Blood laced her sides and spattered her shoulders. Fatigue trembled in her body. Her serpentine eyes pleaded with him.

Corvun walked with broken, jagged steps to where Cephan stood. He stood toe-to-toe with Cephan. Corvun took a chance on Jayren's reckless plan. He pulled his switchblade and swiped it across Cephan's neck.

Too easy. That was too easy, Corvun thought, horrified. He snatched the key from Cephan's belt, his mind racing.

Cephan stumbled back, a hand to his neck as if he feigned mild, *fake* shock. Mocking, always mocking. Blood poured from the deep gash, but Cephan smiled back anyway. He wiped the blood from his neck, and the wound sealed shut as if his finger ran a zipper along the artery. "Well, well, Khlyde," he said. "That was most bold of you. I see why Heaven speaks so highly of you. Chivalry, charming." Cephan raised his arm again.

Corvun decided he'd die before he let Cephan strike Carina again.

Corvun stood his ground. Something jerked him back, testing his balance. A rush of air filled the room. He felt too big, suddenly, and he could feel the blades of the weapons hanging along the walls with his fingertips. No, not his fingertips. His heart fluttered with fear. He saw stark white in his peripheral vision.

Wings fanned out from him to shield Carina. He blocked Cephan from Carina's cowering figure. The billowy tuft of feathers blinked with eyes that nestled deep in the ends of his feathers. He thought fleetingly that they looked similar to peacock feathers. He felt invincible, if only for a moment.

It did not stop the sting as Cephan's nine-tailed whip slashed against him. The whip caught three places on Corvun's face. The stars clung and clawed across Corvun's chest. He swallowed the screams. Cephan jerked the whip back, and Corvun folded his wings and spun. He hit the ground with his knees, wrapping himself around Carina. He shielded her, his lungs filled with the metallic scent of their bleeding wounds. Blood dripped hot down his face.

Cephan struck him again.

He dropped the key.

Pain rippled through him, shuddering through each nerve. Feathers floated from him, rested on the ground by his knees. He gritted his teeth so hard that a headache cracked through his forehead.

"Corvun," Carina sobbed. "He will kill us both."

Corvun put a hand on the floor. He could hardly hold himself up. The next slash burned through his shoulders and spine and wings. Dots filled his vision. He palmed the ground. The small, cool piece of metal found his hand. He yelled out. The tenth lash. Hell's fingertips raked his body like sizzling gunpowder. A star latched into the nape of his neck, and he crumpled into quaking sobs.

'Get up. C'mon, you're stronger than this,' Jayren said.

Corvun couldn't move.

'*Please, man. Please get up. Please,*' Jayren begged.

Corvun pinched the key and reached over Carina's shoulder to unlock her shackle.

Cephan's whip snagged Corvun's feathers and carved deep ravines through his back.

All Corvun could hear was ringing.

His vision faded in and out.

Jayren burst through black shadows straight ahead, the same way Corvun had arrived. Jayren gaped at Corvun. His eyes were so painfully wide.

Corvun *clicked* Carina's other hand free and shoved her forward. Into Jayren's arms.

Cephan hesitated. He stalked nearer.

"No!" Jayren shouted.

A shackle closed on Corvun's wrist.

Corvun pulled, tried to dissolve into his shadowy, black mist to escape, only to find his body wouldn't dematerialize. He was trapped.

The sound slowed Corvun's pulse to a gradual stop. Numbness spread over him. He wasn't leaving. Not the way he came. Maybe not at all. '*Hide her. Take her to Joshuah. Please.*'

Carina covered her mouth.

Jayren's eyes hardened. Jayren shot Cephan a fiery glare then stepped back, slipping away into shadows. Jayren and Carina disappeared.

Corvun flapped his wings uselessly. He flailed in the too-small cage that the walls and ceilings locked him in. The whir of wind from his wings clattered the weapons along the walls. They clapped and applauded Cephan's latest catch. Corvun slumped against the whipping post.

Cephan grabbed his other hand and shut the hard metal around his wrist.

"What will you do?" Corvun challenged. "Kill me?"

"Oh no, I'll let you live," Cephan said. His pale, blue-white eyes grazed the massive expanse of feathers which shone like daylight. "I'll be taking these from you. To say I stole the wings of Michael's son. Imagine what Heaven will say."

Corvun swiped his wings off the floor to flare them out, to bare them like fangs or a brandish of a weapon. But he was only a bird caught in the teeth of a bigger predator.

Cephan snatched his cane from the corner then returned. The cane swirled away into a bright, Heaven-forged sword. "I'll try not to make it quick," he said. He ducked under Corvun's wings and stood between his calves. Cephan clasped a strong hand around the stalk of Corvun's wing.

When the sword touched Corvun's feathered skin, it burned through the soft fuzz of small feathers. It severed his new skin, cauterizing the wound as Cephan sawed up and down. Cephan cut so slowly that Corvun's mind fogged with pain so bright and loud and agonizing. Corvun screamed until his lungs collapsed, then his screams dragged him back to reality, to the endless severing at his back. He gasped, and it felt like he swallowed gasoline, pouring into his lungs and stomach like poison. He heaved and gagged at the sensation of oxygen in his chest. He didn't even want to breathe.

Cephan reached bone. He scraped, carved, chiseled deeper, deeper, deeper…

A pause.

A strike and—

Snap.

Corvun couldn't feel his hands for how hard he pulled against the shackles. His muscles melted in the hot, boiling water of affliction. His head throbbed with pain. His balance, uneven.

Cephan started on the other.

JAYREN OMANS

Black clouded Jayren's vision. He stepped out into that cursed room again, finding that Corvun was still there, still kneeling, still shackled against the whipping post. Jayren had done exactly what Corvun ordered. He delivered Carina to Joshuah, then he returned as quickly as he could. He couldn't leave Corvun alone. But he was too late.

Two huge, white wings sprawled across the ground on either side of Corvun. Limp and separated. They were dirty on the edges. Corvun still sobbed, quiet and fragile. His face was downcast on the metal post. Blood streaked his thin sides. Between his quivering shoulders, there were two bloody-black stumps of bone.

"Corv…" Jayren whispered. His chest caved in. He sank to the ground.

Corvun sniffled, weak.

Jayren looked to the wings again, and his heart sank deeper. *It's all true.* There was no denying it anymore. Corvun had been so beautiful with those wings, so full of life and power. Jayren decided he'd never make escape plans again. He would never make calls for his friends at all. If this was how his plans turned out, then whatever higher power existed surely hated him more than any other stain on the Earth. Jayren heaved himself up, dragged his feet to Corvun. He found the key lying just before the metal post, just in Corvun's sight, as if it had been placed there to taunt him, as if Cephan expected Jayren to return.

Corvun glanced up. His black eyes were hollow and surrounded by puffy, red skin. His lips curled back in a permanent, wry sob, teeth bared. His cheeks were pulled back in a sneer, too. Despite the sweat and blood and bruises, it was the brokenness in his dark brown eyes that cut through Jayren's chest. Corvun's eyes didn't reflect any light.

Jayren's trembling fingers reached for the key, dropped it twice as he fumbled for it. He struggled to unlock the metal jaws trapping Corvun's raw wrists. Jayren pulled Corvun into his arms.

He was heavy, dead weight.

Jayren clutched Corvun. He didn't know what else to do. He sat there holding his friend until Corvun managed the strength to hold on, too. Jayren pulled Corvun through the shadows and back to their dorm. On the floor of their new home, he held Corvun closer to his chest.

FEBRUARY 3RD, 2107 A.D.
NORTHEAST FLORIDA
CARINA BLACKROCK

Fatigue clutched Carina's body. She could not move. She was tied to the bed by invisible forces—of despair and hopelessness and defeat and anguish—like anchors in the ocean floor. She stayed there. Moving hurt her back. Breathing ached in her bones.

Joshuah knocked on her door.

Silence.

She could hardly breathe. Weight crushed her back as she laid on her stomach. She didn't want to think. The night before, Jayren and Joshuah held her in the bathtub as they scrubbed the wounds to prevent infection. Jayren had plucked a piece of his shadow from beneath his arm, as if he'd pulled a coin from her ear in a magic trick. The shadow was a black feather.

"A cloak," Jayren said, "kind of. No one in RUST will find you. Not demons, not Cephan. No one can track you, except me. It's a part of my shadow, so I'll be able to find it. But I'll be the *only* one who can."

She let Jayren tie the feather in her hair. He hugged her then vanished. Carina didn't know if she'd ever see him or Corvun again. The past days had been a whirlwind—of friendship and passion and dread.

"Carina," Joshuah said, bringing her back to the present. "I brought you some tea and some food, if you think you can…"

Carina didn't move.

"I'll leave it, uh—" A tray clattered on the dresser. He cleared his throat. "I'll be downstairs. I'll check on you a little later."

A pause.

"If you're wondering if they'll come back for you, they will. They love you. Anyone could see that, especially after what they did. Risking their lives… Be glad it was Jayren who gave you the feather. It's not always wise to let Corvun find you. I would know," he said.

"Thank you," Carina whispered. She closed her dry eyes.

Joshuah closed the door when he left.

Carina drifted off to the scent of the old, dusty sheets and the steam of lavender tea wafting through the air. Sunlight shone on the soles of her feet, warming her toes. A hot tear slipped out of her eyes as tiredness took over yet again. She had no strength but that to will her mind into silence. Exhaustion consumed her.

OPHIAH JUDE

Are you sure you want to live alone? Ophiah's mother's question rang in her ears.

All of Ophiah's boxes studded the floor to the bright flat like new stepping stones in a garden. She would have all the time and space to weed through her old life here, breaking down old grudges to create a new path for herself. She took in a deep breath, exhaled thinly. It was the first time she ever felt her lungs fill completely.

Someone cleared his throat behind her.

Heart thundering, she spun. She dropped the coffee she held in her hands, and it shattered on the floor. "Jayren," she managed in something not unlike a crack of fear.

Jayren's face was long and drawn and tired, but his features still cut at her heart with accuracy and precision. He cornered her right where he could make a killing blow, had he wanted to. He'd evolved into something far more lethal and dangerous than a garden snake. He glanced down at her spilled coffee with quick eyes. "We'll that's quite the dramatic greeting. Am I that scary?" He waved his hand as if he were wiping a towel over the mess, and the white cup and creamed coffee whisked away into nothingness. He did this all while muttering something inaudible about monsters and closets.

"What are you doing here?" she asked.

"I'm here to help you unpack."

"No," she said.

"In that case, I need a favor." He rubbed the back of his neck. "Corvun—uh—Cephan," he cleared his throat again, "cut his wings off."

"Wings?" she asked.

"Yeah, it's," he paused, "weird? I, uh, don't know. It's definitely not what I expected to be saying when I saw your bedroom for the first time."

"His wings," Ophiah said again. She studied Jayren's blurry face and thick lashes. He'd been crying.

"Shit, what do you want me to say? He *sprouted wings*, Ophiah. I mean, they were massive. *Huge*. Like thirty feet across or something—"

"Do you believe now?" she asked him, licking her lips. The distance between them was coarse, like a crack through dry soil. Their budding friendship had shriveled up. She hadn't decided if she would nurture it back to health yet or try to leave it all behind her and start anew.

"I shouldn't have come here," he said shortly. He turned, and shadows brushed at his ankles like tall grass. He stopped. "Fuck. His back, Ophi. He's torn to hell and back. He *needs* a doctor. You're the only one I could even think to ask. I need North to see him, to make an appointment to amputate the—the—" He rubbed his face.

"Jayren," she said. She followed.

"To amputate the stumps of his wings…" He kept his back to her. He swore.

"Do you believe in God?" she asked him again. She remembered the first time she had. He seemed so much younger then, his eyes so much brighter. It was hard to believe that not even six months had passed.

"Yeah," Jayren said. "I do. And I'm pretty damn sure he hates me. Always has."

Ophiah's heart squeezed in her chest. "I'll talk to North," she said.

Shadows laced up around Jayren like sprouts of vines, gripping and twisting around him until he was covered. The shadows separated, and he was gone.

JAYREN OMANS

Jayren texted her that night. 'I meant to say thank you. I'm sorry I left like that.'

Her text came twenty minutes later. 'I forgive you.'

'I don't want your forgiveness. I just want to be better.'

'Valentine said you can bring Corvun to the North Hospital tonight at ten. Meet him on the roof. They'll take care of him. Don't tell anyone you'll be there, okay?'

'Thank you.'

. . . .

Jayren carried Corvun in his arms—pulled through a nasty black void like a cloth through a gun barrel—to the roof of the North Hospital. He watched Valentine North and another white-haired doctor wheel his friend into the stomach of the building. Darkness crept over Jayren. He waited until he couldn't hear the wheels anymore, then he left.

VENATRIX CANES

Venatrix packed everything into storage. Her parents assured her that she could get it back when it was all over. She had watched her brothers slip unconscious in tubes of metal and glass, and she knew *when it was all over* there would be nothing left at all. She kept nothing but the clothes she wore and the Glass phone in her hand. She felt what was left of her childhood innocence crumble like a sandcastle as she sat in the back seat of her parents' car while they stuck a *FOR SALE* sign in the front yard.

CARINA BLACKROCK

When Carina mustered the strength to rise again, she sat with Joshuah to tell him everything. Jayren visited that day, his arrival announced by the chiming bell atop the door of the Angels' Diner. He walked to the bar and sat beside her. He delivered news about Corvun's successful surgery, and Carina asked for a glass of rum on the rocks.

CORVUN KHLYDE

On the last day of his recovery, Corvun sat across from his father in the North Hospital. Bitter acid rose in his throat. Corvun couldn't stand to look at his father when he gave Corvun details about the plans to plant Venatrix in RUST. Michael instructed Corvun that no one was to know she was a double agent, not even Jayren. Corvun held back retorts about the baby brother he had on the way, and how *he* would never have to face such hardships.

Corvun left the hospital building just to feel fresh air on his face. His post-surgery treatment had not quite ended, and he still had paperwork to finish and to take with him. But when he spotted Jayren standing across the street watching the hospital, he crossed the road and never returned to that prison of ice and gold.

OPHIAH JUDE

Ophiah struggled to pull through to graduation. After her ceremony, Valentine North offered her a position with the North Institute, to be Casper's secretary. It was a slap in the face, and she wondered if Casper had told her father how she rejected him. Ophiah didn't care though, and she held her chin even to Valentine's when they shook hands. He smiled proudly at her. Perhaps he *did* know. Perhaps being the secretary to the new CEO of North Institute would allow her to put Casper in his place, or put her foot in doors she didn't have access to prior. Maybe that's what Valentine wanted for her.

A new beginning, she promised herself. She held fast to that promise.

Somewhere far away, she felt a twinkle in her soul like the birth of a star, like a flutter of notes on a piano. The melody dipped and lulled, but it stayed.

The melodic lifeline plucked at her heart, and it stayed.

EPILOGUE
NAMING THE STARS

Azrael will be named after the ship in the night sky, a vessel to carry the Four Horsemen towards their destiny. She will be named after Carina, which holds the second brightest star in the sky.
— *A History of Hierarchy*

438 A.D.
ROME
ORION

Night fell like sorrow, dark and black, but hope flickered above the lone ship as the ocean lulled it into uncharted seas. The sound of the wind and water lapping at the sides of the ship and its sail were the only noises in the night. A billion stars filled the sky above like white sand, and five gladiators and their captain gazed upward.

Orion shuffled where he sat next to Venatici. She was just far enough that he could not reach out and touch her. With tension from the fight lingering in his muscles and wound, he gave in and laid back onto the damp ropes and fishing nets that scattered the surface below him. To his surprise, Venatici laid beside him. He rolled his head to the side to glance at her.

She didn't look at him. She pointed to the sky, to a bright constellation. Three brilliant stars formed a belt in the sky. "That one—the one with the three bright stars."

Orion watched her passive face, wondering if the moonlight gave her lips a certain taste. (He realized, in studying her face while she gazed up at the stars, that he wanted to kiss not only her lips but the dark, full brow above her thick lashes and slope below her cheekbone, too.)

"It looks like your dagger. See there? The larger forth star is the gem in the hilt, and the three in a cluster are the jewels set in the blade."

He smiled at her. The others spoke softly to each other in Orion's periphery. He let himself relax a little, let their voices fade into the distance. Suddenly he *could*. He was no longer one of the Gemini, the assassin, the killer. Suddenly, he could name himself. He could be whatever he wanted to be, for the moment.

"Did you ever think we'd make it out?" Venatici asked. Her head turned so she could gaze back at him. Her eyes shimmered with ethereal blue in the mix of starlight and darkness. "When Serpens proposed his plan to you?"

"Neither of us had reason to believe him or that his plan would work," Ophiuchus chimed in.

"It was the sweet nothings from the night before that convinced you to trust me," Serpens said, picking his teeth.

Orion heard his sister unsheathe her dagger. He turned to watch.

"Come now, you said my name like it was written in the stars," Serpens said.

"How is your leg, Vena?" Corvus interjected.

Serpens narrowed his eyes at Corvus. "Do you *know* her? You went an awful far way to save her skin."

"Everyone knows me," Venatici said plainly.

Corvus chuckled. "I was her personal hand at her family's estate. I was told to train her in combat, but when she reached the age of womanhood, she figured she could fend for herself and ordered me away, to do her family's dirty work, which she was too cowardly to do. Slave driving, as you know." The laughter on his voice sifted through his words until there was none left.

"When we were little," Venatici started, "Corvus's father always took it on himself to teach Corvus and I the prophecies and of Jesus's life and death. It was never that I was a coward." She sat up too, looked straight to Corvus. "It was because I didn't want to believe it, Corvus. I could see what we were becoming, and I didn't want to accept it. But now? What is there to think? I didn't think *this* is how we would meet them."

"Meet who?" Orion asked.

Venatici turned. "You, Ophiuchus, Serpens. Corvus's father used to tell us that the Four Horsemen and Hades would be named by the stars in the sky. It was to serve as our sign."

"She's right," Carina said. The woman's complexion of sandy, freckled skin had paled a little; her flashing eyes searched the water. Then her eyes met each of theirs, one by one, to settle into Orion's. "As your guardian angel, I would know this. Corvus has known this. I will protect you from the ones who wish to hunt you down, to destroy you. You will be safe with one another, as you will be safe under my watch, too."

Corvus rubbed his face. He hung his head, his brown hair in tendrils of black around his face. "I suppose this settles it." He glanced up from under heavy, worn lids. Far away, light reflected in his eyes, but it shone dully, as if he had slipped beneath the waves of the ocean.

"What do you mean to say?" Serpens asked Corvus.

But the words found their way to Orion's mouth instead, of their own accord, some deeply buried truth that surfaced slowly. "He means we're God's hand of vengeance."

ACKNOWLEDGMENTS

I have to give an extra special thank you to my husband. In these last few months, you've shown me patience and grace, and you've supported me in the ways I've most needed on this journey. God knows—and you and I know full well—that you are everything I ever hoped to have in life. This book, these characters, and this story, is a testament to how much I prayed for you before I knew you existed. You are the man of my dreams. Thank you. I love you.

Thank you, Mom. It's always scary to let the one that raised you read your heart on a page, and I know how much of this story you can relate to our lives. Thank you for supporting me in the early days of this book; it would have never existed otherwise. Thank you for helping me to get to writers conferences, even if nothing big came out of those. Thank you for your tough love; I would not be the writer I am without someone telling me, "You can do better." I love you so much, and I hope one day, I can take care of you the way you've cared for me.

Thank you, Lori and Lisa. Without you both, it's safe to say I would likely never have become a writer in the first place. Lisa, you made reading cool and fun. You made English my favorite subject. The notes you wrote on my vocabulary page drawings encouraged me. Thank you for the extra credit points. Thank you for praying with me (and for me) when I needed it most. Lori, I will never have the right words to thank you. Advanced Writing changed my life. I *would not* have been successful in this endeavor without that class. I am confident

that God put you in my life to guide me to my true calling—
which I believe is this. I admire your grace and poise so much.
Thank you for being tough on me, too. Thank you for
teaching me how to be a Literary Lion. Thank you both for
everything.

Thank you to every single literary agent and acquisitions
editor who turned me down. Yes, all one hundred of you.
Because of you, I was able to tweak this novel to be its best.
Because of you, I realized that I can do everything *you* can do
in the traditional industry. Dare I say, I may be able to even
make a more stunning and unique book on my own, too. You
all taught me resilience like I'd never known. The experience
left me broken, but I was able—by the grace and power of
God—to glue myself back together and make something
more beautiful in the process. (But respectfully, you lost your
chance forever.)

Thank you to my friends and family who've read this book
and given me gentle words of encouragement and correction.
Thank you to my readers. It is an honor to be able to bring
these characters and worlds to life for you to read and enjoy.
Thank you for being here. Without all of you, I'd still just be
a girl with a pen and a dream.

Thank you, God, my Lord and Savior, Jesus Christ, for
giving me the strength, courage, and resilience to accomplish
this feat. I would never be enough on my own. You have put
so many things in my life to remind me that I can be beautiful
in my brokenness. I pray my words and stories can shine a
light into the life of those who struggled in darkness like I did
for all those years before.

ABOUT THE
AUTHOR & ARTIST

R. D. G. Lover is an artist, author, and freelancer. She owns a small business where she sells her original art and takes freelance work for editing services, website design, graphic design, custom paintings, and more. Lover spends her free time stargazing, singing loudly in her car, and working on her illustrated novels about the Four Horsemen of the Apocalypse. She has made it her goal to write and illustrate a novel in every genre.

Her website, www.4pocalypseArts.com, showcases a gallery of all-original art and writing from her stories. To stay up to date with R. D. G. Lover's future releases, be sure to subscribe to her newsletter on her website and follow her on any social media @4pocalypseArts.